THE LIGHT BETWEEN TREES

Anona Rooke is drawn to remote parts of the British Isles and Europe and currently lives in the West Country. She has worked as an environmentalist on various land management projects and her non-fiction has appeared in magazines around the world. *The Light Between Trees* is her first novel.

THE LIGHT BETWEEN TREES

ANONA ROOKE

For my Family with love

PROLOGUE

Y ou came down off the moor as night seeped up the Lutter Brook and the blackbirds chinked their last alarm calls in the valley below. With only a tiny pen torch you found your way into the drift lane, that deep rough cut, littered with boulders and thick with the damp smell of shadow.

You edged forwards, and your fingers recoiled from the leathery chill of the liverwort that clung to the earthy banks. It was the end of the first hot week of summer. Were you hoping to find some kind farmer, a yard tap, perhaps even the offer of a cup of tea? They said that you were both experienced hill walkers; so what series of half-truths were you stringing together to explain your lack of water and fuel?

You came to the barn first and trailed your fingers along the granite wall until you reached the corner and the yard gateway. Your torch was running low, and you couldn't see right across the cobbles, but there was empty air before you and the black shadow of an anxious collie.

The house was in darkness. Why did you go up to it? Why didn't you walk on and leave its secret for someone else to discover? Were you going to knock and then take water anyway; was that your plan?

Berberis thorns caught in your hair as you walked up the path, another warning, but how were you supposed to know? You weren't meant to be there, your feet disturbed the dust and made it harder for the police to tell who else had come and gone.

The longhouse door was open, a black hole, and your voices echoed down the granite cross passage. Did you call out, still hopeful of some response? Perhaps you even stepped forward over the threshold.

The beam of your torch was weak, but it touched the blood, circled it and leapt up to the red pattern on the wall beyond. You stumbled back into the tangled garden then and called the police on your mobile, standing together, faces etched bluish by its tiny screen.

When I returned from my long weekend away, the police were waiting for me in London.

1

There are vehicles pulled up on the verge at every point where it's wide enough, almost from the village, and at least three are emblazoned with the names of familiar TV stations. I edge past them, trying not to scrape the car on the lichen-encrusted trees on the opposite side or catch the eye of the occupants, only to find that the entrance to our lane is blocked by a patrol car. Its bulk half hides the rotten farm sign propped in the hedge. As I nose the Golf up to it, a police officer climbs out and walks over.

"Sorry you can't go up there," he says and looks in through the window at my life laid out in the back. My daughter, Georgiana or Georgie as she has somehow already become, is still asleep in her car seat. Beside her are my bags, too hastily packed for my liking, the first and larger of the two full of clothes and nappies and the second cocooning my cameras in their layers of grey foam. There's an airline label still attached to the strap, and if the officer looks closely, he'll see the name I use now printed across it. The one I chose when I left Devon all those years ago.

"I'm Charlotte Elgin, I'm expected." I feel that I can still keep the two Charlotte's apart. Charlotte South in London, Charlotte Elgin down here in Devon; clean, easy.

"ID?" He bends forward as if to try and read the label then his gaze rests on Georgie for a moment. She is obviously not the usual accoutrement of a journalist.

I hand him my driver's licence and wait while he examines it with exaggerated care. A little eddy of dust rises off the lane and stings my eyes and a man with a camera climbs out of one of the nearer cars.

"I was expecting a Charlotte South." He looks confused for a moment.

"I'm family. Can I go on up?"

"Oh, er yes of course."

The officer reverses out to let me pass, and I ease the car forward in first and steer it around the worst of the potholes. After a short distance, the track swoops sharply right uphill and then divides. Keep left, and you eventually reach what was once my home, bear right along a similar stretch of rough gravel, round a couple of elongated turns, and you come to Sleepers at the head of its little valley, the tattered home of our only neighbours.

I hesitate for a moment at the divide, my attention caught by a flutter of colour attached to the Sleepers sign. It looks like a piece of cloth rather than any blue and white police tape. I'm almost tempted to get out and look, but then I sense the people waiting for me higher up the hill and drive on. Once I knew the line to take to avoid hitting the bottom of the car and knocking out the exhaust or the sump, but years of rains have changed the lie of the land, creating new peaks and gullies, worse drop-offs than there ever used to be.

I'm almost at the top before I can see the longhouse sailing above the valley, seemingly caught between the land and the clouds. I know the precise point that it will come into sight with our three bedroom windows nestled in a row beneath the thatch, but for a few seconds longer I keep my eyes on the surface of the track.

I used to love the dizzying view from those windows so much and the chance to look down on the backs of buzzards and ravens as they flew past. But now even the memory of it makes me feel queasy and scared, as though I'm about to step forward over an abyss and tumble down, down, down, through gorse and bracken and stunted oak to smash against the pale granite boulders in the river far below.

"Honestly Char." I shake my head, surprised and hurt by my old nickname, the one that my adopted brother Simon gave me when we were still speaking.

The yard gate is open, and the spread of cobbles behind the house is full of vehicles. The space looks smaller and scruffier than I remembered. Clumps of nettles push up between the stones in the corners, and an angular wooden figure stands near the garden gate. He may or may not mean that Clare was still making the strange wild dolls that peopled my childhood and earned her a living. Even now, here, I can't bring myself to say, mum or dad. They became Clare and Robert when Simon left, and that's the way they've stayed throughout our intermittent contact over the past twenty years.

For a moment I hesitate looking for a space, and a

strange man comes out of the house and stands watching me. During the drive down I had no clear picture of this moment of my return. Perhaps vaguely I imagined a lone police officer waiting by the barns behind a cordon of fluttering blue and white tape.

Suddenly, I can't face the occupants of all these cars. I feel disconnected, spaced out, as though my body is here in Devon but my mind is in denial, still thinking about work before the police came for me. Full of delicious nervous anticipation of something entirely different, the culmination of fifteen years of effort, the chance of a freer rein than I've had for some time, an opportunity to work in London and then Tokyo, to take pictures of people and places rather than clothes and close up faces. A chance which my creative self leapt towards with joy while the new mother in me struggled along behind, grappling to work out the logistics of it all with a twelve-week-old baby.

"Hell." I still can't quite take it in. Lee and Clare. Clare and Lee Berryman. My mother and her neighbour's thirteen-year-old son. The officers' fears were calmly professional. Four days without news is a long time.

To give myself time I reach into the back and fumble with Georgie's car seat, taking far longer than is needed. She eyes me then purses her lips and releases a little trail of milky sick onto her chin.

"Oh, darling." I dab at her face with a muslin. "This is where I lived when I was your age, it was good then, I'm sure you'll like it. We'll find you somewhere quiet, don't worry."

The air is only a little cooler than in London when I step out of the car, and I realise that, in my haste, I've packed all the wrong things. For a moment I stand still and breathe in the smell of grass and bracken and the warm sweetness of heather wafting down from the hill above. The man, who must be a police officer, gives up waiting and advances on the car.

"Ms South?" He holds out his hand, and I glance over my shoulder as I switch the car seat into my left hand to shake his. When I turn back, I catch the faintest look of surprise and know that he thinks that Georgie is a very young baby for someone of my age. "Detective Inspector Hollinghurst. It's good of you to come down."

"Could you? I mean South is my work name. Everyone knows me as Elgin down here, so I might as well keep things simple." Does my voice give away how little I want to be here, how close I came to turning my back and pretending that I could be of no help to the investigation?

"Whatever you prefer." He gives nothing away. His face is triangular with a broad forehead beneath a receding hairline, and a narrow chin greyed with afternoon stubble.

I look round warily. Beyond Hollinghurst, in a slight indentation on the top of the granite garden gatepost, half hidden by ivy, are two smooth dark pebbles. They were Simon's and my code stones, used to mark whether we were on or off the farm. I can't believe that they're still there.

"The officers in London said that you'd found something you wanted to talk to me about."

Hollinghurst nods. "We need to ask you some questions first. Mr Rawlings has been making us all tea."

His eyes linger on my face a few moments longer than necessary as he invites me over the worn granite step into what was once my own home. For a second I'm surprised, it never crossed my mind that Arthur Rawlings would still be working here, but then again, why not? He was village born and bred, and he loved the farm almost as much as we did.

I take a deep breath, and another familiar but long-forgotten smell fills my nose and sinks down into my lungs, it's a mixture of dust, old trapped wood smoke, damp dog and something flowery. Once it meant home but now it feels thick and suffocating, the kind of air that could trigger an asthma attack.

The kitchen is too warm. Someone (Robert presumably) has forgotten to adjust the Rayburn to take into account the mounting summer heat, but apart from that and a long line of five litre water containers against the far wall, little has changed.

"Ms Elgin may I introduce you to our Media Liaison Officer Amanda Miller and Detective Sergeant Quinn."

I'm sure he puts unnecessary emphasis on my name, and as their faces turn towards me, I'm caught, framed in the low doorway with the summer light bright behind me and Georgie's car seat heavy in my hands. On the beam above their heads is a row of rosettes, mostly reds and blues, from that season of amazing luck that Simon had with Ebenezer. I can't read the names printed on their faces from this distance, but I don't need to. The litany of success rises in my mind unbidden and with it that old confusion of jealousy and pride.

Beyond them all, over near the far door, stands a man in a green boiler suit pulled in at the waist with a leather belt. Our eyes meet across the room. There are so many things I should, I need to say to him, but here, now, his name alone will have to do.

"Arthur."

"I'm so sorry." His hair is grey but still thick, and he must have been wearing a cap earlier, it's left a groove around his skull. In contrast, his body looks somehow diminished, as though he's lost a few inches in height.

"This must have come as an awful shock to you," Hollinghurst says, and his gaze slips downwards to rest among the collection of mismatched mugs on the table top.

He's right, in a way, but perhaps not the way he thinks. I shift the car seat from one hand to the other but make no move to sit down. I don't feel ready for that, not to join the officers at the table as though they're friends who have come round for a chat.

"We're doing everything we can to find them. Forensics have checked the house and barns, and we've had a specialist search team out covering the two farms and the village for the past few days. We've contacted all the local hospitals, every family member we can track down and all her close friends and of course Lee Berryman's as well, but if there's anyone or anywhere you think we might have missed."

"I doubt it." My voice is edged with an irritation that I meant to hide. Their expressions sharpen, eyes switch to my face and lips tighten.

"We appreciate that you've had a long drive," Hollinghurst says. "But there are things we need to ask you."

"I have to change Georgie first. I'll just take her through to the utility room."

I point towards the door and Hollinghurst nods.

Again I take longer than necessary. I lay Georgie down on a faded mat, tickle her stomach and try not to notice anything else, least of all the overpowering familiarity of everything. Even the Belfast sink has the same chip that it always had, a dark little gash that Simon made when he dropped one of the horses' snaffle bits into it that he was rinsing ready for the village show. I wash my hands, cupping my fingers around a green bar of soap that must have recently been smoothed by Clare's palms.

"It's going to be fine," I whisper to Georgie, but she looks away across the room. A dog is scratching at the closed door, obviously shut back out of the way. "We'll be out of here soon, you'll see."

Someone has poured me a mug of tea. It's too orange and sugary, the dregs of the teapot, but I take it gratefully and sit down on the end of one of the wooden benches with Georgie on my knee. Arthur has gone.

"I don't know how much our colleagues in London told you, but perhaps if we go through a few of the details again, you might be able to throw some light on things."

———

This much they know. Clare and Lee were together on Friday morning, not an unusual thing apparently. After Lee's mother and grandmother died, it appeared that he had found something of both of them in Clare. They were clearing a patch of land at the end of the orchard, cutting back the brambles and piling them up ready to burn later. Arthur finished his daily round of the stock and said goodbye to them at 1pm before going home for lunch. At 10.30pm the first police officers to arrive at the farm found a pool of blood on the slab of granite inside the open back door and spatters of it up the wall behind. Tests have revealed that it was a perfect match for Lee's. Neither Clare nor Lee has been seen since.

It sounds different coming from Hollinghurst, his words hang in the room and mingle with the smell of disinfectant still in the air. Everything is suddenly more immediate and inescapable. Mother and grandmother, two generations of Berryman women gone can only mean one thing. A weight drops inside me, and I want to stand up and walk away, out of the house and down the track to the road. I want to keep walking until my legs are tired and my mind goes blank.

"Are you saying that he's Marty's son?" The shortened version of his name slips out of my mouth before I can stop it. A name that I haven't said aloud for so long that it feels alien on my tongue.

"Martin Berryman's? Yes."

"I thought at first. I mean I presumed- Stupid of me."

"Yes?" Hollinghurst waits, and I know that I'm going to have to explain myself.

"I thought that somehow he was Peter's son, not his grandson."

"You know Martin though I assume?" He looks at me steadily until the heat rises in my cheeks.

"I used to." For a second Marty and I are sitting together on a battered rug, aged about eight and nine, eating butter-soaked crumpets. I push the image away. Everyone for miles around knew our neighbours, the Berrymans at Sleepers. They were one of the oldest families in the village as they liked to remind us often enough.

"You must be about the same age."

"He's a year older than me actually but, as you probably already know, I haven't seen him or anyone down here for a long time."

"Okay, and why is that?"

Why? I don't want to think about it, and yet now I'm back it's impossible not to. Every once-familiar item sends a jolt of memory through me, a smell, a taste, a sound of the past. Things that I've tried so hard to forget rush in at me: that terrible night in the oak wood, of course, the shouted exchanges, the bitter looks and then the torment of the silent treatment that Robert, and sometimes even Clare, subjected Simon to for days and weeks afterwards. I should have prepared for this; I can't give these officers the story I tell everyone else and yet every honest answer feels dangerous now.

"I never come back here, I don't get on with my parents," I say at last. Keep it straight, keep it simple, hide the effort, hide the pain.

For a minute or so I'm not sure that I'm going to be allowed to leave it at that. The silence stretches then Miller shifts in her seat. "We think it might help if we got the media involved."

"What?" I remember the terrible moment at the petrol station close to my flat where I went to fill up the Golf before coming down. The same slab of concrete, plate glass and neon light as always, only this time Clare and Lee were waiting for me inside, staring back at me five times over from the tabloids on the centre shelf of the newspaper rack. She's grey now, and he has a small freckled nose and blonde hair edging towards red. I didn't expect that.

I paid for my fuel with cash and turned my three

cards over in my wallet to remind myself not to use them anymore, even when I'm alone.

"Properly I mean, if you and Mr Berryman could go on TV and ask Clare or Lee to make contact."

"Me and Marty Berryman?" I stare at Miller, and a tiny flicker of panic spreads through my stomach ready to flare up at any moment and catch at the back of my throat. "No, no I'm sorry. Is this what you wanted me to come down for? I thought you had something to show me."

"I understand what you're feeling." She lowers her voice. "It won't be easy of course, but it can make a huge difference. People often phone in when they've seen the family."

"Then why doesn't Robert do it?"

Hollinghurst glances at me, and then at his colleagues and from the look in his eyes, I know the truth.

"He's dead isn't he?" A bird flaps its wings inside my skull. "Not at the same time? What happened?"

"We found this; I think you should read it." He holds out a single sheet of paper, but I don't take it. Even from a distance, I can see that it's a typed letter and unfinished, the text ends halfway down the page, and there's no signature. "Miss Elgin?"

"Okay, okay." I reach for the letter and, despite my effort to stop it, my hand trembles as I glance down at the heavy, slightly uneven text that is so obviously the product of Clare's old typewriter.

Dear Charlotte,
  Maybe you've forgotten, or maybe you don't want to remember,

but the valley has an odd beauty at this time of year, perhaps it's the shadow of spring around the corner. I wish I could just write to you about that but I can't. I don't want to say what I've got to say in a letter but better this than an answerphone message I think. I have tried to call you at the flat and on your mobile, but you never answer. I know our last meeting wasn't great and we both said things that would have been better left unsaid, but I hope that your silence means that you're busy and things are going well for you.

I'm afraid that this letter brings bad news. Your father passed away last week; the cancer was too far advanced by the time it was found to do anything about. I didn't know what was coming when I last saw you or of course I would have told you.

The funeral is at 2pm on 9th March at the village church. I realise that this will all be such a shock to you, but perhaps you will be able to be there-

I look up and away, and the air in the room seems to have thickened until I can almost smell the sickness that was so recent, the slow lingering death. Why? I shut my eyes for a few seconds. "It was never posted."

"No. Do you know why not?"

For a moment I think he's going to tell me and my heart speeds up, then I realise that it's a genuine question, he's not as all-seeing as all that.

"But he was always so-" What? Alive, healthy, angry? Surprising images crowd my mind suddenly, and I'm not sure of the truth anymore.

"Miss Elgin?"

"Ten weeks ago."

Hollinghurst nods and the others watch me as the calculation thuds in my head suddenly. Since Georgie was born then. I think of all the times the Northstone number has flashed up on my phone, all the times I've ignored it, putting off the moment when I'd have to tell Clare about Georgie and then imagine her telling Robert.

"Miss Elgin?"

"It's okay." I can't hold my voice level, so I stand up and walk across to the window. The sill is dusty, and a thin film of green mould spreads up from the base of each pane of glass. My fingers are shaking when I dig them into the old putty, and it gives way in four perfect crescents. I twist slightly and bump my left knee against one of the water containers.

There must be a problem with the farm supply. It rises out on the moor above the top wall and runs fast through a pebbly channel onto the Northstone land. Sometimes unknowing visitors used to block it to paddle in until Robert put up a sign, and in winter the storage tank occasionally filled with storm debris. I wonder what's gone wrong this time.

"What exactly happened at that meeting?" Hollinghurst pulls my attention back into the room.

I glance over my shoulder, and he looks at me steadily. Almost too late I realise where this is all going.

"It's a mistake with Lee right? I mean just some kind of misunderstanding. They'll turn up soon." I cling to vain hope.

"Could you tell me what happened at that meeting?"

"It's complicated." I turn back to the view of the narrow, granite-walled back garden. A butterfly dances in the sunlight. "I was pregnant although it didn't quite show yet. I should have told Clare, but I couldn't face it, I knew she wouldn't approve of, well of the way I was doing it on my own and at my age, Robert certainly wouldn't. I was edgy, cross. We argued; I can't remember what about now, it was silly, nothing important."

Hollinghurst doesn't say anything, none of them does.

"I honestly can't remember so it can't have been about much. We haven't talked since though as you know. I told you we didn't get on."

"Okay."

Again there's a long silence, they're apparently waiting for me to say something more but I'm not going to.

"I think we should talk about how we can get the press to help us now," Miller says at last. "We may not have that much time left."

"Could he, could Lee still be alive then?"

"It's quite possible, but he would have been in need of medical attention."

"And there's no record of him in any of the local hospitals?"

"No, but we can't rule out anything right now." Hollinghurst's look holds a challenge, a warning. It forces me to keep seeing myself quite differently. I'm not entirely off the radar as a suspect; it's in all their eyes.

"Look I still don't think it will make any difference if I go on TV, it can't, I mean I'm hardly the beloved daughter."

Georgie's eyes open and a trembly, unhappy noise slips out between her lips. In a moment it'll expand to fill the whole room and then the house.

"Ssh, ssh." I jog her up and down in an attempt to dissipate her unhappiness before it builds up and reddens her face.

Hollinghurst is silent for a moment then he clears his throat and looks at me steadily. "You might be surprised; it could be just what Clare wants. I've got some officers round at Sleepers at the moment. We're trying to set up everything with the TV studio for first thing tomorrow morning."

What does he think? It's hard to tell.

"I'm not doing a press call." My heart races. "I just can't."

"Okay then, what about a few words, pre-recorded, no journalists?"

I think of my Japanese clients, of Dan, my agent, the new flat I was thinking of buying and Lee's pale face on the front of the tabloids all in one freefall of images. Whatever happens, it's probably too late now anyway, someone somewhere will have made the connection, and by tomorrow my face will be plastered across the tabloids alongside Clare and Lee's, a fresh juicy revelation for people to digest over breakfast.

I nod my head slowly and glance at the wood and linen figure on the windowsill, the one with the curly red hair and scar across her cheek. She looks back at me, far from friendly. In fact, she's more like an effigy, waiting to have pins stuck in her. Perhaps if I walked closer, I'd see the tiny holes in her sides. For a moment I remember the other redhead that Clare made at about the same time with Robert's old school friend, who was always somehow known as Uncle Eric, watching over her shoulder. Perhaps his fingers even stroked the nape of her neck while she worked, only we weren't meant to know about any of that.

"Miller will meet you at the TV studio. It would be

great if you could be there by nine," Hollinghurst says and looks at Georgie. "Can you do that?"

I nod. It will happen. Miller will be prompt. We'll meet in some impersonal foyer, and she'll take me to stand in front of the cameras. I don't have a choice anymore.

"And afterwards, what then?"

"Well you're not under arrest, so of course you're free to go."

"I see." I try to focus my thoughts, but somehow I can't think anything through properly. "Can I stay here?"

"Well, there's no reason why not if you want to." Hollinghurst watches me.

Want- The wrong word. I don't want any of this. I want to be back in my flat in London preparing for my new contract. For a second there's a once-familiar voice in my mind, a call that I can't bear to hear. I turn my head towards the window.

"He appears to have been a bit of a loner." Hollinghurst's thoughts have moved on, and I nod again forgetting for a moment who he's talking about, then I shake my head. I don't know that, how could I? "He didn't get on well at school, socially, intellectually he was fine, brilliant in fact."

I stare at him and confusion flares across my cheeks. "You mean Lee?"

"Who else?"

I'm not going to tell him. I don't want to think about it. In fact, all I want to do is go upstairs now, to find a bed and curl up in the darkness under the duvet with Georgie against me. I need to find a resting place inside for all this new knowledge, but they won't let me go yet.

There are more and more questions that cut deeper and deeper into the past. I try to answer them as best I can, but there are things I have never told anyone.

"There is one person who might be able to help," I say right at the end when Hollinghurst is ready to go.

"Yes." He settles back down in his chair.

"Uncle Eric. Have you contacted him?"

"Eric Corderoy?"

I nod.

"A couple of people have mentioned him, but no one seems to know where he is at the moment."

"I've got his number." I scroll through the address book on my phone and give him Eric's mobile number. "I haven't spoken to him for years, so I don't even know if this will reach him."

2

They leave me at dusk with a dry mouth and the sense that, despite my care, I've said too much. For a few minutes the yard fills with people, dark uniformed police officers from the fields and woods returning to roost like a flock of vultures, then as suddenly as they arrived they're gone, the noise of their vehicles dwindling to nothing down the track.

I stand quite still. Without the officers' voices and footsteps filling the space the house is an empty, dangerous land and I'm reminded of that other silence all those years ago. The dense stillness of the night after the air ambulance lifted away over Howden before the owls started to call again and the police cars raced up to the house. Suddenly I have a strong sense of the inevitability of all this, of a terrible unstoppable chain of events linked in some way that I can't yet grasp.

I wait. Somewhere there's a sound. I strain my ears trying to make it out, but it's gone again, not a voice but a movement. The random shift of something in the breeze perhaps. Being the perfect gentleman as always,

Arthur offered to stay the night but seemed relieved when I declined the offer.

Now I'm not so sure that I should have shaken my head quite so hastily. I could have asked him things, like how often Clare went out and whether she talked to the other Berryman's anymore. Did she bake Lee biscuits like she used to do for Marty after Ginny died and Clare had the unerring sense that the male members of the two families were falling out yet again?

"I can't believe it. Tell me it isn't sheep this time? They're not worth it." I can hear Clare's voice full of exasperation even now.

I circle the kitchen once. The single sheet of paper is still on the table where I left it. Why was the letter never finished? Why wasn't it posted?

"Oh God."

Suddenly I pick up the page and fold it in half and then half again and again until it's a thick rectangle not much bigger than a postage stamp. I won't think about it; I can't. It doesn't make any difference now. I wonder if I can burn it or whether that might be classed as destroying evidence. In the end, I shove it under a pile of other papers and look away.

I need, I have to think what to do. I should form a plan that stretches beyond the recording tomorrow, but my brain is a mushy unresponsive mass that refuses to focus, flitting instead from one unsettling image to another. I must be tired that's all; I'll be fine in the morning. I grip my hands into fists of frustration.

"Okay, Georgie let's get you sorted shall we?" My voice sounds too loud in the stillness, and for a second my question hangs in the air around me. But she's asleep in my arms and doesn't even move in reply.

I stoop to lift her bag from a chair and turn from the room, I stop, I walk on again. Each time I cease to move silence buzzes in my ears. It's like that children's game of grandmother's footsteps only now I'm not sure quite what it is that is creeping up behind me.

I haven't felt so alone, so far from another adult, for years and I'm surprised how much that unnerves me. But it isn't only my aloneness that's disturbing. Now without the eyes of the police officers following my every movement I can look properly and see all the things that I have tried so hard to forget. I can think.

My mind jumps across the gap too easily, into the past and back again. Or perhaps it isn't my mind but my body that carries such strong wordless memories of this place. My hands know where to reach for each light switch without me thinking, and my feet have the measure of the uneven steps at once.

A dog scratches at a door again, and I walk through the utility room to let it out, relief flooding through me at the thought that I'm not quite so alone after all. Two collie dogs rush through into the kitchen, one tall and heavy, the other with a mad half and half face, one side white, the other black.

I follow them out into the cross passage and keep my back to the damp patch on the wall. I don't want to know what shapes the blood made but the thin chemical stench of disinfectant pricks at my nostrils and now I'm facing Robert's coat and hat.

"No. No." I don't want to see any of it, and I walk on.

At the bottom of the stairs, I stop again. The first floor hangs above me, silent and remote. I was seldom on my own in the house in the past, and I can't remember spending a single night alone here. I shiver in a sudden cool draught from an unseen open door and search for a memory that isn't there, one time. But maybe my first inclination was right, maybe I haven't spent a night alone here before. The dogs stick close to me now, their warmth pressed against the backs of my legs as though they too are filled with uncertainty.

My head feels muzzy, and I can't think of all the things I've said this afternoon or more importantly of what things I haven't said, what memories I've withheld from public view. But I need to think of them, to keep mental notes so that I don't make mistakes tomorrow or the next day if they ask me things again.

The single naked light bulb on the landing pushes back the darkness but not far, wherever I look there are shadows on the edge of my vision. It should be warmer up here under the eaves but somehow it isn't, and if anything the draught is stronger. At the far end of the corridor, a door bangs and I start.

I'm being irrational. There can't possibly be anything here now, the white-suited figures have run their latex-covered fingers over every surface and checked every centimetre of the old house for what? More blood? A murder weapon? I stand still and listen all the same and a chilly draught of air licks around my bare calves.

"Okay, so there's just an open window somewhere." The dogs cock their ears at the sound of my voice then mill around me as I turn towards my parents' room. Unlike our rooms, it stretched from the front to the back of the house, but oddly it had no window overlooking the valley. The door is closed, and I hesitate outside. The woodwork hasn't been painted for a long time, perhaps not since I was last here, and there are scratch marks from generations of collies that have skulked upstairs and asked to be let in.

I reach out my hand, feel the metal of the latch cold between my fingers and pull back. Not now, not tonight. I don't want to know whether Clare has cleared away Robert's things. I'm not ready to be ambushed by the scent of him still clinging to one of his Fair Isle jumpers or to see his shoes patterned with dust. There are things I need to know, but if I have to look inside to find them, I'll do it in daylight when there'll be sun streaming through the east window.

In the opposite direction were our rooms, Simon's and then mine. I stare along the landing. All the doors are in view, and they're all closed. I used to know the spaces beyond off by heart. I could navigate through them without hesitation after lights out, but now I don't know what to expect. I stop outside Simon's door, and for one crazy moment, I have the urge to knock.

"Fool," I whisper and Georgie shifts in my arms as though my irritation has penetrated her dream.

The door resists my pressure for a second then swings open with a tired groan. For some reason, the curtains are drawn and even before I switch on the light I know that the room is changed. There's a hollow emptiness about the stale air, and my tentative footsteps echo slightly. I flick the light switch. The room is unrecognisable, scoured down to its bones, emptied of everything apart from a bare single bed. I stare at the whiteness of it all; white walls, white woodwork, white floor.

"No way." Something tightens in my stomach and makes me queasy. I gulp and stumble back into the more familiar air of the landing. The tears that refused to come earlier prick at the corners of my eyes and I lean against the thick outer wall and feel the chill of the stone seep into my shoulder blades.

If Simon's room has been totally emptied, then surely my room will be the same. All the paraphernalia of childhood and adolescence cleared away into boxes in the attic or more finally into long gone bin bags. I take a step towards the door then stop. There's no point; I already know what I'm going to find. I walk on again, and I'm almost past the door when I spin round, close my eyes and push it open. A mustiness catches in my nose, and I sense, even before I open my eyes, that the room is unchanged, the space stifled with artefacts from the past.

"What the hell?" I stare at it all in confusion; at the old Indian bedcover, the shelves of model horses, the desk under the window piled with books and I try to make sense of things. Why has Simon's room been emptied while mine has been left ready for my return? I can't believe that on top of everything they've done this. It feels like the final eradicating blow.

The curtains are open, and my gaze flicks to the view out across the head of the valley still discernable in the dusk. There are no other houses in sight, no lights, only dense oak woodland sweeping up to wild moorland and the silhouettes of Hartor and Venn Rocks on the horizon. The village isn't so far away down the valley, but you can't see it from the house, and suddenly I'm glad about that.

I glance along the corridor at the last two doors. The spare room beckons like a welcome oasis but to reach it I must pass a door marked out from the rest by a pair of stylized Indian eyes stuck on at head height. From the time I was eleven, there were three of us; Simon, me and Jamie. Thrown together into a family, destined to share our time and clothes and secrets.

"Jamie." There's a lump in my throat as I clutch at the latch of his door. "Jamie."

Again the curtains are closed, and it's almost the same as Simon's room, painted white and empty apart from a bed, a chair and a small table under the window. There is nothing of any colour apart from a neat stack of school books on the table. The covers are bold, bright and unfamiliar. I open one. There is no name pencilled inside, but the book was only printed three years ago.

Suddenly I know that I can't stay, not tonight or any night; I swing around and head for the stairs, my footsteps echoing through the empty house. The dogs rush after me.

"Oh, God. Look I'm sorry, but you're going to have to spend another night on your own, alright?" I turn into the kitchen to check their bowls. "You've got food and water."

At the back door, I stop. I didn't notice before, but there are two new bolts on the inside at the top and bottom. Shiny silver ones of the kind you can pick up at the farm supplies for a few pounds. I turn round, and there are two on the front door as well. They all look as though they were put on in a hurry. The screw heads poke out, and the bolt sections aren't even straight. They are certainly not Robert's handiwork; he was always so meticulous. I run my fingers over them and have the uncanny feeling that there's something I'm not quite getting yet. Georgie wriggles then mutters towards a scream.

"Okay, okay." I carry her out into the yard and strap her car seat in the back of the Golf, my fingers stumbling as I hurry to make her secure and get moving. What was Clare thinking about when she bought and fixed those bolts? In the past, we seldom locked the doors even when we all left the house, so what changed? Of course, times have moved on, and everyone is more security conscious now, but the newness of the bolts suggests something other than a mere keeping up with a trend. Had something or someone scared her into fitting them?

Almost as soon as I've turned the car and begun to crunch and slide back down the track, Georgie's asleep. After a nod at the single patrol car at the cordon, we turn away from the village and speed through the dark lanes taking a chance and relying on headlights to warn us of other vehicles.

I can't face anyone who might know me, but on my way down I noticed a motel out near the dual carriageway and I head for it now. It seems to offer the perfect mix of transience and anonymity until I push through the glass entrance door. The foyer is a deserted oblong of white fluorescent light above utility Flotex carpet, and the middle-aged receptionist is reading a paper. I turn to retreat, but I'm too slow.

"If you're looking for your husband, he left half an hour ago."

"Excuse me?"

The woman folds the paper on top of the reception desk and looks at me properly. "Oh, I'm sorry I thought you looked familiar somehow. My mistake. The family suites are all fully booked though."

"And the singles?" I glance at the paper, but it's face down on the desktop.

"I'm not sure that I can do that."

"Please?" The darkness presses at my back through the plate glass doors. "I've got a travel cot."

"How many nights?"

"Er, one, tonight at least, maybe more. I'm not sure yet."

Her dark hair has a strange circular parting on the top of her head, and the computer screen is a blue square in her glasses as she consults it.

"Number eleven is free." She takes my work name and cash, then lifts a key card off a board behind her and activates it. "Through that door there and along the corridor on the right. Ground floor."

There's the smell of a bar, and then we're through a swing door and in a long concrete tunnel. One strip light is on the way out, and it flickers and hums above our heads as I count the doors. Nothing is new, and our door has a dent below the handle and scuff marks as though someone has tried to kick it in with a muddy boot.

"I'm sorry Georgie." I kiss the top of her head before letting us in.

The room is a homage to pale rose nylon and mock wood. The carpet, curtains and bedcover all attempt to match and the air smells of stale plastic. As soon as I switch on the top light, I realise that there are no net curtains at the window, only a blank square of dark glass that looks straight out onto the car park. I feel exposed and vulnerable to whoever might be out there in the night and flick the switch straight off again.

"God." My heart pounds and I lean back against the

door in the darkness. This motel was meant to be a kind of safe haven, but it feels as eerie and unsafe as the farm. I know that I'm being illogical, but I can't help thinking that someone could trace me to this concrete box.

Without switching on the light again, I feel my way across the room and pull the curtains shut. Georgie is asleep, and I lower her car seat onto the floor close to the bed. She'll need a feed and a nappy change later, but for now, it seems better to let her remain oblivious to this new arrangement.

I'm too tired to take off my clothes, but as soon as I stretch out on the bed my mind begins to race, and I can't sleep either. Hollinghurst's words are there again. "Socially he didn't get on at school." So what was he saying, that Lee was bullied too? Images that I've tried for years to forget jostle behind my closed eyelids.

3

There's something I haven't told the police. They're alike. Jamie and Lee, Lee and Jamie. I hold the photos side by side in the stuffy early morning motel room and swap them back and forth. The one given to me by Hollinghurst and the other carried always in my wallet. I'm not sure what to make of the likeness yet, but suddenly I'm haunted by another image.

A grassy hillside straight ahead, pale and dry in hard August light, stretching up and up to a distant tor, empty in front but not behind. I should have stopped, I should have turned to face the gang of boys, but I didn't. Instead, I lay down with Jamie, our faces pressed against the turf, a smell of soil and grit, the nickname 'Ginger Bookworm' and their laughter ringing out behind us.

"Don't say anything." Jamie's voice was a whisper through the grass as a handful of stones stung down on us. Footsteps thumped the hollow ground. First close to the left and the right then further and further away. When there was no vibration left, we rolled over and lay on our backs. A strand of his red hair touched my arm. "It's just a game."

A buzzard swung slowly overhead enjoying a thermal. I followed it with my eyes until it was out of sight around the side of the hill. It could probably still see the gang of boys ranging their way back to the village. I shut my eyes for a few seconds.

"Perhaps." But I didn't know how to voice my vague feelings about what might happen when Simon arrived. The suddenness of it all was shocking; we were going from a family of four to a family of five in less than a week.

"I don't think I want a brother," Jamie said, his thoughts apparently straying in a similar direction.

I hesitated catching the wobble in his words. "He won't be a brother exactly though will he? I mean it could be good. We've got to be kind to him anyway, imagine if you were in his position."

"I don't know why they're doing it. Dad always says we get on his nerves and now-"

"Jamie. Come on, you know he doesn't mean that, not all the time."

"Yeh."

"Well seeing as we don't have any choice we'd better just keep smiling and make the best of it."

"Damn." I stuff the photos back into my bag and stand up. It's time to go. I need the automatic preoccupation of driving to blank my mind. I'm sitting in the car about to turn towards town when I remember the dogs; I can't go straight to the TV studio without letting them out and checking their food and water. Guilt flickers through me at the realisation that I haven't even thought about them until now. It's such a long time since

I've been responsible for any animals. I glance at my watch, and my heart sinks. I'm going to be so late.

———

The collies are already barking when I step out of the car in the yard. An uneven cacophony of sound punctuated by the scrabble of claws against old wood. At once my short, disturbed night sinks back and my thoughts snap away from the pre-breakfast gloom of the motel dining room and the sudden scramble of the press as I approached the bottom of the lane. Even though I kept the windows wound up tight, I heard their shouts rise like the bay of hounds on the scent of a fox.

Nerves shoot into the pit of my stomach, and I spin round. The low granite barns, the garden, the orchard, everything is still and quiet in the early morning sunlight. I look more carefully, tracing lines of shadow and arching clusters of shrubs. Two meadow brown butterflies dance in front of the barn and a blackbird darts away over the garden wall, but nothing else moves. Then I remember that I am the stranger here. It isn't Sal or Meg in the kitchen but another whole generation of dogs who don't know me or the sound of my car. I let out a breath and smile with sudden relief.

"Okay, Georgie let's get things sorted." It's going to be hot again, the sky is already a high even blue, and there isn't a stir of wind as I lift her out of her car seat. For a moment she stares at me then her attention is caught by something else, and she turns her head. "We'll let those dogs out then we'll get them some breakfast before we go. I'm sorry everything is a bit different. You've got to be a really good girl this morning, okay?"

I'm halfway up the garden path when I catch sight of a movement out of the corner of my eye, and a figure steps off the lawn onto the cobbles behind me.

"Charlotte?"

I twist round to face the man, and something tightens in my chest. Georgie clutches at me with damp fingers and screws up her eyes ready to cry.

"Marty."

We stare at each other for a moment, playing catch up with all the changes that have occurred in the past twenty years. At sixteen Marty grew past Simon to become a tall man, delightfully so for a few fleeting months of his eighteenth year. Since then his frame has gathered flesh so that now his shoulders and upper arms strain against the cloth of his t-shirt and his belly hangs a little over his belt as he leans towards me.

"I heard you was back. Why?" There are white letters on his breast pocket, 'BJ Slaughterers'.

"Isn't that pretty obvious? Look I'm really sorry and about your wife."

"You can't possibly do anything. You haven't been here, unless-" Marty leans closer. "Do you know something?"

"What?"

"Do you know where my son is, is that it?"

"No, I'm here to talk to the press-"

"Yeh right. He just came round here, it wasn't in him to do anything wrong but all that was left by the end of the afternoon was a pool of his blood. So what's she done, where are they?"

"I don't know what happened." I try to steady my breathing and reassure Georgie at the same time.

"Well someone does."

His face is too close to mine, the forehead wide beneath curly brown hair and lowered in that way that always used to remind me of a Devon bull. There's something sour on his breath, garlic perhaps, I take a step back, and Georgie starts to cry properly.

"Marty-"

"He's only thirteen," he says, and I know the shape and taste of those exact words.

"Ssh, ssh, Georgie darling." I jiggle her up and down. "I am sorry Marty."

"Sorry? Sorry? Is that all you've got to say?" Our eyes meet and then dart apart. "And where's Simon? Is he coming down, is he sorry too?"

"Marty, look I don't know." I shake my head and his gaze shifts back to my face seemingly searching for the glass scar along my hairline. It's such a fine pale streak now that it's hardly noticeable. Everyone down here probably remembers but no one in London would ever guess that I've been in a car crash.

For a second I'm skimming down the field in the old Escort with Simon again. The wild exhilaration of being with him is fizzing through my veins, then Jamie is running out of the woods right in front of the car, face pale, hair a manic frizz of red around the rim of his hood and everything is tilting and rushing towards my face.

Later, much later after we'd come home from the hospital, Jamie told me about the boys in the woods, the ones who'd shouted and chased him. I'd thought the bullying had died down, but it obviously hadn't. I felt guilt suddenly. I should have noticed that it was still going on, but perhaps I'd been too distracted by Simon.

I push the memory away. "I'm here to help."

"Well don't think you can just go swanning back where you came from when today's over and pretend you've done your bit."

"Excuse me?"

"Some of us haven't forgotten."

For a moment I'm not sure, but when I look up his brown eyes are hard.

"Are you trying to-?"

"Let's just say I'm jogging your memory."

My phone rings in my pocket, and Marty glances down then back up at my face.

"I'd best get back to Peter. He's really cut up about Lee as well."

"You're living at Sleepers with him now?" I can't picture it somehow, Marty and his father still sitting down for meals together twenty years on.

"I'll see you later."

When he turns away, I pull the phone from my pocket, but I don't answer it until he's through the gate. Georgie's cries rise an octave almost drowning Miller's voice at the other end. Is she in the TV studio already?

"Ssh, ssh, Georgie darling come on now." I rock her from side to side, but it makes no difference. "I'm sorry I'm running a bit late."

"That's okay, I'm a bit early, so take your time." Her voice is politely professional, but she must have seen things that I don't even know about yet. "I trust you had a comfortable night."

She probably knows that as well, that I didn't spend the night here; the guy on the roadblock will have reported it to the incident room. But I wonder if she also knows where I stayed, it wouldn't surprise me.

"Yes thank you." My hand is shaking as I reach up

to unlock the back door. "I won't be long; I've just got to change Georgie."

"I'll be at reception waiting for you."

It's probably only my overwrought imagination but it feels like she's doesn't quite believe me. Does she think I'm going to flunk it? Have I not quite managed to instil faith in her that I'll go through with this? I thought I'd done pretty well at hiding my desire to flee.

———

Despite my best efforts, we arrive at the television studio half an hour late, and a receptionist with blonde streaked hair and a homemade mini skirt holds open the door of a small waiting room off the main foyer. I wheel Georgie's buggy inside being careful to avoid an umbrella stand. The windows don't appear to open, and the air smells lemon fresh and overheated. Marty isn't there.

"I'm so sorry-"

Miller waves a hand and glances at Georgie. "No worries. Let's catch our breath in here for a moment. Are you happy with what you're going to say?"

I nod.

"If it would help we can run through things now."

"It's alright." My mind won't focus suddenly, and I don't want her to see my fear.

"Okay, but I suggest that you don't speak to the press again after today without me, you know how things can get misinterpreted."

"Oh yes."

"Well if you're sure about this morning I've just got a few people I need to speak to. I'll see you in a minute."

Soft, nylon-covered chairs line three walls of the room and a tall artificial plant of unknown variety leans out from one corner. In the opposite corner a coffee machine gurgles and beside it a rack of leaflets advertises the various showpiece programmes of the area.

"Let's look at these shall we Georgie?" I roll the buggy gently back and forth with one hand as I take one of the leaflets and open it up. The print is poor and chunky; it reminds me of a student's first attempt to promote a college film. Behind me, the door opens, and Peter Berryman is shown in. Surprise hits me as hard as any physical thump, and I swallow back a sudden taste of nausea. I can't tell if he feels anything. He's wearing nylon trousers, and a jumper pulled on over a blue poly-cotton shirt. He looks older but not that much older. I've changed far more.

"Peter."

"What are you doing here?" He stares at Georgie for a moment then turns his head in my direction. "Is she yours?"

"Well yes."

"Someone must have changed then."

"Excuse me?" I try to keep my voice calm, to push away the other images that threaten to overwhelm me then our eyes meet, and his are red and sore.

"Think you're gonna be of help after all these years do you?"

"I-"

"Unless you know something that I don't, I can't imagine why you're bothering."

The past and the future tangle themselves together

in my mind in a knot of pain. I glance out of the window and know that I'm living on the edge now. If I go through with this, if I stand in front of the cameras as Charlotte Elgin then everything that I've tried so hard to forget will surface again and my new life will be smashed apart and yet if I turn away now Lee's pale innocent face will haunt me for years to come.

"Marty's boy is missing, who wouldn't try and help?" It's an effort to keep my voice steady, but I manage it. "I was rather expecting to see Marty here."

"You was always good with words." Peter walks across the room and peers out of the window, taps his fingers along the top of the radiator, turns and walks across to examine the plant. I don't want to look at his hands, to remember how strong they were. "But it might already be too late; Lee could be dead."

"I know. I'm sorry." There's something in the top pocket of his shirt that looks like a packet of cigarettes; it makes a rectangle through his jumper.

"Marty's not so good right now. Said I'd do this for him although I'm no great talker, I told the police that." Peter touches the coffee machine, runs a finger down the line of selections then stuffs it into the coin slot at the bottom. He might have brushed his hair before he came out; it's hard to tell.

"At least there won't be any journalists."

"Scared are you?"

"Peter, look I honestly don't know what happened." All I can think about is Marty's broad bullish head and the accusation in his eyes.

"You look like you've been having a nice time. Shame this has interrupted things eh?"

I stare at him. What have Clare and Robert said

about me locally? There must have been questions and explanations, furtive conjecture if nothing else. I may have been so careful all these years, but I can't account for them. Silence settles between us, thick and heavy, and all the things that I planned to say are gone. Peter looks at my breasts.

"Maybe you shoulda come back before now though, before it was too late."

"Too late?"

"People can get pushed to the brink you know."

I think of Robert grown pale and frail, of my parents' bedroom high under the thatch. Did he die there at home or in some hospice miles away? I haven't been able to bring myself to ask Arthur.

Peter sticks his hand down through the v-neck of his jumper and pulls the packet of cigarettes out of his pocket, looks at them for a moment, shrugs and puts them away again.

"You must've been working out," he says.

"Sorry?"

"To get your lovely figure back so quickly."

The room feels stifling and cold at the same time. I want to get out into the fresh air again, but I have to satisfy myself with pushing the buggy one step towards the window.

"Okay?" Miller is back. "Good, you're here now Peter. If you'd like to come this way, everyone is about ready."

We walk along to a lift, which plunges us down into a shadowy airless space that smells of dusty overheated cotton and floor polish. Peter turns around and around like a cornered badger, then the sound recordist appears from behind a screen and runs through a few details. As soon as he's finished speaking, I can't remember what he said, and Georgie begins to whimper.

"It's alright darling." I lean over the buggy and smooth my fingers across her forehead. She feels rather hot, and another bubble of anxiety wells up inside me.

"Shall I look after her for you?" A tall woman with a bob of dark hair steps forward with a smile. "Isn't she gorgeous. How old is she?"

"Twelve weeks."

"Oh, I've almost forgotten what it's like to have one that age. What's your name darling?"

"Georgie. She's normally so good, but I'm not sure-" I roll the buggy back and forth for a few moments. "This might all be a bit much for her."

"Look, why don't I take you over in the corner there where you can still see your mummy?" The woman squats down and looks into Georgie's face. Georgie stares back, and her mouth puckers.

"I won't be long Georgie." I hold her tiny hand for a moment, and her fingers tighten around mine. "You just be a good girl for five more minutes eh."

Peter is waiting for me now, and I turn towards him, my heart beating fast.

"I'm not having them lights in my eyes," he says as we walk out onto the bright oblong platform that they want to present us on.

"No." I take a deep breath and try to quell the flutter at the top of my lungs. I still can't think what to do.

There are people in the shadows all around us. More people than you would ever imagine such a job should need. I don't want them to sense my fear, but already it's massing in the corners of the studio. I've never liked being in front of the camera, which was partly why, right at the beginning, I found it such a welcome escape to be the one pointing the lens. It was a revelation to be exempt from the family snaps because I was taking them.

"Okay, if you could just stand to your left a bit, that's good." A guy with surfer hair and an ear stud stoops behind the camera and waves one arm out to the side.

The studio is far too hot, and already I feel over-whelmed by it, my throat is dry, and my heart is racing faster still. I glance across at Georgie, but I can hardly see her beyond the glare of the lights. At my side, Peter's neck is mottled with patches of deep red, and he keeps wiping his brow with a handkerchief.

"Do you know what you're going to say?" The sound recordist looks at us with damp brown eyes.

"I …" What can I do? I scrabble for some idea, but my mind is blank. "Yes."

"No." Peter rummages in his pocket for a moment. "Wait, I wrote something down."

"Ah." Another man detaches himself from the shadows at the edge of the studio, walks over to him and rests a hand on his shoulder. "Reading isn't a good idea, it er doesn't look-"

"I'm not going to remember, not with that thing stuck in my face."

Somewhere in the shadows, Georgie starts to cry, and I turn towards her instinctively.

"Okay." The man looks around. "Let's take five guys."

Peter is lead over to a couple of seats in the corner, and I calm Georgie while he has some kind of pep talk. I can't hear the words that pass between them but when we're back on the platform his neck has paled, and his whole face seems more resolute.

"Alright?"

He nods, and we take our places in front of the blue backdrop once again. Georgie is silent but the cameras are like eyes turned towards us and suddenly behind them, I see Dan, the Japanese clients and all the dozens of other people that I've misled over the years. I close my eyes for a moment, but it's no better like that, the pixelated darkness swims and then sharpens into images that I'd managed to forget, and there's the whisper of once familiar voices but no individual words.

"I-" I try to keep my eyes steady and brace my feet against the floor but all of a sudden the studio swoops around me, dark walls and white boards, a snake of cables, the blinding glare of a light.

"Steady." Hands clutch at my arms, holding me up and steering me to the side of the room. "Come on, sit down here, that's it, lean forward for a moment."

The chair is low and hard, and I stare at my feet, or rather just the toes of my thin shoes that poke out beyond the hem of my trousers. Trousers that I bought and wear as Charlotte South. I can't give her away like this. I can't.

"Here, have a drink." A glass of water appears in my line of vision, and I take it carefully, worried that the shake in my hand will show.

"Thank you."

The woman wheels Georgie close again and parks the buggy. I can't look at her or any of them, but I can feel the others gathering around me waiting for a sign that it's safe to advance. At last, when I don't move, Hollinghurst comes over and lowers himself onto an empty chair beside me. I hadn't even realised that he'd come into the studio.

"I know this is hard. Do you just need more time or-?"

"I can't do it." I can't look at his face either. I don't want to see what he's thinking.

"Are you sure?" He hesitates then clears his throat. "Look how about we write out some words, what you would have said, and I'll get an officer to read them out as a statement from you?"

"Would you?" I feel weird, kind of light-headed and sick.

"It seems like the best thing to do in the circumstances."

———

I didn't plan to watch the news. I thought I'd be on the way back to the motel or some other anonymous B&B, safely out of the viewing range of any TV. However, when the time comes, I'm still at the farm, and although I pretend to myself that in less than an hour I'll be on the road, I know deep down that I can't face the bleakness of nylon bedcovers nor the scramble of the press at the end of the lane again.

I gravitate towards the TV set in the living room and lower myself down onto the old sofa in front of it. I thought I'd chosen my words so carefully, but now, read out by the police officer, they sound too formal, almost uncaring. As they twist through the room, they seem to spell out quite another message, so that by the end I'm sure that the whole nation will decide I'm guilty of some terrible double crime.

Heat rises into my cheeks even though I'm alone and I grip both hands into fists. God. God. How long will it take before someone makes the connection and my two names become one? Then Dan, my clients, all my London friends will know. How could I ever have been so naïve as to think that I could sort this out in secret? It's just the kind of thing that the media loves, the kind of story they won't let go of until either Lee is found or someone is found guilty of the crime and even then-

I take a deep breath, but I can't stop the sinking feeling inside me, the sense of where all this is going unless, unless of course Lee is found safe and well soon. But where the hell is he and where's Clare? I look towards the shadowy hallway, and still I can't get a grip on what could have happened there. I don't want to believe that Clare has done something terrible but someone has, and it feels like my whole life is about to be pulled apart in public.

4

The dogs bark suddenly and the sound jars through the dark house and startles me awake.

"What the hell?" In my dreams, I was in some crowded London space, but now I'm disorientated, the room smells unfamiliar, and for a few seconds I can't think where I am, then I remember, and I feel very alone. I lie quite still my heart pounding, and Gel's bark grows more and more frantic. Beyond it there's another sound, someone is knocking on the back door. "Oh God."

I shut my eyes and stretch out my hands, palms to the sheet. The cotton feels cool and smooth against my skin and the blood bounces in my fingertips.

"Go away, just go away and leave us alone." I mouth the words as Gel's brother Bri starts to growl. In a minute all this noise will wake Georgie and then I won't be able to hide our presence. I slip from the bed and wrap a robe around my shoulders. Georgie moves in her cot, clutches one hand into a fist and turns her face to the side.

"Ssh, ssh, it's alright darling," I say and will her not to cry.

A little back from the window I hold my breath and try to picture where I left my mobile phone. It isn't in the bedroom so it must be downstairs somewhere, perhaps on the kitchen table. Wherever it is, it will almost certainly be in full view of an uncurtained window. My heart thumps behind my ribs.

Damn. I should have had a plan for this, Arthur's number written down close at hand or, I shake my head as though to clear the sleep from my brain. Of course, I can phone 999 but how long would it take for the police to get here? In London, I could merely have called to a neighbour or hammered on the floor, but here there is no one.

The knocking stops but the dogs are still barking, and suddenly a thin strand of light shines in above the curtains and slides across the ceiling. For a few seconds, it's there, and I hold my breath, then it's gone. A minute passes, and it's back again. A torch beam shone across the front of the house perhaps. I imagine a figure creeping through the shadows, feet silent over grass; a hand outstretched to feel for a window off the latch. If they come in through the front, I could perhaps slip out through the utility room and make my escape for help across the orchard.

"Go away, please just go."

The knocking starts again and echoes through the empty rooms downstairs redoubling the dogs' frenzy. Their bodies thud against the back door as they throw themselves at it.

"No, no." I lean against the wall, and there's a

strange taste under my tongue. Who the hell is it and what do they want at this time? "Leave us alone."

The knocks grow louder and more irritated, and behind me, Georgie lets out a cry.

"It's okay darling, ssh, ssh." I scoop her up and ease her into bed with me. She starts to feed almost at once, and I press my head into the pillow trying to shut out the sounds from below. Crazily I think that if I stay quite still and silent we'll be safe, like a rabbit freezing in headlights.

Five minutes pass, and suddenly I realise that everything has gone quiet. I lift my head, but there's nothing, no sound of footsteps, no door opening, no restless ranging of the dogs. I try to interpret the silence just as I tried to make out the sounds, and the darkness pulses in front of my eyes.

Georgie feeds and feeds then abruptly snuggles down into the warm cave made by the duvet. It's tempting to leave her there, to cuddle her close and try to stop listening for sounds beyond the room but the warnings about cot death and co-sleeping reel through my head. There's no side to the bed, and she could fall out too easily, so I lift her gently back into her travel cot.

"There you go, darling." For a moment I think she's going to wake, but instead, she settles deeper into sleep.

For a long time, I stand looking down at her and listening. All I can hear is her light breathing and nothing else so eventually I ease myself back into bed. Still, I can't sleep. Who was out there and what did they want? Was it someone come to tell me something that they didn't want the police to know? Or was it Marty or the same person that Clare walked out to meet last

Friday? Assuming she walked out to meet anyone of course.

What if it's her, what if she's the one who has done something terrible? I try to stop that train of thought, but the darkness is too fluid, too empty. All things are possible. The last time I saw her was there anything different about her that I could or should have noticed?

We met in a deli café not far from Covent Garden. Clare wasn't happy, there was tension at the corners of her eyes and in the tightness of her lips but then she never liked coming up to London, and there was always an undercurrent of irritation about that. Robert wasn't there. Sometimes he joined her, sometimes he didn't. It was slightly less strained and superficial when he wasn't there, but not much and I was beginning to wonder why we continued to meet up once or twice a year.

I didn't exactly tell Hollinghurst the whole truth. Everything I said about my pregnancy and not wanting to discuss it with Clare was true, but I do remember what we argued about. Clare wanted me to come down to Devon; she breached our agreement not to talk about it and kept on at me all day. In the end, I'd lost my temper and said that if she didn't want to come up to London anymore, that was just fine by me. Now I wonder if I shouldn't have listened more carefully, had she been trying to tell me something, was her persistence born out of desperation?

Suddenly there's a sound outside.

"Oh God." I sit up straight in bed, the blood racing round my veins as I strain my ears to locate and make sense of the noise. For a few seconds there's nothing, then it comes again, the unmistakable call of a tawny owl beyond the barns. "Phew."

The air floods out of my lungs, and I realise that I'm shaking. Another owl answers from the beech tree near the gate and further away a female tawny screeches in the valley. I lie back carefully to avoid waking Georgie, but it takes ages for my pulse to return to normal, and even then I'm a long way from sleep.

———

I'm still awake when dawn filters through the curtains. With a sigh, I roll over, slip from the bed and head for the landing. The house is silent and chilly, but it's late enough for me to move around without switching on a light. I don't know what I'm expecting to find, but I run down the stairs before Georgie wakes and into the cross passage. Everything looks the same as last night. For a moment I stand with my back against the closed front door. I'm far more out of breath than I should be and I can still hardly believe that I'm here and this is all happening.

In London, I almost thought that I could turn away and pretend that Clare and Lee's disappearance had nothing to do with me; that I'd be allowed to. But now, here, everything is so immediate, so familiar and physically unchanged that I can't hide from the reality of it.

I take a deep breath to steady myself, but it catches somewhere high up in my lungs. What if? What if? My mind races in great dark loops of exhaustion and panic and Georgie starts to cry upstairs.

"Coming darling." Now my words seem to echo the same phrase from years ago, and my footsteps trace others that hurried to pick up a baby. Was this how Clare was with me, with Jamie? And, if so, what lies ahead for Georgie and me? A chill seeps through my skin. I don't want to think about it, but there's no escaping the fact that Clare's genes have shaped half of me, that whatever changes have overtaken her mind may yet lurk within me ready to distort the logic in my brain.

Georgie's face is red with emotion when I stoop to pick her up out of her travel cot, and my hands are shaking. I stare at them for a moment and flex my fingers. Nature or nurture? I've got Clare's thumbs, I've always known that.

"It's okay." I stare across the top of her head to the far wall where one of Clare's collages hangs. It's a strange, unsettling arrangement of purple and black shapes with something that looks like an orange eye off centre. Could she have injured or killed another person's child? Surely not. I try to turn away from the horror of it but deep down a worm of uncertainty wriggles. No sane person would but-

I sit down in the faded denim covered armchair by the west window to feed Georgie. She smells faintly of fresh pee, and after a moment's hesitation, she snuggles in against me as though nothing has changed in her world. I look out towards Longcause Wood and the flank of Howden above and beyond. I don't remember it from before, but now it's possible to see a tiny stretch of the top road before it dips down the hill. Perhaps some trees have been felled or something.

There's a car parked up there, the sun glints off its windscreen, and I have an odd feeling that the occupants could be watching me or at least the house. I dismiss the thought straight away as pure paranoia. Before Georgie's finished feeding there's the roar of an engine much closer. It makes me jump, but it's only Arthur's old Series I Landrover that swings into the yard.

"Oh God." I feel caught out and unready. I need to change Georgie and then myself; I need a shower, breakfast, sleep. All the little mundane things that make a day like this faceable.

I pull on a sweatshirt over my nightdress, push my bare feet into sandals and change Georgie quickly before heading downstairs with her still in the same sleep suit. I once read about a famous actress who sometimes didn't have time to change in the mornings either and wore the same black dress day and night. I'm not sure that I can pull off that look though.

There are dirty plates on the kitchen counter, a split tea bag and a bottle of milk with the lid off. The dogs have pushed their bowls into a pack under the table leaving water spilt across the tiles, but I can't do anything about it with Georgie in my arms, so I carry her out through the back door to the yard.

Arthur's Landrover is beside the stables, but there's no sign of him, so I take a deep, steadying breath of the fresh morning air as I look around. There's no visible sign of last night's intruder, and for a moment I wonder if I didn't dream the whole thing, but the tension in my body tells me otherwise. Someone came, someone up to no good or someone who didn't want to be seen by the police. Whichever way I look at it I feel deeply uneasy.

"Morning Charlotte."

I start as Arthur leads Ebenezer, Simon's old horse, around the side of the barn. Stupid, stupid, stupid. I knew he was here somewhere. I need to get a grip on myself. The horse's hip joints click as he comes to a halt beside us.

"Sorry I didn't mean to surprise you." He looks at me for a moment no doubt taking in my poorly disguised nightdress and unbrushed hair. "Are you alright Charlotte?"

"I think so." I look at him across Eb's dark dipped back, the horse's spine no longer bears the weight of his prominent spreading ribs, and his lower lip hangs loose and rubbery. I touch his nose, and he jerks his head to get a better look at me. "Good boy."

"I know it's a bit early, but I'm giving this old man his breakfast before, well we were due to start cutting the hay this week, it's been such an early year."

"The hay?"

"Perhaps I should be helping to search instead." Arthur looks uncertain for a moment. "I don't want to let Clare down; the contractors are due to bale before the weekend. We can't afford to miss this weather and not have any hay for the winter."

"No."

The shadow of other possibilities hangs between us, and I look away. I have no idea of the farm calendar now, nor of which fields are being rested and what stock should be where, which is surprisingly disorientating.

"Are you sure you're alright?"

"I, er. Arthur, would you like to come in for a cup of tea? I need to talk to you."

"Of course. I'll just put Eb in the stable." I'm not sure if it's only my imagination but his voice sounds guarded.

We walk across the yard, the dogs switching backwards and forwards behind us in sheep-driving mode, and a memory catches me by surprise. Arthur and Simon used to do so much together when Robert was too busy for the farm. They would spend all day gathering the sheep in for dipping or vaccinating, working with slow precision, few words and an odd language of gestures that I could never quite understand. I push the visions away.

"I'll go and put the kettle on."

Arthur takes his cap off when he comes in and sits on the edge of one of the wooden benches by the kitchen table. He doesn't look comfortable.

"I've used the bottled stuff." I glance across the room at the five-litre water containers lined up against the wall. "What's the problem with the water supply?"

In the past, there was occasionally something, a cracked pipe or frogs in the water-collection tank. Simon found a toad leg in the basin once that had somehow come all the way down the pipe and out through the cold tap.

"Nothing exactly." Arthur hesitates. "Clare was very … careful after Robert's death, that's all."

His face is much as I remembered it only more deeply tanned and lined by the sun, there's also a greyness beneath his eyes that was never there before. "She thought that the water caused the cancer?"

"No, no it wasn't anything like that." He traces a knot in the table top. "She said, oh it doesn't matter now."

"Please, go on."

"Well, she seemed to think that someone might poison it."

"What?" I try to catch his eye, but he looks away. "I

mean why? Why did she think that anyone would do that?"

"I don't know. It was just the way she was. It may sound strange, but I'm not sure that she liked being on her own here after Robert died."

He's as wary of me as I am of him. I realise it suddenly, and it's a shock. Have I changed so much? I stretch out a hand and look at my pale, London-smooth fingers. He knows so much more about my family than I do now. He knows how Clare filled her days and where Robert died. He told me the names of these dogs, but he knew the ones before and the ones before that. There are so many other things that I want; I need to ask him and yet now that he's sitting here I don't know how or where to begin.

"Arthur?" He looks at me and the confusion about my near estrangement is there in his eyes. How could I? Is that what he's thinking? Or does it go deeper? Does he resent me being here at all, even now? "Arthur, look I'm sorry I haven't been in touch before-"

"I understand." He raises a hand, but I'm not sure that he does. Whatever, we have to leave it for now, we have to concentrate on the present, not the past.

"Could Clare-?" But there are so many questions that I stop again and try to put them in order in my head. When? How? Who? "Oh, Arthur what d'you think has happened? You were the last to, I mean could, oh God could Clare have, you know?"

His silence unnerves me, and I suddenly have the horrible thought that he might have mistaken what I meant, might have thought that I was inferring that he's in some way guilty.

"I'm sorry, I didn't mean- It's just been going round

and round in my head. I haven't seen her since the end of last summer, and I know she wasn't happy then but-"

"It's okay," he says and looks even more uncomfortable. "But I really don't know Charlotte. The water was one thing, she was tired and upset. Robert's death took it out of her."

"Of course."

I wanted him to reassure me, but I have the sense that he isn't going to.

"She hasn't been out much since the funeral apart from a few shopping trips."

"That's understandable surely; she was grieving, she-"

Arthur isn't looking at me anymore, and he twists his earth-stained fingers until the joints protest.

"What is it?"

For a few moments longer he hesitates then he glances around the room before leaning across the table towards me. "I haven't told the police this, but I couldn't help noticing that Clare had been buying some odd things over the last few weeks."

"Like?"

"Wooden stakes and rolls of barbed wire-"

I let out my breath. Those sorts of odd things. "She probably just wanted to do some fencing to-"

"And shotgun cartridges."

A chaffinch chinks in the garden and I watch it flutter past the open window. Clare never went near the guns in the past, she hated them and wouldn't let Jamie, and I play mock battle games when we were younger. It was only after Simon arrived that all that was somehow eroded. He came with his unlikely interest in the young men of the First World War. Sometimes when we were out on the horses, we became soldiers riding to the front and Simon held up a pole as though it was a regimental flagstaff. He had the looks for it somehow, and it wasn't hard to imagine that he was one of those handsome young men who never came home from France.

The generations of his family were spaced differently than mine, who had all been the wrong age to go to either war, and he'd lost his grandfather and a great uncle at Ypres.

When had Clare learnt about guns? I can't picture her going into a shop and buying cartridges let alone knowing how to cock a shotgun and load them. Was it something that came after Robert's death or before? It adds up with the new bolts on the doors though. Had, I glance around the room as though expecting to see a shadow there, had she suddenly had some reason to fear for her safety?

"I'm so sorry," Arthur says at last, and his tone implies far more than his words. As far as the police know he was the last one to see Clare and Lee alive, and he obviously thinks that there's a strong possibility that she's guilty of something.

"No, I needed to know." Who's right, who's wrong? Or are we both way off the point?

"It doesn't mean-"

"Of course not." But he thinks it does, and maybe the police have already seen through his loyal silence.

Arthur stands up and looks at his feet in their worn dealer boots. What else does he know that he's not prepared to tell even me? "I should be getting on with my work. Eb will have finished his feed by now and-"

"Yes." I watch him walk down the path to the yard, his back stooped and twisted from years of carrying hay bales on his right shoulder. Shotgun cartridges. He saw them but where are they now? Corralled in some room in the police station no doubt along with the guns that used to hang above the inglenook before the days of locked gun cabinets. "Oh God." I sink my face forward against Georgie, but she's almost asleep, so I lower her into her car seat and strap her in. "Your granny-"

I stop myself at once, but I can't hide from the chain of connection now that I'm back. I may have lied to everyone else, but I knew, when I looked at Georgie as soon as she was born, that I couldn't lie to her. One day she would have to know the truth about her relatives, her history. My only consolation at the time had been the thought that that day was a long way off, but now-

"Does she look like you when you were a baby? Is there a family likeness?" The midwife asked innocently, but I couldn't tell her because I didn't know. I had no pictures of any of them apart from Jamie, not even my younger self. Now suddenly I have an overwhelming desire to know whose genes may be strongest in shaping her future.

The sitting room is more cluttered than I remembered and there's a closed-in smell of dust and soot, but the old bureau is still there against the inner wall. It was where Clare used to keep all her letters and photographs and general items of interest.

For a moment I hesitate, then I reach out my hand to lift down the lid. Perhaps it'll be locked, the key hidden from sight, but it opens easily to reveal the tiers of small drawers. The police will have searched them of course, and maybe I'll never know what items have already been taken, but I don't suppose what I'm looking for will have been of enough interest to be removed.

It lived in the third drawer down on the right-hand side. I pull on the tiny handle, and within seconds I can see that it's still there: a battered blue family photo album. My first shots, all carefully posed even then, used to begin about halfway through. Before them were an assortment of school portraits and family groups.

I take the album out with a shaking hand and open it. At first, it seems unchanged. There are the photos of our parents before we were born. Individual shots, including one of Robert at his architectural degree cere-mony when big hair was in, then a few of them posed about the farm, young, carefree dreamers, in front of the house, down in one of the lower meadows, beside a trailer of hay bales. There is even a picture of Clare outside her studio with half a dozen of her figures, wild things with carved wooden faces and string hair.

Fleetingly I wonder who took the photos then I turn the page and find one of me as a baby. I'm lying on my back in one of those 1970s prams with the big wheels, and the canvas fold down hoods. I can't have been more than a few months old. Perhaps the same age as Georgie is now.

Is there a similarity? I glance from the album to her sleeping face, and there is something about the shape of our heads and the baby shortness of our noses. In the album a hand reaches in to me from the side of the frame, Clare's presumably. I feel a little odd looking at the long, slim, youthful fingers, fingers that were younger than mine are now, fingers that may recently have- I flip over to the next page, and still, everything seems normal. There are more pictures of me getting older, riding a trike and then standing with a hobby horse.

Everyone is smiling, a happy family group of three. It's then that it hits me. By the time I was standing like that Jamie had been born. But where are the pictures of him? I turn forward a few more pages to be sure, but there are no photos of him and, further on, none of Simon either. There were pictures of the boys once because I remember taking them, so intent on the overall design that they used to end up looking rather formal and posed, the boys bored and scowling or mocking me with cheesy grins.

There are no gaps though; each page has been painstakingly edited, the photos moved around and restuck to give a semblance of normality. The subtlety of it is chilling. To anyone who didn't know, it would look as though our little family was complete and the boys had never existed.

I stop at a page of summer shots. In the first, I look about eleven, which means it was the year that Simon arrived. I'm smiling down from the back of a grey pony, and Uncle Eric is standing beside me looking away to the left. I can almost remember that picture being taken, the feel of the leather reins stiff between my fingers after the previous day's rain and Uncle Eric laughing because Bethany had nudged him in the back seconds before.

"God." That day was so close to when Simon arrived, the same week perhaps, but before we knew that he was coming.

I turn over the remaining pages quickly, rushing through the years to the end of the album and there is not a single image of either of the boys. Will the police have noticed that? There are no empty pages at the back to give things away, which I can't work out until I look closely and see that they've been cut out against the spine.

I close the album with a soft thump and stand quite still. Why the boys and not me? I don't understand. Why Lee now? A weird sense of unease shifts through me, and I flush although no one is watching. Then crazily I think someone might be watching and I spin round. The room is quite empty of course, and Georgie is still sleeping.

5

"We're getting a good response already," Miller says on the phone later that morning. Her voice has that bright, disconnected professional tone that people take on when they need to do a good job in difficult circumstances. She's updating me because she has to as part of her job, not because she feels for me or even perhaps likes me.

"But is it leading anywhere?"

"It's too early to say yet." She pauses. "But officers are checking all new leads."

"There are a lot of TV vans around still." When Georgie and I went out across the fields for our early walk, I could see the sunlight reflecting off their windscreens far down the valley.

"I'm afraid that there will be with a story like this." Her voice makes me feel that I should know these things.

Hollinghurst arrives soon after lunch in a dark, unmarked car with tinted windows. He's wearing a clean shirt, a pale blue one, but his trousers still hold the creases of yesterday, and his face has a grey sleepless tinge.

"Would you like a cup of tea?" I'm not sure if I'm following the correct etiquette for the situation, but it makes me feel more in control somehow to ask the question. I've reached the end of the bottled water, and I'll have to take a chance with the tap stuff. If Arthur's right and I feel certain that he is, then the problem was all in Clare's mind, and there's absolutely nothing wrong with the water supply apart from the usual blueness of copper stripped from the pipes by the acidity.

"No thanks." Hollinghurst shakes his head. "I won't hold you up for long, but have you seen your brother?"

"Excuse me?" I thought he was going to ask me something else and now I'm thrown.

"Your brother, Simon, has he been in touch with you?"

"Simon?" There's a strange look on Hollinghurst's face, and my pulse speeds up. "No, I, I haven't heard from him for years. I told you and Quinn that before."

For a long moment, he's silent, but he doesn't take his eyes off me. "I need the truth."

"I'm telling it to you."

"Okay." He steeples his fingers. "It appears that he's gone missing as well."

"What?"

"Officers have been round to his houseboat, but there's no sign of him and his neighbours, if you can call them that, haven't seen him since yesterday morning."

Houseboat. It's the first, the only information, I've had about Simon for twenty years. Images flood into my mind. I can't make sense of them or of what any of this means but it doesn't feel good.

"Charlotte we need to find him, so if you've got any information that might be helpful-"

"I told you, I don't know anything about him anymore."

"Okay, I'm sorry you've obviously got things you need to do." He glances down at Georgie who's growing restless in my arms. "But if he does make contact with you or you think of anything that might help us please just call the incident room, say who you are and ask for me, they'll put you straight through."

"Of course."

He's at the door when he swings back towards me with almost exaggerated casualness. "What are your plans by the way?"

"Mine?" I still feel oddly dizzy from lack of sleep and for once in my life, I don't have any clear idea of the day ahead.

"Are you going back to London?"

"Not today now." I don't want to commit myself beyond that, and he doesn't push it.

"We'll keep in touch then. I've got your mobile number."

First Clare and now Simon as well, the ripples of implication are spreading, and I wonder where they'll stop. When the sound of Hollinghurst's car has faded down the lane, I fill a glass of water from the tap and hold it up to the light. It looks quite clear, and it smells fine. For a moment longer I hesitate then I take a gulp. It doesn't taste of anything, and there's no tang of the treatment chemicals that I've grown used to in London.

But what if? I push the thought away quickly. It's fine. I'll be fine.

———

More people have died in the parish now than can fit in the tiny graveyard upriver of the village. However, a little extension has been made in a neighbouring field for the newcomers. I walk through a gap in the original tumbled granite hedgebank and stop in front of the most recent graves. I know that Robert's grave must be somewhere here, but for a few moments, I can't bring myself to look.

Behind me, the church crouches silent and watchful in the shadow of early evening. It has a chimney, but no real tower and I wonder if it's the only church with a wood burner inside. The sun is still up, but we're too deep in the valley to be touched by it at this time.

A car comes slowly down the road, and I stand back against the hedge and wait. Every vehicle makes me edgy now, but this one doesn't stop, and I let out my breath. Further away there are children's voices, a babble on the breeze.

"Okay, Georgie?" She looks at me with steady eyes that might stay blue and might not. It's late for her to be out and about and I know that I'll probably pay for it tonight. "I'm sorry, mummy just needs-"

But I can't finish, I'm not sure what I do need, to see Robert's grave, to be close to him again? A flood of memories rush at me, and I lean back against an old gnarled thorn tree and listen to the river tumbling over the rocks on the other side of the narrow road. Usually, there is a stillness about this place that calms even the most frayed nerves, but now its magic hardly touches me.

All I can think about are the angry words and the relentlessness of Robert's black moods after Jamie's accident, the way he looked at Simon and swore at the dogs. At the time I remember trying to justify his sudden withdrawals while the pain inside me grew and grew. I wanted someone to talk to, to comfort me but whatever I said he merely blanked me, sometimes for days.

The old bleakness rises within me again, and I try to fight it off. It took me months, maybe even years away from the farm to shake myself free of the lingering sense that somehow the downward spiral of events was partly my fault. Even now the old questions gnaw at me. What if I had told Clare or Robert about Jamie's bullies? Or suppose I'd played Scrabble with him that last evening instead of reading alone in my room? Would he have gone out after Simon anyway?

"No." I step forward.

The new graves rise up the gentle slope in front of me. The first few are smooth and green; the headstones fresher than those clustered closer to the church but still somehow settled. Beyond them are the most recent. There are still flowers and gaps marked with wooden stakes. I glance at the nearest, and my breath quickens. 'Reserved, Amy' is written vertically in pen. I hadn't thought that people booked spaces like that.

Robert's grave is on the end of the fourth row. A long dome of green turf with the spade lines still visible, the clods not yet bound back together after their disturbance. A plain granite headstone records the span of his life. Above the dates the three words 'In memory of' say so much in their omission of the word 'loving' that adorns every other headstone close by. It could be an oversight of course, but I think not, who would make that kind of mistake on a gravestone? A single pot of chrysanthemums stands in front of the stone. It obviously hasn't been watered during this latest spell of hot weather, the pale shaggy flowers hang down, and the leaves are curled and brown.

This is it then. His place now. Eternal silence imposed on him as he once tried to impose it on the rest of us. Don't cry. I bow my head as an image rises in my mind: Robert working late under the bright glow of his anglepoise lamp, designing his beautiful houses that were so seldom built. His face intent as his fingers, long and slim for a man, created the drawings in such detail that you could almost feel the dressed stone warm beneath your hand.

"Oh God."

What happened to Robert, to us all? Once we had such big dreams for the farm, for his architecture business, for the things we were going to do together, so what went wrong? Why couldn't we have just talked and worked things out? Why did everything always end in that bleak, terrible silence that left the dogs cowering and shaking under the kitchen table?

I pick up the sad little pot plant, and the children's voices are suddenly close. Somewhere out in the road. Three heads dip behind the wall amidst a cacophony of giggles as I turn towards them.

"Ssh, ssh."

For a few moments they manage to stay quiet then there's more laughter and running footsteps on tarmac. I smile. Whoever they are they can't hurt me now. Even if they're the children of our tormentors, I'm too old for their teasing to touch me. I carry the plant towards a bin I noticed near the church porch. I'm on the narrow gravel path when I hear him.

"Excuse me?"

"Hello."

He's about twelve or thirteen, one of those fit kids, rangy and watchful, dressed in frayed jeans and a Liverpool t-shirt.

"You're the daughter aren't you?" He doesn't look directly at me and his right hand clenches around something, a stone perhaps, or some wooden treasure he's found.

I nod, surprised that he knows who I am. Who has pointed me out to him and when? The sense of being watched all the time increases.

"Is Lee coming back?"

Oh. I hesitate. I don't want to lie to the boy and create false hope, and yet I don't want to scare him either.

"I hope so."

"She won't hurt him will she? My mum says-"

"No, no I'm sure she won't." The shadow of the bloodstain in the farmhouse hangs close.

"He wasn't always bunking off school as they said in the paper." He tosses his stone away, and it arcs into the long grass under the wall. "But his dad had had a letter, he told me."

Suddenly there's a movement away to our right, the catch and swing of light on steel. I spin round in time to see a dark car pull into a side turning. Nothing unusual and yet nerves prickle down my back.

"I've got to go I'm afraid. Don't you think you should go home as well?"

The boy looks in the direction of the car, and his face lights up. "Are we going to be on TV?"

"No."

"My mum was filmed earlier because I'm Lee's friend."

I try to see some likeness in him to friends I had in the village back then, to Vicki or Rick or Tony, but I can't. So many families must have moved in and out since I was last here that it's hardly surprising. I won't ask him his name though and risk my approach being misconstrued by anyone, his mother, the police or even the press.

"We're writing him messages," the boy says. "On Bebo. Do you think he's reading them?"

"I don't know, but that's a nice thing to do."

The boy smiles for a moment then spins around on one heel. His converse trainers are muddy. "I'm going back across the fields. I've got a special way."

For a moment longer, he hesitates looking at Georgie than he turns and runs away through the gap into the new graveyard, over the wall and on up the field beyond. I watch him until a sound behind me catches my attention.

"Miss Elgin?" A small man with a dark moustache is at the church gate, one hand on the cool steel the other steadying the camera slung around his neck. "Miss Elgin can-?"

"No." I swing away from him with a hand up to my face. I know the shot he wants, and he's not getting it, but I've been stupid, he's blocking my escape now.

Ahead of me, the old church door stands dark and solid. I don't think the man will follow me inside. "I'm sorry Georgie I know it's past your bedtime."

It's cool and shadowy in the church, and there's a deep stillness. I stand for a long time near the back of the narrow nave. The barrel roof arches above my head as it has done over countless generations, the old carvings at the joints a little wormy and aged now but still discernable as three rabbits linked by their ears. Clare told me the story behind them when I was quite young and a little scared of the church for some reason, but I can't remember it. Suddenly that seems careless. I should know it to pass on to Georgie. In fact, there are so many things that I should remember for her sake, so many things that I might; I would have done differently if I'd know I was going to have her. Is it too late now?

I sink down onto one of the pews at the back. The wood is cold and slightly damp through the thin cotton of my skirt. Is it too late? For a moment I feel safe within these thick granite walls, beyond the reach of all the people who are clamouring for my attention, and my head clears a little in the stillness. If Clare is still alive somewhere how will this all end and how will we come to terms with what has happened, with what she's done?

At best she and Lee will be mostly unharmed physically, but mentally? There'll be police, lawyers, psychiatrists, a court case, prison even and everything will be splashed across the tabloids. At worst. I shut my eyes, and now there's another image behind my closed lids: Simon.

"Oh God." Georgie shifts in her carrier then lets her head flop forward against my chest.

I can't make sense of what Hollinghurst's words could mean, of how Simon might be involved in all this. I'm almost sure that Clare hadn't been in contact with him since he left, at least up until I last saw her over nine months ago. The sadness of it was in her eyes although we never talked about him. So what's happened since then? What do the police know that they're not telling me? What perhaps does the whole village know that I don't?

It could be a coincidence, of course, he could have gone away quite innocently, unaware of what's happened, but even I have to admit that that seems unlikely with all the press coverage. What else then? What other possible explanations are there for his 'disappearance'? An odd, edgy feeling niggles at me. It's as though there's something I should know that's just out of my reach, some connection I should be making that I'm not.

Instead, all I can see suddenly is Simon's younger self as he slowly eased out of the grief that had enveloped him when he first arrived at Northstone. Day by day, month by month the pain receded, and we ran lighter and more carefree down through the fields. Sometimes he would grab my hand and force me faster and faster until my feet seemed to skim above the grass and the sharp granite boulders flashed by beneath us.

"Come on, come on." It was a chant, a challenge. He could do it but did I dare?

All my fears about him descending on our family were gone in the wild excitement of having him around. Suddenly I couldn't even remember what it had been like before he arrived, that time seemed distant and somewhat dull. Marty was still around of course, but he became a background figure, someone who joined us at the weekends if it was a game for three or four. He was slow and solid compared to Simon and didn't get the new fleeting jokes that stretched to places beyond the valley.

"We're going to London," I told him once, and he just laughed as though I'd said that we were flying to Russia.

That day jabs at me now. I'd spoken almost teasingly in the yard at Sleepers not knowing how soon and in what circumstances my words would come true. Marty was mending some implement, a chain harrow I think, his hands and face covered in mud and grease. For a few moments with the mask of work, he was almost middle-aged, and my mood felt heavy. He always reminded me how much there was to do, then Simon came running along the track and the day changed. There was still lots to do of course, but we could whirl through the jobs to freedom, to a gallop over Howden or a swim in Devil's Cauldron.

"Come on."

There's a noise outside the church, faint but unmistakable through the thick walls and heavily leaded windows, a vehicle starting up and moving away down the road. I shut my mind to all else and listen. It slows, surely for the bridge, then the gears change and the sound of the engine deepens as it pulls away up the hill. Fainter, fainter, fainter and then it's gone. I let out my breath and wait until I'm sure that it isn't coming back before easing open the door and looking around. Its dimpsy outside but the churchyard seems deserted and the road beyond.

"Sorry Georgie, let's go now." My heart is beating hard by the time we reach the car, and still, no one has appeared. All I need to do is strap Georgie into her car seat, and then we can go but my fingers are clumsy, and nothing does up the first time. "Come on, come on."

Finally, we're both in and secure. I slam the driver's door and start up the engine, but we can't go back to the farm. It's too remote, too dangerous after dark, in my head but maybe also in reality. There was someone there last night. However much I try to reason it away, I know that I wasn't mistaken.

I'll have to phone Arthur about the dogs, that's all. I reverse the Golf out of the little grassy pull-in beside the churchyard and turn away towards the village. The lane ahead is deserted now, but there's uncertainty around every bend, and I drive faster than I should. What if the journalist has stopped somewhere to wait for me?

"I'm sorry Georgie, I'm sorry," I say when I have to brake abruptly to avoid a rabbit.

I reach the outskirts of the village without meeting another car, but there are a group of marked vans parked along the edge of the tiny green, so I take the narrow left turn that'll bring me almost back round on myself.

Did anyone see me? I keep checking my rearview mirror, but for the moment I seem safe. At the next junction, I turn right and then I'm away heading south towards the open anonymity of the dual carriageway.

"Phew."

For a second I relax and swing the car around another corner. The road straightens out between high granite hedgebanks and dips gently downhill. The sudden familiarity of this particular stretch clutches at my throat.

It was right here in the dark all those years ago- I remember the lights coming up fast on full beam, dazzling through the night so that they filled the whole of the narrow lane and I couldn't see anything beyond them.

"Wait," Simon's hand on my arm held me still.

A cow lowed behind us, mourning the loss of her calf. The air was cold against my cheeks, but I was sweating beneath my jacket, and my breath grew tighter and tighter as a hot, sour taste spread under my tongue.

"Now."

We ran out, flinging ourselves from the bank to the hard tarmac below, four wild jarring strides and then into the hedge beyond, thorns tearing at skin and eyes dazzled and blind in the sudden darkness.

"I felt its heat," I said.

"We did it."

Simon held me tight and breathless in the wet grass, smothering my giggles with a hand across my mouth as we listened for a falter in the engine. There was a smell of exhaust fumes and lanolin, and I didn't dare move my hand in case there was sheep shit as well.

"No brakes."

"Ten out of ten?"

"Eight."

"Why?" I picked a stem of bramble out of my hair.

"We could get closer."

"But I felt its heat."

"So?" He stood up. "You have to touch it."

"What? I can't do that, it's dangerous. We'll cause an accident or, or be killed."

"Are you scared?" He stepped away, and a sweep of cool air slid between us.

"Oh God." My heart is beating hard even now. I glance in the rearview mirror, first at the road behind, then twisting my neck slightly, at Georgie. The road is empty, and she's asleep so- I turn my attention forwards again, and there's a dark figure already in mid-air out from the right bank. "Shit."

I slam on the brakes, there's nowhere to go, I'm too close already, I'm going to hit him. The car squeals to a stop less than a metre from the jean-clad legs and the man looks at me over the bonnet with one arm behind his back. For a moment longer, he's a stranger, and I have the crazy feeling that he's got a gun, then he smiles.

6

———

"Simon."

He walks round to my side of the car, and I wind down the window.

"Fancy-"

"What the bloody hell? I could have killed you. I've got a baby in the back." Adrenalin fizzes in the tips of my fingers.

"I'm sorry I didn't mean to scare you." He brings his left hand from behind his back and holds out a large bunch of flowers. "I brought you these."

"What are you doing here?" I don't take the flowers. They aren't from any service station; there are lightly scented roses, snapdragons, larkspur and others I know but can't name, garden flowers from someplace warmer and more sheltered than the moorland garden around the farm.

He's wearing washed out jeans and a checked shirt and he's thinner than before, there are grooves down his cheeks, and there's something else about him that I can't put my finger on. A breeze blows a strand of golden hair across his eyes, and he brushes it away with a hand that is suddenly so familiar that I catch my breath.

"Simon, what-?"

He ignores me and turns instead to look back up the road. I glance in the rearview mirror in time to catch sight of a dark car coming round the corner. I'm not sure if it's the same car as earlier, it might only be an innocent traveller and then it might not.

"Get in."

"What?"

"Quickly."

The car speeds up behind us, and I'm sure that I can see a camera in the hands of the passenger. As soon as Simon's in the Golf I pull away.

"Bloody press."

I have to concentrate to drive safely through the lanes. Once or twice I catch sight of the dark car behind us then it's gone again behind the high hedges. I accelerate as hard as I dare and turn left and then right a few times through the maze of roads. I'm surprised how well I remember them.

We don't speak for a long time, but I'm aware of him sitting there beside me, within touching distance for the first time in twenty years. The flowers lying across his lap fill the car with a light scent of summer.

"How-?"

"Don't-?"

When we're finally out on the dual carriageway, we both start to speak at the same time and stop.

"You first," Simon says.

"How did you know that I'd drive along there then?"

"I've been waiting for you all day."

"But-"

"I heard your message on TV. I had to see you alone Char, and there are too many police officers around the farm."

I can't look at him for a second as we've run into a sudden knot of traffic, one of those unfathomable go-slows, but his words make me uneasy.

"So?"

"Don't you like the flowers?"

"Simon, it's been twenty bloody years. I didn't even know whether you were still alive. You never called, not once, so you can't just come crashing back into my life now and expect me to behave as though nothing's happened." I take a deep breath to steady myself. We're so close that I can smell his skin, warm and slightly earthy, the scent at once familiar even after all this time. "Why are you here anyway?"

For a moment he's silent, then he rolls up each sleeve of his shirt, in turn, revealing deeply tanned forearms. I can't stop myself looking, and it's there, a straight scar across the back of his left wrist. He's so casual about exposing it that I think he must have forgotten.

"What's going on?" He keeps his eyes straight ahead.

"You've seen the news."

"Of course, but that's probably all spin, what's really happening? Why was it a statement from you and not Robert on TV?"

I pull out from behind a lorry and speed up in the outside lane. Suddenly I want to go faster and faster, to put a huge distance between us and the farm, but I know that I won't.

"Simon, Robert's dead." I glance sideways at him, but his profile doesn't change.

"I see," he says at last.

"And the rest, well it's like they're reporting, they've gone, Clare and Lee, there's no sign of them anywhere."

"And?"

"That's it, as much as I know."

"But-"

"I haven't been back here for nearly twenty years either."

"Yeh right." He pinches his fingers together in turn as he works out the mathematics of what I've said. "When you were fifteen?"

"Just sixteen."

"But-?"

"I've met them off and on when I've been in the country. Mostly Clare and Robert came up to London. I haven't seen either of them for nearly a year."

"You're serious?"

"How would you know? I mean how the hell would you?" My voice rises. "If you'd flown to the moon you couldn't have vanished any more successfully."

"Charlotte."

"For God's sake Simon, you were the one that ran away, and now you come back here with a bunch of flowers as though-"

"I'm sorry. Pull into the next service station, and I'll get out."

"What? No, no don't be silly. It's just- Look let's go to Newton and get some food."

We drive on in silence to the next slip road then turn off and head for the market town that was once our nearest shopping centre. The main road is rougher and bendy, and after a few miles, Georgie wakes with a cry.

"Ssh, ssh darling." I glance in the mirror at her.

"Who's the father?" Simon asks.

His abruptness makes me want to tell him that it's none of his business, but there's something else about his voice that catches me off guard. "There isn't one, I mean obviously there was but we've got an agreement, he isn't involved in any way. My choice."

Simon is silent for another mile or so until we're on the edge of town.

"You disapprove?"

"No actually I'm, I think you're very brave."

"And you? Does anyone share the houseboat with you?"

His attention snaps away from the road. "How on earth?"

"The police told me." I turn left and then right, and we park up in a side street around the corner from a row of shops that we used to frequent as teenagers. "I'm going to have to feed Georgie first."

"Georgie?"

"Short for Georgiana. She is a girl."

"Okay."

Now that we're able to look at each other properly we're suddenly awkward, and we keep our gazes everywhere but on each other's faces.

"Simon why?" I didn't mean to ask the question yet, but I can't stop myself.

"It's maybe not the time." He glances back at Georgie whose cries are rising, then fingers the flowers in his lap. "Are you hungry? Shall I get a takeaway?"

"Fine, yes, good idea."

I open the door and stand up on the pavement so that I'm better able to unstrap Georgie and lift her into the front for a feed.

"She's beautiful," Simon says watching me for a

second with that smile that I sometimes didn't understand even back then.

I look away. "D'you want to see if that pizza place is still around the corner? Anything veggie is fine with me. My wallet is in the door pocket there."

"It's okay, I've got some money. Maybe not as much as you but I think I can buy a couple of pizzas."

"I'm sorry, I didn't mean to imply anything." Georgie's cries are agitated now, and I have to turn my attention to her.

"I'll see you shortly," Simon says and walks away down the street.

"Oh God." I feel oddly shaky as I unbutton my shirt. I need to think what to do before he comes back. I should phone Hollinghurst of course but I can't right now because of feeding Georgie. Anyway, for some reason, I'm not sure that I'm going to, not yet anyway.

Several pairs of teenage girls walk past down the street, but none of them looks right in at us. Each pair is rather alike, and I wonder whether Georgie will have the kind of girlfriend that I never had. Will they wear the same style of shoes and swap clothes in their bedrooms? How different will it be for her to grow up not sandwiched between two brothers?

Simon's back quicker than I expect and he pulls open the passenger door, two pizza boxes in his right hand.

"It was still there I- oh sorry." He stops when he sees Georgie feeding and averts his eyes.

"She takes her time."

"Shall I wait outside?"

"Don't be crazy; she could be another twenty minutes anyway."

"I got two vegetable gardens." He says using the term from our childhood. I wonder whether he's said it since or whether he's only remembered it because he's back. "Can you eat now, shall I tear you off a piece?"

"Thanks."

Is this how we're going to be? Super polite, skirting over the surface of things when there's so much else to talk about? I take a bite of pizza, it's oily but good, the kind of comfort food that I need right now.

"I was thinking about what we used to do on that stretch of road back then," I say at last.

"So was I."

"It was mad."

We slip back into silence for a while, and Georgie drinks away steadily. The windscreen steams up above the pizza boxes balanced on the dash, and the car smells of hot tomato and also faintly of fresh pee. Georgie needs a nappy change as soon as she's finished eating, that difficult manoeuvre on the back seat where everything threatens to roll off onto the floor.

"Do you want another piece of pizza?" Simon asks at last, and I nod.

"The police want to speak to you urgently."

"To me?" Simon's surprise looks genuine.

"I'm supposed to call if I see or hear from you."

"And have you?"

"No, of course, I haven't." Our fingers touch as he passes me the pizza and I pull my hand away.

"Why not?"

I watch him for a moment. He looks tired suddenly. There's a dryness about his skin, and the grooves seem to have sunk deeper into his cheeks.

"I looked for you you know, in the papers and later on the Internet."

"You did?" He doesn't smile, and there's something in his eyes that I can't define.

"I never found any trace of you though."

"I, I couldn't." He stops and takes a swig of cola from one of the cans he brought back with him. "Fuck."

"What is it?"

"Nothing." He rubs a circle in the condensation and looks out of the side window at the street.

"What are we going to do now then?"

"Well-"

"I don't want to go back to the farm; there was someone there last night. I heard them."

"You didn't answer the door." He watches a car glide past and stop at the junction behind us.

"Of course not, but-"

"It was me. God Charlotte."

"You." I don't know whether to be angry or relieved. "What on earth?"

"I'm sorry. I needed to talk to you; it was stupid, I didn't think-"

His feet on the cobbles, his hand on the door, his torch beam sliding across the ceiling. "We'll go back then. I wasn't looking forward to staying in a motel again, to be honest."

Simon shoves the pizza boxes and cans into a bin while I turn the car around then climbs in beside me again. Such a simple act that feels so weird after all this time. I glance sideways at him then away again.

"The police obviously think you've done a runner."

"What?" It takes a few moments for the implication to sink in. "Oh God, I was just coming down here."

I wait, there's something that still doesn't quite add up.

"Where's your car then?"

"I haven't got one. I er don't drive anymore. I caught the train and cycled. My bike's in East Wood."

I think of the old farm Escort with its rusty wheel arches and the way he used to fling it around the corners so that the wheels spun on the wet grass and my breath caught in my throat. Why doesn't he drive anymore? There's a darkness behind his words that stops me asking him outright.

We leave town. Beyond the reach of the streetlights dusk has swept in. I switch on the headlights and drum the fingers of my right hand on the steering wheel. Now that we finally have the silence of a wide dark road we're both speechless, unable to find the words to span the intervening years. We have to talk though. I scan through my mind trying to find a way in that won't seem overtly accusatory or suspicious and time slides by.

Beyond the dual carriageway, the road rises steeply, and the fields on either side are dark and mysterious. The odd house light only serves to make the spaces in between feel more remote and unwelcoming. I don't remember this sense of alienation before, and I wonder if I haven't become too urban for this place. Beside me, Simon moves restlessly in his seat and stretches out his feet in the footwell. He never was a good passenger. I smile.

"What?"

"Nothing."

"You had that look." He pulls at his seatbelt then lets it snap back.

"What look?"

"The one that always used to drive me mad."

A weird fear lurches through me. "I did that? I see. You never told me."

"Char."

I push the car forwards up the last steep hill then we're dropping down towards the river again.

"We can't go up to the farm together," Simon says when we're half a mile or so away.

"No."

"Look I'll get out in a minute, walk around and meet you at the house."

"But-" Will he? Or is he going to disappear again? He's right though. If we drive up to the cordon together, there will be all sorts of questions, and I'll have to explain why I haven't called Hollinghurst. I stop the car in the next field gateway, and Simon climbs out.

"I'll see you soon," he says then hesitates and leans back into the car. "Honestly."

When he's gone, I clench both hands around the steering wheel and rock back hard against the seat. I can't believe it. I can't believe that we've travelled the best part of fifteen miles together without a proper word.

"Hell."

There are no obvious journalists or TV vans, but I can't shake off the sense that someone is watching me, even now at this hour, driving carefully up the potholed hill. As I approach the point where our two tracks divide my headlights pick up a patch of brightness around the Sleepers sign, and I slow down even further.

The piece of cloth that I saw before has been joined by a teddy bear tied to the post and several bunches of flowers. There are also cards and pieces of paper attached to a thorn tree nearby.

"Oh God." It's too like a memorial, and it fills me with terror about the way things may turn out, the final blow of the evening. I won't read the messages, but I can imagine them written in the childish scrawl of his friends.

Georgie is still asleep when I reach the yard. I park under the garden wall and sit still for a few moments. Will Simon come back? And if he does what exactly are we going to do? I try to make sense of things in my mind but somehow I can't. Perhaps I'm in shock, or perhaps I'm exhausted. I know that if I don't move soon I'll get stuck, so I unload the car as quietly as I can and carry everything into the house before going back for Georgie.

"Ssh, ssh, gently darling." I ease her car seat down onto the centre of the kitchen table out of reach of the dogs' flailing tails, and I'm about to fill the kettle when there's a slight sound outside. The dogs jump towards the door barking, and Georgie wakes with a jerk and starts to cry.

"Oh no."

"I'm sorry, I'm sorry." The familiarity of him standing there in the doorway his golden hair tousled by the wind hits me so hard that for a few moments I can't speak. "Char are you alright?"

"Fine, fine. I'm going to have to feed Georgie and get to bed now." I turn away from him.

"We'll talk in the morning then."

———

It's late when Georgie is finally asleep and back in her travel cot. I lie in the deep darkness under the thatch but once again sleep alludes me. It feels surreal to be here, the two of us together in this house after so long, surrounded by acres and acres of emptiness. I try to picture the last time we were both under this roof then stop myself; it's best not to go there.

Instead, I let my mind range out from the house across the shadowy land beyond, skimming over grass and heather, bramble thicket and bracken. At the moment the nearest people are surely Marty and Peter and beyond them, who knows, although it's likely to be a police officer.

I'm not sure which room Simon has taken. I heard him come upstairs, but I couldn't tell which door he opened. Now I try to sense where he is in the stillness. For a long time, there's no sound then a board creaks and a latch inches up. He's being careful not to wake Georgie or me.

He walks along the passage and opens another door. This time unmistakably I recognise the squeak of my old hinges, the bane of my teenage life whenever I tried to sneak anywhere after our parents were asleep. No amount of oil ever seemed to silence the old metal for long. There's the click of a light switch, and I know what he'll see and what he'll no doubt deduce from that.

"Oh God." I want to go out to him, but I don't, I lie quite still instead. What could I say anyway? That I wouldn't blame him if, if what?

After a long time, the door closes, and Simon's footsteps move on along the corridor to the next room; Jamie's. For a moment he hesitates then I hear that door open as well and the faint creak of boards as he walks inside. Again the click of the light switch and this time I know how it'll flood hard cold fluorescent throughout the room, bouncing back off the whiteness of everything. What's Simon thinking? About the last time he was here or about that night in the woods?

I don't want to think about it, but it's too late, disturbing fragments of memory flash before my eyes. All the thoughts and harsh words of accusation that I've shut out for so long crowd around the edges of my mind again and suddenly all I can think about is the blood. There was so much of it on him, and it seemed darker and thicker than any I'd seen before. Somehow I knew that it was human blood, but not Simon's.

7

Georgie wakes early, feeds and goes back to sleep again. Usually, I would force myself to get up and snatch some time for myself, but there's a heaviness behind my eyes that threatens to turn into a headache, and I pull the duvet up to my nose instead. Despite the summer heat, it smells musty as though the bed has been made up for a long time, but no one has slept in it.

When Georgie next wakes me the sun is streaming in through the curtains, and there are voices in the garden below. For a moment I feel disorientated then everything comes flooding back.

"Okay darling, okay." She's making that anguished hungry cry, and yet I need to be downstairs talking to whoever it is who has arrived.

I pull on a robe and head for the door, which only makes Georgie cry even harder. "Just a minute darling, please."

Simon is coming out of his old room in the same checked shirt and jeans as last night, and his feet are bare. He looks as though he hasn't slept at all, his skin is grey beneath his tan, and his hair is all roughed up on one side.

"It's alright; I'll go down," he says. "You just do what you need to do with Georgie."

"But it's probably the police."

"I'll have to talk to them sometime, so it might as well be now."

"But-"

"It's okay."

He goes down, and I hear doors opening and closing and Hollinghurst's voice and another that is probably DS Quinn's. A dog barks but is silenced almost at once then there's the squeak of one of the benches being pulled out across the tiled floor in the kitchen.

"Come on then Georgie." I feed her in bed with me and listen to their voices going on and on down below, too far away to be clear but near enough to keep me on edge. Suddenly I'm reminded of that other time the police came for Simon all those years ago after the fire on Howden when Robert banged out of the house, his actions incriminating Simon more than any careless words of Simon's ever could. I stuff the thoughts down but it's too late, they've left a nasty chill in the pit of my stomach and a sense of time closing in again.

They're still talking when I've finished feeding and changing Georgie, so I sit on the edge of the bed with her and wait. After a while, she grows restless, and I rock her gently back and forth in my arms.

"Row, row, row your boat …. Merrily, merrily, merrily. Life is but a dream."

I'm quite light-headed from lack of food, but I don't want to go down while Hollinghurst is still here. At last, when I think that I can't wait much longer the voices stop, a door opens, and after a few minutes, there's the sound of a vehicle turning in the yard behind the house.

Simon is sitting alone in the kitchen when I go down, and his shoulders are hunched.

"So, what did they want? Is there any news?"

"Not really." He smoothes a hand across his face and doesn't look at me.

"Then-?"

"D'you want a cup of tea?"

"Thanks."

He walks across the room to the empty water containers then turns back to me.

"The tap stuff is fine."

"But-?"

"Clare thought someone was going to poison her. But I've drunk it."

"Okay." His eyes narrow but he doesn't say anymore as he fills the kettle from the tap.

We drink Earl Grey black and finish a packet of cornflakes from the cupboard dry because there's no milk left only dozens of tins of ravioli and canned pineapple chunks. I stare at them for a moment before closing the door. They don't strike me as the kind of foods that Clare would like or even buy. She was always one for fresh vegetables and fruit from the garden and even when she came up to London, she carried her homemade food with her. I almost ask Simon what he thinks, but he's concentrating on his bowl.

"I did like the flowers by the way," I say, at last, looking at them in a cream enamel jug in the window.

For a second Simon glances in my direction then he sighs and examines the scarred surface of the table.

"Did Hollinghurst want to talk to me as well?"

"No." He stands up abruptly. "Do we need to let the hens out?"

"What?"

"Do we have hens in the arks at the top of the orchard anymore?"

"I'm not sure; I suppose we could look."

The grass is ungrazed and uncut. Simon walks ahead flattening a narrow pathway and sweeping off the worst of the dew with his jeans. I tread carefully in his steps holding Georgie against me.

"What did Hollinghurst actually say?"

We reach the arks, but they've sagged into the ground, empty and rotten. A rat has gnawed a hole in the boarding on one corner, and the glass in the tiny windows is smashed.

"No hens here then." Simon turns back to face me and his gaze shifts between me and the horizon and the grass at our feet every couple of seconds. "Not a lot. He asked me if I knew what had happened."

"Just a routine question then."

Simon's lips tighten for a second then he looks away across the valley to the distant shimmer of the reservoir.

"Simon?"

"It was like he knew I was here somehow."

"But he can't have done, can he?" I follow Simon's gaze for a moment then swing round. There's no movement up on the hill, but the sense of being watched is suddenly intense. Somewhere, somewhere there's a sniper whose weapon isn't a gun but a pair of binoculars or a telephoto lens. The only reassurance is the thought that they can't hear us.

"Who knows?" Simon shrugs. "I don't want to talk

about it. They obviously have their theories. Lee's Marty's son, remember."

"I suppose we're all suspects to a certain extent." I stroke the top of Georgie's head and she makes that strange little birdy noise of hers.

"Yeh, but you'll be alright. They'll leave you alone just as Robert and Clare did."

"What d'you mean?"

"I've seen our bedrooms; I'm not stupid."

"Oh, Simon." I can't think of any words of comfort as the old pain slips between us again.

"They obviously wanted to forget that I ever existed."

He's probably right. I bow my head trying to force my mind back to a time before all this started, to conjure up even one happy memory, but it's hard.

"I've been watching you anyway." He looks straight at Georgie for a second. "Well not you exactly, but your work."

He knows what I've been doing all this time, but he's never tried to contact me. I don't understand, but I feel oddly uncomfortable. "How? I mean-"

"Charlotte South. That was clever."

"Not that clever. Can you imagine what'll happen if this gets out? No one I work with knows who I really am and they won't understand why I changed my name. I can't do anything else. They might even-" I curl a finger against Georgie's cheek for a second as a vision flits across my mind: strange hands reaching out to take her from me.

"Char-"

"Why did I ever come down here? God. It just didn't

feel like I had any choice after the police contacted me and I saw Lee's face-"

"You did the right thing."

"What if it isn't though? What if-? Simon they could take Georgie away from me."

"No one's going to do that."

"How d'you know?"

"Because I do. Anyway, I'm the one who could have done it, the one who-"

"What?"

"Oh, it doesn't matter."

"The one who what, Simon?" There's something about the evasive downward slide of his gaze that scares me. "If you're talking about the past, about what happened to Jamie, that was an accident."

"Yeh."

"So?"

"I live alone on a houseboat; I don't drive." He digs at the ground with his heel for a moment then tips his head back and watches the swallows wheeling in higher and higher circles. The mist is clearing, and it's going to be another of those perfect blue days.

"And?"

"These things-" He stops. "Shit. I'm the one who shouldn't have come here."

"Simon?"

"They want me to make an appeal on TV as well."

"I see. What did you say?" I can't quite get my head around this new request.

"There's no point; you know that."

"You refused?"

He nods, and I have an odd feeling that he's made a big mistake. "Was that wise?"

"I don't want to go back to that time, Char. I can't. I've got things to do anyway."

He swings away across the grass and heads down towards the yard.

"Simon wait." I hurry after him with Georgie in my arms. "We were going to talk."

"I've got to go."

"Well at least let me drive you down to get your bike."

"I'm okay, I can walk," he says and stops to open the yard gate.

Something else has happened to him since he left. It's there in the harsh edge to his words and in his eyes.

"What?" He darts me a look.

"Simon, what's happened to you?" I try to imagine what his life has been like. Has he always lived on a houseboat? What does he do for a living? Does he have friends, a partner, children even?

For a minute or two he's silent, and he doesn't move.

"Simon, please?"

"It isn't pretty." He stuffs his hands deep into his pockets and won't meet my eye.

"I'm sorry." I wait, but he doesn't say any more. "Look before you go you should know, Jamie's still alive, he's in a residential care home, Uncle Eric told me, and I've been to see him. I've been every few months."

"So have I."

"What?" This time he's caught me by surprise. "But the staff never-"

"Good. I asked them not to."

Patient discretion. I think of the carers in their blue uniforms and the long polished corridors. It isn't meant to feel like an institution, but it always does. "I can't believe Jamie's thirty-five now, and he was thirteen then, the same age as Lee Berryman."

"What are you saying?" His eyes narrow against the sun.

"I'm not sure, it just feels like it should make sense somehow, but I can't work it out, what d'you think has happened to them?"

"Just let me go now."

"Simon?" I'm falling into that old trap, and I can't stop myself.

"Don't you understand? It isn't you; it was never you. I just have to go."

He walks away across the yard and out through the gate onto the track without a backward glance. I hold Georgie against me and watch until I know that he isn't coming back.

My phone rings and I jump.

"Charlotte?" The voice so familiar, so not here that it disorientates me. "Charlotte what the hell is going on? Is it true what the papers are saying, that you're really Charlotte Elgin, that-?"

"Dan." I stagger backwards and sit down on the grass. I can hear the office in the background, the busyness of computers and other urgent calls securing deals and discussing artistic direction. "Look, please-"

"Sorry, sorry. It is true then?"

"I haven't seen the papers." I try to keep my voice strong, to push back the tears that threaten to overwhelm me.

"Where are you?"

"Where d'you think?"

"I don't understand. I mean why? We, I trusted you, I'm your agent and the father of your child for goodness sake, didn't you think I had a right to know who her grandparents were, that they were still alive?"

"Dan please, I never, look don't be angry with me. We had a deal remember, so you can't start wanting to get involved now."

"But-"

"No Dan, you have to understand."

"No, you have to understand where I'm coming from, it's all over the tabloids. Have you any idea how many calls I've had this morning already?"

"Dan I didn't have a choice. The police asked me, the boy-" A bird calls over and over from a tree near the gate, but I don't recognise it anymore.

"This isn't about the boy; you know that. Some warning would have been nice. Why the fuck didn't you tell us?"

"I thought, I thought I could-"

"Keep this quiet? Get real Charlotte. They're saying it could be murder. That you're 'helping with enquiries'."

I can't listen to anymore, so I put my phone down on the turf and stare at it.

"Charlotte? Charlotte?"

"What?" I pick it up again.

"This is just such a shock. Look, I'm coming down."

Dan, here. He doesn't fit. It won't work, I'm sure he said once that he was allergic to dogs, perhaps to all animals.

"No. What good's that going to do now?"

"We have to talk this through properly. I need to see Georgie anyway."

His voice sounds almost proprietorial, and I'm scared suddenly. He's never held Georgie, touched her or even really spoken to her, so why this hint of posses-siveness now?

"She's fine. She's right here in my arms at the moment."

"Charlotte, I don't know who you are anymore."

I switch off my phone and sit quite still breathing hard. Could Dan take Georgie away from me? I'm sure he can't, he isn't even named on the birth certificate, but what about DNA testing, what if he suddenly pushed for that? Georgie's got his eyes, there's no denying it, and perhaps later she'll have his hair and-

"No way darling, no way, you're my baby."

I thought I'd covered every eventuality in our pre-birth agreement but I never even came close to thinking about anything like this. Mostly we'd discussed the possi-bility of Dan suddenly having fatherly feelings, but he loved his single life, and we'd always ended up laughing. Dan wasn't a family man whichever way you looked at it. He was too attached to his immaculate bachelor flat, his nights out with the lads, his freedom to come and go as he pleased and to travel to the winter sun whenever the fancy took him and work allowed. I felt safe about it all then, but now-

He'll come down. The papers will no doubt have contained enough information for him to find me. I look round in a panic thinking of everything I've told him in the past, the web of lies I created as soon as I left here, even when I was still working in the veggie café before my photography was 'discovered'.

I told him, as I told everyone in London if they asked, that my parents had died when I was sixteen and that I was an only child. It seemed easy enough to say those things right after it happened when I needed to

escape from the numb dark evenings with rain running down the windows like tears and seeping through thin patches in the thatch to map new continents across the pale ceilings. Oh yes, it seemed easy, but I didn't know then how your own words can twist themselves around you and cut you off from everyone, even those who think they're your friends, can become your public history as it were.

"Damn, damn, damn." I can't think straight, what to do, where to go, what to say and then suddenly all I can think about is Simon, of his heavy tiredness and the drawn lines of his cheeks, of the things we never got a chance to talk about and of where he's going now.

We weren't meant to grow up together. We had met a few times years before, but that was all. It was one of those agreements that your parents make with their best college friends feeling sure that it will only ever be hypothetical, we'll take care of your child if you take care of ours should anything terrible happen, and then the two cars hit and spun hundreds of miles away from us.

There was the call later in the evening than was polite, the silence, the rush of expected words and then again the silence stunned and heavy. Two days later with the echo of clashing metal and sirens still in his ears, Simon burst in on the game of cards that Marty and I were playing.

———

I don't want to hear the news, but I have to know what's being said to prepare myself for Dan, so I go indoors, unpack my laptop and plug it into the slow farm dial-up while Georgie's feeding and then sleeping. What I read leaves me clenched tight inside.

Who is Clare Elgin? That's what everyone seems to be asking, and the photographs and profiles create a disturbing picture of a life lived in increasing isolation. Vicki from the village shop (whom I once considered my best girlfriend) gave an interview on the previous evening's local news describing Clare's aloof behaviour and strange and sporadic shopping trips, while other villagers, Jack Pengelly, Martha Endworthy and Arnie Symthe to be exact, eagerly offered supporting sound bites. Their faces, familiar and yet different, catch me by surprise. I've tried so hard for so long not to think about any of them, to make it a habit rather than a painful act of will to forget, but now after a mere glance they're all back and with them another whole flood of memories.

I stand up, go to the fridge and drink down half a litre of orange juice without taking a breath. As soon as it hits my stomach, I feel sick, so I sit back down in front of the computer. The reporter even managed to dig up a small-time art critic who claimed that he had always felt that there was something 'other' about the figures Clare crafted.

"The figments of a disturbed mind," he says to the camera, smug at his turn of phrase and authority on the matter. I click the disconnect button and turn away from the screen, but minutes later I'm back logging on again and scrolling through the entries. Suddenly it's there in black and white; the link between me and Clare and Lee, my near estrangement from my family, laid out for the world to see, described by the online version of one tabloid as 'the unhappy previous life of top photographer Charlotte South'.

"Bloody hell." My heart starts to pound. Although Dan warned me, I'm still not ready for it, not for the inflammatory words and the spin.

When you're a child, you often accept the way your parents are as normal until someone says something. It never even occurred to me that Clare had anything that might be classed as a 'problem' until Marty asked why she never left the farm.

"She does," I said, but then I couldn't remember a time to tell him about, and he laughed.

"You see."

"No, no you don't understand." It was before Simon's arrival, and we had been playing Gin Rummy in front of the fire at Sleepers. I stood up and splayed my cards into a mess, but as I lingered there above him uncertainty niggled through me, and I realised that it was probably me who didn't understand.

I look back at the computer screen and flick to another site. There's more of the same and a sense of dread flutters in the pit of my stomach as I read. Suddenly there's a knock at the back door. I swing around, my first impulse to reach the door before the visitor wakes Georgie.

"Who is it?" I think it's going to be a police officer, but instead, I find Marty standing on the doorstep.

"Where is he?"

"I'm sorry?"

"Simon. I heard he was back and I need to talk to him." His face is flushed, and he smells hot as though he's been running.

"News travels-"

"Oh come on."

"Marty, I'm sorry, but he isn't here."

"Yeh, yeh. Told you to say that did he?" He sweeps a hand through his tangled hair and takes a step forward. "You know they've found her blouse over near Long-cause Wood, soaked in blood."

"What?"

"I was there."

I can see what's going through his mind. "Whose blood?"

"Isn't that obvious."

"You don't know." I feel shaky, and the past and the future are suddenly slippery, changing even as I try to make sense of them.

"I'm telling you, so now are you going to tell me where he is or has he run away again?"

"Marty I don't think we should carry on with this conversation." I try to keep my voice steady, but all I can think about is that wide tumble of mixed woodland stretching from Howden down to the river. It was where we spent so much time when we were younger, first the three of us, me, Jamie and Marty, then Simon as well for a while. It was where we camped and cooked out, the smell of it clinging to our skin in a delicious spicy mixture of oak leaves, crushed peaty earth and woodsmoke.

"You haven't changed either; you always did try and protect him, always. But then you were in love with him weren't you?" He stares at me for a few moments longer then turns away down the path. Before he reaches the gate, he swings back. "My lad could be dead by now you know."

———

There was a time, a crazy, wonderful, crowded time that caught me by surprise then just as its memory startles me now. We were all together in Robert's Landrover, he was driving, and Jamie, Simon, Marty and I were all squeezed into the back on the hard metal seats that jarred up through your coccyx whenever he went over a bump. Surprisingly Clare was there as well up front in that beautiful, green, flowery dress that she sometimes wore with wellies. We were going to buy a ram as you do, but why the hell we were all going I can't remember.

It was hot outside, and the heater was jammed full on as well. Robert cursed it but good-naturedly and in the back, we all began to strip off clothes, one layer at a time.

"I'll do the talking," Marty said. "I know what I'm looking for." And he did, he knew his sheep better than the rest of us put together. Even Simon had to admit that.

"Charlotte must go in first though." Simon laughed and pulled off his sweatshirt.

"Why?"

"Because the farmer is bound to be a man and he won't charge us so much for the ram when he sees her."

"What? You sexist pig." I kicked him in the shin but I had sandals on, and it hurt my toes more than his leg, and he laughed.

"You're right. Good plan." Marty slapped him on the shoulder, and then Robert swung round a corner rather fast, and we all fell against each other in a confusion of giggles.

"We should offer to pay him by weight," Jamie said when we'd recovered.

"Sorry?"

"If we set our figure right he'll think it sounds like a good deal. I bet you he's sure his ram weighs more than it does."

Typical Jamie. I grin, but deep down it's still painful. It's always like that now, the good memories and the bad hurt in equal amounts but different ways.

In the end for some strange reason that again I can't remember now, perhaps we'd just got the day completely wrong; we didn't go to buy a ram at all but drove down to the beach. There were ice creams all round and Clare and Robert went for a walk along the cliffs hand in hand. We hadn't brought swimming costumes, but the lure of the sea was too much, and we had to go in. At the far end of the beach, we stripped down to our underwear and jumped off a low rocky promontory.

"Whoa." Simon hit the water first from twenty feet up, followed by Marty. Jamie and I were much more cautious, and in the end, we both paddled in from a spit little more than feet above the beach.

"Come on you chickens." Simon and Marty were elated, and Simon dragged me up onto the rock beside him. "Remember you need to hit the water with your feet, straight down, no belly flops, or you'll be." He slapped his hands together and made a face.

"Don't."

"It isn't that hard." Marty was on the other side of me. "Come on I'll show you."

He jumped again and then so did Simon. Higher and higher they went each time, another band of rock, another ten feet and I crept upwards at my own pace. Only Jamie seemed happy to potter about in the shallows at the edge of the beach.

We burnt that day and later Simon had to rub oil into my back to soothe it. He'd won the competition for the highest jump with a final mad dash off the very top, startling the seagulls as he went down paddling the air with his feet and then hitting the water perfectly straight. I'd hardly been able to watch.

"Next year," Marty promised, his eyes full of excitement, but by then he and Simon couldn't be in the same room as each other let alone spend a whole afternoon together.

8

"We need to talk some more if it's convenient." Hollinghurst is back later that afternoon and stands firm in the kitchen doorway. He doesn't look as though he'll be easily diverted or take no for an answer. "And then I need to talk to your brother again."

"He isn't here."

"Okay, when will he be back?"

"I'm not sure. What is this about? Is there news?" I don't exactly mean to be antagonistic but Marty's visit has put me on edge, and the vision of Clare's blouse wet with blood is going round and round inside my head.

"Why didn't you call me?"

"I don't know what you're talking about." I'm playing a dangerous game but his words are pushing me into a corner, and I can't think what else to do.

"Oh come on. When Simon came back why didn't you call me as I asked you to?"

This question was bound to come sooner or later. I glance back at Georgie asleep in her buggy and finger the hem of my shirt.

"Well?" Hollinghurst's voice is verging on the impatient.

"Because it was late, I was tired, and I had to look after my baby. I was going to phone you this morning, but you arrived before I'd had a chance."

Hollinghurst is silent for a moment. Then he sighs. "I hope you're telling me the truth because anything else could be classed as obstructing our investigation and that's a criminal offence. I might even begin to think that you didn't want us to find your mother or talk to your brother for some reason."

"Well, you'd be wrong."

"D'you understand what I'm saying?"

I nod, but he hasn't finished yet, his eyes are too intent.

"And another thing. Why didn't you tell me about the gambling?"

"The gambling?" Oh God. I'm wrong-footed again and have to drag my mind away from Simon and Long-cause Wood. Does he mean what I think he does? I glance down at my hands, smooth not nicked, scratched, muddy and always smelling faintly of horses as they were when I was last here.

"You know what I'm talking about. Your father and Peter Berryman." He eyes me without a smile, and I know that I'm not going to get away with bluffing anymore.

"I didn't know you wanted to go back that far."

"Let's let me be the decider of that, shall we? I'll go back as far as I need."

"Okay." Did Peter tell him or was it Marty and why has he brought this up now?

"Is it true that your father and Peter Berryman used

to play Poker together on a regular basis and that your family acquired a good proportion of Peter's land in payment for a gambling debt?"

"Yes and no. I wasn't there." I wasn't, but I've imagined that evening often. The low light in Sleepers' kitchen that was sliding into chaos with Ginny already dead for months, the tobacco smoke and the back draught of coal fumes from the ancient Rayburn. The four of them sitting around the table: Robert, Peter and the Hemsworthy brothers.

"So?"

"Robert wasn't playing anymore. It was all getting a bit too serious. Peter lost to Keith Hemsworthy. Robert gave him the money to pay off the debt in exchange for the land." The detail of it has never seemed so important. I look at Hollinghurst steadily, but his face gives nothing away. "He helped Peter."

"Did Peter see it that way?"

"Robert gave him thousands of pounds." But as I say it I'm not thinking of Peter but Marty stumbling away down the darkening track the following afternoon, his words flung out behind him.

"It should have been my land, my future."

Georgie shifts in her buggy parked in the hallway and I look back at her anxiously. She'll wake soon and cry for food.

"It wasn't even good pasture. It was too steep, and the bracken was encroaching."

The truth, or is it? The soil may have been thin and sandy and ridged by generations of stock walking around the valley, but it still grew a tight, wiry turf that gave the ewes a bite when they most needed it after a long hill winter. The acreage, stretching as it did from the moor wall to the valley bottom, was the difference between subsistence and a family living.

"Peter might have had to sell the whole farm otherwise."

As things turned out would that have been better?

"What did Clare think about the gambling?" Hollinghurst stretches out one hand and examines his fingers as though the question is really of little importance.

"I don't know. She never said much about it." Not to me anyway, although I was aware that she thought it was a mistake to buy more land. That we could hardly look after what we already had properly. Perhaps she talked to Uncle Eric in more detail. He seemed to be on extended leave from his engineering job in Bahrain around that time and was always at the farm or taking parcels of figures down to the Post Office for Clare when Robert didn't have the time.

"Is there anything else?"

"What?"

"Anything you may have forgotten to tell me before." He looks at me hard, and I don't like the inference behind his words. "And you might want to take your time before answering."

"There's nothing else," I speak fast without thinking, the easy way to lie.

———

When Hollinghurst has gone, I carry Georgie up the stairs. I have to look. I've glanced into Clare's room already, but I didn't step beyond the doorway, something stopped me. This time I walk right in.

The space is plain, the walls thick and uneven, plaster bulging over unseen granite work behind. It smells a little musty and closed in, summer air that's almost damp but not quite.

There's an old pine double bed with a cabinet on each side, an unmatched pair that was probably some fleamarket find in the seventies, a built-in wardrobe that Robert made out of old doors, a chest of drawers and a rocking chair in the north window. There are few ornaments, an unusually shaped rock on the windowsill and a stoneware vase full of dried flowers on top of the wardrobe.

I stand on the long striped rug that I remember from my earliest years. It was supposed to be made out of camel hair, and it prickled against my bare knees. The bed is only casually made, there are creases in the pale duvet and a dent in one pillow, but the forensics team will have been in here, so it's hard to tell what signs were left by Clare and what by them.

One bedside cabinet is bare; I bite my lip and turn to the other. Beneath a pottery lamp with a paper shade, there's a novel by Helen Dunmore, a book on embroidery techniques, a pair of reading glasses and an old-fashioned wind-up clock that has stopped at 10.45. Am or pm? I stare at it for a moment. Does it matter, would it tell me anything if I knew?

What did I think this room would reveal anyway? I stoop to open the cabinet, cradling Georgie's head with one hand as I do so and she looks up at me with wide, startled eyes.

"Sorry. I won't be a moment."

There are magazines inside, all the same quarterly fabrics journal, and a basket of wool and cotton oddments. Nothing unusual, nothing out of the ordinary, nothing to suggest a life about to capsize. I stand up again, and Georgie fidgets and pulls at my top with one hand.

"Okay." For a moment I hesitate, and then I lie down on the bed to feed her.

Light dapples the ceiling, and it's oddly peaceful. I didn't expect this. I can see what Clare saw so recently, the room and through the north window the narrow view of tree branches and the top of Howden beyond. The space feels more personal to her than the rest of the house despite the fact that she lived here alone. Lying on Clare's bed I suddenly feel closer to her, can remember how she was before any of this started, before Simon arrived if I'm honest.

That was the young Clare, the one who still used to run and laugh, whose red hair flamed before the wind, the one who dug the garden, strained honey, made soap and would even kill a chicken on occasion. She still had energy then, excitement, dreams and in the evenings her hands worked on, creating the wild, beautiful dolls that made her not exactly famous but well known in certain circles.

Was it Simon who changed things or all of us? When was it that her silences and sudden bouts of irritation became the norm? She still laughed with us of course, but in between, she was tired and withdrawn.

I try to trace the line from then to now, from that to this, but if there's any connection, the detail of it eludes me. Of course when viewed with hindsight Clare 'lost' more than one child in the oak wood the night of Jamie's accident. She lost all three of us. But how does Lee fit into this? Did Clare even tell me about Lee's arrival? I try to think back. Thirteen years ago I'd have just returned from Canada. I can't remember her saying anything.

When he was born, did she feel jealousy or sadness? Looking out of the east window of this room towards Sleepers did he remind her of the children she no longer saw, of the grandchildren she might never see?

Was his thirteenth year a turning point for her? He'd reached the age that Simon was when he arrived and Jamie was when he was lost. It feels as though it should make sense, should give me a clue as to what might have happened and where to find them but still it doesn't. Every time I think, or perhaps hope, that there might be some innocent or at least well-meant intention behind all this, I think of the blood.

When Georgie has finished feeding and is blissed out and sleepy, I roll over. It's then as I lean closer to the surface of Clare's bedside cabinet that I see the marks. I didn't notice them before because of the dark wood, but every item has a black pen line around it, the base of the lamp, the books, even the glasses and the clock. There's also another empty outline, a long thin shape like that of a serious hunting knife.

"Oh God."

Did the police mark out where these things were positioned and take the knife, or was it Clare? It's like a horizontal version of the pin boards you see in meticu-lously tidy workshops, where every tool has its place drawn out so that it's easy to spot what's missing. Such tidiness isn't Clare's style though, and there are no other similar outlines in the house.

I take a deep breath and run a finger across the empty space. What was Clare thinking if these marks were hers? Did she need these visual cues to stop herself forgetting something like the knife that made her feel safe, that allowed her to sleep even?

Suddenly the room doesn't feel so peaceful anymore. I lift Georgie into her sling and carry her back downstairs. I'm tired, but there are still a dozen things I need to do before I can rest. I've hardly even started them when the call comes through on my mobile. It's the police officer on the roadblock to ask if I know and am expecting a Dan Richer.

"Yes," I say although a cowardly part of me wants to pretend that I don't know him and have him sent away.

Ten minutes later I hear his Mercedes in the yard and go out to meet him. We stand quite still looking at each other without a word as though trying to find a way to bridge the new knowledge that hangs between us. He's got the kind of features, a strong nose, high cheekbones and dark hair, which grab attention from afar. It's only when you're up close that you realise that something about the proportions of his face is exaggerated and he isn't classically handsome at all.

Tonight he also looks tired, and there's an odd red rub mark on the side of his neck. I imagine him worrying at it with his immaculate office fingers on the drive down, fingers that belie the fact that there's a tattoo of a serpent hidden up his sleeve.

"Hardly Scotland as you can see." I try to make light of the false identity I've given him, to laugh, but the sound comes out all wrong.

"You could have told us." Dan doesn't smile.

"How could I, not when-?"

"Bullshit." He glances at Georgie. "Sorry."

"You'd better come in." There might be someone up

on the moor with a telephoto recording this meeting even as we linger here. I glance up. I know where the best place would be, a little above the wall where it dips down into our land. I can't see anyone, but it wouldn't be so hard to hide in the bracken there.

Dan has to duck through the low doorways and the concentration of that and avoiding the slathering attention of the dogs, silences him until we're in the kitchen, the room that I've made home for the moment with an assortment of essential baby items.

"After all the time we've spent together. I don't understand." He looks around at the piles of muslins, the car seat and the string of shiny toys and beyond at Clare's things, the worry doll on the windowsill and the seventies decorations. "Was it a joke? Have you been laughing behind our backs?"

He's too close, and as always his height surprises me. I step away towards the sink to fill the kettle, and the dogs run in a restless arc around the room stopping for a moment to whine and then growl below the window.

"It wasn't like that at all. It was just, well like a pen name."

"Yeh, of course, it was." His thin-soled, square-toed city shoes look all wrong on the flagstones that are more used to Wellington boots and his aftershave clashes with the scent of dog and dust. He looks at the collies warily and flinches when they get too close.

"Dan I don't need this right now." I put the kettle down on the hotplate aware how close to the edge I am, how even a few more of the wrong words from him will make me flip. Closing my eyes for a second, I take a deep breath. I need to be strong, stronger than this. "Look I think-"

There's a noise outside, and the dogs run through into the central passage barking. For a moment I can't hear anything above their agitation then there's the unmistakable sound of the back door opening and footsteps approaching. Seconds later Simon appears in the kitchen doorway his hair windswept, and his chin shadowed with stubble.

"Leave her alone."

Dan is visibly startled and looks from Simon to me. "And you are?"

"I'm Simon, Charlotte's boyfriend." He steps between us before I have a chance to say anything and slides an arm around my back, his hand coming to rest on the curve of my waist. For a moment it feels strangely familiar. I think of Marty's words and something quivers in the pit of my stomach.

"Charlotte?" Dan's gaze flicks to my face. "Another little surprise eh? You told me there wasn't anyone else in Georgie's life."

Confusion sweeps through me, and I can't think what to say at all now that I have the opportunity. I know if I hold out a hand it'll be shaking.

"Well?" Dan's irritation fills the room.

"It's getting late; perhaps we should talk about this tomorrow." I step away from Simon, pretending that it's a necessary move to see to the kettle on the stove.

"You think we can leave this overnight? Have you any idea how much damage the press can do in that time? Charlotte we have to make a plan now. We need to issue a statement before I get completely tired of saying 'no comment'."

"Say what you like then. Ditch me publicly if you want to. I don't care anymore." I imagine him deleting my name from the agency website and with it the chain of my images that I love, the ones I'm most proud of from Brittany and Vancouver, Cape Wrath and Budapest. The ones that aren't what they seem at first glance, that show the element of illusion that has become my trademark.

"Charlotte?"

"And give Liv the Aoki contract."

"That's yours, and it's just as well you're such a good photographer."

"What do you mean by that?" I'm close to the edge.

"I think you should leave," Simon says from across the room.

"Charlotte?"

"It might be best."

Dan hesitates, his anger barely concealed, then lifts his jacket off the back of a chair and walks out of the door. "I'll speak to you in the morning then."

I wait until the car headlights have disappeared down the track before turning on Simon.

"What are you doing here and what the hell was all that about? You've just made everything ten times worse. Dan's-"

"Georgie's dad, yeh I could see that, and also a git. Charlotte I couldn't leave you here on your own."

"You don't know a thing about him." My fingers sting across his cheek, and he ducks away from the pain. The jerk of movement disturbs Georgie, and she lets out a little cry.

"Shit."

"Oh God. Sorry. I shouldn't have." I can't believe I've hit him at all let alone with Georgie in her sling and I step back with my head down.

"It's okay," he says and takes hold of my wrists. "Char it's okay."

Suddenly I haven't the energy to resist as he folds Georgie and me into his arms but I can't relax, and we stand together stiffly, like acquaintances at a railway station.

"I need to talk to you," he says.

"I'm too tired Simon. I have to get Georgie ready for bed anyway."

9
_____

I 'm too tired even to sleep it seems or at least to sleep properly. Between Georgie's feeds, I drift in that grey no man's land that isn't quite a dream but doesn't seem real either. Sometimes I'm in the room and sometimes not. For a while, in the deepest darkness, I'm riding with Simon. It's late, and we're far out on the north moor, land that Simon knows somehow, and I don't. The horses are evenly matched, and we're galloping across a rough hillside, faster, faster, faster. Hetty's power surges beneath me, and the wind whips back my hair as adrenalin spikes through my veins.

"Come on." Simon pulls ahead kicking Eb and turning downhill towards the stream.

The ground steepens through a tumble of rocks and Hetty's quarters slide beneath her. Faster, faster, faster until I think we must fall and hit the sharp granite then suddenly we're at the bottom on the flat again, and Simon is laughing.

"See it wasn't so hard."

The horses are hot and lathered white with sweat,

and we stand side by side drinking in the wet salty smell of them. It's only April but a prolonged spell of early sun in March has bronzed Simon's skin, and the winter feeding has left him hard and fit.

"You look fantastic Char." He leans close and catches me by surprise, and suddenly there's music jinking through my veins, and we're dancing not there but in a dark barn that smells of straw and alcohol. Our faces are black, and there's a caller with a fox's mask. We know each other so well that our bodies fit together and we spin faster and wilder than anyone else. So fast that everything is a blur, the people, the walls, the lights and again I think I will fall but Simon has my arm, and there's a spark in his eyes that I don't quite understand.

I want the moment to go on forever then the music changes, and somehow I'm in different heavier arms, and when I look up, it's Marty's face that's close.

"You look stunning tonight," he says his fingers on my bare shoulder as we arc away across the barn past Simon sitting alone on one of the straw bales against the wall with his chin in his hands.

———

I wake chilled down one side with the duvet half off me. It's light, and a bird is singing outside the window, but Georgie is still asleep. For a moment that feels like a luxury and I lie quite still then an odd, uncomfortable feeling presses close and I sit up. There's something I can't quite grasp, a memory from the night that slips away even as I try to focus on it, something beautiful turned sour.

I dress in the bathroom more carefully than

yesterday in linen trousers and a grey merino jumper. As an afterthought, I put on my favourite coral necklace for confidence. When I return to the bedroom, Georgie's still asleep, so I pick up the baby monitor and creep down the stairs. There's a smell of coffee and toast coming from the kitchen and Simon turns from the Rayburn when I push open the door.

Our eyes meet, and for the barest second we're back before any of this ever started and the old excitement leaps between us, then reality closes in again.

"I've made you some breakfast," he says. "There's enough tinned ravioli for a siege and dog food for that matter but not much else unless you want pineapple chunks on your toast."

"No thanks." I take the mug he holds out, but I don't sit down. A siege. Is that what Clare was preparing for? It feels like I've been given another piece to the puzzle, but I can't see how it fits together yet.

"What?"

"Oh, nothing." I shake my head. The room is chaotic with stuff, mostly Clare's but some of mine now as well, baby things that need tidying and washing. I have to get a grip.

"I'm sorry about last night," Simon says with his back against the stove.

"Yeh." I glance at his hands. He could ride so well, God I never even came close to matching his skill and daring.

"I-"

"Forget it." I don't mean to be rude, but I find myself examining him without thinking. Looking for clues as to how the intervening years have treated him. My first impression was right, he is much thinner, almost to the point of gauntness but he'd still make you look twice although the wild edginess of his youth is tamed somewhat by age, a cheap checked shirt and a slightly harsh haircut. "If you've known where I was or who I was all these years why didn't you call me?"

"Char."

"Simon I looked for you, I would have called you if I could." I take a gulp of tea; he's remembered exactly how I like it with a dash of cold water.

"I thought. Well, I thought you didn't want me around anymore, that you wouldn't want to hear from me."

"Oh, Simon. You could have tried me." His excuse isn't enough; it doesn't feel right, I'm not getting something. My anger flares suddenly. "Every night I used to wonder where you were, what you were doing, who you were with, and all that time you knew where I was."

"I'm sorry."

"I don't know what to think anymore." Suddenly I can't stay in the room. I turn and carry my tea out into the garden. It's going to be hot again, a perfect blue day. I sit down on the wooden bench under the south wall and below me the valley shimmers, an undulating green sea of early summer oak leaves.

Someone was once said to have described this spot as the most idyllic place to build a house in the whole of England, and I used to agree with them, but now every vista holds too many painful memories.

After a while, the front door opens, and Simon walks across the lawn.

"May I sit with you?" He's made a fresh plate of toast thick with golden honey.

"If you want."

We gaze at the view in silence then I take a piece of toast, and it tastes perfect.

"I had such a great weekend just before all this happened," I say. "I hired this cottage that I go to in Wiltshire and left my phone and computer in London. Georgie and I spent four days alone there; it was bliss."

"Four days of innocence before all hell broke loose."

"Something like that. I didn't think about Clare once, well about any of you actually, sorry." I watch a buzzard drift by below us. "How funny, it takes such an effort to shut everything out nowadays, but it's still just possible. Although you seem to be much more successful at it than I am."

"That isn't always such a good thing." His voice is sad, and I glance sideways at him.

"Where's your houseboat?"

"It's a barge. I've been doing it up for years." He tells me the name of the nearest village, and I can picture its narrow main street not ten miles from the Wiltshire cottage.

"I don't believe it; I drove through there last Friday." We were so close it feels uncanny. What chances kept us apart then but have brought us together now? How often have we circled within miles of each other without knowing?

"I missed you so much," I say without really meaning to, without looking at him.

Simon is silent, and a light breeze blows down off the moor. It makes me anxious and restless suddenly.

"Oh God, what a mess. Simon, we have to find out what's happened to them." I stand up abruptly. "Come on."

I turn left along the narrow stone path that leads

around the corner and under a ragged archway of rambling roses to a small granite building with a green door. There's something nailed to the wood in the centre at eye level. Something that looks horribly like, I take a step closer, something that is a severed paw, possibly of a badger.

"Euh." I turn away. "What's that all about?"

"I don't know." Simon reaches for the twisted iron ring that forms a handle. I think it might be locked but the door swings open. "It's probably some superstition, a guardian spirit or sacrifice or something."

"Don't." I shudder at the thought and follow Simon into the cool granite space. At first glance little has changed and the familiarity of it makes me edgy for no reason that I can pinpoint.

"Clare used to spend such a lot of time out here, d'you remember?" Too much time it had seemed to us on occasion, mostly when we wanted something. Often she'd claimed to be too busy with orders to come to school events, but as I grew older, I'd started to wonder if it wasn't something else. She'd never liked crowds or the clique of school mums, and the studio was her refuge where she was not to be disturbed. "Do you think she's, well lost it completely?"

"I don't know Char."

"How are we going to cope if? Well, whatever she's done."

"Can it be any worse than this?"

"Don't."

The air has a damp musty smell, and I wait a few seconds before I switch on the light. It doesn't feel to me as though Clare has been here for a while, perhaps not since before Robert's death. Did she have any help nursing him or in the end was it just the two of them and their memories holed up together in dusty granite stillness?

I step further into the room, into Clare's space, and it feels as personal as looking at someone else's emails and as uncomfortable.

"Where are you?" My voice sounds hollow, and for a second I think Simon's fingertips touch my shoulder but when I glance around his hand is back in his pocket.

The studio appears to hold everything and yet nothing of Clare. Or perhaps it's only that I can't read the messages here. Line upon line of sculptural worry dolls sit festooned in cobwebs and harbouring all kinds of dead insects. Behind them lurks a pile of wooden oddments while swathes of unused material drape down from the ceiling.

They're not the kind of dolls she used to make. These aren't even all human; some have animal faces and thin dark eyes. To the right is a group dressed in black, to the left a row with real animal skulls as heads; more mice or rats, I'm not sure which.

The police have been in here, of course, looking at the sadness of forgotten work, the piles of paper sketches curled like leaves and the spiders spinning and bobbing in the corners of the ceiling. There are dirty footprints in the dust on the floor and faint dust-free shadows on the shelves where dolls have been moved and not replaced in quite the same position.

Gel comes padding in behind us, her tail waving against my legs as though she expects to find someone else in the room. She circles the space once then sinks down onto her haunches at our feet.

This is where Clare came to dream, to plan, to get

away from the stresses of motherhood. Again I'm aware of how much I and perhaps every child takes for granted about family life. As a child, you don't notice the pure numbing exhaustion that you cause through endless nappy changes and questions, through sleepless nights and nightmares, through the things you do and the accidents you cause. I look round the room again, scanning everything.

Along the far wall are several rows of large paint cans. They look new and unopened. I examine the labels. "They're all black. What on earth? I just don't understand any of it. God, God, God." I slam my fist down on the edge of Clare's workbench again and again until a red hot pain spreads through my hand. "It's hopeless, where the hell are they?"

"Char." Simon steers me back out into the sunshine. "Look I'm going to help with the search today. I should have gone out yesterday, but I wasn't thinking straight. I saw Arthur on my way back, and there's a group of them starting on the other side of Longcause."

I think of Clare's blouse and the blood. Was there a mark on the ground? Darkness on the leaf mould or splashes of red on the dried leaves?

"I wish I could come with you, I wish I could do something, but there's no way with Georgie's feeds and everything."

"No one would expect you to."

"I know but-" My phone rings and I fumble in my pocket for it. "I'd better take this; it might be Hollinghurst."

But it isn't, it's Dan. I turn away from Simon and face the valley again. "You're still talking to me then?"

"Charlotte I've written a statement, it's gone out this

morning. We've confirmed your link and requested privacy at this difficult time. You know the sort of thing."

"Thanks."

"Now what about the Aokis?"

"They still want me?"

"Yes, but we might be able to reschedule. I'll give the clients a call." His voice is cold and professional.

"There's no need. I'll be there."

"Are you sure?"

"Dan I want this job, and I'm going to make a success of it, okay?" The buzzard we watched earlier is back swinging effortlessly on a thermal. Perhaps it's got a nest out below Hartor again. "You may not trust much else about me right now, but just remember I was the one who did all the work for this contract, who stayed up until two in the morning for a whole fortnight putting the portfolio together because Georgie wouldn't sleep during the day."

"Alright, alright."

"I'll talk to you later." I snap the phone shut.

Simon is watching me. "Dan and I aren't together okay and never were. Not that it's any of your business."

———

The house feels weird and empty when he's gone. I feed and change Georgie, play with her and then settle her back down for her morning nap. When she's asleep, I log onto the Internet and search for news. The press has found a new angle and changed tack.

Marty. Martin Henry Berryman, the slaughterer. Full height, front page on more papers than you'd care to buy. It isn't a good shot or a good look. His shirt is smeared with something that could be mud or blood, and the angle has somehow emphasised his heaviness and the dour expression that sometimes crosses his face. If people are meant to feel sorry for him as the father of a lost boy that photo makes it hard, instead there's a suggestion of a latchkey lifestyle.

I glance at Marty's picture again, and I feel for him despite everything. He always meant well. I can see that now. He may have been methodical, unimaginative, even boring at times, but he never set out to do any harm back then. How many hundreds of times did we wait for the school bus together, playing mock cricket to keep warm in the winter or rolling up our sleeves to tan our arms when the sun shone? How often did we toast bread in front of the fire at Sleepers and cast about the woods for chestnuts to roast?

I'm sure that people thought that we'd stay together, become childhood sweethearts and live happily ever after in the narrowness of the valley, or at least they did until Simon arrived. Did we think that? I can't remember ever dwelling on it, but perhaps Marty did in secret.

Was I cruel to him when Simon came? I never intended to be but Simon was so much more fun, and we fitted together better than Marty and I ever had. Simon loved horses and riding and running and speed. With him, life was suddenly a whirl of possibilities.

What possibilities has Marty had in his life, other than the round of farm work and the killing of animals? There was Emma of course, but she was in and out of his life tragically quickly by all accounts. She gave him Lee and died a couple of years later in a pile up on the dual carriageway. There's a small black and white photo of her, grainy and dark.

I scroll down the screen, but suddenly I can't go on reading the unkindness there. I need to do something to help instead. There are also half a dozen domestic things that I should be doing, but they seem fiddly and inconsequential compared to what's going on outside up and down the valley and beyond.

There must be something constructive that I can do. I stand up and pace from room to room. I don't know these things, I have no medical background, but how long could Lee survive in his condition? Hours, days, weeks? Is his time already up? I count the lapse on my fingers; it's over a week now and all the while the grandfather clock in the hall ticks off the minutes like blood dripping from a wound.

The farm phone rings once, and I jump to answer it. There's a strange man on the other end, and instinctively I know that he's a journalist and slam down the receiver again.

Ten minutes later Hollinghurst calls me on my mobile. They'd like me to answer the farm phone if it rings again and keep talking so that they can track the caller.

"And don't give anything away," he says. "I'm sure you're good at that."

"Thanks."

What exactly are Arthur's group doing on the search? I try to imagine them spread out across the wooded hillside, footsteps beating down the undergrowth. Are they carrying sticks? Do they have dogs, perhaps the retrievers from Hartor Barton if they still breed them there or some spaniels running round in constant excitement? Will one of them stumble across something?

I close my eyes for a moment against the vision of another blood-soaked article of clothing caught on a bramble bush or worse, the dark crumpled shape of a body. What if they do find something? What then? Shame surges within me for a moment as I remember the times I've wished that Robert and Clare would just disappear.

In the otherness of London, it seemed the answer to all my problems, for them to be erased from my life. But did I mean dead? I recoil from the selfishness of my younger thoughts. I didn't mean this, never this, not Robert's cancer or- I shake my head as a nasty little thought worms its way into my mind. Could I have brought this on? Is it a wish come true in an awful, perverted way?

"No." I grab a load of Georgie's things and begin to sort through them in crazy haste. "No."

But the thoughts won't stop now. Clare tried to make amends in her way, didn't she? All these years, all the times she came up to London, her long red plait oddly bright and wild among the commuters at Paddington Station, when she'd much rather have stayed at the farm, and I did nothing but resent her visits.

"God."

What if she's dead and I can never say sorry? Or what if she's been driven to do something terrible because I, because no one was there when she needed them?

I find her letter where I buried it beneath other papers and unfold it again. The words are even more painful now than the first time I read them. I sit down on the end of one of the kitchen benches and rest my head in my hands. Why didn't she post it? Was she so scared of another rebuff that she couldn't face it? Was it more tolerable that I wasn't at Robert's funeral because I didn't know than because I'd chosen not to come?

Would I have gone if I'd known in time? I try to be honest with myself, but my thoughts are slippery and tainted now. Well, would I or was Clare justified in her fears?

Georgie wakes suddenly with a scream as though she's picked up on my turbulent thoughts and I run to her almost gratefully. One of the best and the worst things about babies are their all-consuming needs. When you're deep in the run of nappy changes and feeds and more changes and washing you can blank your mind to everything else and numb yourself with tiredness.

She won't sleep again until bedtime now so I put all ideas of cooking a meal for Simon out of my head for the moment. I've tried to cook with Georgie in her sling, but it's awkward and uncomfortable for us both so we'll have to wait for food.

I'm upstairs feeding her when Simon comes in. The dogs bark once then there's the skitter of claws on the hard floors and the slam of a door. I think he might come up to find me, but he doesn't so I go down with Georgie in my arms. He's standing in the shadowy kitchen with his back to me.

"Simon?"

For a moment longer he doesn't turn, and then he does, and I catch my breath at the sight of his face.

"Oh my God, what's happened?" There's blood everywhere, smeared across his cheeks and down the front of his shirt. For a moment I can't see where it's all coming from then he puts a hand up to his nose and it comes away covered in blood as well.

"I expect it looks worse than it is," he says, and his voice is thick and slurred.

"Yeh, right. Look I'll just, I'll put Georgie in her car seat, and then I can help you." My hands are shaking as I ease her down and strap her in and her face tenses towards tears. "Darling look here's your caterpillar, come on he wants to keep you company."

For a moment she seems undecided then her eyes fix on the soft toy hanging above her, and she stretches out a hand towards it. I smile at her quickly then turn towards the utility room with Simon, my heart racing.

"So what happened? Who did this?"

"Shit." He leans forward over the Belfast sink and blood splashes onto the white ceramic.

"Simon?"

"I was only trying to help."

"Okay." I soak some kitchen roll in cold water and start to clean his face. The bridge of his nose is red and puffy already, and there's a nasty looking split in the skin. An area of dark bruising is also growing around his right eye. I hope nothing is broken.

"Ouch."

"Sorry." I wait for a moment. "Look perhaps we should go to A&E."

"No, I'm alright."

"But-"

"I'll be fine."

I take a deep breath, and I can feel the tension tightening across my shoulders. "Was it Marty?"

He shakes his head without looking at me.

"Then?"

"Does it matter?"

"Oh Simon, come on."

"Alright, it was Tony, Tony Pearson."

One of the rugby lads. I close my eyes for a second remembering his heavy shoulders and broad flat face. "And did you-?"

"What was I supposed to do? He said some things. I couldn't just let it go."

"But-"

"I know. I know."

Behind me, Georgie starts to cry, and I swing away from him. "And Tony, what does he look like tonight?"

"Sore."

"Oh God. Couldn't you just-?" I pick up Georgie and hug her against me trying to steady myself with the sweet familiar baby smell of her.

After a while, Simon comes back into the room. Most of the blood is gone, but his face is a mess of puffiness and bruising. Tomorrow it'll probably look even worse.

"I'm sorry," he says without looking at me.

"It's a bit late for that now."

"Char?"

"Well for God's sake. What's going to happen after this?"

"It'll be alright." His voice is tight.

"You think so? You really think that?" Georgie shifts unhappily in my arms, and I glance down and smooth a finger across the top of her head. "Sorry, darling."

"I saw the posters today."

"What?" I feel sidetracked for a moment.

"They're everywhere, on telegraph poles, on people's

gates and cars, on trees. Lee looks so like Jamie doesn't he? It's uncanny."

"Yeh." My heart is pounding although I've hardly moved. "It's the hair."

"Someone said that Marty's wife, Emma I think her name was, looked a bit like you. I can't believe that."

"I suppose they meant she had red hair as well." For a moment there's silence apart from the tick of the grandfather clock in the hallway. Another day, another night. I hug Georgie tighter.

"So what are we going to do?"

"Do?"

"Simon I'm scared. I mean now-"

"It'll be okay."

"How can you say that?"

"Char, please? Come here." He holds out his hands to me.

For a moment I hesitate then I take a step forward, and his arms feel lean but strong around both of us, and I let my head rest against his chest. Georgie seems oddly reassured, but tears are suddenly running down my cheeks.

"I'm sorry, I just can't stop thinking about Lee. He's only thirteen, the same age as Jamie when-"

"I know." Simon's grip tightens around us, and we stay like that for a long time, but he doesn't say anything more, and in his silence, I sense his fear. He still smells of the search, of peaty earth, young bracken and blood.

10

————

Again I can't sleep and neither it appears can Simon. Every so often there's the creak of a board and the soft pace of a foot, once or twice the faint squeak of a door opening and closing but the darkness is between us now, isolating us with our thoughts. In the early hours, it's Jamie and Lee that I keep thinking about. Lee and Jamie. Two evenings quarter of a century apart. The beginning and the beginning of the end?

"Was there a gun?"

Hollinghurst refused to comment either way, but I'm sure he knows. I heard that other shot through my open bedroom window, but I didn't know what it meant. I thought it was only the boys shooting rabbits far down the valley and I turned my face into the pillow. I hated to see the tiny limp bodies afterwards with their blood-spattered fur and blank staring eyes.

It was only later when I heard the running footsteps and shouts in the garden below and saw the blood on

Simon, that I knew that something was wrong. But it was a good half hour before I knew how wrong.

Simon loved Jamie, of course, he did. I remember how they used to sit in the evenings, heads together on one side of the kitchen table as they laboured through their homework. Or at least Simon worked while Jamie flew through his then turned to point out Simon's mistakes, not sarcastically but with an amiable prod of his finger against the paper. He wanted to help, and Simon didn't care how he got his done as long as he did for there were horses to ride afterwards and sheep to tend.

What happened was so unfair, so cruel, so unlikely. Jamie shouldn't have even been there.

"No, no, no, not shooting, not yet." That's what Simon had said to him over and over again. I'd heard him on more than one occasion that week, and yet still Jamie had followed him out into the darkness that last Saturday, slipping from the house while none of us was watching. I must have been upstairs somewhere, reading or sorting through my photographs. I can't remember now for it had started like any other Saturday evening. We rambled through the house and farm, together and then apart, casual and careless. There was no reason to be otherwise.

He'd jumped Simon on the edge of Queen's Wood, in the deeper oak darkness. That's what Simon had told the police afterwards and me when we sat for so long in the plastic overheated waiting room at the hospital. He stepped out of the shadows smiling.

"No." Don't think about his smile. Don't think about the way his lips curled away from his teeth in a crazy mix of childish innocence and teenage maturity. He was going to be a paediatrician; he knew it without a doubt. Nothing was going to stop him, except Simon.

Jamie wouldn't leave Simon. He wouldn't go back. There was something in him that night, village voices that chased him on, only Simon didn't know it then, not until afterwards when I told him. He would show them; he would, the gang with their watchful eyes and words like knives. He'd show them he could shoot to kill too, rabbits anyway.

The black tide of forbidden memories laps closer and the capsized images bob. Red hair in torchlight, eyebrows so neat they were almost feminine. No wonder they had it in for him. He was too different; it's easy to see that now, too earnest for his age, too clever. But it was Simon, wasn't it? Simon who loved him who did the real damage, Simon who ended it for him in a cruel twist of fate.

I wasn't there that night, but I'd felt the sway of mist close to the brook on numerous other occasions, cold against skin. We all used the shortcut. Simon, Jamie, me and Marty. Home from the village, down the dip, past Crow Tor and up the other side, rank couch grass, alder grove and bracken stand. Silver birch roots like snakes in the torchlight, in the grass. It should have been a quick walk for Simon that night, but there was something there.

Jamie was the one who switched out the light apparently. There was no moon. Simon had one chance. The shotgun was ready in his hand for the fox that never came. There were footsteps instead, too heavy for an animal; a familiar silhouette crossed the clearing. Marty. What happened then has never quite made sense. There was an argument between Simon and Marty, shouting, a struggle, they'd both admitted to that. The gun went off accidentally, and somehow Jamie was shot. It had all seemed so unreal. Of course, Simon could be wild, but he was usually so careful where guns were concerned.

Why wasn't the safety catch on? I went over and over it in my head back then and still; I couldn't work it out. How could Simon have let such a thing happen? Whenever I tried to ask him, he clammed right up. Even now, all these years on, there is something that doesn't quite make sense. Something that shivers around the edges of my mind and scares me. Of course, Simon and Marty hadn't always seen eye to eye but surely- Yet that's how it happened. That's what they both said.

I don't know the exact words that passed between them that night. Only three people do know that, but I can imagine almost how it was. Jamie wanted them to stop; he shouted out catching Simon's attention.

"Jamie?" Did Simon call his name? Breeze against face, darkness pressing close. Did he turn? Leaf mould, wet earth, stub of rock, lurch of air. Fuck, the gun, don't drop the gun. Blast of sound, kick through the arm. A scream in the darkness, Simon's or Jamie's?

"Jamieee."

Total stillness. One second, two, three. Unbearable to look. Oh God no. Slow turn. Staggering breath, leaves, trunks, block of rock, patch of earth. Searching for something, for anything. Knowing the worst. Black gaps between his thoughts, spreading outwards.

He'd have called him mate. That's what he always said. "Mate."

———

Georgie wakes screaming as though she's had a terrible dream. The noise is different, somehow edgier than her usual cries. It drags me out of bed into the cool grey light of early dawn. She's lying on her back in her cot, and her eyes are wide open, but she hardly seems to see me.

"Hey, hey Georgie, what's the matter? This isn't like you." I lift her up as her face grows redder and redder and wet with tears. "Ssh ssh now, mummy's here. Georgie, Georgie."

Usually, I can calm her quite quickly, but now her cries rise another octave, shimmying around the room and out through the open door.

"Georgie, Georgie, Georgie what is it?" I press her cheek against mine, and her skin is burning hot between the tears that run down into the corner of my mouth. "Please darling, ssh, it's alright now, it's alright."

I open my top, but she doesn't seem hungry, so I carry her across the room and pull back the curtains with one hand. It's still on the verge of darkness outside, but I rock her up and down in front of the open window in the hope that the fresh air will calm her. If I look hard enough, I can just pick out the white blobs of sheep grouped under the garden wall. There seem to be more of them than yesterday, but I don't try to count them.

"It's alright darling; we're going home today. Later."

I try to push away all thoughts of Dan and the drive, the last minute arrangements that still need to be made, like what time I'm going to meet Pam my childminder not to mention the model who is bound to phone in sick and the props that will have gone astray. There's too much to fit in, and suddenly I don't think I've got the energy for half of it.

"Georgie, it's going to be fine, just fine."

The door scrapes behind me, and I turn. Simon is there wearing the same jeans as last night but then perhaps he never undressed properly or never slept. His right eye is puffy, and his face ranges from red to black. He winces as he pulls a jumper on over his head and walks into the room.

"What's wrong with her?"

"I, I don't know. She's probably just upset by all the changes. Georgie, please ssh, ssh. How are you?"

"Fine." He stops as another blast of screams fills the room, then steps forward. "Can I do anything?"

"Do you know about babies?"

"You could show me."

"Okay, look, oh Georgie please." I rock her backwards and forwards, and her noise undulates around my head. "I don't know what you want darling."

"Why don't we take her outside? Isn't walking meant to be good for them?"

"We? You don't have any children then?"

For a second there's that edgy look on his face again, I've touched up against something, and then it's gone. "I want to help Char."

A cold breeze eddies in through the open window. I need to get dressed but putting Georgie down again will only make her worse.

"Watch she doesn't slip."

Georgie's screams hesitate for a moment as I hand her over and then she opens her mouth even wider and pumps out the sound.

"Hell."

I wrap a shawl around her then Simon turns his back discreetly while I pull on a skirt and jumper.

Outside the air is damp and cool but the first birds are already singing in the trees behind the house, and the sun isn't far below the horizon.

"We could go into the orchard." He spins around on one heel and looks up at the fields. "No, let's go down the track, it'll be drier."

The granite is loose and angular beneath the thin soles of my sandals, and twice I have to stop to shake a piece of gravel out from between my toes. When we're level with Rocky Platt, the first rays of sunlight spread over the horizon and we pause to look out across the valley.

Robert never quite managed to clear the field of boulders and now they lie like so many slumbering animals. Above them a flock of gulls wheel in from the west. I remember with an odd sense of familiarity that they always used to fly inland at this time of year after the hard golden backed coch-y-bonddu beetles.

"Where did you go?"

"Up the back of Longcause and-."

"Not yesterday, back then, when you left."

"Christ Char, why do want to know now? I walked, I hitched, I got to the edge of Brum. So what?" He rocks Georgie up and down as her cries rise again.

"I've always wanted to know. Ssh, Georgie, ssh. Shall I take her?"

"I'm alright. It got late. I came to this café, and I went in because I was cold and I needed a coffee. I stayed there for five months frying sausages."

"Was there?" I turn to study his face. "Was there a woman?"

"There was Felicia. She took me in and gave me pot."

"Good." A cool breeze blows across the grassland, and I want to think about this, not anything else. "You needed someone to look after you; I'm glad she was there."

In the brighter light, his nose looks so sore, and there's an odd swelling over the bridge of it that makes me think it might be broken. "Char I'm sorry."

"It wasn't your fault." I turn away from him, and we listen to a car moving slowly through the lanes in the valley below.

"And you, how on earth?" He looks down at my expensive London shoes.

I shrug. "An amazing chance, that's all."

His eyes are full of disbelief, and I know that I've oversimplified the years of trying, of working at the veggie café until my feet ached and my stomach churned with black tea. Day after day of it followed by long evenings walking the streets and catching the other side of London through the one lens that I could afford: tired night faces, the flick of shadows across paving slabs and under awnings, the sense of people never quite seen but always active.

The amazing chance, of course, was the exhibition that the café manager let me stage under my new name and the gallery owner who happened to walk in and see it. After that, it was still a few more years before I served my last cappuccino and dared to call photography my job, my career.

"I'm supposed to be going back to London today." I hesitate. "Oh, God. It was all arranged weeks ago. We have to fly out to Paris tonight. It's the first part of a big contract. I've waited such a long time for it, but it doesn't seem right, not now."

"Char, you have to go."

"I don't know, I mean-" Georgie is quiet at last, and the car below us is the only human sound in the dawn. I feel edgy suddenly. If I am going, I need to go back to pack.

"She's stopped crying." A smile twitches at Simon's lips and his fingers move against Georgie's arm, a shy tentative gesture.

"Thank goodness. I don't think I could cope with her crying all the way to London." I stop. "Oh God, I don't know-"

"Char you've got to go. I'll stay here."

"It shouldn't be you. Clare shouldn't, this isn't fair. None of this should be happening."

"Char-"

"I always meant it when I said it wasn't your fault you know. I never lied to you." I study his beautiful, damaged face, everything about it is different, but the same and suddenly I wonder what he knows about that night in the oak wood long ago that I don't. We're both scarred by it. I can still hear his panic-stricken shout beneath my bedroom window and see the front of his jacket soaked in blood, but what terrible visions of the minutes before does he hold within him? Or the minutes after for that matter when Clare ran out, her face taut with terror, and Robert's bellow echoed through the still night air.

"Jamie's what?"

I try to shake free of them, but the images linger, poisonous as ever. Something convinced the police that it was an accident and there were never any charges but all the same.

"I never lied to you," I say again, but I don't think

he believes me and suddenly the car is much closer. It idles for a moment beyond the lower hedges then the throb of its engine changes and deepens under pressure. It's coming up the track towards us. I glance at my watch and feel exposed.

"It's only six am for God's sake."

"There must be news."

We look at each other, and I feel another quiver of the past, of long forgotten times when we stood together waiting for a visitor to negotiate the hill. Time has formed a loop around us but rather than being comforting it makes my heart pump faster.

The dogs bound in over the dew-laden grass, lips spread wide and tongues lolling and Bri barks once sharply as the nose of a dark car swings around the corner. The tyres spin on the loose gravel and then it's alongside us, and the window slides down.

"Good morning," Hollinghurst says. "Looks like you've got an early riser there."

"Have you found them?"

"Not as such," he says, and I don't like the expression on his face as he and Quinn climb out of the car. "Simon Elgin, just the person I was hoping to see. We're arresting you on suspicion of the abduction of Clare Elgin and Lee Berryman. You do not have to say anything, but it may harm your defence if you do not mention when questioned something which you later rely on in court. Anything you do say may be given in evidence."

"What?"

"You heard."

"But-" I turn to face Hollinghurst but he won't meet my eye, and the air is suddenly less clear than it was before as though an early mist has slipped between us.

Simon bows his head for a moment and looks down at Georgie. "I've told you everything I know."

"Come on now." Beyond Hollinghurst, Quinn straightens his shoulders.

"You'd better take Georgie." He eases her back into my arms.

"Simon?"

"I don't know anything about Lee Berryman; you do believe me don't you? Char?" His face is so close to mine that I can see the blood starting to ooze out of the cut across his nose.

"I'll come with you."

"No, you've got your photo shoot."

"But-"

"Promise me you'll go. I'll call you tonight on your mobile, okay?"

"Simon."

He turns towards Hollinghurst and takes a step forwards. The dogs agitate around his legs eager to carry on with their walk. "What exactly makes you think it was me?"

"Mr Elgin."

"You're wasting your time. I've told you what I know, which is nothing in case you've forgotten."

"There really isn't any need-"

"To take an attitude? Is that what you're saying? I don't need to be concerned that you've come here to arrest me at six am? Is that so?"

Hollinghurst glances back towards the car and Quinn takes a step forward. "You're not helping your-self here."

"Seems you've already decided."

"Come on now." Hollinghurst's shirtsleeve has a small dark mark just above the cuff that appears out of a fold of cloth as he reaches for Simon's arm.

"For Christ's sake, get your hands off me." Simon flicks his arm up and out, and Hollinghurst leans away.

"Mr Elgin I have to warn you."

"You're all the same."

"Simon."

"Let's go then. I don't know anything about it, so this is just a bloody waste of time. Time when you should be out looking for them."

Quinn steps close, there's the crush of metal against flesh, then he steers Simon into the back of the vehicle. Simon's face looks battered behind the dark glass, and his black eye is visible even from a distance. I wonder how many journalists are already at the bottom of the lane and wince.

———

"Shit."

It's warmer in the kitchen than outside, and the old oil Rayburn hums. Georgie's obviously hungry now and starts to cry again, but I have to find my mobile first and make a call.

"Hi, Dan it's me."

"Charlotte." It's early; I've surprised him, it's all there in his voice. "Is everything alright?"

"There's been-" I pause and think about Simon's face again and the handcuff closing around his wrist. I didn't promise- "Look I can't make it this afternoon."

"What?" There obviously hasn't been anything in

the news yet. "Charlotte you can't be thinking of flying out in the morning."

"No, I mean that I can't make it at all."

There's a moment's silence. "I see. Do you want me to try and reschedule? The model is probably on her way already but-"

"I know, and I'm sorry. There must be someone else who can do it though, isn't there?" Tokyo slides away from me as I speak. All that effort, all that planning. I press my cheek against Georgie's head and close my eyes trying not to think about it, but the knowledge settles heavily somewhere deep inside. I'll lose a lot of money of course. But it isn't just the money, it's the chance of doing something different, the chance to stretch out and claim my style.

"I'll see what I can arrange." Dan's voice is tight, and faintly behind it, there's the whine of a police siren. It puts me on edge even though it's unconnected with anything down here.

"Charlotte?"

"Okay. Thank you." Georgie starts to cry properly, and her cheeks redden. "Look I'm going to have to go."

———

I sit in the rocker, and there's no shock of cold air against my skin as I unbutton my top. Georgie is hungry but grouchy because of the delay, and her attention wanders away from my breast over and over. Today of all mornings I need her to drink quickly. I stifle my impatience as I stare across the familiar room.

Last time the police came for Simon after the shooting all those years ago, the cars rushed up the track, blue lights cutting through the darkness. There were what seemed like hours of questions before statements were signed and we were back together again in agonised silence.

Last time. There's something in the back of my mind, some sense of connection between then and now that I'm still not getting. I let my thoughts drift for a moment as though that way I might catch myself out and suddenly I'm thinking about yesterday, about the search and Simon's face. What did Tony say to Simon yesterday and what made him say it?

"Come on Georgie." I stroke the top of her head. I need to go and find Arthur. He will surely know what happened. Georgie pauses for a moment, and I'm about to do up my top again when she decides that she's still hungry after all. "Okay, you win. Just another five minutes though."

I reach across and switch on the radio. Clare and Lee's disappearance is still a top item on the news, and I hear edits of Peter's and my words again and again. More people have phoned in, and there's been a sighting of Clare and Lee in London, Glasgow, Manchester, Penzance and Mallorca. I can't make sense of them, can't even begin to think how they could have got from here to any of those places without being seen or why they would try. My hopes rise though; surely if they're still alive out there, Simon can't have been involved or at least not in any negative way.

A red blonde boy was seen getting on a train at the Gare de Lyon in Paris, and someone emailed a grainy photo of a boy's red head at Malaga Airport to the police and a tabloid at the same time. By chance or otherwise, there's a woman in her sixties standing beside him.

At last Georgie's finished and I carry her upstairs to get her ready for the day. On the chair by the window is my camera case. I hardly dare glance at it. Two weeks, no less than that, just over a week ago, I was so excited about the prospect of the photo shoots in Paris and then Tokyo. I'd planned them so carefully in my head, thinking up ways to overcome all the challenges I thought I might face, the childcare issues and lack of sleep, but of course I never even imagined something like this happening.

"We have a few things to do now darling so will you be good for Mummy?" I hug Georgie to me and tickle her bare toes, but the look she gives me doesn't promise anything either way. "Right, first of all, we have to go and find Arthur. You know the nice man who helps here."

The dogs pad restlessly at my heels, and I know that they want to come too, but I push them back when we reach the kitchen door.

"Good dogs, we won't be long." I reach down and rough their heads. Gel closes her eyes for a second and waves her tail half-heartedly but her ears are still cocked and her spine taut. "We'll be back soon. I promise."

Are they just missing Clare or is there something more to their watchfulness? What did they see? I glance over my shoulder towards the hallway without meaning to. It's silent and shadowy now.

"Come on Georgie, time to go." My words sound edgy even to my ears, and the back door grinds as I pull it shut, the grit beneath it adding a reluctance to the movement that I try to ignore. I turn the old key in the lock and drop it into the terracotta flagon beyond the bench, we've used the same hiding place for it since I learnt to walk. Bri makes an odd sound, half whimper, half whine and I turn away.

Eb is sunning himself by the yard gate, his dark coat dusty and his ribs a light corrugation beneath his skin. He's apparently waiting for his breakfast, but I don't know what he has now. I try Arthur's number as I walk across the yard, but there's no reply.

"We'll drive down and find Arthur, okay?" I kiss Georgie's forehead and a damp finger digs at my cheek for a moment. The total trust in her movement makes me want to cry. "It's all going to be fine."

We're halfway down the track when Arthur's immaculate old Landrover noses around a corner into view. I slam on my brakes too hard and the Golf skids on the loose gravel. For a few seconds I sit still, my nerves jittery, then I lean forward to open the door.

We both climb out of our vehicles at the same moment, and Arthur is considerably stiffer than I am. For a moment he leans back against his door and looks around as if expecting to see someone else.

"Morning Charlotte." His gaze comes to rest on my face. "Is everything alright?"

"I tried to call you." I flush suddenly for no reason. His Wellingtons are spotlessly clean, and he's wearing fresh overalls where anyone else would make the same pair last all week. If you didn't know him, you'd think that he'd prepared himself especially to be filmed by one of the TV crews hanging around. How he's survived working here for so long is a mystery to me. But perhaps his meticulousness perfectly offset Clare's vague, random ideas all these years.

"I'm sorry I'm a bit late. I had a few things to see to first." Arthur's smile is wary for a moment.

"Are you? No, that's not- Arthur I need to talk to you about yesterday, about-"

"What happened on the search? It was most unfortunate." He takes off his cap, smoothes a hand over his hair then replaces his cap again. "How's Simon?"

I hesitate for a moment. Arthur wore the same make of green overalls and belt twenty years ago and every day since? I can't lie to someone who lives life so straightforwardly; I can't lie at all right now the tears are so close.

"Oh, Arthur the police have arrested him."

"For that? I thought it was rather busy down there on the road this morning."

"No," I glance over my shoulder as though there might be someone behind the hedge listening to our conversation. "Look could we go up to the house?"

There's nowhere wide enough to turn, so I end up reversing all the way back to the yard. Arthur follows in his Landrover, and the dogs greet us with a wild flailing of paws.

"Okay, okay." I push them back before they start to alarm Georgie.

"Shall we have a cup of tea? I'll make it because you've got your hands full."

"Thank you." Arthur obviously knows this kitchen as well as I used to and he finds everything we need without hesitation. When the kettle has boiled, he pours two mugs, and we sit down on either side of the cluttered table.

"So what exactly's happened?" He twists his mug between his gnarled hands. There are deep stained grooves across the edge of his index fingers from years of outdoor work.

"It's all a horrible mistake." I rub a hand across my face and try to pull myself together again. "It's got to be."

Faced with recounting the details of the morning I suddenly can't do it. Bluntly it was a police raid, one of those events that you read or hear about then move on with scarcely a thought for the people involved, the obviously guilty people caught by surprise in their beds with no chance to run. That's what it would have been like for us, perhaps how Hollinghurst planned it, only Georgie had other ideas.

"They arrested Simon for the abduction of Clare and Lee," I say, and Arthur watches me. "It's got to be a mistake. They can't think. I mean, what happened yesterday?"

"Yes," Arthur sighs. "I had a word with Tony afterwards. What he said was well out of order."

"Did he start it then?"

"Well-"

"Please Arthur, I need to know."

"I don't like to repeat it, but he suggested that Simon might not lead us in the right direction." Arthur glances away from me.

"You mean that he inferred that Simon knows what happened to Clare and Lee, that he was somehow involved? But why? Why would he think that? I mean surely after all these years." It doesn't make sense. I close my eyes for a moment.

"I never saw him," Arthur says thoughtfully.

"What? But you just said he was with you on the search yesterday."

"Oh yes, he was, of course."

"Then?" I frown.

"Sorry, I didn't mean-" He takes a purposeful sip of tea. "It's nothing."

"Really?" A weight drops inside me for some reason, and I feel slightly shaky suddenly. "Arthur you would tell me if there was something-"

"Of course." He doesn't look at me.

"I'm going down to see Tony."

"You are? Is that a good idea?" An expression I don't understand crosses his face and is gone again almost at once.

"I have to find out why- I mean the police have arrested Simon. He could be charged and go to prison."

Arthur is silent for a moment then he finishes his tea and stands up. "Look I'm sure the police'll check everything out properly. They have to. In the meantime, you be careful eh?"

I know he only means well, but suddenly it feels as though he's stepping away from us. After he's gone out into the yard to feed Eb and start on his other farm jobs, I sit quite still for a few moments. Despite his warning, I feel that I have to go and see Tony. I need to find out what's going on and why he thinks that Simon's involved.

———

I've never seen anything like the end of our lane for real. Cars and TV news vans block the road and people are standing around everywhere. As soon as they clock the sound of my car, they rally into a group, which surges towards me. Even with the windows wound up tight I can hear their shouts like the bay of hounds on the scent of their prey.

"No. No." For a moment it looks as though they'll swamp the few uniformed police officers. I put my foot down and don't wait to find out, and in seconds I'm clear of them and heading away through the lanes towards the village, my heart racing.

Tony used to live on a farm out to the east, and as the eldest son, I guess that he might still be there or at least nearby. However, when I reach the end of his track, it looks so different that I almost think I've made a mistake. The banks have been bulldozed right back, and the whole track is wide open. In fact, one hedgerow is gone, and there's a new vista across the fields to the granite farmhouse. Even from a distance, I can see that that has changed as well. There are two modern barns alongside that dwarf the house itself.

Suddenly I feel less confident, so I stop the car once we're off the road. Behind me, Georgie agitates at one of her hanging toys.

"Okay, okay I know, it's just-" I close my eyes for a second. Just what? Don't I want to find out what's going on? Am I scared? "We're going now. Okay?"

I ease the car forwards down the track, but my heart sinks a little when I reach the yard and see several newish pickups parked there and a large blue tractor. It's too late to turn back though for there's someone at the open farmhouse door.

I climb out, gather Georgie into my arms and walk across the yard. "Hello."

The woman on the doorstep is so young that she could be Tony's daughter. She sweeps a strand of dark hair off her face but doesn't come forwards or answer.

"Hello," I say again. "Is Tony in?"

For a moment longer she stares at Georgie and me then she shakes her head. She's wearing a low cut sleeveless top, and despite the heat of the summer, her skin is pale and sun-starved. I wonder if she's a cleaner or housekeeper, although the way she's standing there feels more proprietorial.

"Will he be back soon?"

"We thought one of you might come round," she says, and I suddenly feel at a disadvantage. She obviously knows who I am, but I don't know for sure who she is. "To apologise."

"Apologise?" My heart speeds up.

"Tony's in hospital having his arm set." She pauses and narrows her eyes. The look makes her seem much older. "Right at the start of the summer."

We both know what that means for a farmer. No heavy work. No tractor driving. No haymaking or harvesting. I swallow. It feels as though I'm looking down a kaleidoscope and the pattern at the other end has just changed without warning into something that I can't see clearly.

"I'm sorry to hear that," I say as calmly as I can although the words seem all wrong. "I'll come back another time."

"We're going away." She flicks at her hair with one hand again. "Majorca. At least we can still lie in the sun. Is there anything I can help with or do you want me to give him a message?"

"No thanks, it's alright." I can't think what else to say, and we look at each other in silence for a moment. Does she know what's happened to Simon? Somehow it wouldn't surprise me if she does. "I'd better be getting back."

I turn towards the car, and she stays where she is on the doorstep until we're driving out of the yard. Even then glancing in the rearview mirror, I can see her still standing there.

———

I switch on the radio as soon as we reach the road, but I can't concentrate on a programme about fly-tipping, so I flip through the channels and hit the local news. Suddenly it's there.

" … new development in the case of the missing schoolboy Lee Berryman, we have just learnt that the police have made their first arrest. Our reporter Patsy Forest is at the scene. What can you tell us, Patsy?"

"Thank you, Vince. Yes, I can confirm that the police have arrested a 39-year-old male who is believed to be Simon Elgin, son of the other missing person, Clare Elgin, on suspicion of abduction-"

"Oh my God." I switch off the radio and stare at the empty lane ahead. It'll be everywhere now. My heart beats hard, and there's a strange taste in my mouth. Simon gave Clare flowers on Mother's Day, even the first one after he arrived. I think of those early tufty battered bunches of daffodils half crushed in his fist. Simon has broken Tony's arm. "Bloody hell."

My phone beeps twice on the seat beside me, and I reach over to read the text.

R U okay. D

I wait for a moment then click the speed dial.

154

"Charlotte I've seen the news." The familiarity of Dan's voice jolts through me.

"Have you sorted the shoot out?"

"What the hell is going on?"

"I don't know."

"But they're saying that your brother, the one who-"

"Dan, please." I grip the steering wheel hard with my right hand. "I know what you're going to say, but there are just some things, look I can't explain now. I'm sorry."

"More things? Good God."

I slow for a blind corner, and the hedges rear high above the car heavy with summer foliage.

"Charlotte?"

"And like I said if you don't want me on the team anymore that's fine."

"Charlotte are you driving? Look for Georgie's sake please just pull over."

I end the call and stare straight ahead. Immediately it begins to ring again.

"Dan, I'm fine to drive, so let's just leave it for a bit shall we?"

11

The police station has moved. I can't remember exactly where it was before, but now it's in our old secondary school. There's a group of people waiting outside the main door who might or might not be journalists. I drive past without slowing, and I don't think anyone notices me.

Half a mile on I turn into a side street, pull over to the kerb and call the incident room number. A man answers with the usual official spiel.

"It's Charlotte Elgin, please can I speak to Detective Inspector Hollinghurst?" I try to keep my voice steady, but my palms are damp. "It's important."

There's a pause for a few seconds. "I'm afraid he's busy at the moment, can anyone else help you?"

What now? I try to think quickly. "Can I speak to Amanda Miller then, please?"

Another pause and I'm ready to be fobbed off, but instead, Amanda comes on the line. "Miss Elgin, what can I do for you?"

"How?" I swallow and fight back the urge to shout.

"It's only been a few hours, so how on earth? Did you tell the press about Simon?"

"We haven't released any updates yet," she says carefully. "But-"

"What?"

"Your brother has been arrested. We can't deny that."

"But it's a mistake, and now, now it's out there everywhere." I swallow. Simon has also broken Tony's arm. I don't want to think how or how it will look when that gets out as inevitably it will.

"I'll be monitoring what's said."

"And?"

"I do understand how hard this is for you."

"You have no idea." Behind me, Georgie picks up on my mood and starts to cry. I snap my phone off and sit with my eyes closed for a few moments. "God, God, God."

What to do now? I unstrap Georgie and lift her onto my lap for a short feed to calm her, but she's having none of it.

"Please darling, please." I kiss the top of her head and try to calm myself as well as her. I need to talk to Hollinghurst, but he apparently doesn't want to speak to me right now or can't which rather suggests that he's still interviewing Simon.

I stare up at a single gull gliding across the cloudless blue and my phone beeps on the passenger seat. Another text. I reach for it with my left hand and tip it away from the glare of the sun to see the screen.

Call me when you can. D.

The car is still in the shade of the building, but it's stuffily hot inside. I put my phone down again and sit with the door open while I feed Georgie. I'm thirsty as well, but I've forgotten to bring a bottle of water so I'll just have to stay that way. When Georgie's finished, and I've changed her, I put her back in her car seat and drive out of town.

The holiday traffic is on the move heading for the beaches along the south coast with their promise of a cool breeze and perfect domes of local ice cream. We get stuck in clot after clot of cars, and each time we slow almost to a stop I think that someone in a nearby vehicle will recognise me, so I keep my head down. It takes us far longer than it should, but at last, we're clear of the dual carriageway. Georgie is hot and restless, and she threatens to scream.

"Ssh, ssh darling, I'm sorry, but we're nearly there, nearly back at the farm."

The road from the village is chaotic with news vans and cars, and there are people everywhere. Some are reporters with cameras slung around their necks, but there are others whose business is less obvious. I have to slow down to a walking pace to get through. Hands slap the side of the car and faces press down close.

I flick the locks and keep my eyes straight ahead. "It's okay Georgie; it's okay."

A man steps out in front of the car, and for a second I have to stop. Immediately he's joined by others, and I'm surrounded. Fear clutches at me, and someone tries to open my door.

"Miss Elgin, is it true, is-?"

"Where is he?"

"Go away."

I don't know what to do. If I drive forward will the people move? I rev the engine and someone laughs; then there's a lens pressed against the glass centimetres from my face. I put a hand up to hide my profile and Georgie screams.

"Ssh darling, ssh." My fear turns to anger. How dare they do this to us? I put my hand on the horn and hold it there, and Georgie's screams turn more distraught. A few minutes later a police car appears around the corner, and the reporters step back to the sides of the road.

I'm through but my heart is pounding, and my palms are damp against the steering wheel. Never, ever do I want to have to go through that again. I turn into our track, and within minutes you'd have no idea what lies behind. The sun shines on the pale gravel and two butterflies dance above a patch of flowers on the side.

It's tempting to stop to take in the normalness of it all, to breathe, but I keep moving. I'm nearly at the junction where the track divides when a dark green Landrover comes round the corner towards us with Marty at the wheel. The absolute last person I feel like meeting at the moment.

"Oh no."

He drives right up to us and stops, but he doesn't get out. Instead, he sits with his arms folded and the engine running. The track is too narrow for us to pass and it's a long way for me to reverse to a wider spot. I still feel on the right side of everything. Clear. I can look Hollinghurst in the eye and let his suspicion glance off me and yet somehow it already seems as if my innocence is an irrelevance to him, to the reporters, to everyone.

It happens in slow motion. My hand is on the gear

stick ready to push into reverse, but I reach to open the driver's door instead.

"I won't be long Georgie."

I walk between the two vehicles to Marty's window. There's a new dent in his door as though he's opened it too fast and carelessly into something solid, a granite wall perhaps. For a moment I think he's going to keep the glass between us then he winds it down.

"Is there news?" His face is red from the sun, and his hair is unwashed and unbrushed. It hangs against his forehead in damp, greasy strands. Has he seen the papers today?

"You know there is." Keep calm, keep calm, keep calm. I swallow and away to my left a bird calls over and over. "We need to talk."

"About?"

"What you've said to your friends and the police." He's above me up there in the cab, and I have to twist my head to see him properly. "What did you tell them?"

"What did-? Ah." He leans back in his seat and stares at the roof then he laughs in an odd harsh way and sticks his arm out of the window. I think he's going to hit me and step away, but he's merely gesticulating. "You see that back there, all them notes, they're to my boy, my boy."

"Marty?"

"This isn't my fault. Don't you think Simon showed his true colours yesterday on the search?" He hesitates and a sudden look of satisfaction curls at the corners of his lips. "I just told the police what I know."

"What you know or what you think?"

"He's only a child."

Heat swells in the base of my throat and rises

upwards. "What happened in the past is over; we can't change it, any of us, and stirring it up again isn't going to help now."

"I wasn't talking about the past."

For a second I remember how we used to be together before Simon came, how easily we talked and laughed and how once or twice he held my hand in the hazel shelter of the lane on the way back from the school bus and then again years later. The clarity of the memories surprises me, he's closer than Dan, closer than any of them and the blood rushes into my cheeks.

"If you've said anything to the police that isn't true-"

"You'll do what? Get your London friends to sort me out?" He rubs his forehead with the heel of his right hand.

"You bastard."

"This isn't about that night. I saw him with my own eyes."

"What?" A sudden chill licks across my bare arms. I don't understand what he's talking about.

"He has told you, hasn't he?"

"Oh that, yes of course he has."

"Really? And don't you think it's a bit too much of a coincidence? He comes back, and then Lee and Clare disappear."

Does he know where Tony is now? My shoulders tense.

"I mean, I've been thinking. Clare mad as a hatter, and we may have had our differences but she came to Lee's christening, and she wasn't one to go off of her accord now was she? It was unusual to even meet her down at the shop. Do you see what I'm saying?"

He's right. I look away. Clare tried to fit in and not

show her fear when she came up to meet me in London, but she'd talk about leaving before we'd been together half an hour. The trains worried her and driving back to the farm in the dark. Staying over with me was never an option. She used to throw her plait over her shoulder and pretend that she had too much work to do.

"Where are they?" Marty's tone changes abruptly and there's a dark patch of sweat at the bottom of the v of his neckline

"What?"

"Tell me what you know."

"I don't know anything." We're closed in by the tangled hedges here, out of sight of the roadblock, of anybody.

"Oh come on. Simon must have said something by now."

"I don't know what you're talking about Marty." There are smears of mud on his shirt as though he's been carrying something over one shoulder. "But I don't like what you're inferring."

"Why? Why Lee? Why now?"

"Marty." I wonder how I ever felt close enough to him to tell him family secrets. "Marty I need to take Georgie back to the farm."

"Of course you do." He stares at the car for a moment. "But just imagine what it would feel like to lose her."

———

There's an armoured police van in the yard and an unmarked car, and the back door of the house is open.

Did I forget to lock it or do the police know where the key is kept?

"What on earth?" Georgie starts to cry as soon as we stop and I lift her out of her seat and into my arms. "Come on darling; it's alright."

A man waits beside the door now in smart casual clothes, and he looks at me uncertainly.

"What's going on?"

"And you are?"

"Charlotte Elgin. This is my mother's house." Beyond him, a figure appears down the stairs with a clear plastic bag in his hand, and there are sounds in the kitchen.

"Do you have any ID?" He holds out his card.

"What? Oh, come on." I'm tired, I'm hungry, Georgie needs a nappy change, and I've had enough.

"I'm sorry but-"

"Okay, okay." I go back to the car and fumble in my bag. "I've got a credit card, will that do?"

"Well."

"Oh and my maternity card." I remember it suddenly.

"Fine." He looks at them quickly.

"So what's going on?"

"We have a warrant to search the house."

"Again?" I don't understand. "It's been searched already and the land and-"

It hits me suddenly. They're not looking for clues left by Clare but by Simon. Another officer appears from the living room. There's something about his narrow face that looks vaguely familiar, and I think I must have seen him the first evening.

"Miss Elgin, I'm sorry, you've obviously got your

hands full." He makes a fish mouth at Georgie then looks back at me. "But is that your Golf outside?"

"Yes."

"D'you mind if we just take a look at it?"

"Carry on." I'm sure I can't stop him even if I wanted to.

"Oh, and could you tell us where Simon Elgin's vehicle is at the moment?" The question is thrown casually over his shoulder as he heads for the door.

"He hasn't got one. He came down by bike."

"Oh, okay, where's he parked that? We didn't see it earlier."

I point to it now leant up against the barn wall, and the man laughs, but the sound isn't one of real amusement.

"Come on let's not play games."

"I'm not." I turn away from him. "And I need to feed my daughter somewhere quiet."

I watch from the living room window while I feed Georgie. Two officers search my car inside and out, front and back. They appear to take samples of something from all the seats, then one of them spends minutes on end leaning into the boot. Finally, they examine each of the tyres.

A thought hits me out of the blue. What if they find something? I know it's clean of course but suppose, suppose somehow it isn't?

All the things I've ever seen or heard or read about police investigations whirl through my head in a confusion of anecdotes and images. This isn't good; it isn't good at all.

"Miss Elgin?" An officer stops discreetly in the doorway. "Do you mind, could I have a word?"

"Of course." Georgie has finished feeding, and I adjust my top.

"Is the laptop in the car yours?"

"Yes." A horrible feeling sinks inside me. I know even before he opens his mouth again what's coming next.

"I'm afraid we're going to have to take it away with us."

"No, no, you can't, I'm a photographer, it's got all my work on it, I need it." I stand up abruptly, jolting Georgie without meaning to and she starts to cry. "Heh Georgie, Georgie. Look please?"

"I'm sorry."

"When?" Panic surges through me. Clients are waiting for images that I need to send them. What will I say even if I can email them from my mobile?

"I can't tell you at the moment I'm afraid."

When they've all finished and driven away with Simon's small rucksack of things and my laptop I can't stay in the house. It smells of them, of aftershave and washing powder and although it looks the same, it feels different, sullied somehow. Everything has been touched, turned over and replaced again.

I lift Georgie into her carrier and walk down through the fields with the dogs, but I hardly notice anything until I'm almost at the river. I can't believe it. How could they think? My laptop.

Without planning to, I arrive at one of our old favourite spots. Great slabs of granite stretch out into the water, smoothed by generations of winter floods, but they were dry and warm beneath our bare feet the last time I was here that freakishly hot May day.

We cast off our sandals where the short-cropped turf

of the bank gave out, and Simon walked right to the edge of the rock and stared down into the dark, peat-stained water. After a moment or two, he pulled his t-shirt off over his head. Underneath he was golden brown and almost thin. Knobs of bone stood out on the tops of his shoulders, and I could see the edges of the muscles stretched across his belly. I wanted to touch his shoulder, but I sat down instead.

"It's good to be out here isn't it?" Wasn't that what I said with childish innocence?

The opposite bank rises steeply up into a patch of oak woodland and the nearest trees stretch out across the water. Back then a rope hung down over the pool, ending a couple of metres above the water. It was a piece we'd filched from the bale stack the previous summer and Simon had spent a whole morning balanced among the branches choosing just the right place for it.

It's gone now of course. I can't even see the branch it hung from, so perhaps that has also been torn down by a winter storm.

I had wanted to swim later, to let the cool water take me in its grasp and wash away the scents and sounds and feelings of the hospital but I wasn't sure whether we would or not.

Further downriver there's a car park and an ice cream van, and back then the rocks were covered in families soaking up the sun, but up here above the tangle of barbed wire and rhododendrons it was our place, quiet and hidden. Once I used to dream that we could write messages and float them down to all the people below us, I imagined what I might write and who might read it.

Simon was silent. Not so long before we'd have been planning something, how to reach Hew Tor in half the time by jumping a locked gate or when to slip away on a school evening without our parents noticing. That day Jamie's shaded hospital room hung between us and the tubes that fed him filled us with horror and guilt. It seemed wrong to do anything frivolous or fun while he was in there.

It's so quiet, the water slides by with the minimum of fuss, and for a second I imagine that there's a thin figure standing on the edge of the rock. He looks so miserable, so vulnerable that I want to reach across the years to him and hold him tight, to stop him running blindly into the future.

Back then I wanted him to rub sunblock into my bare shoulders, but his fingers dithered against my skin their pressure uncertain and unwilling.

"I can't do this," he said. "I can't do any of this. It's, it's shit."

Two mallards slop by on the current, jigging up and down as they follow the turbulence. Will they rise up and away when they come among people further down or will they just paddle faster with their wide, webbed feet?

That day Simon threw all his sandwiches into the water without warning. I watched my careful preparation float away downstream.

"Aren't you hungry?"

He stared at me for a moment, and I thought I saw water gathering against his bottom eyelids. "Char, don't you understand anything? Why the hell are we here anyway?"

"Simon."

"I can't be doing this. Look, I'm going back."

"Simon, please wait. I'm sorry. I was only trying to, I thought being here might help." I can still feel the acute pain of my younger self.

"Help?" "You really don't have any idea do you?"

Do I have any idea now? Well, do I? I wrap my arms around Georgie and stare down into the dark water. It swirls past my toes streamed with tiny white bubbles and every so often there's something else caught up, a twig or a leaf, that bobs and spins.

All that time ago and yet standing here the memory is so fresh, so painful still. If I had only done something different could I have averted what happened next? Could I have stopped the chain of events that has somehow led to all this now?

I turn away from the water and back up the hill, pushing myself on until I'm breathless and hot. Eb has wandered down into Rocky Platt, and I stop beside him for a while, partly to regain my breath and partly in the hope that his steady grazing will somehow calm me.

"Where's Hetty?" I stroke his dark neck feeling the tightness of old muscles and wonder what happened to my mare. Is she still alive somewhere, sold on to another family or do her bones lie here beneath the wiry turf on the farm? Eb lifts his head and rubs against me, friendly in that distant thoroughbred way of his.

Back at the house I let myself into the shadowy kitchen and feed the dogs. Every sound that I make is strangely amplified through the silent building reminding me of my aloneness, of the fact that everyone else is gone now, even Simon.

Hours later I think I hear a vehicle on the track and look out but there's nothing there and, curled up by the Rayburn, the dogs don't share my concern.

12

Simon doesn't come back that night, and the weird half insomnia has me well and truly in its grip. Once again I drift through the surreal twilight world of our past between Georgie's feeds. In the room and then out of it again, in the house and then far beyond.

There was a time when the snow fell deep and early, and the views from our bedroom windows were alpine. Even the tallest grasses that poked through the crust were rimed with ice. Simon must have been about sixteen, which meant I was fourteen. We walked across the valley to the reservoir, one, two, three mornings and on the third, there was no creaking when we stepped on the edge.

"Okay." Simon looked out across the silver-grey sheet speckled with snow crystals and a smile curled the corners of his lips. "Come on."

At first, I couldn't do it. I dithered at the edge like an overfaced horse, and Simon carried on without me. Ten feet, fifteen. He walked with exaggerated care at first, testing each step but there was no sound. The freeze had gone in deep night after night, and behind us, beneath the snow, the ground was hard and rutted.

"Come on."

It was weird, scary and exhilarating at the same time. I stepped out but then I stared down at my booted feet and imagined all the dark water beneath me and almost I stopped again.

"Char." Suddenly Simon was back, and he grabbed my hand. "It's good."

Further, further, further out we went, and still, there was no sound. In places the ice was smooth and glassy, in others, it had frozen in ripples. My breath was high up in my lungs, and I felt hot and slightly dizzy despite the cold breeze in my face.

"Wow." We reached the middle and held up our hands. It was a wide white world. "Yes."

After that, it was mad and easy. We danced, we slithered, we ran, and all the time we held hands, laughing and pulling each other up when we nearly fell. I didn't want to reach the far bank, but suddenly we were there, and we fell giggling onto the snow.

"We did it; we did it." Simon was elated then he pushed a handful of snow down my neck, and I got him back, and we rolled over and over until we were damp and exhausted.

"I'm hungry." I sat up and fumbled in my pocket for the bar of chocolate that I'd brought.

"Wait, we can have that later." Simon pulled two newspaper packages from his pockets. "They're a bit squashed, but they'll be fine."

The air around us filled with the delicious scent of hot baked potatoes and newsprint, and we leant back against a rock and ate in contented silence. Melted butter dripped through my fingers and despite the cold-ness of my toes I'd never been so happy.

"We'll walk back round over Hartor," Simon said, and my heart soared. It would stretch out the perfect day of snow almost to dusk, long beautiful hours alone together before the round of feeding and the content-ment of horses crunching hay in the frosty darkness.

For minutes on end, perhaps even nearly an hour I slip down into sleep then suddenly the air smells of heather smoke, and I'm running away from someone and towards someone, a thick dark plume rising off the flank of Howden behind me.

"Simon. Simon." I shout but no one comes, and his code stone isn't on the garden gatepost. There's a smell of smoke even indoors now. "Simon."

I can't find him anywhere, and yet the sense that I've just left someone is close. Minutes before I was talking but not to myself. I grapple through the darkness of this night and that, but I can't find Simon or the other person.

"Where are you?"

Blue lights spin and flash through the trees, and suddenly there are voices, and he's in the yard in stained jeans and a black t-shirt. My mouth tastes of plastic water and soot and I know that much earlier Peter lifted my hand, blistered from beating out the flames with a long wooden stake, and looked at my fingernails. Peter. But it wasn't him that I'd talked to.

"Simon." For a second he seems surprised, almost perturbed to see me. Two frown lines dip between his eyebrows and I don't understand, then Robert's behind us with his glasses hanging around his neck and a sheaf of papers in one hand. We've disturbed his work, and now his temper will flare easily.

"You've gone too far this time, way too far." His words smash through the shadows, and suddenly we're all dazzled by blue and white light. "How could you have been so stupid? Someone is bound to have seen you."

"No. No."

I turn away from them now although I couldn't in reality. The sunlight was different earlier, as though it was shining through cellophane onto our faces as we talked, but who was I talking to? Who?

"If it was you, if you lit the fire-" Robert's words were aimed at Simon, but they hit my skull.

"No. No."

"For God's sake, of course, the gorse was getting too high, we all know that but there was going to be proper swaling next week." A small fire kept in check by all the local farmers, nothing like the one that swept wildly across Howden above us.

"Why, why is everything always my fault?" Simon's beautiful face is stained with ash, and the whites of his eyes are red from the smoke but who was I talking to earlier?

"It's hardly surprising, is it? After your recent behaviour."

"That's not the same. I'm no arsonist. I didn't do it, alright."

The police are in the yard again, different officers, vaguely familiar. A routine visit. Yeh right. For a second Simon's scared then, he sweeps the expression away with the heel of his hand and looks far too intelligent, too golden to do anything stupid.

In the morning my eyes feel gravelly, and I can't think straight. It's an effort to get up and make breakfast and the list of other things that I need to do stretches out in front of me in panicky succession. I should do some work, there are calls I have to make, but I can't face them. Instead, I make a strong black tea and sit down on the back lawn with Georgie asleep in her car seat beside me. Far above us on the top road, the sun sparks off the windscreen of the same dark car that I've seen parked up there before, but I try not to look at it.

On the hour I know that I could catch the news but I won't. I breathe deeply and watch a blackbird pulling at a worm under one of the shrubs. Beside me, the radio lurks ready. No. No. I reach out and turn the knob and the same newsreader as yesterday is there on the lawn with me. At first, it seems that we could be old news, there's been a big fire in a block of flats in Torquay that may be arson and then-

"And now other news. We can confirm this morning that the man arrested yesterday in connection with the disappearance of schoolboy Lee Berryman is Simon Elgin, adopted son of-"

There's a sound on the track up the hill, and I switch off the radio. "Bloody hell."

A Landrover swings into the yard followed by a patrol car and stops in front of the barn. The Landrover is newer and shinier than Marty's, and for a moment I think that it's an unmarked police vehicle but the man who jumps down from the driver's side is far too untidy to be a plainclothes officer. He's tall, dark and vaguely familiar and he's wearing a boiler suit that flaps open to the waist. There's someone in the passenger seat as well, but they make no move to get out, and I can't see them properly through the reflection on the windscreen. The end of the local news report blares out through the open window.

I stand up, and the man advances towards me, tongues of green nylon hanging out over the tops of his Wellingtons. He's heard everything, everything. The officers in the patrol car sit and watch.

"I thought I should come round in person," he says, and his gaze sweeps around the yard to the police and then back to me. "Darren Collier."

For a moment longer I can't place him, then I have a vision of the school bus, of Marty sat up near the front playing cards endlessly to while away the journey. Playing cards with-

"We were booked to bale here later this week, but if it's all the same to you, we won't be coming now."

"I see."

"Marty is a good mate of mine, and I wouldn't want my chaps up here in the circumstances." His eyes are hard, and he looks around the yard again as though to satisfy himself of something.

"Okay."

"You may want to find a contractor from out of the area, everyone around here is very busy, if you understand."

"Point taken." I grip my right hand into a fist to steady myself. "Thank you for letting me know."

When he's gone, I stumble back to Georgie hardly noticing where my feet tread. She's still sleeping, and I watch the gentle rise and fall of her chest. It's something I do so often without thinking to check that she's breathing. I know all the statistics about cot death, but it's still a lingering dread at the back of my mind that seems heightened somehow since I came back to the farm. Perhaps I'm afraid that this sudden stress will be too much of a shock for her tiny heart or that somehow it will loosen her tenuous baby grip on life.

I hardly thought about motherhood before she came along, or only vaguely, and it never even occurred to me to wonder what it must have been like for Clare to suddenly have Simon thrust into her life, to become responsible for another body and soul. Now I can't stop thinking about it. She had Jamie and me far younger than I had Georgie so she'd have been about my age when Simon arrived. Would I do what she did? Could I cope? I can't imagine having two children, let alone three, at the moment.

Far away there's the sound of a tractor. Without really thinking about it I notice it falter and then drop into a lower gear and growl against the hill. The stock has to be checked and fed whatever. I sit down on the grass. All I want to do suddenly is watch Georgie. Perhaps it's all I'm capable of doing.

Other than the possible likeness between her and the photo of me at the same age that I found in Clare's album, I've never really been able to see myself in her, a little of Dan perhaps around the eyes. Now studying her features relaxed in sleep I'm sure that she's got Jamie's chin. The small almost pointiness of it has passed across the generations from him to her. Jamie looked more like Clare than any of us, which means that one day Georgie may look like her grandmother.

The tractor is suddenly much nearer, and there's a smell of exhaust fumes in the air. I stand up in time to see it cross the field beneath the house and pull out onto the track. Peter Berryman is at the wheel.

"What the hell?" I watch as he climbs down from his cab and walks stiffly across to the garden wall.

"I thought I should come round."

"You too." Tension prickles down my back as he bends to pick up something from the dust and fingers it for a few moments. It looks like a nail or a screw.

"Sorry?"

"Nothing."

"You wanna watch things like this, or the police'll be getting punctures in their fancy cars."

"Yes, thank you."

Peter digs about in the dirt with his toe as though there might be some other hidden danger there. "So the police came for another look in the house did they?"

"You obviously know they did." Someone's spread the word. It must be all around the village by now.

"At Simon's room?"

A black beetle scurries across the grass at my feet, stops, turns at a right angle and heads for a rose bush.

"Are you going to tell me what's going on?"

"I don't know any more than you do."

"Like hell." The lines of his sunburnt face tighten.

"Excuse me?"

"I think we should stick together over this, Marty's boy could be dead."

"Okay, I know." I dig my nails into my palms to stop myself saying anything I'll regret.

"How's Simon been spending his time all these years?"

"What?" My gaze snaps back to him, and he's watching me with a nasty little half smile.

"I'm not stupid; I can use a computer as well as the next man. Have a little look on the web like."

"He's been leading his own life."

"Ah is that what you call it? And where is he now then? Dropped back out on his lonely little houseboat?"

"I have to go and change Georgie." I pick up her car seat and turn away from him.

"They've got frogmen searching the reservoir again."

I don't look round. I want Peter back in that cab and out of the yard now.

"I owes you an apology as well," he says.

"For what?" My heart thuds.

"For the other day, for suggesting that your mother-"

The back door is open. I keep my eyes on it and my feet moving one after the other, left and then right, but I can barely walk in a straight line.

Inside the house, I kick the door shut with my heel and sit down in the living room for a long time with Georgie cuddled in my lap. After a while Gel and Bri come in to join us and lie on one of the faded Indian rugs.

All around us are surprisingly familiar things which I no longer have any share in. I let my head sink back against the cushions and try to think where I would go if I left here in a hurry with a bleeding boy and I didn't want anyone to see me. Where? Where? Where? The whole moor, the whole county for that matter, seems impossibly fraught with danger in that situation.

"Oh God."

I remember something suddenly. Besides her worry dolls, Clare used to create simple embroidered books depicting scenes from farm life. The first ones were perfect presents for young children, with bright stick figures and bulbous cows, but as the years went by the subject matter became darker. Uncle Eric teased her about that, and even I began to wonder where the lurid and sometimes bloody scenes came from.

She kept sketchbooks of ideas for them in a deep drawer in her studio. I knew where but I never looked. Now I walk straight in and tug at the brass handle. Will they still be there? The drawer sticks for a moment then judders open. It's full of dusty sketchbooks of various sizes.

I lift them out one after another. In typical Clare fashion, some have dates, and some don't, but I try to establish their approximate age by the state of the cover and the colour of the pages. The oldest are indeed tattered and yellowed, their pages foxed and creased, but from the middle of the pile upwards it's hard to tell. I can't believe that Clare always replaced them in order, so it isn't as simple as taking out the top one and knowing it's the most recent. They aren't all completed either. She appears to have moved between them on a whim depending on what size she felt like using.

I open the top batch on Clare's work table. There are books of tiny sketches, mostly individual people with strange, expressive faces that don't tell me anything. I turn to the larger sketchbooks and catch my breath. Inside are the scenes I remember or something like them. Some are recognisable as places on the farm, Eb appears in quite a few, and there are cows and flocks of sheep.

Summer, winter, spring the seasons change as I flip through, detailed with bright, simple markers. Daffodils for spring, a big childish sun for summer, a snowman, even clusters of holly.

The people are different, less stick-like and more blobby, some young, some old, even a few tiny children and a baby. I pause on that page. Could it be that somehow Clare knew? But no, that's not possible. It's pure coincidence. I turn over the page, and it's there, the word starting with a big curly 'G'. Granny. A little further down the page: Gran, Grandma. Experimental writing, the kind a teenager might do, or a newlywed. In fact, anyone trying out a new name or title.

I swallow. How? Did she know about Georgie or was she merely doodling, perhaps even thinking about Lee? Do these words suggest her feelings for him and if so what clues about her intentions do they offer?

The harder I look the more confused I feel so I pick up another sketchbook and begin to leaf through. This one is darker. Clare has used more paint and less pencil. There are pools of red and black, but the scenes are not recognisable as the farm or even as local places. I study the people, but they too are vague. You couldn't possibly suggest that they represent anyone I know. Tired and frustrated I bundle all the books back into the drawer and slam it shut. Somewhere in the distance, the helicopter is circling again.

13

The dogs rush in across the yard with a dead, partially dismembered rook that evening. First Bri has it then Gel wrenches it off him, and they run round snarling and snapping, the bird jerking this way and that as though in some strange final flight.

"Drop it." I stop them at the door, but Gel won't let it go. A damp wing feather falls onto the granite step, and I look away for a moment. I've never been very good at things like this. In the past, it was always Simon or even Jamie who put the mangled rabbits or injured toads out of their misery and disposed of them. "Drop it."

Georgie's asleep so I fetch a pair of rubber gloves and keep on at Gel until she lets go of the bird and I'm able to pick it up and avert my eyes as I carry it to the dustbin.

That night I dream of the rooks.

They drop out of the edge of Longcause Wood one after another in a black tide that heads for the carcass on the snowy ground. More and more of them come until the field is almost hidden by them and their calls fill the air. Suddenly I'm in among them, and their beaks snick about my head. Closer, closer, closer and then they're not rooks at all but ravens with heavy shaggy necks and eyes that can see a mile or more.

The cow shouldn't be dead. She was beautiful and young, a heifer really, and now here she lies bloated and dull, her eyes already gone.

"Where the hell were you last night?" Robert shouts, breath pluming in the cold air and Simon turns around, his hands clenched in the pockets of his waxed jacket.

"I checked her before I went. You were going to look at her last thing, you said."

The party down at Hartor Barton hangs between them. Up close Simon's breath and skin still smell of it, a mixture of alcohol and stale tobacco smoke, but he's trying hard to keep his sleepless night at bay.

"You can't be a part-time farmer Simon. I'm tired of it."

"That isn't fair; I do every bloody thing around here and-"

"Simon don't talk to your father like that," Clare says but her voice is low. We all know who's right and the accusation makes me want to cry. Simon tries so hard, and now he's standing over the dead cow as though her death is his fault.

"Well, what are you going to do about it?" Robert's face is red from the wind.

"I'll phone the knackers." Simon spins round on his heel and heads back down the hill his feet crunching on the snow.

"This can't go on." Robert glares at Clare. "I'm

going to sell the stock as he's not prepared to look after them properly."

"Robert."

"No. I've had enough this time."

"Darling, it was just a misunderstanding." Clare puts a hand on his arm, but he shakes her off.

"I don't want to talk about it anymore."

We stand in an awkward silence for a few minutes. The sun has almost set, and the temperature is dropping rapidly. I shiver suddenly and stamp my feet on the frosty ground.

"Charlotte, go on in, or you'll catch a chill," Clare says, and I turn away from them and follow Simon's footprints back down the hill. I can't believe that Robert will carry out his threat and yet already I can see the cows and sheep lined up ready to be sold.

"No, please no," I whisper, and I don't want to see Simon because then I'll have to tell him, but he comes running back up the fields to meet me. From a distance he looks young and tanned, his hair flipped back by the wind in a golden mane, but as he grows closer and taller, he ages and his stride becomes stiffer.

"I couldn't find you," he says running past me, his breath rasping. "I've been looking everywhere."

His face isn't tanned at all but dry and scorched by the wind, the whites of his eyes stained yellow. He looks tired and ill, but I can't keep up with him until he slows metres from the bloody stretch of snow. The ravens must have worked fast for the body on the ground is smaller and darker now. We walk towards it and Clare and Robert are gone.

"Don't." Simon tries to hold me back with his hand,

but it's too late I can already see that it isn't a cow lying on the snow now but a child with reddish hair.

"No." The blood spreads outwards, seeping fast through the crystals to my feet and then onwards down the hill. "No."

I turn towards Simon, but even as I do so I know that I'm alone; the rasp of his breath lost in the wind.

―――

"You have another brother don't you?" Hollinghurst says across Ebenezer's back the following morning. "A blood brother."

I keep the brush contouring around Eb's belly with even pressure and breathe in the rich, dusty smell of him, a mixture of field earth and hot hair. I don't like the way Hollinghurst emphasises the word blood, releasing it into the air so that it flows like it did from that wound in the past and drags my nightmare close again.

"James Graham Elgin, now residing at the Fairfax Community. Charlotte why didn't you tell us about him?"

He must have known about Jamie all along so why is he asking me this now? Ebenezer is thin despite the rich summer grass. When I press my fingers against his side, I can feel the corrugations of his ribs just beneath the skin. He's old, but he should be looking better than he is. I smooth a hand down his hollow neck and make a mental note to buy him a mineral supplement.

"Charlotte you haven't done yourself any favours you know."

183

"Favours? Oh, I didn't realise that I needed to redeem myself in any way."

"Charlotte." Hollinghurst walks around Ebenezer leaving an exaggerated distance between himself and the horse's head as though he expects the poor old man to jump forward and snatch at his shirt with his teeth. "I thought, well I thought that we had an understanding."

"An understanding?"

"Yes. I thought that whatever has or hasn't happened between you and your family you'd tell me the truth to help find Lee."

I push the brush across the metal teeth of a currycomb several times then flick away the pale grease. I need to know what Hollinghurst has done with Simon. "The blood on the blouse, whose was it?"

"What?" His attention sharpens and his eyes narrow.

"Or can't you tell me?"

He shakes his head. "We haven't had the results yet."

Enough time has elapsed surely. Hollinghurst's lie disturbs me. It means something I don't want to think about, and I turn back to Eb.

"Your brother James-"

"Okay, okay. I didn't tell you about him because he can't possibly have anything to do with this." I tap the currycomb against the top of the door to release another drift of grease. Some of it lands on Hollinghurst's sleeve, and he shakes it away. "Sorry."

"You weren't trying to hide the fact that you have another brother then?"

"Of course not." I shake my head as I think of Jamie's pale swampy face. I know the feel of his hand now, heavy and damp, fingers clinging to mine with an awkward twist. Hollinghurst probably thinks that I didn't tell them about Jamie because I also wanted to hide the facts about what happened to him. But he'll have known about that night right from the beginning; everything will still be on file somewhere so any attempt at deception would have been pointless.

"Some things are just private."

"We're going to see him."

"No, no you've got to leave him out of this. He won't, just don't go there, please."

"Time is moving on, and we can't leave any gaps Charlotte."

"You don't care, do you? You don't care if, if, talk to the staff but don't go and see Jamie."

Eb moves restlessly, and Hollinghurst hovers near the door as if ready to make a hasty retreat, only he doesn't, he turns back to face me instead.

"There's just one other thing. Martin Berryman," he says, and my hand stops right where it is with the bristles of the brush pressed against Eb's bony side. "I understand that you and he once had a … relationship."

"We were teenagers together, friends."

"And?"

"That's it."

"But you were close, closer than say, you and Tony Pearson."

"Perhaps, for a short time." I keep my eyes on the horse's dusty coat. "Why are you asking me this?"

"Let's just say that I'm trying to get a clearer picture of how things are."

"Were."

"Sorry?"

"How things were. It was over twenty years ago for

God's sake." My voice rises, and I take a deep breath to steady myself. I have to keep calm.

"And what would you say your relationship is with him now?"

"My relationship?" Something catches at the back of my throat. "Well, I haven't seen him for years before this."

"But you have spoken to him."

"Recently, you know that. Not before."

Hollinghurst looks at me hard for a moment. "What did you talk about?"

"Lee, Peter." I shrug. "What would you expect us to talk about right now?"

"Why did it end?"

"Excuse me?"

"Your relationship with Martin, why did it come to an end?"

A mote of stable dust spins lazily between us, caught in a bar of sunlight from the one small window. Long ago people might have hidden in here, feeling safe behind the thick granite walls. Then the window might have been more like an arrow slit or a gun hole. I don't know what people or why they might have been hiding, but I know how they felt.

"We were just friends, I told you."

Hollinghurst is silent for a moment then he reaches over the door for the bolt.

"Was Clare being threatened?" I ask, and he stops, his hand poised in mid-air.

"What makes you ask? Do you think she was?"

"I don't know. I just wondered. Clare never liked guns."

"I see." There's silence for a moment then he draws back the bolt. "I need to talk to Simon."

I stare at him confused. Surely that's what he's been doing for the past two days although- Somewhere at the back of my mind a random piece of information stirs. I'm sure I read something that said it's hard for the police to detain someone for longer than twenty-four hours without charging them. I might be wrong though.

"It wasn't his fault, about Marty I mean," I say too quickly, and Hollinghurst turns.

"Is he in the house? I'll just go over."

"He isn't there." The blood bounces against the tips of my fingers as all my presumptions about Simon still being in police custody fall away.

"Where can I find him then?"

I stare at the static in Eb's coat; a grey film of dust and grease still clings to the surface. "He's out."

Hollinghurst says goodbye at last as though it has merely been a social call and I stand in the full sun and listen to his car rolling away down the lane. The engine idles at the bottom for a few minutes and then eases away to nothingness along the valley floor.

"Damn."

The air around me smells of the rich, sappy scent of drying grass. I try not to breathe in too deeply or to look out across the meadows beyond the barns. It's almost perfect haymaking weather, although perhaps a little too hot, but Arthur phoned earlier to say that he had an infection and wasn't feeling well. He sounded terrible, but there was a hesitancy in his voice caused by something other than his illness.

"Thanks for letting me know."

When he'd gone, I continued to hold the receiver in

my hand as though everything he hadn't said might yet pour out of it. Without even his support the days ahead looked truly bleak.

I try not to think about it, to turn my attention instead to the immediate problem of the hay. In this sort of sun, grass left to lie for too long without turning can burn to dust on top and go yellow and fermented beneath. I know these things deep down.

In another few hours, all Arthur's hard work will go to waste. As I walk into the house the muscles across my shoulders tighten in a spasm of anger. After I'd spoken to Arthur, I called a dozen people and failed to find even one contractor who wasn't 'too busy' to come over. Half an hour later it felt fruitless to carry on, as soon as I said the name of the farm I knew I'd get the same response. No one wanted to have anything to do with us.

I can't see what else I can do with Georgie in tow, so I make myself a cup of tea and sit down. The sun shining through the window is hot across my bare arms. Arthur's voice bugs me again. He looked tired to the core yesterday morning, all the effort and worry of the previous week scored across his face in deep, dry lines, so I'm not surprised that he's feeling ill. But it wasn't only that, in fact, I sensed that his illness was almost a relief, giving him the perfect excuse not to come up to the farm for a while.

Was it the fight between Simon and Tony that changed things for him or Simon's arrest? I try to stop those thoughts, but they're there in my head, as real as the contractors' replies. I can't face the humiliation of this much more personal rebuff, so I stand up and walk outside.

There's a broad headland of uncut turf around the

edges of the fields and the smell of timothy and cocksfoot and all the grasses whose names I've forgotten almost overwhelms me. I sink down into the meadow and run my fingers through the patchwork of plants. Suddenly I'm crying for the impossible, filled with a desperate wish for things to have turned out differently and a deep longing never to have had to leave, never to have forgotten the intricate details of this place.

I kneel there with my head bowed and the tears running down my cheeks, and I think of the expression of smug certainty on Darren Collier's face. Suddenly I can't bear the thought of everyone looking up the hill, seeing all our hay going to waste and knowing why.

"Oh, Clare what have you done?" I think of the photos of her in the album looking so young and carefree, her mouth curled in laughter more often than not and then of the outline of the hunting knife drawn on her bedside cabinet. "Why, why, why?"

After a while, Georgie grows restless and begins to whimper, so I stand up and walk back towards the house. I know what I have to do. I can't; I won't be beaten like this.

Back in the yard, I look up at the mud-spattered windscreen of Arthur's tractor. I'll have to use it whether he likes it or not and I can't hide behind ignorance, I've turned hay before, not for a long time of course, but I know how to do it. I run through the procedure in my mind. All I need is a safe place for Georgie in the cab.

"No more excuses then."

Arthur's tractor is monstrous in comparison to our own old Massey, but the controls are surprisingly sensitive. So sensitive that I oversteer and send it juddering and jumping across the yard. For a moment I think that we'll take the gatepost with us, then I have the machine under a little more control, and we roll out into the meadow in a reasonably neat arc.

"Sorry, Georgie." I lean over to give her a kiss in her car seat wedged into the space beside the controls where other drivers carry their dogs. She waves one hand and doesn't appear at all disturbed by the jolting, so I sit quite still for a moment to steady my nerves.

I grew up haymaking, but although the basics of the job are imprinted on my mind, there were always other people to take control in the past. I lower the hay bob, but tiredness forces me to drive slowly so that everything takes twice as long as it should and I only finish turning the grass in the first two fields in time for a late lunch.

Georgie is hungry before we finish, but then perversely she drinks so slowly that I almost fall asleep with her under the old damson tree in the corner of the orchard. The shadows have lengthened by the time I'm able to advance on the tractor again and hoist Georgie's seat back up into the cab.

"Only two fields left," I promise but the greeny yellow grass seems to stretch away from us in a mesmerising, never-ending, untamable sea. I should use this time to think, to make a plan but somehow I can't focus my mind on anything other than the tractor and the hay and I shake my head in frustration.

"We have to do something." I stare through the tinted glass measuring my distance from the last strip of turned grass, trying to keep a straight line. Usually, I'm not like this. I've trained myself to think quickly, to be decisive, but now, when I need to come up with an idea of what Clare might be thinking and where she and Lee might have gone, I feel strangely numb. It's like I'm looking in on my new life and listening to my words as I would a stranger's. "God."

We're almost on our last circuit when the dogs detach themselves from the tractor's wake and dash off towards a figure standing in the gateway.

"Simon." The tractor spews out a dark cloud of diesel fumes as I press it harder up the slope towards him and swing open the cab door. "Where on earth have you been?"

For a moment he doesn't say anything, and his face is an unreadable mess. The bruising has spread out and changed colour so that it runs from dark blue in the centre to a nasty yellowish around the edges. His left eye is still half closed.

"Well?" Sweat runs down the side of my face, and I dip my cheek against the sleeve of my t-shirt suddenly aware of the dust engrained in my clothes and hair and skin.

"What are you doing?"

"Isn't it obvious?"

"But you shouldn't be back yet. What about Arthur and the contractors?" He looks up at Georgie wedged in the cab. "Oh God, let me take her."

"She's alright, but you look like shit."

"Thanks."

He flinches away from my words, and for a second there's something beaten and helpless about the way he rubs the palms of his hands down his thighs and turns from me. He would never have allowed himself to look like this when we were growing up, not even during the rare times when he went down with something. As a rule, he was always infuriatingly strong and healthy.

"So what's going on?" He squares his shoulders, and the look is gone, he's in control again.

"Remember Darren Collier?"

"Darren-"

"You know, Marty's friend. Well, he was the contractor, but he won't come out here now. I've tried others, but no one wants anything to do with us." The pain of that digs in again.

"Char."

"I couldn't sit around and have everyone looking up here and thinking-"

"Fuck them."

"Yeh well I'm just about finished, and I need something to eat."

He's wearing the same clothes, and when we're close in the kitchen, I can tell that he's been too hot for a long time. There's a kind of weird scent about him as well, a chemically stale smell.

"Simon, what happened on the search? You didn't tell me you'd broken Tony's arm."

"How? Is that what he's saying now?" His eyes are glittery with tiredness, and they shift and shift again as he tries to focus. "Oh well, it doesn't matter."

"It does. Come on, you can tell me." I haven't been able to face Clare's stores up to now, but there's nothing much else left, so I take a tin of ravioli out of the cupboard and begin to read the label to see if it's vegetarian.

"It was a mistake, alright."

"A mistake to break Tony's arm?"

"No, I didn't mean that. I didn't break his arm anyway, he missed me and caught it on a branch."

"Right."

"I didn't tell the police everything," he says avoiding my eye. "They kept asking, but I didn't tell them about, well you know-"

Does he mean what I think he does? I look down, and things skitter out of my hands, sliding away across the wooden work surface. At our backs, the dogs pad from side to side waiting for their dinners. "Simon, what's going on? I need to know. The police came to search the house again and my car. They took my laptop."

"Shit."

There are a few tomatoes left in the fridge along with a cucumber and half a pepper. I begin to slice everything ready for a salad. "Well?"

He picks up the pieces of vegetable that I've already cut. I expect him to arrange them in the salad bowl, but instead, he corrals them at one end of the work surface.

I glance across at him and the knife slips and slices into the flesh of my index finger as though it's no denser than the flesh of a tomato. I grip the cut with the other hand then bend over and shut my eyes against the pain. "Damn."

"Are you alright?" Simon's hand touches my back for a second then he turns on the tap and rushes cold water into the sink. "Look, get it under here."

"No, no not yet."

"Come on Char." He pushes me forward, and blood spatters against the white ceramic turning the water red as it swirls down the plughole. "It looks deep. Just keep it under there while I get a towel or something." His hand trembles and there's a freshly scabbed cigarette burn just behind his knuckles. I didn't think he smoked.

193

"It's alright; I'll find one." As soon as I take my hand out of the water the pain throbs through my finger.

"Here." Simon bunches a piece of cloth around the cut, but the blood soon soaks through and drips onto the floor.

I sit down on one of the wooden benches and the tiles slide away from me for a moment. "It's going to need stitches isn't it?"

"I don't know. Look, I'm sure it'll stop bleeding in a minute."

"But, but what if it doesn't? Simon, I don't think I can cope with anything more."

"Don't cry, Char." He sits down beside me and slips an arm around my shoulders. "I'll make you a cup of tea."

"And then what?"

"If it hasn't stopped bleeding we'll get you to a doctor, okay."

I want to let him take control, to sit back and feel the safety of his words closing around me. "How? I can't drive like this and, do you have a license?"

For a moment he doesn't say anything then he stands up and moves away to the sink to fill the kettle. "I can drive."

"But-"

"I killed a horse." He keeps his back to me. "And I was done for drink driving, that's why I don't have a car and why I don't drink anymore."

"I see." I remember the way he used to ride Eb, his hands gentle on the reins, holding in the gelding's excitement until he danced across the turf.

"It was years and years ago although I'm not trying to defend myself. It wasn't a good time, but it shouldn't have happened." When he finally looks back at me his face is strained.

"Where have you been the last two nights? You can't have been with the police all that time."

"I thought you were in London until today."

"And?"

"I walked around. I don't know where I went. I had to think."

For a long moment, we stare at each other in silence, and even Georgie and the dogs are still.

"Why didn't you phone me? I'd have come to fetch you."

"I didn't know."

Have we been apart too many years to understand or help each other now? A great wave of sadness overwhelms me, and I concentrate on unwinding the bloody piece of cloth from my finger

"Did you tell them about Jamie?"

"No."

"But Hollinghurst asked me like it was new information."

"They must have known about him all along. Arthur would have said, anybody, would."

"Then why did he wait until now to ask me? I don't understand."

"He's trying to catch us out." Simon stops. "When exactly did he ask you?"

"He came round earlier today." I grip my finger tight against the throbbing pain.

"Oh great."

"Simon?"

"Did you tell him how long I'd been away?" He slumps down on the bench opposite me and rubs a hand across his face. The skin drags into dehydrated lines.

"Of course not, I just said you were out. It was fine."

"Are you sure? Do you think he guessed? I should have been here overnight. It's one of the conditions. Fuck."

"Conditions?" I can't take my eyes off his face. His lips are chapped and sore as though he's bitten them over and over again. "What conditions? I don't know what you're talking about."

"Bail. I've broken my bail conditions. I should hand myself in." He stands up.

"Bail? Why?" I grip his wrist as he reaches for the phone on the windowsill. His skin is warm and dry. "Simon wait."

When we were young, I seldom tried to stop him doing anything. He had enough energy for both of us. It was wonderfully exhilarating and totally unlike anything I had shared with Marty or anyone else locally. Simon carried me along like a bird slipstreaming a ship. Now we're more evenly matched somehow.

"Char I, look perhaps I'd better just go."

"What have you done?"

"I don't want to mess things up for you again."

"Simon, what have you done?"

"They think, because Lee's Marty's son, because of me and Marty in the past. Because of what happened on the search." He pulls away from me and stands rocking from side to side. He looks like he needs to lie down.

"Oh my God. No way."

"It makes perfect sense to them."

"No."

"I'm sorry."

"But why, I mean-?" I cover my eyes with my hands for a moment, and I'm shaking. "Simon, have you-?"

"Have I what?"

I open my eyes and glance at his face and just for a second I catch that tired wary look again and I know that I can't ask him the question that haunts me. Have you been back here in the last twenty years, have you been back recently?

"Have I what?"

"Nothing, nothing, it doesn't matter." I turn away from him, and Georgie starts to cry in her car seat over by the window. "Hey, hey darling what's wrong? Where's my smiley little girl gone?"

I unstrap her and lift her up above my head and down again, something that has always made her at least curl her lips but her dark eyes are full of tears.

"Simon we've got to do something, but, oh Georgie please." I try to dry her tears with the tips of my fingers, and she presses her face into my shoulder. "I'm so tired. I, I can't think straight, I can't even-Hollinghurst also wanted to know about Marty and me."

"Really?"

"I told him that we were only ever good friends, but I'm not sure that he believed me."

"I wonder why?" Simon's voice is harsh suddenly, and he looks away from me.

"Simon. Whatever you think, it's true. Marty wanted it to be more."

"Yeh, I know, everybody could see that."

"He never touched me though; he was the perfect gentleman." I wipe another tear off Georgie's face.

"Oh, of course, he was. Char you don't have to go on pretending with me."

"Pretending? I don't know what you're talking about."

"That afternoon, the last winter, you know when it was all snowy, and you went round to Sleepers to look for Meg. I know what happened." Simon's voice is strained. "I wasn't blind. I, I just didn't know what to say to you. I, God I was so angry."

"I don't want to talk about it." I swallow and turn away from him. He knew. Even after all these years, I feel the old flush of shame rise within me. Meeting Peter again stirred up memories of course, but somehow I managed to shut them away. Now Simon has caught me off guard and slammed me back into that terrible week. The smell of Sleepers kitchen cloys in my nose. That combination of dirt, wet dog and coal fumes, a strangely masculine smell with nothing pretty to take the edge off it, no flowers or scents of spring.

I'd knocked on the back door expecting Marty to answer but it was Peter who opened it. He smiled at me in a strange way and hardly seemed to hear my question about Meg. Suddenly he grabbed hold of my arm and pulled me in over the doorstep. For a few seconds, I was too surprised to struggle against him.

"Kiss me," he said. "I'll pay you."

"What?" I tried to shake free of his arms but he held me tight, and the next moment he was caressing my face and hair with his gnarled, work-worn hands. Rough tags of skin scratched against my cheek.

"You're a little lady now aren't you? Quite grown up in so many ways." His hands moved downwards, and I fought against the pressure of them. "My Marty doesn't know how to show you a good time, does he? But I do, oh yes."

"Peter." I tried so hard to fight him off, but he was stronger than he looked.

"Come on; you'll love it. I've been watching you for so long, your beautiful little body, your legs. I can't wait for spring when you'll wear those shorts again."

"Peter, no, please, leave me alone." My coat and jumper were gone, and my shirt slid to the floor. Peter pushed me across the room onto the sagging sofa in the corner. The old rug scratched against my bare back, and my wrists burned, but suddenly the clothes on the floor seemed to belong to another person who was nothing to do with me. I was high above them, looking down, safe, untouchable distanced from everything that happened next.

"I'll make this worth your while," Peter said, and his smile was confusing, it was the one I'd seen so often before. I'd thought it was just him being friendly and I'd smiled back when I'd met him on the farm, warmth passing between us.

There was a noise outside and a dog barked. In an instant, Peter was across the kitchen and holding out my jumper and coat.

"Here you go. I hope you find your dog. I'll get Marty to give you a call if your dog comes round here." It was like nothing had happened, nothing at all, or that what had happened was quite normal, how adults carried on.

"Char?" Another hand on me, another time but I shrink away instinctively, and tears are running down my cheeks as well as Georgie's. "Char, I'm sorry, I didn't mean to upset you. I just don't understand. I mean how could Marty, you'd been friends for ages? And you, why do you go on protecting him?"

"I don't."

"Char. What I did, I know I got carried away, that it was totally irresponsible, such a stupid, unforgivable schoolboy error, but I was so angry, I just couldn't bear to see you that upset. He had it coming."

Something tightens behind my ribs, and I turn back to stare at Simon. "What are you talking about?"

"That night in the oak wood. I wanted to teach Marty a lesson, you were being so strong, but don't think that there isn't a day that goes past when I wish it hadn't happened. When I wish I-"

"Oh my God, are you saying?"

"What?"

"You thought- That was why you went for him. Simon, it wasn't Marty." I close my eyes. If I'd told him the truth-

"I don't understand. Something happened. You went round to Sleepers didn't you?" He hesitates for a moment, and I glance at his face. His lips tighten. "Oh no, don't tell me, it was Peter?"

I nod.

"Shit. Shit!"

"Simon?"

"The bastard. He, he was just sitting there in the kitchen when- Right, I'm going round there."

"Simon, no."

"But-"

"Please, there's enough damage done already, just leave it now. It's all too long ago."

He stands by the door for a while as though he hasn't heard me then his shoulders slouch and he presses his face into his hands. "Okay. You're right. I- I just can't believe. Oh, fuck what a mess."

"Yes."

"I should apologise to Marty though, shouldn't I?"

"I think it's probably too late for that."

"Char? I was trying to help."

"Were you going to shoot him? Did you mean to?" My hands are shaking, and his momentary hesitation fills me with terror.

"Of course not. I just wanted to scare Marty that's all."

Georgie shifts in my arms and her cries rise again. "Ssh, ssh darling." I press my cheek against hers in the way that should calm her, but it doesn't seem to make any difference.

"I'm sorry."

"What are we going to do now?"

"I don't know," he says quietly.

14

I catch sight of Simon by chance as I glance out of the landing window on my way to the bathroom. He's halfway along the ridge of the main barn, barefoot and stripped to the waist. For a second I can't move or breathe. The early morning sun makes his hair glow, and he holds his arms out straight on either side of him as he flexes each foot in turn. He's been up there before, many times, but I can hardly bear to watch. Twice I turn from the window only to spin back seconds later.

I know he's doing it not to show off but to forget. It was always the same, balanced between sky and earth he could only focus on one thing: the precision of each step. The soles of his feet felt for the ridge tiles, and his eyes held the horizon.

Watching him now I can't help noticing that he's as lean and fit as he ever was and for a strange, heady moment it feels like I'm looking out on another summer day long ago. I press my nose against the coolness of the glass so that I can't see my reflection and the passing of the years marked out in the lines beneath my eyes.

Simon. Simon. I want to open the window and call out to him, but I hold back my foolishness and wait until he's reached the end and dropped out of sight before I run downstairs and switch on the TV.

There are no more possible sightings of Clare and Lee, and subtly the mood of the breakfast news report has changed. It begins with an aerial view of the farm and the village, and I'm filled with a momentary terror that we'll somehow be on screen, but the photo pans out into a fly-by over the reservoir across the valley. The police vehicles are easy to pick out even at several hundred feet, grouped like a mass of predatory insects in the public car park. The shot zooms in closer again, and suddenly the police frogmen are there with search dogs along the water's edge. The reporter's voice takes on a professionally grim tone in suggestive reverence.

"What are they saying?" Simon appears in the doorway. I didn't hear him come in and I switch off the TV. "Why did you do that?"

"Because." I flush.

"In case I hear something about myself, is that it?"

"No, yes. Oh, Simon." He's put his shirt back on, but for a second I wish that it was twenty years ago again, that we were still here but about to eat a different breakfast with Jamie thundering down the stairs and Clare singing in the yard.

"It doesn't matter." Simon stares at the blank TV screen then sits down opposite me. He takes the lid off the strawberry jam and twists it back on again without helping himself to any. There's a restlessness about his limbs that makes me uneasy. In a minute I'll start thinking things I'll wish I never had.

"Could they still be alive?"

His gaze flicks to my face, and I hold it. I won't be the first to look away.

"Well?"

His face is tight and pale with a strange red mark across one cheek like a slap, the slap of Robert's words against his face all those years ago. "You bastard, this is all your fault, get away from my son."

"I know what you think I'm capable of." He stands up and walks to the window, flicks the catch and pushes it open. There's a noise outside, a vehicle on the track. My head aches and I feel as though I've been punched in the face, but I listen. "It's the police."

I turn to Simon, but his eyes slide away from me towards the sound.

"What can they do?" Crazily my mind jumps to how today might have been in London. I'd be preparing for the next part of the Aoki's photo shoot of course. I try to think about it, but everything feels slippery and disconnected, as though the whole contract was a fantasy that I held in my mind, one of those things that you dream about over and over when you're starting out, in the hope that the repeated vision will eventually be made real.

"I can't be locked up." It's a plea, not a statement, and his lips are drier than ever and cracked, a streak of blood smeared like lipstick.

"They'd have to have something on you surely." I watch him closely and again the question that I can't ask hangs between us. I have to keep believing that Marty was lying otherwise everything will start to fall apart.

Simon rolls the hem of his shirt between finger and thumb. His silence scares me. I try to catch the expression on his face, but he's still looking away towards the sound. I don't always understand his looks now anyway; they're clouded with something from these past intervening years. We've both got an unshared, uncharted history, places where there is no common strand of intimacy and recollection.

"Simon?"

The sound is louder now and heavier. A tractor. My relief only lasts a few seconds.

"What the hell does he want?" A flash of reflected sunlight flicks along the wall as Peter opens the cab door and steps down into the yard.

"Simon, remember what we agreed yesterday. Don't you dare say anything."

"I won't, but you can't expect me to be polite to him."

We've finished our breakfast croissants pulled from the hoary depths of the chest freezer in the utility room and defrosted in the Rayburn oven. The last golden crumbs are cold and dry between us now. Simon glances down at them then clatters the plates together into a pile in the sink.

I see the kitchen as Peter will, it's shadowy and dusty, and Bri has tipped over his bowl again scattering food across the tiles. We should be outside. The sun is high and heading west, and the fields of cut grass dry slowly to dust. Back then we would never have stayed indoors on a day like this, Simon's feet would have run restlessly over grass stubble and dirt, and the sound of tractors would have dragged out through the long, clear day.

Peter's step crushes something on the path; we'll let him come to us, come right to the closed door and knock. The dogs jump up. They knew he was there already, but now they have to act.

"Mornin. I thought you might need a hand with the haymaking seeing as Arthur's ill and all the contractors are so busy," he says from the doorstep, and his eyes linger on me as though they're feasting on something that gives him secret pleasure.

"We're managing fine on our own," Simon says behind me, seemingly unaware that he's brushed up against one of Robert's old coats. "But you might move your sheep while we've still got some grass left."

"I hadn't realised they were causing a problem. I'll bring the dogs around when it's cooler tonight."

"Sure."

"Where shall I start turning? Did Arthur cut Great Acre first?"

Simon's anger is hot and metallic; it squeezes out through his pores with a smell of blood. I can feel the heat of it sweeping past me to push Peter back. Or perhaps it's just the tang of fear.

"Thanks, Peter, but look, there must be other things you need to do. Simon's right, we're doing fine."

"Without my trailer?" There are purple stains beneath his eyes.

"We're going to borrow one."

"Not before the rain, I shouldn't think."

He turns back to his tractor satisfied with his answer, shoulders stooped slightly to the right, left knee cocked in that direction also. He's an old man, a tired old man with age spots creeping across the backs of his hands. He should have had a future, young arms to wrap around the burden of poor pasture and rain, foot rot and scab that he has to pass on from father to son to grandson.

"He's not staying," Simon says behind me, but his

voice is tired. "I mean this is crazy, Marty's son's missing, and he's round here baling our hay."

"Perhaps he wants to get away from Sleepers."

"It won't be as simple as that." Simon stares across the yard for a moment. Suddenly there seems to be nothing else for him to do but take Arthur's tractor and follow Peter out onto the parched field. He drives the machine forward hard, belching black smoke through the exhaust pipe into the clear blue air.

What can I do? It feels like we've all taken a weird dip back into normal life only it isn't like it used to be. It can never be like it used to be. If it wasn't for Georgie, I'd join the search that's ranging further now despite the police assurances that things are best left to their specialist teams. I've seen the bands of villagers treading the skylines and heard their calls spreading through the woods down the valley, but mobile reception is patchy here and it's harder to check the news on the internet without my laptop. I feel more out of touch with the local mood already.

In the end, I take Georgie out in her sling so that she can watch from the shade under the hedge. She's grown so much that her weight pulls at the small of my back. The first blackberries are tight green clusters along the bank and a song thrush darts into a patch of thorn ahead of us. Georgie stares at it for a moment then her gaze drifts sideways, and I think she might be looking at the glare reflecting off Simon's windscreen.

I watch him take the higher side of the field. He drives fast, and the winnower fluffs the hay out in a cloud of dust. He's opened the back window of the cab, and he glances behind him over and over again, up and away beyond the trail of grass. I want to warn him not to give himself away, but I don't do anything until he draws up alongside and opens the door. Sweat stands out across his face, and he's breathing hard.

"Why haven't the police come?" he says.

"Maybe it's no big deal."

"Jesus Christ. He mustn't see." He looks across at the other tractor.

"Just keep going then."

"Why the hell is he here anyway?"

"Simon."

———

When the heat of the sun creeps in beneath Georgie's sling, and her face begins to go red, I walk back to the house to get lunch. However, in the kitchen, I realise that there's nothing left to make it with, no bread, no fruit and no tins that look remotely appetising among the limited array at the back of the cupboard. The moment I've been putting off has come, but I still can't face the village shop. If I hurry, I've probably got time to reach the supermarket on the edge of town and whip around before Georgie's next feed.

I feel exposed and nervy as I ease the Golf down the track. There are more reporters than ever with a fortune of camera equipment at the roadblock and at least half a dozen news vans with familiar initials emblazoned on their sides. The single police officer struggles to hold them back as I turn out onto the valley road away from the village.

All the way to the place where Simon jumped out on me I keep expecting someone to appear around the next corner and every open stretch of tarmac brings a fleeting moment of relief. It's only as the roads widen and the thickening traffic promises me anonymity that my heartbeat finally slows and my shoulders relax.

"Phew." I let out a sigh of relief but then there's the space to start thinking about Arthur again. I tried to call him several times earlier to see how he was but there was no reply, and it feels more and more like we've lost our only ally.

The supermarket is busy, and Georgie is edgy, too close to a feed to settle properly. I know that I'm risking an all-out bawl, but I strap her car seat onto one of the special trollies and head through the main doors. To my left rises a bank of newspapers and magazines. I keep my head down. I won't look, I won't and then-

Simon's face is there splashed across several tabloids, caught in a moment of tired wariness. Where was the picture taken? For a moment it's all I see then the headlines jump out at me.

"Secretive Simon."

"Family feud abduction."

"We love you, Lee."

"No." I swing the trolley around. I can't go on. I've forgotten to get cash, and someone will recognise me. I'm going the wrong way now; there's a wall of people heading inwards. I look at the floor; dodging feet and tears prick at my eyes.

"Charlotte?"

Not me, a chance call for another person.

"Charlotte? It is you isn't it?"

She's about my age with long blonde hair and a little boy holding her hand.

"Sandra." We stare at each other for a moment, and I think that I'm going to cry right there in front of her. I bite my lip and glance down at the little boy. "How are you?"

"Fine, thanks, but what about you? Toby this is my old best friend." She touches my forearm so gently that it almost undoes me. "I'm sorry. It can't be easy at the moment."

"Thanks." I try to rally my thoughts, to push away the images of Simon's tired face. How did they manage to capture that look, just the one that makes him appear capable of the worst? "Are you still living down here?"

"No, unfortunately, we're in Kent now, for work, but mum's in the same house." She turns, and there is her mother aged of course, greyer and plumper, but still recognisable. I think of the times I spent in her kitchen making peppermint creams and that other speciality of ours: nut brittle. All that sugar, all that fun.

"Charlotte. How good to see you. Are you bearing up alright?"

I nod, not trusting my voice and she looks at Georgie.

"What a dear baby. She must be a real blessing at the moment." She doesn't spell it out, but the remark is double-edged, she means right now and at my age. I tense. Behind her, unseen, are the others: Vicki and Tony, Jack Pengelly, Martha Endworthy and Arnie Smythe all ready with their opinions and sound bites. "I'm glad we've met. I just wanted to say that I really feel for you. It's such a terrible thing. Clare was always so good to Lee."

"She was?"

"Oh yes, right from when he was quite young but particularly after his mother died."

The supermarket lights are very bright even in the

foyer. They seem to blaze down on us with the heat of the sun. What other important things did Clare and I fail to talk about? I try to remember her even mentioning Lee's name in the past few years, but I can't think of one time.

"It's not what you become, but how you are, that's important." Clare's words float into my mind. Why do I remember them now?

"And don't take any notice of what people are saying."

"No." My mind spins away from them into another space high above the farm where the buzzards wheel and the sun is clear and bright. "Look I'm sorry, but I must get going."

They glance at my empty trolley, but I don't care. I have to get out of here, away to a place where there are no people, no cameras, no police.

"Oh God." As soon as we're back in the car, I can't stop myself running her words through my head again. What was she inferring? That Clare wasn't responsible for what's happened? And what are people locally saying exactly? Does she, do they really think that Simon-? I press the tips of my fingers into my temples until the pain jumps out. "No way."

———

I wish that there was another way back to the farm without having to run the gamut of the reporters but of course there isn't. They see me coming this time, and men are running down the road with cameras, hands on the car, faces close to the glass.

"Miss Elgin?"

"Miss Elgin, can you tell us where your brother is now? Is it true that-?"

I press my foot down as hard as I dare and swing into the track with a shower of gravel. Behind me the patrol car reverses across the gap, thank God.

We make it the rest of the way back to the farm without meeting anyone. The tractors are still out in Five Acre, and I sit for a moment and listen to the innocent summer sound of haymaking. A sound that I grew up with and used to love but now everything is changed, spoiled and even that sound is tainted with unease.

Georgie wakes abruptly and starts to cry and although it's almost lunchtime I have to feed and change her before I can do anything else. When she's finally settled again, I delve into the freezer for some food and find a bag of pasties. The shapes of Clare's fingertips are imprinted in the homemade pastry. I stand quite still. Are they a clue, and if so, to what? Clare's thoughts, her intentions? I stare at them. If anything they suggest an unchanging resolution to stay at the farm, a desire to remain as self-sufficient as possible and not even have to venture out as far as the village shop. So what does that mean? I shake my head, I can't, I won't go there, but Sandra's mother's words and the shadow of blood are close.

In a rush, I put all the pasties in the Rayburn oven and stand back in the stagnant air of the kitchen. There's something ominous about the sky beyond the open window. It's too clear somehow, a hard, bright, perfect blue.

I've never trusted perfection even though I always try to create it. I can't help looking for the flaw, the insidious creep of a mark or scar, the disintegration around the edges that needs to be cropped or hidden.

I should go on looking for clues while I wait for the pasties to cook but staring around at the clutter of Clare's life I've no idea where to look next or why I even think that I might see something that the police have missed.

After a moment I take out my phone instead and scroll through my contacts list until I come to Eric's number right at the end. I've never called it before, and I look at it for a long time before pressing the speed dial button. There is silence as our two phones try to connect through the ether then a slightly American voice intervenes to say that the number is unobtainable. I try again straight away in case there was some mistake, but the result is the same.

"Damn."

When I go out Simon looks at me as though I've cooked the pasties myself along with the big slabs of dry fruitcake from the tin in the larder. We sit down on the grass near the barn, and I spread out the greasy lumps of hot pastry.

"Are you okay Char?"

"Of course." I glance away so that he can't see my face.

Without work, we are suddenly awkward. The whole occasion feels absurd, our families too at odds to be together like this. Simon leans back against the rough granite wall and stares up at the swallows high overhead while Peter fetches something from the cab of his tractor. A tabloid. I tense and watch in horror as he unfolds it and silently and deliberately places it face up on the grass beside Simon.

"Secretive Simon." The words, the photo, just as shocking as the first time I saw them little more than an hour ago.

For a second there's nothing but the call of a buzzard across the valley then Simon jumps up and walks away without a word.

"So-" There's a smug grin on Peter's face.

"Get out."

"What?"

"You heard. I don't want you on this farm anymore, and take this filthy pack of lies with you." I grab the tabloid and stuff it at his chest, twenty years of pent up anger rising to the surface.

"You don't believe-?" His gaze fixes on my face.

"Too right I don't."

I have to find Simon. I sweep a startled Georgie up into my arms and head after him, the dogs bouncing at my heels then running off around the side of the barn. In the distance, there's the sound of a helicopter again, and I glance up in time to see it swing in over valley. It's lower than usual, not much above the trees of Longcause and the sound of its rotors throbs through me.

"Go away, just go away."

I think he'll be in the house and he is, up in his old room. He's sitting in the single chair in the window with his head in his hands. He doesn't look up when I enter.

"Simon?" I put a hand on his shoulder, and he flinches slightly. "Simon I've got rid of him."

After what seems like minutes he looks up at me, and his face is gaunt with tension. "Fuck."

"We-"

"Should get on with the haymaking, I know."

"I wasn't going to say that." The helicopter passes

low over the valley and way down beneath the trees the news vans wait.

"I don't know what to do," he says.

"There are people who can help us."

"They don't live around here then." He laughs harshly.

"I've seen their websites."

"No." Simon shakes his head. "I know their type. It'll be a con."

"We'll get one who's a proper lawyer."

"I can't afford that. I'm just a gardener." He steeples his hands over the bridge of his nose and breathes deeply. "My life- well you've seen what they're saying. I am a loner, an introvert, I live on a houseboat, and I don't drive because I had a fucking breakdown. There, now you know the truth."

"Simon."

"I've done drink and drugs. Char, it's all there on a plate for them."

"But-" I search for something, anything to suggest but my mind's numb.

"I haven't even got an alibi for that night. I was out, alone."

"I see." I stroke the top of Georgie's head.

"I have to be outside. I'm no good at offices, I'm not much good at anything, apart from cycling. I'm as fast as the best." He grins momentarily, and there's a flicker of the old Simon, bold, mischievous and competitive.

"I've never seen your name."

"Oh, I don't compete. I've cycled the routes though, mostly at night, the time trials and the hill climbs."

I imagine him alone in the darkness speeding along the empty roads, his head down and his legs pumping. If it was anyone else, if I read about him I know what I'd think.

———

The weather has been so hot that the hay has cured in a day less than normal. We work all the rest of the afternoon, or at least Simon works and I dip in and out around looking after Georgie. Despite the stench of diesel fumes and the pure hard graft of turning and baling the hay it feels almost relaxing to be out there together doing something that we used to share summer after summer.

By six the fields are dotted with bales. The sun is much lower, and a breeze whips dust and hayseed into my eyes when I carry out a jug of chilled apple juice.

"Georgie's asleep so I can help for a bit again," I say to break the silence.

"We need to get the bales into stacks; it'll be quicker to pick them up then." Simon drinks his juice in one gulp and sets the glass down under the hedge. "It's going to take ages with only the link box."

I park Georgie's buggy near the gate where I can see her and walk out across the shaved grass to the first trail of bales. My arms aren't used to lifting anything much heavier than Georgie or a camera bag, and long before I'm even halfway across the first field, they grow weak with exhaustion.

"You want to swap?" Simon asks leaning out of the back of the tractor cab and watching me struggle to heave a bale into line. "It'd make sense if you drive for a bit."

Georgie is still asleep, so I haul myself up the narrow

iron steps and onto the torn vinyl seat. Inside the glass space, the air smells of fresh sweat and Border Collie and the afternoon takes on a more threatening hue through the tinted windscreen. The clouds seem much nearer suddenly and the storm inevitable. I drive at walking pace for a while then Simon runs up alongside and pulls open the cab door. "Char we need to go a bit faster now."

We're loading the link box for the last time when the air chills and darkens. Up and down the hedgerows blackbirds chink their evening alarm calls, and a rising wind sends last year's dead leaves scurrying across the shaved grass.

"Here it comes." Simon looks up at the sky and begins to run. "I'll drive if you go and get Georgie."

The first hail hits us as I rush the buggy into the shelter of the barn and the noise on the tin roof is amazing. Georgie stares out with wide eyes, and within minutes the ground is white. Simon reverses the tractor in until it's under cover then cuts off the engine.

"Look at that for timing." He stretches out his bare, grimy arms and rolls down his shirtsleeves.

Hail bounces off the edge of the roof and pools in front of us, while away to the west somewhere lightning flashes and I begin to count as I wait for the thunder. Simon looks out towards the track, and from his stillness, I think that he's heard something, then his shoulders slouch, and he digs at the floor with his toe. With the work over for the moment, everything else presses close again.

"Let's go in. I need to get Georgie to bed."

The rain comes up behind us as we cross the yard and run up the path into the house.

"God, look at it," Simon stays near the kitchen window, but he's not there to watch the rain. His gaze flicks towards the lane, and he leans sideways until his cheek is against the cool glass.

"Simon."

"I know." He puts his hands up in a casual dismissive gesture and forces himself away from the window into a circuit of the room.

Once we would have gone down to the Ring of Bells, crowded into the oval snug room and ordered great baskets of oil-drenched chips. I long for the comfort of that, for the carelessness of letting someone else fetch and carry.

"Are the police watching us?" Simon says, and I fill a glass from the tap, letting the water run until it's as cold as the underground granite. "Is that what this is all about? Are they watching to see if we break from cover?"

"I don't know what you mean."

"We're like those rabbits in the hayfield, the ones that wait until the last moment, until it's too late and they get crushed."

The sky is a strange greenish colour and rain courses down the west windows. I try to steady my breath, to pull it into the pit of my lungs, then let it out again, slowly, and the water drains in a cold line to my gut.

"Simon-"

"I'm not going to run."

Dan told me something once about guilt and bravado. I try to remember his actual words, but I can't even hear his voice now. I'd caught an edge of emotion in one of my early spreads of photos quite by accident. When we looked at them in the design room, it was like looking into the model's soul. Dan loved it, but I felt awkward, as though I'd purposefully stolen something that wasn't mine.

"I've got nothing to hide."

He's like that now. One minute I think I know him, the next he makes some gesture perfected during our years apart, and he's a stranger again. He walks away to the window and leans on the sill with his back to me. His shoulders are narrow and clenched.

"I'm going to feed Georgie and get her to bed."

When I come down again, he's still there, and it doesn't look as though he's moved at all.

"I should go and check Eb," he says rousing himself as I enter the kitchen.

The early, storm darkness swallows him up for a long time, and I'm just beginning to worry when the door flies open, and he leans into the room, soaked to the skin.

"Simon? Is Eb okay?"

"He's fine, but I need the big torch, this one's flat." His face is grim.

"What is it?"

"There's something out there. At the top of the orchard." He sweeps a strand of wet hair out of his eyes.

"What sort of thing?" Nerves lurch through my stomach.

"I can't see, there's a smell. Something dead."

"Oh God."

"I won't be long."

"Simon wait. I'm coming with you." I glance at the baby monitor on the table.

"But-"

"She'll be fine. It isn't far, and we'll lock the door."

We shut the dogs in the kitchen, and I grab a coat from the hooks in the hall. It's an old waxed one of Clare's. Too late I realise that I have no hood or gloves and within seconds my hair is plastered against my skull, and I can feel cold rivulets of water trickling down my back.

Another night, another time and almost the same steps. What were we looking for then? I remember a cold wind and high clouds, Simon's hand around mine pulling me forwards up the hill. This time we're a little apart. The torch beam slices through the wet darkness and my heart pounds. The wind has got up, and the old apple trees sway and groan.

"It's somewhere up here," Simon says as we skirt along the hedge.

"It can't be anything. I mean the police searched the whole farm." I stop as the smell hits me in a wave of rain-soaked air, thick and choking. "Oh no."

"You wait here."

"No."

The smell grows stronger still and then fades a little, and we turn back. A bramble grabs at me, and I bend down to pull it free of my jeans.

"It's in the hedge." Simon scans the tangle of thorn with the torch beam, and I can hardly bear to follow its progress. "Somewhere, here."

He lets out his breath in a rush and steps forward.

"What is it?"

"Don't look."

"Simon." Panic clutches at the base of my throat. "No."

"It's a fox."

"A fox?"

"It's not very nice though. I'll come up and sort it out tomorrow."

"Oh God." I feel shaky suddenly and stumble on an unseen lump of turf.

"Char are you okay?" He reaches for my arm in the dark.

"Yes. Yes." I take a deep breath and regret that almost at once. "I'm fine."

We walk back down to the yard, and somehow Simon's arm is around my shoulders. I'm not sure that I need it, but he does shield me from the wind a little. In the kitchen, the lights blind us for a few seconds while water runs down our waterproofs and spreads out across the tiles.

"Here, use this." Simon tosses me a towel that was airing over the Rayburn, and I rub my hands and face. It smells of the dogs.

"I'd better check Georgie." I peel off my wet jacket and jumper and step out of my wellies before tiptoeing across to the table to pick up the baby monitor. She's still asleep, her breathing steady and even. Relief floods through me.

"We can sort out all this wet stuff in the morning."

The water has reached my skin, and I shiver as Simon opens the pantry door and lets in a flood of stale cold air.

"Give us your jacket." He holds out his hand for it, then stops. "Hey, Char are you alright?"

"Yeh, yeh I'm fine." I can't stop shivering now, and when I try to undo the buttons of my shirt, my hands won't work. "This is stupid, I know it was just a fox but-"

"Come here." He wraps the towel around my shoulders and reaches for the first button. "You never were any good in the cold were you?"

We're so close that I can smell the coffee on his breath and see individual grains of mud in the lines beneath his eyes. The air fizzes between us and the muscles around my shoulder blades are bunched and tight. In the morning I'll wake with a pain down the side of my neck.

"Char it's me, I won't hurt you." Simon's fingers slide up under the towel and feel through the thin wet cotton of my shirt. He digs deeper and deeper until he catches a knot in the muscle and I start with pain.

"Not so hard."

"Sorry."

His jumper is still dry, and it smells of hay dust. I press my cheek against it and close my eyes.

"Oh Char," he says quietly, and then I'm looking up, and his lips taste of rain and mud.

His embrace is oddly familiar, and a rush of memories floods my mind; other long-forgotten nights when our joint warmth was a matter of survival out in the lambing shed, the feel of his hand over the back of mine as he showed me how to massage a horse, the scent of his young sundried skin after we'd swum in the peaty pools far below the farm. I pull back.

"I'm sorry."

"Char, what's the matter? That was meant to be nice."

"It was, it is, but ..." I twist away across the kitchen and pull the towel tighter around my shoulders.

"But?"

"I don't know. Simon please?"

The landing window is open and cold, damp air

eddies down the stairwell and into the hall. Beyond, in the garden, rain drums on the tin roof of the utility room. For a moment I pause and stare at my face in the old mottled mirror hanging beside the coats. Sunburn flares across the bridge of my nose and along my cheekbones and a line of tiredness dips between my eyebrows.

"Oh God." I press my face into my hands for a few moments, and when I glance up again, I look flushed and confused.

15

_____

Where are they, where on earth are they? There must be something more that I can do. I spin around in the morning light and the horrible uncertainty, the waiting, the not knowing claws up my back. There must be something-

My mobile rings and I grab it, sure suddenly that it's news. Hollinghurst's voice sounds edgy and evasive. He wants me to meet him at the station this morning if at all possible. He won't give me any details, but I sense his urgency.

"I have to do a few things first, for Georgie, but I'll be there as soon as I can."

Beyond the window the yard is littered with storm debris, a tide of pale granite gravel washed down out of the drift and piles of battered twigs and leaves. The sight of it all makes me feel exhausted and anxious. What else has changed overnight?

Simon is still asleep, and I don't want to wake him, so I turn the radio on low and listen to the local news. We're the third item. "Police have today renewed their appeals for information about the missing schoolboy Lee Berryman. Lee disappeared thirteen days ago while visiting a neighbour and neither he nor his neighbour has been seen since."

"Someone out there knows what has happened to Lee." Hollinghurst comes on, and his voice is measured and professional, but that same edge that I heard on the phone is there. Is it frustration? Anger? "If you believe that you have any information relating to this case please call the incident room as a matter of urgency."

I switch off the radio. The dogs are sniffing around in the yard, tails waving absently. Someone is out there. Are they watching us even now? I glance up at that spot on the moor above the curve of the wall, the closest public point to the house, but nothing moves in the bracken. Behind me, the grandfather clock in the hallway is still ticking off the minutes, the hours, the days.

"Shit."

Is Lee dead now? Is that what Hollinghurst thinks, what they want to tell me? Is Clare? Is it too late, have we been too slow?

"Char?" Simon is in the doorway watching me. I didn't hear him, and I flush. I can't even think about last night now.

"I have to go down to the police station." I start to grab my things together. There's always so much to take with a baby.

"What for? Char, you haven't had any breakfast." Simon is close suddenly, and he catches hold of my bare arm. His hand is warm. "About last night."

"Simon." What do I need? Nappies, food, muslins. "Look, I can't-"

"I'll come with you."

"Sorry?"

"Just give me five minutes, and I'll be ready. You'll need someone to look after Georgie won't you?"

"Yes, yes, of course, thanks."

He remembers the things that I forget, a bottle of water for us and some crackers and spread, the dregs of the cupboard. We shut the kitchen door in the dogs' faces and go out to the car.

"So?" He twists round in the passenger seat while I secure Georgie's car seat.

"Hollinghurst called, he wouldn't tell me what it's about, but his voice, it was different."

"Perhaps-"

"No, please." I hold up a hand. There are enough terrible images in my head already.

"Char."

"What?" I don't look at him. Last night is too close, too confusing. I sweep a curl of hair back behind my ear.

"You said, 'I can't.' Can't what?"

"Simon." I'm too hot suddenly, and I roll up the sleeves of my shirt before I climb into the car. Now he's so close again, his bare arm centimetres from mine, his jean-clad knee, his-

"Char look I, I wasn't trying to take advantage of you last night."

"I know."

There was another time, another gunshot in the dark and my finger was on the trigger. It was the summer before the end, but he probably doesn't remember it. We were at Cameron Mackenzie's leaving party in the ugly red brick Victorian house on the edge of the woods that his parents still just owned. They weren't around, so perhaps they'd already gone to Edinburgh.

Cameron's sister Abby was there in a halterneck bikini. It was her gun and her Barbie dolls on the wooden blocks at the edge of the wood that we shot. Simon was angry with me for some reason, and he walked away to the other side of the house.

Much later I found him there sitting in an old deck chair. I was so tired by then that my legs felt weak and I had to lean against him for support. He put his arms around me and then somehow I was sitting on his lap. Our faces were so close that he was all out of focus, then our lips met. Just for a second, the tips of our tongues touched. He tasted of charcoaled food, and something slightly minty and Marty's spiked orange juice raced through my veins.

"Then?"

"Please." I concentrate on turning the car out through the narrow gateway and down the track. The storm has cleared the air, and it promises to be another day of almost unbroken blue. Difficult light to photograph in unless you want those hard over-exposed shots that make even the innocent look guilty of some undefined crime. Perfect weather for the guys at the roadblock then.

We slither down the steepest part of the track and out past Lee's shrine. For a second I glance back at it in the rear-view mirror. If anything it has grown even more. There are buckets of flowers now and a big red teddy bear. The colour seems horribly wrong, too like blood-soaked fur.

"He might not be dead."

"Sorry?"

"That teddy, look. I mean how could anyone? Don't they think at all?"

"Char." His hand hovers above my knee, settles for a moment then lifts off again.

"And now." The urge to turn round before we reach the wall of reporters, to abandon the car and flee away across the fields almost overwhelms me. It's too much, all these people, all the cameras.

There are several police officers, running figures across the road, hands, a flash. Simon ducks his head and in the back Georgie starts to cry again.

"Char hurry up."

"What?"

"Just drive on."

More people appear around the next bend, a group of ten or so spread out across the road, forcing me to slow again. I flick down the locks something I usually do half way along our track now.

"Keep going."

I realise with a jolt of shock that they aren't all reporters. Vicki's there and flat-faced Tony near the back, but there are other strange faces with mouths stretched wide. I can hear the sounds of their voices but no words, then a man steps up and bangs his fist against the passenger window on my side. For a moment his skin goes white and bloodless against the glass. Georgie flinches and lets out a little cry.

"Ssh darling, it's alright." My foot hovers over the brake. "I don't want to hit anyone."

"Just keep moving, they'll get out of the way."

There are jeaned legs and bright splashes of coloured t-shirts, the dark, unblinking eyes of camera lenses and then we're past and speeding away between the high granite hedge banks. Simon lets out a long uneven breath, and I glance at him.

"It's even worse than before. Oh God, what's happened?"

———

"What's happened?"

Hollinghurst comes out to meet me in the foyer. He is much edgier today, and his movements are hurried and angular as he shows me through to an airless room with a long table and a screen on the far wall. Quinn is sitting in front of the screen, but he stands up and comes over.

"How well do you know the moor?" Hollinghurst asks, and his voice is taut.

"Er, well I haven't been down here for a long time but-" Is he trying to trick me in some way? To find the chink between truth and lie. Another officer comes into the room, and I watch as he fires up the projector. For a moment there's a blank oblong of white light on the screen.

"We've got some photos." Hollinghurst sits down in front of a laptop and clicks several keys. "I was hoping that as a photographer you might be able to say whether they're straights and also if you recognise any of the places."

The first shot is of a patch of woodland, mostly broadleaves with a band of conifers in the background. There's a low stone wall patched with moss and the edge of a gate. The trees are in full leaf, and the photo looks recent. Hollinghurst holds it on screen for a minute or so then clicks through to the next one. It might be of the same woodland and then it might not. It's a different angle anyway. There's more open ground and clumps of grass. The third shows a stretch of moorland, heather, bracken, a few boulders but no sky.

They're bland pictures, the kind of shots that you'd normally delete without thought, not save and send. Their very nothingness serves to heighten the sense that there's something sinister just out of the frame, beyond the reach of the camera. If you could only turn a little, you'd see it, the disturbance of earth, the shape in the undergrowth, the movement in the shadows. But you can't, all you have are these clear innocent patches of sunlit ground.

The fourth and final shot is much poorer than the others, overexposed and way out of focus. There are splashes of green in the foreground that look like vegetation caught close to the lens and obscuring most of the frame. What's behind them is hard to make out. Harsh white light almost obliterates a blurred dark red and black shape.

"So?" Hollinghurst waits. What does he think? What does Quinn think? It's hard to tell, but a sense of unease hangs over the room

"I, I don't know. Could I look at the first ones again?" The shapes, the growth patterns of the trees, are they familiar? I cast my mind back, sifting through images in my head. Comparing and discarding. I'm not sure I can pinpoint exactly where the photos were taken, but there is something about them, something that makes me think that they are true representations, that I've been to the places they show. "The first three might be of Longcause Wood, up at the top end below Howden. Where did they come from?"

Hollinghurst hesitates for a moment and glances at Quinn. "We were emailed them anonymously. We're trying to track the account at the moment."

"Was there a message?"

"For information. That was it."

Two words, usually so innocently, so helpfully sent. The kind of words that almost stop you reading on if you're busy. The email beyond can wait.

"And you think Clare and Lee might be there?" I swallow, and the final shot fills the screen before us. The uniformed officer tries to adjust the focus, but it makes no difference. The picture could be of anything, the blur of redness merely a piece of material, a jacket or something much more sinister.

"We hope not of course, but it's a possibility that we have to follow up." His words are heavy. "It could also be a hoax; we need to check both angles."

"A hoax? You mean someone would-" I shake my head, I can't believe it. "Why?"

"You'd be surprised."

Quinn leaves the room, but a few minutes later he's back with a map, which he spreads out on the table.

"Could you show us where you think these shots were taken?"

Longcause Wood. So close. I lean forward to study the map. I find Northstone and a little to the west the familiar blocks of woodland.

"About here and maybe here." I place my finger on the map in a couple of places. "But I'm not sure."

"Thank you, that gives us a start." Hollinghurst stands up and turns towards the door his energy once again focused beyond the room. "I'd appreciate it if you could keep this to yourself."

"Of course."

———

Georgie is crying. I hear her as soon as I step out of the police station. The noise rises across the car park and out over the chain link fence tattered with trapped rubbish. She's fine with Simon, of course, she is, but I start to run.

"Oh come on darling." Her face is red and wet, and I lift her out of Simon's arms and hold her against me. Suddenly I'm close to tears as well.

"She hasn't been crying long," Simon says. "I wasn't much good at stopping her though, sorry."

From this angle, our old school building looks harsh and uncompromising its sharp, ugly lines perfectly suited to its new job.

"Char? Are you okay? What's happened?"

"I had to look at some photos. Ssh, ssh darling." They're still imprinted on my mind, and I examine them again. Was I right? Were they really of Longcause and, if so, who sent them and what do they mean?

"Photos?"

"I'm sure Hollinghurst thinks they're dead now. He's looking for their bodies, isn't he? A grave." I strap Georgie back into her car seat. She doesn't like it, and her cries rise, but for once I ignore them.

"What were the photos of?"

"Longcause. I think they were of the top corner."

"Shit."

His lips tasted of mud last night and the rain. He

hasn't shaved since and there's a light golden stubble on his chin.

"Let's get out of here."

Even on the edge of town, people are thronging the pavements. Ordinary people doing ordinary things, their faces clear for a second then gone. Sometimes my gaze connects with a stranger's through the glass and across space and once a child smiles at me. I don't smile back, and the kid scowls instead. Ordinary people doing ordinary things, shopping for food perhaps or clothes, knowing who their friends are and what's going to happen next in their lives.

"I wonder who sent them." I glance in the mirror at Georgie. She's quietened down again now that we're moving and suddenly I want to keep driving and driving, numbing my mind with the constant flow of everyday road images.

"Didn't they know?"

"Hollinghurst said it was anonymous email account. Just numbers or something. They're trying to trace it though."

"Pull over." Simon leans forward and puts a hand on the dash.

"What?"

"Into that car park over there."

I find one of the few remaining spaces in the multi-storey and park up. It's shadowy outside the car, and there's the rumble of other vehicles spinning up through the tiers.

"I don't want to go back yet," Simon says looking straight ahead at the safety mesh.

I can't face it either but now that there's nothing else to divert our attention our silence becomes awkward.

"I'll buy you lunch or tea or whatever." Still, he doesn't look at me.

"Thank you."

It's loud and busy, and bizarrely Georgie falls straight to sleep in her sling as soon as we step onto the hot dirty pavement outside the car park.

"Do you mind if we walk for a bit?" Her face is so delicate and perfect resting sideways against the strap, and I lift the hood to protect her soft baby skin from the sun.

Simon shakes his head, and we blend into the crowd of shoppers. The multi-storey sits flanked by a battalion of small bars and cheap cafés. Neon and plastic adorn the street in equal measure in some hopeless pretence at Americanism, and the drains smell like hot urinals. I still have a map of the town in my head somewhere, and I dredge it up as we walk.

"It's got to be a hoax," I say suddenly. "Apparently some people do things like that, I dunno why."

"Char."

"I'm sure it wasn't a body. It could have been anything. It looked almost photoshopped to me, deliberately blurred."

"A body? I thought you said they were of Longcause."

"Three were. The fourth. It could have been anything, that was deliberate, I'm sure of it." A cruel trick. But why?

"I need a coffee." Simon steps into Twiggy's, a narrow strip of café pressed in between a burger bar and a Chinese takeaway still shuttered against the after-noon sun. A sixty-a-day woman wheezes out onto the pavement to take our order and doesn't seem to recognise us.

"A fair old morning," she says staring across the street towards a group of Japanese students with backpacks. I try to smile, but my cheeks feel stiff.

"I guess so." Simon is better at playing normality.

The drinks when they come are insipid, more chlorine than tea or coffee and still, we don't look at each other properly.

"Where would you go with an injured child?" I ask. In the distance, there's a bus trying to manoeuvre between a lorry and a poorly parked car. Suddenly I want to run down the street to it, to jump on and be carried to wherever it's going. I'd get out then and walk through some sixties housing estate to an insignificant semi with a strip of grass out the front and a rabbit hutch at the back. My house. I'd walk in, and no one would look or care. Pure glorious, anonymity.

"To a hospital."

"Well of course, but if you didn't want to be seen." I slide a hand around Georgie to make sure that her back isn't pressed against the tiny sticky table.

"To someone who could do first aid-"

"Serious first aid, they'd have had to be medically trained I should think."

"Oh Char this is crazy, we don't know it was like that. It could have been anything."

"What, like murder, like being buried in Longcause Wood?"

"Char." His hand comes to rest on my knee under the table.

"It has to be something else. They have to be alive

still." The panic is there again threatening to overwhelm me.

"You'll make yourself ill."

"I've got to walk, Georgie will wake up again if I sit still any longer."

There's a park at the end of the street; a swathe of grass interspersed around the edges with flowerbeds and crisscrossed with tarmac paths. Away in the distance a tiny tractor and trailer are parked by one of the borders and two council workers unpack a new display of bedding plants. Closer at hand, a teenage boy, throws a ball for a young black Labrador and a toddler staggers along the path on uncontrollable legs. I can still smell the chemically-treated air of the police station on my hair.

Beside me Simon is golden. People notice him. It was always like that, even when he first arrived women looked. He was oblivious then, but now his jaw tightens, and he walks on fast. There isn't even the faintest suggestion of a breeze and the heat drills into us so that by the time we reach the far side of the park our faces are damp.

"Is that enough walking for you?" I want to see his face properly, but he's looking away towards the street. "Would madam like some lunch?"

We're in the trendy quarter now. Café land with a difference, with clean silver tables and liveried cushions on the metal chairs, with bright awnings and pot plants.

"Indoors or out?"

It's dark, anonymous and cool indoors at the back of an Italian cafe. We find a corner seat, and I feed Georgie under a muslin.

"I need a drink." Simon studies the menu, and I

think he means juice, but he orders a bottle of red wine instead.

"But-?" I stare at the condensation on the glass, and although I don't say it, the dead horse and the mangled car are suddenly close. What came before and after? He hasn't told me, but I know what he was like drunk, first wilder and funnier than usual but still eloquent then steadily more and more out of control, swinging between silence and aggression.

"I'm alright. A couple of glasses of wine won't hurt."

We order bowls of pasta as well, and I hope that the hot spicy sauce will mop up the alcohol that I can't share. Simon drinks quickly, one, two, three glasses and everything in the street is bright and remote at the end of the dark tunnel of the café.

"Should we go back and help look?" Suddenly it seems obscene to be sitting here drinking while the search continues so close to the farm.

"Don't be crazy. I wouldn't be allowed to and you, well you can't help with Georgie." His eyes are bright and restless. "If they're dead we'll hear soon enough."

"Simon."

"Sorry." He sinks his face into his hands. "Oh, Char I really am sorry, for everything."

The waiter is watching us. He's young with a floppy dark fringe, and he looks a bit French. Does he know who we are? Has he worked it out yet? Will he save up these images of us to share with his friends?

"There's no way; you know that don't you?" Simon stretches his hand across the table towards me. "Please say you believe me. Char?"

After school, all those times, just us alone together. I never had a boyfriend.

"Just say it. I need to hear you."

"Simon, you're drunk."

"So what?"

"I think we should go. I need to change Georgie, to get her back to the farm."

"But I need another drink."

It's further back to the car than I thought but Simon hasn't caught me up by the time I reach it, and there's no sign of him when I look back.

"Oh God." What do I do now? I can't leave him. Irritation and fear mingle in my veins. I hang around in the car park for a bit then I buy another ticket and head back into town. It's even hotter now, a thick, sultry heat that last night's storm hasn't shifted.

Simon isn't in the café, and this time I'm sure that the waiter does know who I am in my new capacity as the daughter of a potential criminal. A headache swoops in from nowhere and gnaws at the base of my skull.

"I'm sorry Georgie." Suddenly someone grabs me from behind and spins me around, and Simon's there laughing in my face.

"What are you doing?"

"I thought I'd lost you. I'm sorry. Look, can I take you out for tea?" He's a little flushed, and his hair is dishevelled and damp.

"We've only just had lunch." I don't want to feel like this.

"Oh go on." We walk on, and suddenly there's someone following us, a man in the crowd, a walk more purposeful than the rest.

"Simon." I glance back.

"That's crazy." But he grabs my arm and pulls me into a side street. Left, right, left again. Our footsteps echo between blank brick walls, and there's the smell of hot cloth at the back of a dry cleaners. "Let's go down to the river and see if that place that used to do chocolate truffles is still there."

It was one of our favourite after-school haunts. The place we went to while Tony Pearson and some of the others stopped off at The Cider Bar. A group of swans used to drift around outside waiting for crumbs, and sometimes there were ducks under the tables.

It's gone. The tables, everything. Without a word we walk past the padlocked gate and on down the river, following the concrete pathway close to the backs of houses and unknown streets. If we walk far enough, we'll come to the funny little pub under the pylons. It never moved on with the times.

"One for the road?" There's a single tired wooden picnic bench outside, and I sit down on one side with Georgie while Simon pushes open the door. The smell that wafts out is the same, stale alcohol and lemon air freshener. The previous customer has discarded a tabloid. It flaps in a sudden breeze, but it can't escape from under the ashtray.

"It hasn't changed at all." Simon sits down with a pint of cider and passes me an apple juice. "Some things don't."

16

Martin Henry Berryman. No holds barred this time. There are more unflattering photographs of him and the house. Sleepers looks run down and untidy. There's a crack down the front wall, and the window frames need replacing. A collie dog snarls at the photographer, and the press has found one of those anonymous friends prepared to speak out about his fatherly capabilities. He's a grafter, a licensed killer of animals. His hours are long, and afterwards, he drinks hard on a Saturday night. He used to play football with the local team but not anymore, not since Emma's death.

Lee roams, and he lets him. He thinks people haven't noticed, but Social Services are onto him. Lee's school attendance was on a decline; there had been unanswered letters from the Head. Not good.

It's late, and there are fewer vehicles along the lane but

great stretches of churned up verge. We drive past quickly, and I'm aware without really looking of figures sitting waiting in the pale glow of interior lights.

"Don't they ever sleep?"

Beyond them, the lane is a dark tunnel of oaks alongside the river with huge moss-covered boulders lurking in the undergrowth like sleeping animals. I watch the brake lights of the patrol car glow red in the darkness as the driver reverses back into place behind us and feel oddly and unjustifiably safe.

The headlights catch a tawny owl perched low on a branch and something else, a dark shape at the side of the track.

"What's that?"

"Where?"

I jab on my brakes. There's a person in a black jacket leant against a tree trunk. For the merest fraction of time before my brain has registered things properly I think that it might be Clare, then I see that the figure is far too large to be her. It's a man with his head down. He doesn't move even with my headlights full on him and then I catch the glint of a bottle at his feet.

"Stay there." Simon opens his door and steps out. He's nearly up to him when the man raises his head. It's Marty.

For a moment they're both motionless then Marty lunges to his feet with the bottle in his hand and takes a step towards Simon. I slip off my seatbelt and jump from the car.

"Where's my boy?" Marty's voice sounds slurred, and a muddy mark stretches across one cheek.

"Marty."

"Well, where is he?"

"I don't know." Simon stands his ground, but his back is stiff.

"Have you seen? They're saying that I neglected him, that it's my fault. Fuck them."

"Come on Marty."

"They think, that bloody Headmaster, what does he know? I mean who the hell is he to-?"

"Marty we'll give you a lift home."

"What?" He looks at me properly, his eyes focusing for a few seconds before his gaze drifts back to Simon again.

"No thanks. I'm not getting in a car with a liar like him." He waves the whisky bottle at Simon's head.

"What did you say?" Simon takes a step back, his voice is cold and steady, but there's alcohol speeding around his veins as well.

"Tell her, go on. Why don't you? You've been back, I saw you. What have you done with them?"

"Marty."

"You were always trouble, right from the very start."

"Is that right?" Simon's shoulders are tight, and there's a look on his face that scares me.

"Come on both of you; this isn't going to do any good." I glance back at the car listening for Georgie but the lights dazzle me, and I can't see anything.

"Why don't you tell us what you know?"

"Fuck you."

"Simon."

"I've had enough of this, I-"

A cold breeze blows down off the moor, and we're out of shouting distance of anywhere.

"Simon please, you go back to the farm, and I'll give Marty a lift home."

"But-"

"Go on. We'll be fine." Our shadows rear up into the trees, and I'm scared that Georgie will wake alone in the dark car. "Simon, go on."

Still, he hesitates then he turns and vanishes out of the dazzle of the headlights into the deep darkness beyond. For a while I can hear his stumbling footsteps then those too fade away. I should have told him that I keep a torch in the glove box, but it's too late.

"Come on Marty."

"It's him. I always knew, right from the beginning." He leans back against the tree again and takes a swig out of the whisky bottle that's half empty already then he starts to slide downwards and disconcertingly grabs at my hand. "I may not have been the best father, but I never meant to hurt him. I had to work; it isn't easy on your own, you'll see. Maybe I've worked too much."

"Look, let's get you back to Sleepers." I pull on his arm, and he staggers up again. His breath in my face is a mixture of alcohol and yesterday's garlic.

"Charlotte we may have had our differences but you know that I'm not a bad man, don't you?"

We used to play cards together, share our packed lunches while we waited for the school bus and buy each other crisps at the village shop with our pocket money. A montage of innocent childhood images slides before my eyes.

"Okay, look Marty you're drunk, why don't you just get in the front here." I hold open the door for him. He stoops forward as though to climb into the car then he sways upright again. "Can't you see what he's like?"

"Sorry?"

"Simon. It was always the same, right from the start."

"Marty I'm not listening to this." In the back, Georgie stirs with a cry.

"Fuck it Charlotte; he could have killed you in that car." How much do those thoughts hurt him? That I was saved while his wife died; two separate crashes divided by years but not by so many miles. Seemingly random events linked together by his life.

"Marty just get in."

He sits still and slightly bent with the bottle gripped between his knees as we make our slow way up the hill and suddenly doesn't seem inclined to say anything more.

"Marty, look I'm sorry about Lee, I really am."

"Of course you are, you-"

"But listen." I put my hand on his knee to get his attention, and he's shaking slightly. "Marty you've got to get this thing about Simon out of your head. He doesn't know anything more than I do."

"That's what he's told you, but I saw him out by Longcause."

That name. Always that name now. I think about the photos, and the headlights catch Lee's shrine, great bunches of golden chrysanthemums glow in the dark among the myriad of cards and letters. Beyond, up our track, there's a figure, shrinking back from the light even as it touches him. Marty's looking slantwise across the fields, and I don't think he sees Simon, but it feels good that he's there and Georgie and I aren't so totally alone in the darkness with Marty.

"I wish I knew where Lee was. I wish I could help you; you've got to believe that. Marty, I'm a parent too and if I could do anything to bring him back safe for you, I would."

He's slumped sideways against the door, and I'm not sure whether my words sink through his alcoholic haze.

"Marty." I don't want him passing out on me, and I stop at the entrance to his farmyard. "Will you be alright from here?"

For a moment there's no response then he raises his head and looks at me."I love that boy."

"Of course you do."

"When Emma died-" He takes another swig of whisky.

"Marty you should go in. Get some water or some milk. Wake Peter if you need to."

"You and I-"

"No. No." I'm not having this conversation, not here, not now, not anywhere. What might have been is a long, long time ago now, a lifetime ago. We're different now, Simon has changed us, or at least me.

He opens the door suddenly and lurches out into the darkness. "Thanks for the lift."

"No problem." I wait until he's crossed the yard to the back door and disappeared inside before reversing up and going back for Simon.

I'm part way along the lane when I see him running towards me in the brake lights and stop.

"Char, Char are you alright?" He pulls open the passenger door and climbs in beside me breathing hard.

"I'm fine."

"Oh thank goodness. I thought, you and Georgie, I should never have left you, I'm sorry."

"Simon it's alright."

"No, he, he could have-" Suddenly he leans across and pulls me against him. "Oh God."

We kiss in a tangle of arms, a twisted awkward position across the gear stick but it doesn't matter, nothing else matters and then it becomes too uncomfortable, and I pull back

"Simon, you're drunk."

"A little, but maybe I needed to be to-" He kisses me again a mere brush of lips then smiles. "I've wanted to do this for so long, and I thought I'd blown it last night."

"Of course not." Behind us, Georgie shifts in her seat and lets out a little sleepy cry. "Look we'd better get back."

The yard and house are dark and remote, and a cool breeze sweeps down off the moor. It's as it should be, as it has been for years and yet-

"I have to get Georgie to bed." We stand on either side of the car and look up at the sky, clear now and thick with stars. After years of city life, I've forgotten skies like this.

"Okay."

I wait, but he doesn't look at me or say anymore, so I turn towards the house. I think he might follow me but he doesn't, and the kitchen feels lonely and empty.

Georgie wakes when I change her and then it takes her a while to settle back to sleep in her cot. For once I want to rush through the whole ceremony of it and leave her, and I feel guilty.

"Night, night darling." I stroke the top of her head. Is this what it's like being a mother? Will I always feel this conflict between needing my own time and yet not wanting to leave her? Will I always wonder and worry when she's not close to me? Is near-constant guilt a part of it all?

Walking back down the stairs I have the sudden sense of what it must have been like for Clare when we were gone, the house empty and silent. The back door is open to the thin darkness; someone could walk in, anyone, someone did walk in. I take a deep breath and put a hand on the cool plaster. It's still there, the faint stain of blood on the paintwork. It must be something to do with the shadows because it's hardly visible during the day.

"Simon?"

There are no lights on. I stand in the hallway and listen. Nothing.

"Simon?"

The Rayburn ticks quietly to itself in the kitchen, and the warm glow of its heat reaches me even in the doorway. I step back and trace the shadows through to the living room, hand on wall, fingers trailing the rough plaster. Everything seems a bit jumpy and out of focus.

"Simon?"

The darkness is thick and empty. Back in the hall-way, I stop again. There's a noise outside, the rush of paws as Gel scuds out of the shadows with her crazy half and half face. I cup my hand behind her ear, and her coat is silky against my palm. She plumes her tail at me then turns back towards the open door.

"Simon?"

There's a half moon, and shrubs loom out at me in strange almost human shapes. A sudden thought, a mere flicker of the past, pulls me to the garden gate. I put my hand on the top of the right gatepost, and my fingers brush over the two smooth pebbles. I ease them into my pocket and follow Gel around the side of the house to the front garden. The air smells of greenery and something else, a thin pure strand of scent, sweet as a distant memory. Simon is sitting on the grass staring out across the valley.

"Char?" He glances around and holds out a hand to me.

"I didn't know where you were."

"Come here."

For a moment longer, I can't let myself go but I need him so much, and I sink down beside him.

"Simon, hold me, please."

"Oh Char, I really thought-" He slides his arms around me. "Last night-"

"It's okay."

"No. Look I'm sorry. I would never, ever take advantage of you Charlotte, not like that and I don't want-"

"Simon shut up. It was me. I don't know, I just, oh God."

He's shaking as we kiss, but his mouth tastes familiar and when I close my eyes the whole of our past is behind my lids. I can see him at thirteen when he'd just arrived, his face aching with the effort not to cry, at fourteen, inches taller and already far more confident and at fifteen, bronzed and fit, daring me to run faster and ride harder.

"I thought, I thought you hated me," he says when we come up for air. "All these years."

"Simon, I could never do that.

There's no breeze in the garden. The dogs are moseying away through the tangled undergrowth, and there's the purposeful rustle of something else, a hedgehog perhaps. I sit back a little.

"What if Hollinghurst is right about those photos and they're buried out there? What if we never have a chance to speak to Clare?"

"Char."

"Just like we'll never speak to Robert again. Simon, dad's dead, he's not coming back."

"Ssh, I know. Come here." He pulls me against him. "You're exhausted, Char."

"I can't-"

"Don't try. Let's just stay out here for a bit. It's a beautiful night." He slips off his jacket and spreads it out on the grass behind us.

"If-"

"Char."

"No, please, hear me out. If Clare is dead, you know I don't think I'll ever be able to forgive myself. Simon, all this time, I thought, hell I've been so angry with them, so horrible to her."

"It's alright."

"But what they did to you-"

"Let's not talk about that." He touches the ends of my hair then runs his fingers along the edge of my jaw. "It doesn't matter anymore."

"But-"

"I love you, Char. I think I've always loved you."

"Oh, Simon." I cling to him suddenly, and he eases me gently back until we're lying full length. The ground feels wonderfully supportive, and I relax into it. Our heads are in the grass, but there's hardly any dew, so it doesn't matter.

His face is pale in the faint moonlight, and his skin is cool beneath my palm. Somehow I can't stop touching him. I trace the curve of his forehead then run my index finger downwards over the bridge of his nose to the stubble on his chin.

"Simon, Simon."

There are thin sharp bird cries in the darkness of the valley below us and a cow lows in some distant pasture. It makes me feel scared for no reason.

"I've never injected," he says.

"And?"

"I just wanted you to know that, in case. Hell. I was scared of needles alright." He was. I remember he even hated injecting the horses under the vet's guidance. He'd avert his eyes at the last moment so that he wouldn't have to see the needle puncture their skin.

"What do you want to do?"

"You tell me."

"I'm doing the asking." I lick my lips and shiver slightly as he undoes the top button of my shirt and then the next.

"Okay, I don't think you should be alone, not tonight."

"In case I get nightmares?"

"In case of anything," he says, and I remember something: the two of us in dusty shadow at the back of the barn, my skin smooth with lanolin from fleece rolling. I'd kept up with the New Zealand shearers all day.

Simon had me by the arms, pushed back against the huge poly bags of new fleeces, finger and thumb tight around my narrow bones. "You're fourteen; you should know what you want to do."

"Why? Because you and Jamie do?" The spongy warmth of the fleeces pressed against my back.

"Because you need to think now or you'll waste your

life, get married and, did you fancy them? Did you fancy the shearers?"

"Of course not." But I had a little, the blonde one with the shy grin in particular.

"I don't believe you."

For a moment I felt the imprint of his slim, taut body down the length of mine. His weight pressed in on my chest, and the warm smell of his skin was all around me. Just for a moment, then he let me go and turned towards the light and the sweet powdery scent of wall-flowers.

"That time when we were shearing. I think I knew how you felt then, only I didn't admit it," I say and wait to see if Simon still holds that incident inside him. For a few moments he looks blank then his eyes widen just perceptibly. I only notice because we're so close.

"That was a long time ago."

"Yes." I unbutton his shirt. Cloth can hide a lot. He's thinner than I thought but it doesn't matter, nothing matters as I press my cheek against his skin and listen to the beat of his heart.

"Char." He twists slightly bringing our faces level and then our lips. "Are you alright to do this? I mean after Georgie, I don't know these things."

"Simon, I'm fine."

"You will tell me if I hurt you? We can stop any time."

But I know as I reach for him that we can't, already it's too late. To stop now would tear us apart and leave a wound too deep to heal. Saltwater wouldn't do the job, nor antibiotics or alcohol. There'd always be a scar.

"I love you."

"Oh, Char."

Suddenly our fingers are stumbling and snatching at zips and cloth in their haste to reach skin and trace the lines we only know through clothes. Birdcalls pierce the darkness again as we press our mouths together and I think I hear wings moving fast, a flock of strange small bodies that we'll never see.

Simon's eyes are shut and then open in my face, so close that they're out of focus as I must surely be to him. His lips taste of something that I only half remember. I search back and back, but I can't think what it is as we turn slightly, hips feeling the warm, dark soil uneven through the thinness of his jacket.

We kiss harder and harder, the heat of bruising spreading along our lips in the darkness and still our tongues press deeper into the past reaching for the truth until I'm breathless and dizzy. I never thought about this when we were young, or did I? I try to think of one time with clarity, anytime, but all I have are fragments, odd sensations and cursory moments, shadow touches.

But this is us now. Suddenly I'm crying and all the lies I've ever told slip away into the darkness.

"Char?" His breath brushes across my face, and just for a second the feeling is there, clear and bright and glorious as mountain air, something forgotten and now remembered, a flash of perfect tranquillity. I can count the times on my fingers that I've felt it before in the whole of my life. "Char, are you alright?"

"I'm … I just can't believe after all this time."

"You're so beautiful."

He pauses then brings his hand up beneath my skirt, catching the folds of cloth with his arm and tracing a line through the darkness upwards from my knee. His fingers are warm and gentle, almost hesitant; he doesn't want to make a mistake, not now.

We are so close that I know everything and nothing about him. He's slept with other women, but I mustn't think of their faces, nor their bodies, perhaps thinner and more angular than his once. That bit of our past doesn't count. We're going back, way back to a place where no one can see us, dodging up through acid-smelling bracken, his hand on my arm pulling me onwards, keeping me to himself.

A June bug whirs close past our faces as I spread my legs wide and he lowers himself into me. For a moment his weight against my hips is too much, I tense, and there's a sharp little thread of pain.

"Char?" He pulls back.

"I'm okay." I'm ready for him now, ready to admit what I've never fully admitted even to myself before. I link my hands behind his back and pull him down until he's crushing me into the soil and there is nothing but the two of us swimming through the billowing darkness as one, the smell of the night garden all around us.

———

Afterwards, we lie side by side not quite touching, the ground hard against hip and shoulder and a cold easterly breeze spreading between us. I feel the chill of it run up my legs and catch in the pit of my stomach, twisting into a knot. For a second I feel a nameless, blind panic. "Please don't ever leave me again."

"Char? I'm not going to. I couldn't; I love you too much." His jacket is gone, and his hand feels across the grass for me, searching for my hand until our fingers link and squeeze tight. "You're cold."

"Not really." I stare up at the sky, and for a moment I can't find the words for what I want to say. "This doesn't feel wrong does it?"

"Of course not. It isn't. It's right, totally right, but you are cold."

"Perhaps we should go in."

We stand up and stagger against each other for a second, drunk and disorientated by the darkness and our new knowledge. At my side, the small pale face of a rambling rose nods in the breeze.

"I found something." I press a hard oval into his palm. "My stone was there too, can you believe it after all this time?"

"I know."

"We should use them again."

I close my fingers around the pebble. "Let's put them back; now we're both here."

The moon goes behind a cloud, and the garden is dark as we place the stones in their old place. For a moment our hands rest together on the cool granite.

"I'd like to go and see Jamie tomorrow," Simon says.

17

W e shouldn't have, we shouldn't, we shouldn't, we shouldn't. There's a helicopter low and close, the pressure of its rotors throbs through the house, and something rattles on a shelf in the kitchen. Is it the police over Longcause even now at this early hour? I press my hands against my face, covering my eyes until the darkness blooms but the gloriousness of last night is still there, the warmth of Simon, the imprint of his arms around me, the taste of his mouth against mine.

A cool breeze eddies in through the back door. Did we leave it open? Were we really that careless? I try to think, but I can't remember, then Gel comes bounding in, her coat pointed with dew and her paws muddy.

"Good dog." I wait for Bri, but he doesn't follow. "Where's he gone then?"

I need a strong black tea, the sourness of tannin with a kick of caffeine. I set the kettle to boil on the Rayburn, and the helicopter flies in closer still, now it's right over the house and Gel runs out barking.

Should I go out? Should I run across the fields and over the low wall into the wood while Georgie's still sleeping? Could I find what they're looking for? The photos are in my head again, and now I'm certain that I was right, they were taken from the moor looking back towards this house, only it was obscured by the trees.

"Oh God."

Gel runs in again alone, and this time there's something about her restlessness that catches at me.

"Where's Bri then?" I carry my tea to the open door and call him, my voice floating out across the yard weak against the drone of the helicopter quartering to the west. I wait until it drops away behind the hill then I shout again.

Nothing. I glance up towards Howden without really wanting to, and the dark car is there on the horizon. It could belong to a habitual dog walker, of course, someone with a favourite route across the hill, but I don't think so. It feels more sinister than that.

Gel darts out behind the buildings into the orchard and starts to bark. Is she trying to lead me on? I push my bare feet into a pair of old wellies and head after her.

"Bri, Bri, come on boy, what are you up to?" Perhaps he's got carried away, as bored collies often do, and cornered some stray sheep that he won't let go. "Bri."

The helicopter comes in again, so low overhead this time that all the small birds scatter out of the hedges and I suddenly feel hunted like them.

"Hey." Gel barks at it then runs off again towards the old chicken arks, and I think I catch the edge of a dark shape beyond. "Oh God."

I start to run, and there's Bri lying at an odd angle

behind the nearest ark. He tries to lift his head at the sound of my approach but somehow he can't, and there's a patch of crushed grass around him as though he's been struggling.

"What's up boy?" I crouch down beside him and stroke his head. His muzzle is wet with foam. "Aren't you well?"

For a moment he rolls his eyes at me then he moves and tries to pull himself to his feet. His hindquarters go one way, and his front legs splay out as though they're bending in all the wrong places. After a moment or two, he gives up and paddles the grass feebly with his front paws.

"Okay, okay." He's too big and heavy for me to lift. "You stay right there, and I'll be back very soon."

I run down through the orchard and across the yard. There's a smell of fresh coffee wafting through the house now. "Simon, Simon."

He's in the kitchen dressed in jeans and a grey t-shirt, freshly showered, his hair slicked back and dark with water still, his skin golden. He smiles as soon as I appear and something lurches inside me.

"Simon."

"Come here; I didn't know where you'd gone." He slips an arm around my waist and tries to pull me against him. I want to let myself go in his arms, to taste the coffee on his lips and feel the warmth of him again but I stand my ground.

"Simon, you've got to come quickly, it's Bri, I, I don't know what's wrong with him."

He's exactly where I left him, and Simon stoops to stroke his head. "It's alright boy."

"He looks almost drunk. I mean he tried to get up, but his legs went everywhere."

"He might have been poisoned." Simon's face is grim. "Or bitten by a snake."

"What? Oh God." An image of the rows of plastic water containers in the kitchen leaps into my mind. Did Clare know something? Was her fear justified after all then?

"We need to get him to a vet quickly. I'll carry him if you open the gates."

Bri is heavy and awkwardly floppy. Simon staggers under his weight, but he makes it back to the yard without dropping him.

"Georgie isn't ready." I open the boot of the car for him. "Can you go on your own? What about insurance?"

"Fuck that; we need to get him down there now." Simon pads round the dog with an old blanket then stops. "He looks just like Gyp doesn't he?"

I nod. I'd already thought that, but I didn't want to say. Gyp was Simon's first dog given to him by Robert when things were still good between them, and Simon was to inherit the farm.

"I'll get him down to Abbeyford as quickly as I can." He hugs me for a second, and it's a gesture that promises so much in its casual naturalness. "He'll be alright Char I'm sure he will."

"Let me know as soon as there's news."

I watch him go with an odd feeling deep inside. Of course, he'll come back, of course, they both will and yet- I push the feeling away and go in to find Georgie.

———

It's a restless morning. I can't concentrate on anything indoors, not the jobs I need to be doing or even on the continued search for clues. The latter feels a little pointless now for beyond the window the helicopter circles. In the end, all I can do is watch it from the west window in the spare room, which overlooks the stretch of our fields right out to Longcause Wood, and wait for Simon's call.

Again and again, the helicopter passes across the wood, down the valley and then up and away over Howden only to reappear minutes later. After half an hour the circles grow smaller, and it begins to hover low above the woodland. The sense of foreboding grows intense. What's happening out there? What have they seen? What lurks beneath the canopy?

I sit on the bed and tickle Georgie with a dried flower head. She dabs at it with one hand that is slowly beginning to unfurl as she discovers her fingers and relinquishes the sticky handfuls of fluff that she's clutched at every day for weeks.

A little before eleven Gel starts to bark and bark as though there's someone there and I carry Georgie to the landing window expecting to see the Golf swing into the yard. The cobbles are deserted, and there's no sound of a vehicle pulling up the track.

"Gel, Gel." Still, she barks, and now there's the skitter of claws as she races through the hallway. "Gel."

Downstairs on the mat beneath the letterbox is a rolled up newspaper secured with brown tape. I stop, certain that it wasn't there before. Gel jumps, spins around and barks once.

"Okay. Good dog." I pull open the door. "Hello, who's there?"

The path and yard are deserted. The only movement a blackbird pulling at a worm in the flower border. There's no sound either, no hasty footstep on gravel, no metallic squeak of a gate latch but Gel runs out and round the side of the buildings as though she's heard something. I follow as far as the garden wall, and I'm in time to see her wheel around the beech tree and head back towards me. Glancing up at the flank of Howden I think for a second that I catch a movement in the crook of the moor wall, but when I look again, there's nothing but bracken and gorse.

Back inside I have the sudden urge to slam the door and run the bolts home before I stoop to pick up the paper. My name is written in neat capitals on the brown tape securing it, but there is nothing else, no address, no stamp, no note. I lean back against the door breathing hard. I should bin the paper as it is unopened, unread. I look at the handwriting again as though I expect it to be familiar in some way but of course, it isn't, anyone could write like that, and hundreds do.

In the kitchen, I pull out Georgie's car seat and strap her into it. For a moment she looks like she might cry and her face reddens then her toy octopus catches her attention, and she settles down again.

"Who was it Gel?" I look out of the window uneasily then back down at the paper in my hand. I should throw it away. I hesitate then I slit open the brown sash with my thumbnail. The tabloid unrolls to reveal a photo not of Lee or even Marty but of Simon beneath a lurid headline.

"Oh God."

I don't want to read the text but odd words jump out

at me, and suddenly I can't look away. Yesterday the press was behind. What they said about Marty was bland compared to this. Now they seem to be racing ahead of the police, making connections as they go.

Paragraph by paragraph I'm drawn into the supposed otherness of Simon's world. From the things I know, the death of his parents, his adoption into my family, the incident in the oak wood and what the journalist has called his 'attempted suicide' in public to his endless partying, drinking and drug taking. It's all there, the things he's told me and the things he hasn't.

After the parties came the almost inevitable crash, the death of the horse and the conviction for drink driving. But those are only the starters; the journalist obviously relishes the next bit. His turn of phrase paints a darkening picture of events, a period of deep depression, another conviction for minor shoplifting and then the move to the isolated houseboat 'beyond prying eyes'.

Here it's suggested that Simon has lived alone for years with infrequent visits from men and boys but never women. The inference of homosexuality is there and also of something darker and more sinister. I slam the paper down on the table and stare across the room. I feel dirty for even reading it, like a distasteful eavesdropper. But then I can't stop myself picking it up again and carrying on from where I left off.

The story continues inside the paper. The journalist has managed to track down some of Simon's 'neighbours' among the transient waterborne community, and here he pieces together some derogatory snippets about Simon's aloofness, his strange night-time behaviour and long unexplained absences in the early hours of the morning. There is no mention of his passion for horses, his cycling, his fitness and his need to be outdoors. Everything is twisted and somehow made to read like the story of a completely different person.

By the time I reach the last paragraph I'm shaking, and I can hardly focus on the images that intersperse the text. There's a dark picture of the houseboat, which manages to make it appear sinister and unwelcoming although in reality the stretch of river is probably beautiful and silent, and another photo of Simon looking tired and wary.

"Oh God."

My phone rings and I jump as though someone has looked over my shoulder and caught me reading something that I shouldn't. It'll be Simon. I fold the paper over before answering.

"Charlotte." It's Dan. He's read the story then. I grip my left hand into a fist.

"It isn't true."

"I'm sorry?"

"What they're saying in the tabloids, it's, it's slander. You mustn't believe it." Gel comes up close and leans against me, and I caress her head.

"I haven't read the papers today, should I?"

"No, please don't."

"Charlotte, are you okay?" As always there are office sounds in the background, other calls, other people, some perhaps listening in.

"I'm fine." I take a deep, steadying breath. He's checking up on me before the Warwick photo shoot. I don't blame him. "And yes this time I'll be there."

"It's only four days away. Are you sure?"

"Of course." I'll be able to do it, to focus my mind and hold a steady hand. It won't be easy, and I'll have to fetch my desktop from the flat or borrow another laptop if I don't get mine back from the police, but I can't afford to let this job go. Whatever happens, I'll blank my mind to the thoughts reeling around the beautiful old rooms; I'll see what I need, the shapes, the images, the nuances of light. It's only one day after all.

"Liv is quite happy to do it if you can't."

I'm sure she is. It's her chance. My work ending in her glory. "I'll be there, don't worry."

———

When he's gone, I look at the paper again. There's no hope of fairness for Simon now. These words, these images will be in everyone's minds.

"Damn it."

I dial the incident room number and wait. "Amanda Miller please."

She comes on the line almost straight away, and her voice is calm as though nothing is wrong.

"You must have seen what they're saying about Simon. I don't care what you said last time, you've got to do something about it."

"I do understand how upsetting this must be for you." Her voice is professional, measured. She's been trained well for this.

"Stuff that, it's just wrong, it's defamation, inflammatory, prejudicial." I need to keep my voice down, or I'll wake Georgie.

"What exactly do you think isn't true?"

I cast my eyes over the article, and suddenly I see how cleverly written it is. There's nothing that you can quite pin down; it's all suggested by omission rather than written out, perhaps the dark accusations are only in my mind.

"It's harassment." I bite my bottom lip.

"Do you want to lodge a complaint?"

"If you had any idea, any idea at all. God, there's probably someone watching the house right now." I take a deep breath, I need to stay calm, but the tears are close suddenly.

"Can I speak to Hollinghurst?"

"I'm afraid he isn't here right now."

"Okay, thanks." I shut off my phone, and for a moment I can't move then I jump up and stuff the paper into the dustbin. "Leave us alone, just, oh please."

But I know that they won't. Not while Simon's on bail. While the possibility of guilt clings to him, the reporters will keep digging and finding all the filth that they want or twisting around what they do find until it sounds unhealthy, sinister, criminal.

There's the sound of a vehicle on the track, and I go to the window in time to see the Golf swing in through the gateway.

"Simon." I watch him climb out of the car; weariness makes his limbs stiff and his movements careless. He slams the door and pushes his fingers through his hair before turning towards the house. There's no sign of Bri with him, no black and white collie face pressed to the window behind him, and something tightens beneath my ribs.

"Where's Bri? What's happened?" I meet him at the door and for a second before he reaches out to me the journalist's words dance between us. I don't want to think about them, but they're lodged inside me now invisible yet insidious. Who were the men, the boys who visited his houseboat?

"Char." He holds me tight, and I rest my head against his chest, the clean, familiar scent of his shirt is laced with the chemical smell of the vets now. "I've had to leave him there I'm afraid. They think he might have been poisoned, but they're not sure. It could be something else, a tiny fracture in his neck. They did loads of tests, but the results were all coming back negative."

Poisoned, deliberately. The possibility hangs between us. The why and the who. I stuff the thoughts down. We don't know.

"And? Is he going to be alright?" I've only known the dog for such a short time, but already he's grown familiar and loyal in his own aloof way.

"The vets have done everything they can; we just have to wait now and see how he is later. But if-"

"No." I step back. His face is hard, the muscles in his jaw clenched.

"He's not going to get away-"

"Stop Simon. Don't say it." I think of the rook suddenly and the fox, innocent victims or the real targets? On one level it hardly matters which, the danger is real enough and the poison could be anywhere on the farm, a baited rat, soaked chocolate drops lying in the grass. On another level though, the intent makes all the difference. It means something that I don't want to think about.

The idea hits me as I stand there and suddenly it seems the only thing to do, a possible solution to all of this. "I've got to go out."

"What? Where?" He looks surprised and then wary. "Has something else happened?"

I shake my head. I don't trust my voice.

"I'll come with you."

"No, no I need to be on my own."

18

The house was never beautiful; it was modernish back then, pebble-dashed and surrounded by tarmac. Sandra's mother was always trying to soften it with plants, and now all her efforts have paid off. In fact, the garden has taken over so wildly that for a moment I wonder if I heard wrong in the supermarket. Has Helena left the house empty and moved on?

I park up and lift Georgie out of the car aware that there might be unseen eyes watching me. When I turn round the front door is open, and Helena is standing on the step.

"Charlotte, how lovely to see you." She smiles, and her warmth appears genuine, but does she mean it? "Come in; I've got the kettle on."

The kitchen is the same as my vague memory of it, and the smell is at once familiar. As she pours tea into two yellow mugs all I can think about are the peppermint creams we used to make in their childish tin foil wraps, rounds of sickly sweetness.

"So?" After the compulsory baby cuddling moment

we sit down, and there's another Siamese cat, generations on but equally friendly. Georgie stares at it, and it opens its blue eyes extra wide at her. "What a time you're having."

"I hope you don't mind me coming round." I feel awkward suddenly. I still haven't been able to get hold of Arthur, and his silence bugs me more than I'd care to admit. It feels as though no one locally trusts us now.

"My dear, I'm glad you have. Sandra will be so sorry to have missed you. She's gone back to Kent now of course. I do miss her, but she comes down as often as she can."

Her words are spoken without deliberate intent I'm sure, but they fill me with guilt nonetheless, and I concentrate on my tea for a moment.

What I need to know, what I have to ask. I look up again.

"What you said about Clare the other day, it was true wasn't it? About her and Lee?"

"I'm afraid that I only actually saw her once after Robert's funeral and she was rather, distracted. She phoned-"

"Yes?"

"In the middle of the night several times."

"Oh." Despite the sun shining in through the window, I feel cold.

"She thought she'd heard someone outside. I told her to call the police, but I don't think she ever did."

I think of Simon knocking on the door and of his torchlight running across the ceiling.

"I'm sorry."

"No, it's alright."

"But before that, well she obviously really cared

about Lee." Helena's face is soft beneath a sweep of thick grey hair caught up at the back in a French knot with a pencil. "She used to worry about him being on his own so much. I know Marty had to work and Peter was always out on the farm, but it was such a lonely life for him. Boys of that age, they need friends, adventures. Goodness, I know my three were up to no good if you left them alone for five minutes. Not that I'm suggesting that Lee- Actually I think it was rather the opposite."

"How do you mean?" I feel even warier suddenly.

"If you don't mind me saying, I think he was a little like Jamie used to be. You know, always doing school work." She lowers her head, takes a sip of tea then looks straight at me. "She never got over that. I don't suppose any of you have."

"No. Have you told the police this?"

She nods, and I wonder what else she said to them. She'll know other things I'm sure, things that I can't ask Arthur now. She'll know whether Robert's dream came true, whether, in the end, he ever felt that all his hard work had paid off. I dig my fingers into my palms. To know or not to know?

His dream was a great glass building reaching high into the sky. So high that when you were standing right outside it, you couldn't even be sure that you could see its roof. The point where it appeared to give way to the sky could have been a false peak like some mountains have.

It was an impractical building for anywhere locally; it belonged in a city, perhaps not even in England. He used to arch his hands above his head creating the roofline for me. I remember having to squint against the sun to see what he meant. Sometimes he'd even describe it in such detail that I could trace the drops of rain, the prints of unknown fingers, even the grains of dust on the glass.

"Dad's big project?"

"There was some interest," Helena says being gentle. "I think a firm in Canada was looking at the plans."

Too late. I sigh. Oh, Robert, why couldn't we have talked properly? Why didn't I ask you the same question I've just asked Helena? I had the chance last time you were in London, but all we did was storm round the Tate in time for you to catch your train back to Devon. I didn't even buy you a coffee that day, you were too busy being angry about naïve young upstarts who you said were cube builders rather than architects, and I was too full of irritation about that.

"I can't believe that Clare would ever have intended to do Lee any harm," Helena says, and I study her face. It's more lined but still familiar after all this time. Is she trying to tell me something? I stroke the top of Georgie's head and take a deep breath.

"Did Simon come back do you know? Did Clare ever mention it?" As soon as I've finished speaking my cheeks burn. There is in the questions far more of an admittance than I care to make and I feel like a traitor.

Helena is silent for a while then her hand comes to rest on my arm. "I didn't see him, and no, Clare never mentioned it. I've heard the rumours of course, but you can't believe everything that's said. You must ask him though because if you don't, it'll eat you up."

She's right. I sink my face forward against Georgie and smell the sweet warmth of her hair.

"I'm scared."

"Of course you are, we all are."

We sit in silence for a few moments and I stroke Georgie's cheek with my index finger.

"I've got some peppermint creams," Helena says at last, and we both smile in recollection. "Sandra's boys helped me make them but to be honest I don't have such a sweet tooth anymore, and I'm struggling to get through them. Why don't you take some back for Simon?"

"Thanks."

They've made the same funny little silver trays that we used to and probably think that they look as grown up as we did, although, in reality, they are quite obviously odd cardboard boxes covered in tin foil.

"Look after yourselves and do let me know as soon as there's news. I miss Clare."

———

I make a decision and drive on into town. Georgie needs a feed first, so I give her half an hour in the car park. While she drinks a memory surfaces in my mind, one that I haven't thought about for a long time.

We jumped hand in hand off the top of Little Hartor the day I broke my ankle. It was glorious for nanoseconds and bad luck that the rougher ground was on my side, it didn't look that way from above.

"Shit." Simon's face was white as he leant over me in the grass and his fingers were clumsy; they pressed in all the wrong places and made things worse. Hot pain rushed up my leg, and I knew that I was with the wrong brother.

Uncle Eric was there when we got back to the house.

No one had told us that he was coming down and both he and Clare looked hot and surprised when we finally tracked them down and staggered into Clare's studio.

"My darling." Clare gathered herself together in seconds, swept back her plait and straightened a crease in the front of her shirt. Uncle Eric's hands were far gentler than Simon's, he'd been a paramedic in some previous life. He wrapped an ice pack round my ankle and gave me some arnica before the trip to the hospital.

Uncle Eric drove because Robert was out until the evening and for a few strange hours we were like a different little family unit. We were so natural together that if anyone had looked at us, they would surely have thought we belonged together in a way that we never did.

———

When Georgie has finished drinking I buckle her sling around my waist and lift her into it before hooking the straps over my shoulders. Hopefully, she'll stay calm. I take a chance and walk into the police station.

"I need to speak to Detective Inspector Hollinghurst." I give my name and wait. It takes him five minutes to come out to me.

"Charlotte."

"I need to talk to you."

He shows me into a different room this time, a blank little interview space with a low ceiling and a single scarred radiator. Was this where he brought Simon, where he spent the twenty-four hours that he won't talk about? It's starting to feel like a mistake being here when the door swings open, and Quinn comes in. Our eyes meet for a second, but he doesn't smile.

"So?" Hollinghurst's edginess is closer to impatience today. Things are changing, moving on.

"Is there any news?" I don't sit down at once. There's a table between us, sticky with coffee rings.

"We've been up to Longcause Wood. I think you were right about the photos, but we haven't found anything yet." He's not giving away any other information; his expression is clear about that.

"The media aren't exactly helping." I have to be careful to keep the anger out of my voice. I need him on my side, trusting me.

"I understand how you're feeling and I believe you've been talking to Miller about it. I promise you we are monitoring the situation."

"Thank you." It's hard to stop myself saying any more.

"You have something to tell me though?"

Like the grandfather clock at Northstone the digital square on the wall here is flicking over the minutes. Measuring out the time between Lee's life and death, eroding the possibility of anything else bit by bit by bit.

"Well?"

In my head, in Simon's arms this seemed like a good idea, but now with the two of them in the room-

"Miss Elgin, could we come to the point please because we need to get on."

What I'm about to do is for the best, I know it is, for everyone. It can't harm Lee if anything it could help him.

"It's about Simon." I sit down, and his eyes don't leave my face.

"Go on."

"I-" Now that I'm here with his full attention the words tangle themselves up in my mind. I take a deep breath. "I need to be sure that this won't appear in the tabloids tomorrow."

"It won't come from us."

"There is something they haven't found out, something that I should have told you before, I'm sorry, but it's rather personal." I stop, and he waits silently. "It's about Simon and me, we, well we're together."

"I see."

"It isn't illegal because he's my adopted brother, but we keep it quiet. No one down here knows, and our parents certainly didn't." Even as I say it, I'm not sure that it's the truth. There was something in Helena's eyes. I think she knew.

"Okay." He steeples his fingers and rests his chin against the tips. For a second it looks as though he's engaging in a silent prayer and I'm disconcerted.

"Why I'm telling you this, well the night that Clare and Lee disappeared Simon was with me in the Wiltshire cottage I'd rented."

"Ah." He lets out his breath and smiles. "Now I see where this is going. Can you prove it?"

"Sorry?"

"Did anyone see you together there?"

"Well no, that's the whole point, I pay for the isolation, and usually I don't even see the owners. I pay online, and they leave a key hidden for me. We didn't see anyone all weekend."

"How convenient."

He doesn't believe me, and I can't look at Quinn. I feel hot suddenly, and I want to run from the room and away down the street. Instead, I force myself to sit still and calm my breathing. He may not believe me, but he can't be sure that I'm not telling the truth. If he tries to check up, he won't be able to prove things one way or the other. No one did see me the whole weekend.

"And another thing, someone's poisoned one of our dogs."

"What?" Hollinghurst's expression sharpens, and I tell him about Bri.

———

I call the vets before I leave town. Bri has come round, and they think that he's going to be alright, but they want to monitor him overnight to be sure.

"Oh thank God." At least one thing has gone right today.

When I reach the farm, Simon is pale and distant. He hardly smiles when I come in nor when I tell him about Bri.

"What's up?" I put my hand on his arm, but he snatches it away. "Simon?"

"Nothing."

"There's obviously something."

"I don't want to talk about it." He turns from me, and it isn't until much later that he comes into the room and slams the tabloid down on the table in front of me. "Where did this come from?"

I've prepared some proper food at last. I had to go shopping for nappies on my way back from the police station, and I bought us some treats: fresh pasta, sundried tomatoes, artichoke hearts, olives and focaccia with mango sorbet for dessert. I even drizzled olive oil and balsamic vinegar into a saucer for dipping.

I wanted to pitch it right, not too formal or over the top for the situation but something a bit special to mark last night. I thought, I hoped we might have a quiet meal together. Not romantic in the circumstances but somehow companionable.

"Oh, Simon."

"Well, you've obviously read it." He won't meet my eye.

"No, yes. I'm sorry, I didn't mean to, I shouldn't have done."

"What does it matter, everyone else will have. I mean what the fuck now?"

"It's so unfair, so wrong. It's not you." I put my hand out to him, but he turns away.

"Isn't it?"

"No."

"Where have you been today?" His voice is dull.

"Shopping, I told you." Now it's my turn to be evasive.

"And?"

I close my eyes. I don't want to tell any more lies. "I went to talk to Hollinghurst."

"Great. To tell him how much of what they're saying is true I suppose?"

"Simon. I told him that you were with me the night Clare and Lee disappeared."

"You did what?" His expression changes and his gaze locks onto my face. "Char."

"I thought, well you needed an alibi."

"But they'll check up."

"So? It was a remote place, that was the whole point. No one will have seen anything either way."

"Oh God, I don't believe it." He stands up and walks across to the window. "How could you?"

"I thought it was the best thing to do."

"To lie?"

"I'm good at it."

"So it seems." He grabs his plate from the table and dumps all the beautiful uneaten food into the bin. "Any other nasty little secrets in here then?"

"Simon."

"I'm going out." The door slams behind him.

———

He doesn't come back for hours and suddenly this night is too close to another, the twenty years between nothing but a blink of time. How did that journalist find out about the so-called 'public suicide attempt', that terrible row in The Ring of Bells? Who has he talked to? Someone around here, someone close by.

"Bloody hell."

I can still feel the drizzle of that evening on my face, the late winter chill followed by the wall of heat as I walked into the pub and all faces turned towards me.

Robert hadn't told me what was happening. There'd been a phone call half overheard from the top of the stairs, and he'd left the house suddenly in silence as he often did, only that time I'd sensed that something was very wrong and that it involved Simon.

"I'll be there in ten minutes," Robert said, and that was my only clue. Surely it meant that Simon was in the village somewhere. I took a chance. It was possible to beat the car to the village if you ran really fast down the shortcut or at least Simon had.

I grabbed my coat and ran but I was slower than him, and Robert's old car was parked outside the pub by the time I arrived on the green out of breath and trembling slightly from the jarring descent through the oak wood.

I had a horrible feeling as soon as I saw it there. I'd smelt the alcohol on Simon's breath for the past few weeks, and his eyes were often bloodshot and his hands less steady.

Barry Southway was at the bar, I can picture his tattooed forearms even now, and the others, Vicki, Rick, Tony, Howard and Paul, were crowded around tables near the inglenook. There were strangers too, but I hardly looked at them. All I saw was Simon holding a knife in Robert's face, six inches of darkened abused steel that we usually used to slice open bales of hay.

"Simon." My voice floated across to him, and he looked right at me then shook his head.

"Simon don't be an idiot, put the knife down." Robert's jacket was damp across the shoulders from the rain.

"Just like that?" Simon smoothed the blade through the air and Robert tried to take a step back, but he was pushed up against a table.

"Simon listen to me now."

"Me listen to you? Hah, is that a joke?"

"Simon." I tried to get his attention again, but he wouldn't even look at me. His face was flushed, and his golden hair was tangled and damp. "Simon."

"Put the knife down now."

"I didn't mean it to happen, but perhaps you're right, perhaps it would be better if I wasn't here."

It seemed to take place in slow motion, or perhaps that's only how I remember it now. Simon raised his left hand until his arm was at chest level, turned his wrist and ran the blade across the back of it in one smooth movement.

"Simon, no."

The bracelet of blood sprang out instantly, and within seconds it was dripping onto the floor.

"You idiot." Rick jumped forward first, but Simon was quicker than him and shook himself free. The next moment he was running right at me.

"Simon." For an instant I had his arm then he wrenched the door open and swept out into the darkness. "Simon."

It was raining hard, and my torch battery was low, the light feeble. Simon's footsteps echoed on the tarmac for a few strides then they were gone. I swung the torch beam and caught his back disappearing through a gateway.

"Wait." I reached the gate but the field beyond was blank empty darkness that my torch barely caressed and there were no distinct sounds beyond the rain and the wind in the trees behind the shop.

"Charlotte. Charlotte." Robert was behind me calling me back to the car, to the farm, to my new life without Simon, only I didn't know that then. We all thought for days that he would come back, if not sooner then perhaps later, but as the time stretched out my fear and anger grew.

"No way." I don't want history to repeat itself and yet I seem unable to stop it. With Georgie, I'm trapped in the dark farmhouse. I can't run out calling through the fields or even really drive around the lanes with her at this time. It wouldn't be fair; her sleep is already disturbed enough as it is.

For an hour or more I pace through the shadowy rooms downstairs fingering items of Clare's that I've seen a hundred times before, a worry doll, a half-finished piece of embroidery on a round frame, a shepherd's crook propped in a corner, but I hardly see them and think even less about them. My mind is out searching the darkness, wondering where he is, how far he's gone already and whether he has any intention of returning this time.

Georgie wakes as usual, and after I've fed her, there seems no point in waiting up any longer. In fact, a dull certainty that he won't come back settles over me. I'm lying alone in the bed that we've only shared for the one night with the pillow that still smells faintly of him pressed against my face when Gel stirs, and I hear something in the yard. I've locked the doors, so I go down. Simon is standing on the back doorstep with his head hanging.

"Can I come in?"

I hold the door open for him, and he steps into the hallway where we stand close but not touching.

"I'm sorry," he says, and suddenly we're in each other's arms.

"I thought you weren't coming back."

"Char. I'd always come back to you."

There's a fresh scratch on his cheek. I wipe away the blood with the tip of my index finger. "But-"

"I know, I know. But this is now."

"Please don't do that again."

"What they said, you know it isn't true don't you?" His gaze flickers across my face then away to a corner of the room and back.

"Shoplifting?"

He sighs and strokes my hair. "It was stupid; I don't know what came over me. I, I can't explain. One minute I was in the shop and the next- I didn't keep the necklace, I gave it away."

"You stole a necklace?" I feel cold suddenly.

"I could have paid for it, I meant to, so I don't know why, I had the money. It would have looked beautiful on you."

"On me?"

"The partying wasn't much fun either," he says, and I feel sad for him. He was so young and good looking that the party scene should have been his for the taking.

"And the drugs?" I can imagine him stoned if I try or high on some coloured tablet, his movements manic and his mind racing with a hundred different ideas at once while his words slurred out. But the aftermath, that's harder. I don't want to think about the times he might have lain ugly in recovery, his skin sallow and his eyes bloodshot.

"Okay, but the big things aren't true. That's what I meant. You know that don't you?"

"I think so."

He's silent for a while, but when I look up at him, questioningly he smiles.

"Do remember that time you held me in the stable? Just before-"

"You ran away. Yes, I remember." I can still taste the salty darkness and hear Eb's hooves dancing on the cobbles, crazed from galloping after one of those hard, solitary rides that left him run up and dark with sweat.

"That meant so much to me."

"Really?" He'd been thin then as well but it was a different kind of thinness, an unhealthy thinness and his skin was reddened and chapped from the wind. We hadn't shared a meal for months, and I wondered when he was eating.

"I just couldn't tell you."

"And I thought you were angry with me for trying to get you to talk to Robert." I'd flung out my arms encircling the 'everything' that we never talked about and scared Eb with my sudden movement. He'd jumped away to the corner of his box, and Simon had had to calm him again, his hands gentling down the narrow, damp neck with more confidence than he showed over anything else by then.

"Well I was, but that hug." He stops and fingers the hem of his shirt. "They blamed me Char, and I thought you did too."

"No way. Never." I'd put my arms around him and pulled him against me. His jacket was all caught up, and the end of the zip stuck into my neck. I do the same now, and he slides his arms around my back and grips me as tight as he did then only there's nothing but thin cotton between us this time and I can feel the warmth of his body.

"Is this what it was like with Marty?" That's what he'd asked then catching me off guard. "When you were together, is this how you hugged?"

"Simon?" I took a step back from him and looked up at his face. "We never."

"I don't know that's all. I've never been with a girl."

282

He'd lowered his head and begun to dig at the straw with a toe.

Now he looks down at me, our faces close. "I know they wished that they'd never made the stupid offer to adopt me."

"Simon, that isn't true."

"Isn't it? If I hadn't come into your family none of that and maybe none of this would ever have happened."

"You can't think like that."

"You thought I might be gay that night, d'you remember?"

"I was rather wrong, wasn't I?" I laugh, but it tails off into silence.

"And you thought I was sleeping around, that I was with someone all the nights I spent at Simpson's barn."

It was true. Simon hadn't brought any girls home, but he'd slept away from the farm on countless nights. I'd felt sure that he must have had sex by then, probably more times than he'd care to admit. It was then that the gay thought had dawned on me.

"Is that where you went? I never knew, but I always wondered. You looked so terrible."

"Like now?"

"Don't be crazy; you don't look so bad now."

"The photographs-"

"You can make almost anyone look terrible with the wrong lighting." But there's beauty in his edginess; even the poorest, roughest shots haven't been able to obliterate his good looks.

We're both silent and now as well as the photos, words from the tabloid float into my mind, I don't want them, but they come anyway tainting my thoughts. Here we are again, up against the apparent absence of women in his life. A lack that is somehow made to seem unnatural because of his good looks, suggestive of something else, something seedier.

"The boys." He knows what I'm thinking now as he so often did in the past. The colour rises in my cheeks as he brushes the hair off my forehead and runs a finger across my temple. "They're my Godsons, Henry and Ed. One's into cycling, and the other loves boats, so it's great, their mother left for another man when they were three and four."

"Bloody Kyle what's his face." I curse the unseen reporter.

19

W e fetch Bri from the vet the next morning. He's limp and washed out, but he wags his tail and can stand for a minute or so.

"He should be alright now, but watch him closely for the next few days. If he starts to go downhill again bring him straight back in. He's been lucky." Old Hemmings the vet studies our faces, checking to see that we've understood what he's said but also for something else. Is he looking for the truth in us? His hair has thinned to nothing on top, and his face is deeply tanned and lined from being outdoors in all weathers.

Simon and I spent many hours with him in the past helping at a difficult calving or holding an injured horse. I close my eyes for a second. If we'd stayed, if things had been different, people like Hemmings would have been part of our lives. We'd have paid them money and toasted their successes. Simon might have worked with them, and for them, hands close together on the rough stone of a fallen wall, skin slicked with rain. I'd have known their children and spoken to their wives.

"I can't say for sure, but it looked to me like some kind of poisoning." Hemmings strokes Bri's head one last time. "I'd keep a close eye on your other stock as well at the moment."

That would normally be Arthur's job, but there's still no sign of him coming back to the farm. We'll have to go there now, across the fields stretched out in the sunshine where the unseen danger lies.

"Thank you."

––––––––

"That's it, he's gone too far this time," Simon says as soon as we're back in the car.

"Simon."

"He's not going to-"

"We don't know for sure, so please leave it." I sink my face forward into my hands and take several deep breaths. "Can't you see what this is doing to us all? It's, it's getting just like before, it's got to stop."

"But-"

"Simon, no."

He jerks his seatbelt and then his seat and stares out of the side window with his lips set in a line. It doesn't look as though he's going to speak to me all the way back to the farm. I'm tempted to switch on the radio, but I don't. I haven't logged onto the Internet either since the previous day. It's slow and frustrating on my mobile and only forces me to remember where my laptop is.

Even though it's only a few hours without news, I feel out of touch. Hollinghurst hasn't called, and his silence unnerves me. He's sure to have been checking up on my story. I can't think of any way that he can be sure about that weekend in Wiltshire, and yet I suddenly have the niggly feeling that there's some clue to my solitary stay that I've forgotten.

"I'm sorry I didn't eat that food last night," Simon says abruptly, depressing the window and keeping his face turned away from me. "It looked great, and it was such a lovely thought as well."

"Not insensitive in the circumstances?"

"Eating junk or starving ourselves isn't going to bring them back."

When we reach the farm, we settle Bri in his bed by the Rayburn with a bowl of water close by and then suddenly there's a gap. A stretch of time until Georgie's next feed and nappy change which has no preordained activity to be crammed in. We look at each other recognising the limbo and feeling the discomfort of it. Surely there must be something that we can do, anything to help.

"We were going to see Jamie," Simon says. "I haven't seen him since last month, so perhaps one of us should still go."

He's right; it's been longer than that since I was last at Fairfax what with Georgie's birth and everything and guilt pricks at me.

"He might not have realised how long-" My voice trails off. We don't know that; we don't know anything for sure about Jamie's thoughts now.

"D'you want to go? I don't mind looking after Bri if you do." Simon's hand comes to rest on mine. His skin is warm and smooth.

"Of course I would, but I think it would be better if you went this time. I'd have to feed Georgie first and then, well I'm not sure if it would be a good thing to take her. I mean not yet. I want her to meet Jamie one day, but perhaps she's too young right now."

"Okay, if you're sure."

"I'll phone my insurance company and get the car insurance updated."

He leaves after a quick snack, and the house feels empty and silent without him. I know it was my choice to stay, but I suddenly feel trapped and powerless none-theless, the dusty silence claustrophobic. I try to busy myself with mundane domestic tasks, but I can't settle to any of them. All the time I'm listening for the sound of a vehicle outside, for an engine, for the helicopter, for anything that would give me a clue as to what the police are doing now.

Once or twice I go up to the spare room and stare out of the west window, but there's no sign of any activity over at Longcause today. Were the pictures a hoax then after all or-? I push the other thoughts away and spin round. I need to prepare myself for the photo shoot anyway, to clear my head a little so that I can focus on the job ahead.

"It'll be fine Georgie, good for us." But again it feels wrong to go, like leaving a sinking ship while there's still a chance to check for survivors. But I have to earn a living and what the hell can I do for Lee now?

———

The police helicopter comes in low over the garden at teatime, and I start. For a few moments everything trem-bles under the shock of sound then the helicopter rises up and away and begins to quarter back and forth over the higher fields. Bri stands up, and Gel runs out barking, chivvying a group of Peter's sheep up into the top corner of the orchard and on through a gap in the hedge. I stand in the open doorway and whistle, but she's not listening.

"Gel, come on."

After a day of conspicuous absence, this sudden police activity is unnerving. I can't work out what it means, but I wish that Simon was here with me. I stand at the landing window with Georgie in my arms. Her skin looks oddly pale in the sunlight, and a niggle of anxiety worms its way beneath my ribs.

"You're alright aren't you?" I hug her to me and run my index finger around the stripes of her babygrow. "Just tired eh?"

The helicopter flies down over the house again, and Gel runs back, her barks high and anxious.

"Okay, okay." She races up the stairs to me, and I stoop to catch hold of her collar. "You stay here now."

Bri barks in the kitchen, a sore restless noise. I don't blame him. The sound of the helicopter is under my skin now as well. It makes it hard to concentrate on anything else. I'm either trying to work out exactly where it is and what it might have located or waiting for it to return. Gel lies down beside me then bounces to her feet again almost at once.

"Look you two." I know that Georgie won't settle to feed with the dogs agitating around, so I carry her into the spare room and lie down on the bed with her. It's the only room in the house that contains few memories, and usually, it soothes me spending time with her like this but now I'm on edge, listening to the sounds beyond the room. First, the helicopter circling again, then the calls of restless sheep, closely followed by the dogs barking and Gel padding up and down the stairs.

Georgie drinks intermittently and seems equally distracted. After little more than twenty minutes she's done, and I carry her back downstairs. The sun is sinking and, although on the surface it's a near perfect evening outside, there's an eeriness about the sudden silence that puts me on edge. I used to love being out on Howden at this time with the whole valley laid out before me and the scents of bracken and heather filling the air as the dew settled, but not tonight. Who knows what might be hidden in the bracken up there or who might step out from behind the wall.

For some reason even the Northstone fields feel unsafe, the hedgerows shady alleys of danger, high and tangled enough to hide a grown man. I don't want to be alone here suddenly but where's Simon? I thought he'd be back by now. I check my watch and make a quick calculation. It would surely only take about an hour to drive to Fairfax from here and another back. Once there he'd be unlikely to spend more than an hour with Jamie. So, going by that, he's already several hours late.

The delay makes me uneasy and all at once Marty's words are in my mind. "I saw him with my own eyes. Don't you think it's a bit too much of a coincidence? He comes back, and then Lee and Clare disappear."

"No way." Why am I thinking this now? I must be tired that's all, and yet the more I try to reason myself out of it, the more this weird sense of paranoia clutches at me. If I concentrate, I can still feel Simon's arms around me and the pressure of his lips against mine and yet now the memory is edged with uncertainty. What if I'm wrong about him? Suddenly other words bubble up in my mind, something else Marty said long ago. "You've changed since Simon came, you're different when you're with him. I don't understand you anymore."

I have to pack ready for the photo shoot. That's what I need to be focusing on, not these crazy random thoughts. I start to check my things, but I can't concentrate, and my thoughts drift away again almost at once.

The last time I visited Fairfax, just before Georgie was born, when the steps up to the front door were steeper, and fog clung to the grey stone, Jamie seemed much the same as usual. He grinned at me from beneath his red fringe as though he might know me and linked his arm through mine as we walked up the long carpeted corridors. But when we turned a corner, he leaned on me more heavily than before, and his face glistened with sweat.

I tried to tell myself that his weight gain was only a natural progression. Didn't every man begin to spread in his mid to late thirties, the tightness of youth replaced by blossoming middle age? On one level I could make myself believe that, but on another, I had a sense that something bigger and more frightening was happening to Jamie.

Simon took my mobile and was going to call when he got there, but now his silence unnerves me. I glance at my watch then go downstairs and pick up the house phone. My mobile rings outside on the garden table.

"Oh God." I put the house phone down.

By the time I reach the lawn my mobile is ringing again. For a few seconds I'm taken aback and confused, then I pick it up. I don't recognise the number that flashes across the screen.

"Charlotte." Simon's voice sounds breathless and panicked, and there are other people in the background in a large echoey space. My heart starts to thud.

"What's up? Where are you?"

"It's Jamie."

"Jamie?"

"He's, he's. God, Charlotte can you come? We're at the last services off the M5, in the petrol station."

"We? What the hell's going on?"

"I couldn't leave him there."

"Oh no, Simon. No way."

"It was fine until I had to stop for fuel."

"How could you?" I stare down the valley, and the distance seems to fold in on itself in the heat.

"He won't get back in the car."

"What were you thinking?"

"Is Bri alright? Can you come out here in Clare's car? Charlotte?"

"Okay, okay. Just go and keep talking to Jamie. Have you let the staff at Fairfax know? Simon, this could be classed as abduction."

"Will you call them? Please?"

"Oh for God's sake."

———

There's a tailback on the motorway and another on the roundabout before the services, but at last, we're there. I peel off into the petrol station, and it takes me a moment or so before I spot the Golf parked over near the air machine and vacuum. Simon and Jamie are sitting a little way away under an ornamental maple sapling on the steep grass bank. For a second before Simon notices us he's a stranger and there's tension in every line of his body, then he glances in our direction and waves before stumbling down to meet us.

"Thank God you're here Char." He stares at me through the open window, and his eyes are jittery. His expression reminds me of his photo on the front page of the tabloid. "He just got out of the car when we stopped, and now he won't move. Don't be angry, please."

What if? I should open the door and reach out to him but dark thoughts circle round me and somehow I can't. A weight drops inside me, and I try not to think about last night.

"Char?" A look of uncertainty crosses his face.

"How the hell did you get this far?"

"We went for a walk in the garden, that's all. We were near the car park, and Jamie wanted to look at the cars. I didn't plan this, honestly. He just sat in the Golf and then, well there were no nurses around, they were all busy indoors-"

"Fairfax isn't happy; they were about to call the police."

"Oh God."

"Is that all you've got to say? I thought you might have grown out of this sort of thing." I grip the steering wheel hard for a few seconds.

"I see." He takes a step away from me.

"Do you though? We're not teenagers anymore."

"Meaning?" He swings back, and his face flushed.

"Fairfax don't mind home visits for goodness sake, but they have to be planned. There's paperwork to fill out and-"

"It's like a prison then." He glances over his shoulder at Jamie who isn't even looking in our direction.

"No. The carers just have to be sure that their clients are safe."

"Behind locked doors."

"We'll drive him back now. I'd better go and talk to him."

"I'm not taking him back there, it is like a prison, a beautiful prison, I've always thought that. We can't-"

"Simon he needs special care." The muscles between my shoulders tighten and a headache throbs from nowhere.

"He needs real life."

"Like this?" There's a smell of burnt petroleum in the air and the constant roar of traffic passing less than fifty metres behind Jamie's back. "I'll go and say hello if you keep an eye on Georgie."

The bank is steep and slippery with long rank grass. Jamie watches in silence as I stagger to stay upright and eventually give in and put one hand out to steady myself. He's wearing shapeless jeans and a baggy white t-shirt, and I'm reminded of an inmate. Even from a distance, there is some indefinably different quality about him, something that would make you wary if you didn't know him.

"Hi, Jamie. How are you doing?"

There's a flurry of litter beyond him, old crisp packets and drinks bottles, even a couple of takeaway cartons. I don't want to look too closely at what else might be lurking in the grass.

"It isn't very nice up here, why don't you come down?"

Simon is watching my back. I can feel his eyes on me, but I don't look round.

"You know who Simon is, don't you? Come on, let's go down and join him."

Jamie's face is pale, his jawline lost in a swell of fat that has thickened a little more each time I've seen him over the past few years.

"I'm sorry I haven't been to visit you for a while, but you remember that I told you I was going to have a baby, well she's here. Georgie's in the car."

He moves his feet, digging his heels into the damp turf and dislodging a can that rolls away down the slope and eventually settles on the concrete pad at the bottom.

"We can't stay up here all afternoon. Please, Jamie." I hold out my hand to him, and he looks at it for a long time before taking it. When I pull back, he's a dead weight, and I think we'll stay trapped on this grotty patch of grass by his silence. "Come on."

We reach the forecourt in a jarring rush, and Jamie leans against Clare's car to catch his breath. Inside Georgie squawks at the sight of me.

"Hello, darling." I wave at her through the glass and Jamie follows my gaze then makes a strange deep noise in his throat and swings away.

"Hang on Jamie; it's alright." Simon reaches for him, but he's too slow, and Jamie dodges around the side of the Golf.

"Jamie that's Georgie. I told you about her. Please, look she just wants to be your friend."

"Oh, Char." Simon glances at me, and for a second his eyes are bleak.

"He'll be alright in a minute. It's just sometimes, new things, well you know."

Jamie stops at the air machine, and I take his hand again. His palm is hot and damp.

"You're not going to mind my baby are you?"

People are watching us, a couple in a VW camper van parked beside the nearest pump and the woman at the till. They'll all be making up their own version of events. I lead Jamie gently back towards the car. He's taller than me but he moves like an ungainly child, his head down and his shoulders rounded.

"Would you like a coffee now?" Simon asks, but Jamie just digs at the concrete with the toe of his white plastic trainer.

"I don't think so. Let's just get going." Suddenly I can't bear all the eyes upon us. "Clare's car doesn't have any airbags, so I'll put Georgie in the front. Look, Jamie, why don't you sit in the back there?"

Jamie looks at me blankly. It's so hard to tell what he understands. The nurses told me that it might be much more than we think, there have been specific indications, nuances of movement, which suggest that much is still hidden behind his grey-green eyes.

"I could do with a coffee though," Simon says.

"No, come on."

"Char?"

"I just want to get out of here." I don't trust my movements suddenly. They feel awkwardly self-conscious, giving me away with every turn and look.

Jamie climbs into the back of the car and sits with his head bent forward towards the floor. Simon glances at him before walking round to my side and closing the passenger door.

"Before you say anything, we can't take him back. Char I'm not going to do it." His face is drawn, and his hand shakes slightly as he sweeps his fingers through his hair.

"Simon he needs special care." I look away from him.

"I'll do whatever he needs."

"But-"

"You don't understand, do you, even now?"

"We can't do this Simon." I splay my hands out against the side window and stare at my fingers. "What about his medications and his, his personal needs?"

"We have to do it. I owe it to Jamie. I can't take back what I've done, all I can try and do is make a difference now."

"Oh, Simon." I lower my head as uncertainty sweeps through me again.

"Alright, we'll go over to Fairfax and talk to the manager, say it's a holiday, just for a few days, and pick up his stuff."

20

The reality of what we've done hits me as soon as we walk through the back door. Seeing Jamie there in the passageway, his red hair as bright against the exposed stonework as it always was, is almost too much to bear. I glance at Simon, and he looks as stunned as I feel.

Last time- Is that what we're both thinking? Last time we were all here together, Jamie was young and fit and healthy with a whole other life ahead of him, and we had no inkling of any of this. I clench my hands into fists. Only Jamie seems unaware of the significance of the occasion. He wanders into the kitchen and bends over to stroke the dogs as though he was here just yesterday.

Is that how it feels to him? Is time an irrelevance, contorted and convoluted in his brain so that it no longer has any meaning? On the way here I worried about this moment and whether seeing the farm and being back within these walls would raise painful or turbulent memories and upset him. But he doesn't seem phased by it at all.

"I have to go and get Georgie."

She's contentedly asleep after the drive, but I need an excuse to step outside. Once I'm out there I'm not sure that I can go back in.

"Shit." I lean down behind the wall where no one can see me. All I can think about is how things might have been in terrible contrasting detail.

Jamie was brighter than any of us. Everyone could see that as soon as they were close. His movements may have been slower than either Simon's or mine, but beneath his red hair, the synapses in his brain flashed messages as fast as light. When he got going, I couldn't understand half the things he said.

For a second I see how it could have been here and now, this arrival quite different: Jamie coming in to meet us for a rare snatched chunk of time together. Each of us successful, fulfilled, happy. Jamie tired and jet-lagged after his latest career high, his briefcase beside him on the kitchen floor, full of papers that he'd written and presented at some medical conference. He might have just flown in from the States or Canada, perhaps even Australia.

And Simon? Well, he'd have come in off the farm somewhere, smelling of soil and cows, his face radiant from the wind and sun, his eyes a little proprietorial as he thought about all the things he wanted to show off, the changes he'd made on the farm since Jamie's last visit.

I don't want to think like this, but it's too late, the images of what might have been are lodged in my head. They fill me up and take me over so that I can't even look across the yard without seeing the car that Jamie would have driven here, a large dark hire one, fresh from the airport pick-up point. Behind me suddenly are voices, ours in that other life, carefree, normal, spiked with laughter as we share a sudden in-joke, perhaps one that has run through the years.

"No."

Jamie could have been a consultant by now. I sink my face into my hands, but Robert's there as well now, mellowed by the intervening years, old and proud. His hair is thin on top, and his hands are a bit shaky, but he smiles, enjoying having us all together again even if only for a few days. He's cooked for us because Clare's been too busy and there's a cake on the table and more in the freezer. Jamie teases him gently, too much sugar, it'll hit us hard, make us hyper and rot our teeth and they laugh together.

What about Simon and I? How might we have been? Together for years, parents, married even? I won't go there.

"Char?" Simon comes out into the back garden. "Char?"

I can't face him. I stay still, concealed by the wall. Whatever I say at the moment will be too painful for either of us.

"Are you alright?" I don't hear the gate latch, and he comes up behind me silently. His hand on my shoulder makes me jump. "Char?"

"I can't- I'm sorry." I look up at him, and there are tears in my eyes. "It's just seeing him here; it brings everything back."

"I know."

"Everything."

It isn't only how things might have been now, but how things were, that night and before. Things that seemed so inconsequential at the time, little family rituals, have with hindsight become beautiful and precious beyond words. I clutch at them as though they might save me from the other thoughts, but they slip away in the face of the sudden bleakness that overtakes me as I think about the terrible chain of events that caused all this. Over in the car, Georgie starts to cry in a sudden rising wail, and I turn towards her, forcing myself back into the present.

"Georgie, hold on darling."

My hands are clumsy as I unstrap her and when she's in my arms, I have to stand still again, scared that I'll drop her. Simon's there on the edge of my vision watching me, but I can't look at him.

"I'll take her upstairs to feed her. It's probably past her bedtime." I can't remember exactly where we are in the day, my brain won't read the signs, and we float through the warm air towards the house without really knowing what comes next.

"Charlotte, hang on." Simon's at my side and he slides an arm around my shoulders. Everything suddenly seems steadier, firmer and I can feel the cobbles beneath my feet again. "I'll come with you."

"But-" Jamie's here, that's what all this is about, why these memories have forced themselves to the surface again. But we've got to look after him now, I've got to get a grip.

"He's in the kitchen with the dogs; he's quite happy." Simon hesitates. "Can I carry Georgie upstairs for you? Will she let me?" He takes her, and she doesn't seem to mind, which makes him smile fleetingly. But when he looks back at me his face is serious and concerned. "You go first. I'll follow."

He thinks I'm going to fall and in fact, I do stumble several times. I don't know what's wrong with me; my reactions seem all out of sync. In the bathroom, Simon lays Georgie down on her changing mat, and I realise that he's going to do her nappy.

"It's alright; I can do that."

"No, you sit down and instruct me." He pushes me gently into the old rocking chair in the corner. It's the one that Clare always intended to mend but somehow never did. The seat is half broken but a big cushion fills the gap, and it's only slightly uncomfortable.

When Georgie's clean and in her night things Simon pulls me to my feet. "Are you okay? You looked terrible."

"Thanks."

"No, Char I didn't mean, you know you'll always be beautiful to me." He kisses the end of my nose, but I don't know how to react suddenly. It's as though I'm an innocent country teenager again.

"I need to feed Georgie," I say at last, and Simon lets me go, but I can feel his eyes upon me until I've turned into the spare room.

———

Much later he holds me in his arms wordlessly. I know that he's done everything this evening, looked after Jamie, cooked us all a meal, fed Eb and kept his eye on Bri without once asking for help.

"Thank you for sorting things out," I say at last and his grip tightens around me.

In the shadowy stillness under the thatch, I'm

suddenly thinking about Peter again. I force myself to face the memories and not flinch away. I don't have to tell anyone the details if I don't want to, not Simon, not the police, not anyone. It's too late for the telling to make any difference.

I go back into the Sleepers kitchen as I am now and try to reach out to my younger self. I want to tell her that it's going to be alright. That despite the pain she'll be sensible, she'll remember that she's got forty-eight hours to go and see a doctor and she'll do that. He'll think that she's messed around with a teenage boyfriend but he'll give her what she needs and that part of that terrible week will be dealt with successfully.

If only I could tell her that that was the end of it, that after she left the clinic and slipped the tiny pills, everything would be fine. If only- I shift in the bed and Simon moves his arm a little until we fit together comfortably again. I can't lie anymore, not to myself, not to Simon, not even to Dan.

21

There's a crash in the darkness and the splintering of broken glass. I hear it before I'm properly awake; it thrusts in on my dream and drags me to the surface of consciousness. Cold air sweeps down my side, and there are running footsteps on the bare boards.

"Simon?" I grapple for the light switch but nothing happens, and he's already out of the room.

"Jamie, Jamie."

There are other sounds now, a scrape and a thump that jars through the walls, a muffled shout outside somewhere, then more footsteps. A shadow passes the open door, running, and heads for the stairs. Georgie starts to cry, opening her mouth wider and wider until it's a full-blown howl.

"It's alright darling." I'm out of bed and lifting her against me before I've even begun to make sense of the sounds. "Ssh, ssh."

It's deeply dark and chilly, but I manage to pull a robe on over my shoulders, one arm at a time, and push my feet into a pair of sandals without putting Georgie down. The dogs are barking wildly, although Bri's attempt is still oddly hoarse and feeble, and there's a jumble of footsteps downstairs. I hurry out onto the landing, but again nothing happens when I flick on the light switch.

"What the hell?" I feel my way down the stairs and a sweep of cool air floods in through the open back door. "Simon? Simon, what's going on?"

There's no one in the kitchen, and the dogs are in the yard now, I can hear their barks growing fainter. Bri shouldn't be out yet, my heart lurches, and my right foot crunches on something. I take a step backwards again.

"Simon?"

"Char, careful."

He's back in the room and the torch beam swings across jagged shards of glass to a block of granite on the floor, then up to the yard window. The night swoops in through the broken panes.

"Oh my God."

"Stay in and lock the door after me."

"Simon, what-"

"Jamie's gone. Don't call the police." He spins around and disappears back out into the night.

For the moments it takes my eyes to adjust to the sudden darkness again I can't see anything. I wrap the robe around Georgie and tiptoe to the open door, one hand out to guide me away from the furniture. At first, there's nothing, then one of the dogs barks sharply away to the left down the hill. "Oh God."

Dawn is still some way off beyond the horizon, and the barns are no more than solid blocks of deeper shadow. Who's out there in the night? My mind races and for a moment longer I stand and listen. There's no sound now other than the whisper of the breeze through the Scots pines. I turn back inside and slam the door shut before running the bolts home.

My hand shakes as I search through several drawers for candles and matches. At last, we have a wavering light in the room, and the damage jumps out at us again. There's more glass than I thought and splinters of wooden window frame scattered across the work surface. The block of granite is about the size of my head, and it's gouged a hole in the floor tiles where it landed.

"It's alright Georgie; it's alright."

We wait for what seems like hours but is probably no more than ten minutes, and she drifts between tears and sleep. Did we give Jamie the right medication last night? I snatch the sheet of instructions off the table and stare at it, but it takes my brain a while to focus. Yes, it looks like it. I put it down again. Still, there's no sign of anyone returning, and suddenly I'm terrified. I push my bare feet into a pair of wellies that are a little too big, pick the heavy old torch off the passage shelf and unlock the front door. My back prickles as I scan the darkness beyond the garden. Nothing.

"Simon, Jamie."

A breeze chills against my face, and for a second I think I catch the bob of a light moving down through the lower fields, but then it's gone. A memory from that other night long ago flickers but I force it away.

"Simon, Jamie." I walk to the garden wall and swing the torch beam back and forth across Lower Five Acre, then more slowly along the hedgerow. Nothing. They must have gone on along the same route as before, the shortcut to the village, the last path that Jamie ever walked here as a teenager. I shiver and swing the torch beam again, straining to see something, a movement, anything that will give them away.

This time I pick up the sudden blue, green spark of eyes close to the ground and catch my breath. I hold the beam steady trying to make out a shape, but the next moment they're gone, and I know that they belong to something wild and wary, a fox perhaps.

Bri is the first one to come back. He's been running harder than he should, and his flanks are wet. He pushes in under the gate panting.

"Where are they then?"

The collie touches my outstretched hand with his nose then flops down at my feet. For a second I'm worried that he's going to keel over, but he seems alright. I strain to see or hear anything in the darkness behind him, but my eyes feel gravelly and refuse to focus on the undulating shadows, and Georgie starts to press her head against me and cry, a sure sign that she's hungry.

"Simon." They must be coming back. I ignore Georgie for as long as I can, but there's only one thing that will calm her now and eventually I have to return to the house. The candle flames fan low when I walk in through the kitchen door, then flare up illuminating the damage.

"Hold on Gel." I push her back with my foot while I sweep up the mess of broken glass as best I can with one hand. My heart beats fast. Who came out of the darkness to do this and where are they now? I feel exposed in front of the uncurtained windows as I open my top for Georgie and all around the house, the night presses close. "It's alright, Simon and Jamie'll be back soon."

It grows chilly as I sit and suddenly I'm reminded of

another evening in this very room, after Jamie's accident. The shadows were almost the same and the air as static with tension. I heard Clare and Robert from above, their voices hushed but still clear in the empty house. I didn't want to listen to the individual words, but I couldn't help it, even with my head pushed into my pillows they floated up to me.

"Robert, why do you think Simon's never at home now?"

" … he should …"

"No, it's your fault, you can't go on blaming-" There was a sudden movement, the scrape of hurried steps, a sharp intake of breath and a slight moan.

I went down then, and they were standing over near the Rayburn, fully dressed. Dad had his head at an odd angle as though he was trying to hear something outside the room and there was an ugly red mark across Clare's cheek.

A sound outside pulls me back into the present, metal against metal. Gel and I hear it at the same time, and she barks with a sharp, anxious edge. Nerves jolt through my body, and I stand up with Georgie in my arms and turn towards the window.

A torch beam wavers across the yard, and they appear around the corner of the house and stagger across the cobbles. Simon has his arm around Jamie's shoulders, and Jamie leans against him, but there's nothing companionable about their progress.

I look through the broken window. "Oh thank God. Are you alright?"

"We followed the lights and got to the village, didn't we mate?" Simon tries to keep his voice steady, but he looks done in.

"Torchlights?" Not Marty then but others, a swell of hate reaching out of the darkness towards us.

Simon nods, beside him Jamie's face is streaked with blood from a scratch above his left eyebrow, and his breathing is laboured. He makes a strange little grunting noise in his throat.

What the hell are we going to do?

————

The police helicopter passes over the house before breakfast. It's high and travelling in a straight purposeful line. Simon watches it from the window then, before either of us has had a chance to get dressed, Jamie careers out of his room, down the stairs, across the yard to the woodshed and locks himself inside.

"What about his medication?" I stare at Simon in a panic.

"It's alright; I'm sure it won't matter being a little bit late."

"But-?"

"Char, I'll go and talk to him in a minute."

A breeze fans through the broken kitchen window and the gouge in the tiles looks pale and raw in the morning sun. All the other debris is gone, but the rough block of granite sits on the end of the table beside my camera case. Simon looks at it. "It must have caught the light bulb and tripped the fuses. I've reset them, and we've got electricity again now so-"

"Thank you." I shiver, and he pulls me against him. "Char we'll sort things out, I promise. Look why don't you go and get dressed."

"We'll have to get someone in to fix the window and-"

"I know. I'll call a builder in a minute." For a second he's the old Simon, practical and organised, knowing what to do and what tools are needed.

"And the police."

"No." He leans away from me.

"Simon."

"They'll just find some way to blame me."

"That's crazy." I touch the piece of granite with the tips of my fingers. It's rough and pale, and I wonder where it was unearthed from. "They'd-"

"Char, I don't fucking know anything." Simon steps away, and the sudden hardness of his words surprises me. They remind me of how he became towards the end when he did eventually speak after days of silence and how I felt. I don't want us to be like that with each other again.

"But you have been back." I wait, and something digs in beneath my ribs making it hard to breathe.

"How?"

"Why didn't you tell me? Simon, why?"

"I couldn't; I didn't." He sinks his face into his hands then raises his head again. "Okay, yes I came back, to say sorry, but I bottled it. I couldn't face them."

It sounds like the truth. It has to be the truth. I walk across to the window and touch one of the sharp points of broken glass with the tip of my index finger. "Just the once?"

He hangs his head.

"Why, after all these years?"

"I'd been thinking about it for a long time. I know that sounds lame. If I had, I'd have seen Robert."

"Don't." I raise my hand. I can't go there. "Is that partly why the police think, why you're on bail? What else haven't you told me?"

"There's nothing else." He avoids my eyes. "Don't you believe me?"

Do I? Don't I? Does it make any difference? Not to Jamie anyway. His world isn't the same as ours now; it makes its own sense. His expressions are unreadable, his thoughts unknown. How long he thinks he's spent in the woodshed and why may be utterly different from our perception of that time.

When Simon eventually manages to persuade him out of the dusty depths, they go for a walk up through the fields. I watch them from the top window while I feed Georgie, but I can't even pretend that things are almost as they were. Even from a distance, there's an uncertainty about Jamie's gait that gives him away. It's as if the rules of adult behaviour are nothing to him.

Two, three, four times they stop and each time the pause grows lengthier. The last time Simon looks back towards the house and half raises his hand to me. Is it a wave or a gesture of bewilderment? I move my hand in reply, slowly so as not to disturb Georgie, and I can't see where any of this is going.

No builder will come out. The name of the farm is enough to put off all of them in the same way that it did the contractors. After lunch, I sit with Jamie and Georgie in the garden while Simon attempts to patch up the window with a piece of rigid plastic from the barn.

Our conversation is stilted. Kept to the basics for Jamie's sake although I'm sure that even he must notice the chill between us. Georgie certainly does if her restlessness is anything to go by.

"Please darling, please you must sleep." I gave up on the travel cot when her screams didn't falter, but the car seat is little better. I rock it with my foot for what seems like an age, but still, her eyes are wide open. "I'm going to have to take her out in the buggy."

Simon doesn't stop what he's doing, and I'm not sure whether he's heard or not.

"Is that alright with you?"

"Whatever."

"Please?" Still, he won't stop cutting strips of duck tape with infuriating deliberateness, so I settle Georgie in her buggy and wheel her down the garden path. This is so familiar, so painful still, as though nothing has changed in the leap across the years.

Simon visited Jamie in hospital as often as he possibly could. I knew that, but our parents didn't. He said that school made no sense anymore and he couldn't add up the strings of numbers in maths or make sense of the chemical formulae that danced before his eyes. Within a term, his grades plummeted, and I knew that he wanted to give up altogether, to get out in the 'real world' as he called it.

In the meantime, he caught a bus to town and then another out to the hospital and padded down the long corridors to the head injury unit. I'm sure that the nurses brought him cups of tea where he sat holding Jamie's hand and reassuring himself that the blood was still pulsing through his brother's veins.

When Jamie came out of his coma, I saw the leap of hope in Simon's eyes followed the next few days by a terrible lingering silence almost as deep as Jamie's when he realised that the change in consciousness was so marginal.

"It's only the drugs," I said. "I'm sure that soon-"

"What?" One word in a sea of hopelessness.

"He will get better."

I never quite knew what happened when Robert found Simon at Jamie's bedside in the middle of a school day. They came home separately, and the coolness between them spread outwards to include Clare and me. It was after that that I began to smell alcohol on Simon's breath and he took to staying away from the farm for increasing lengths of time, sometimes night after night.

"Simon." Georgie is asleep by the time I get back, and I take his arm and pull him into the house. "We've got to talk properly I don't want to go back there."

"You're right." He knows what I mean and rests a hand on my shoulder, but he isn't concentrating or even really thinking about it.

"Please?"

The three of us eat together, but it's a strange meal. Simon and I talk and Jamie watches us. Without knowing how much he understands it's hard to know whether to include him in the conversation or not. When we try, the gaps that should be his to fill stretch out into awkwardness and when we don't it feels rude and insensitive.

Simon's hands are clumsy. He catches a glass with his knife, and the sound sings out through the stillness then later he drops a bowl, and it smashes on the tiles.

"Oh God, I'm sorry." He stoops to pick up the pieces, and I want to cry. This isn't how he should be. What he did back then was a moment of craziness but nothing more. If things had been different, if he'd stepped fractionally to one side or the other, or if Jamie had, then our lives might have faltered slightly, but moved on again almost without a ripple. A near miss to be gaped at, talked about, and then forgotten. What cruel alignment of movements brought everything together in that moment like that?

"You know that I've got a photo shoot booked the day after tomorrow don't you? I'll need to go up to London."

He nods, and Jamie looks at me. Does he understand what I'm saying as well?

"I could try and change it."

"And risk losing the work? No, don't do that."

"Are you sure? I don't want to go. It, it doesn't- Well not at the moment. Will you be alright with Jamie?"

"Of course." He smiles, and his voice has softened. "We'll have a great time won't we mate?"

Perhaps he will, but it's a long time to be on your own with Jamie, and I wonder as the hours stretch out how he'll feel.

"I'll have to travel up tomorrow afternoon so that Georgie gets enough rest." The logistics of it all niggle at me. I can't rush around as I used to, grabbing food and sleep when I could. Everything has to be planned out around Georgie's feeds and nap times.

"We'll be fine."

When Jamie's gone to bed, we kiss in a long, slow embrace that puts me on edge even though, or perhaps because, it feels so natural, so right. The room is in darkness when I pull back to study Simon's face, and it's hard to see him clearly.

"When this is over, however it turns out, we will stay together won't we?" I can't imagine going back to my old life now, not to how things were, to the long hours of work and the briefly thrilling but ultimately empty encounters with good-looking men who never quite understood me. Or perhaps it was me who never understood myself. A cool draught needles in from somewhere and I wrap my cardigan more tightly around my body.

"You'll visit me in prison then?"

"Don't say that." I tighten my grip on his hand as though I can hold him close and safe forever.

"Let's go out." He slides an arm around my shoulders and steers me into the front garden. It's a still soft night. Not quite as warm as lately but so clear that we can see the outlines of the trees on the horizon across the valley. A low V of Canada geese honk their way overhead towards the distant silver strand of the reservoir, and suddenly I'm filled with a sense of vertigo, of things slipping away from us in the darkness.

"We've got to do something."

"What?" His arm tightens around me.

"We can't go on like this. I mean what's being said, it isn't right. You shouldn't still be on bail."

"There's no point in getting a lawyer."

"Why not? Simon, I don't understand." There's a car out on the lonely moorland road beyond the reservoir; its headlights cast a double beam through the darkness.

"We've been over this before."

"And I said that I'd pay."

"This isn't just about the money. Charlotte you seem to think you can buy anything you want."

"No, I don't." I feel rebuffed and pull away from him.

"Char."

"Leave me alone."

We stand a little apart in the darkness and the breeze is cool against my face. In the distance, the car stops and I wonder why. What has the driver seen out there?

"I'm sorry." He touches my arm then runs his fingers upwards to the side of my neck.

"Simon." I want to shrug him off, to ignore him still, but I can't. "Is that what you really think of me?"

"Come here."

It's safer in his arms, and the slippery, out of control feeling recedes a little. "I only want to help you."

"I know."

"We can find someone good or-" There's Liam. Why didn't I think of that? Beautiful, blonde Liam who I used to share picnics on the Downs with and quiet nights in West London. This may not be his speciality, but he'll know someone good.

"No."

"Simon."

"I won't talk to them."

"Oh God." I hit the palm of my hand against my forehead. "Please?"

"Char."

The geese are calling again but further away this time, out on the reservoir now. Suddenly I don't want to argue, so I stop and take a deep breath.

"I'm going to miss you tomorrow."

"And me you."

22

A little beyond the frames of the photos there are patches of dark, disturbed earth and the untidy debris of clear fell: piles of brash and jagged remnants of discarded trunks stretching down almost to the far reservoir edge. It all makes sense now. These are the things the photographer teased us about, the things he hinted at through the pure blandness of the shots he did take and send. I thought they were pictures of Longcause and without the glint of water in the distance that was an easy mistake to make.

I stumble as we step through the deep double ruts left by the forwarders and logging tractors. Behind me, there's the snap of a twig, and Hollinghurst's footsteps falter and then speed up again. I turn around, and as I do, so I realise that there's something wrong about the light. The sun isn't directly overhead but we haven't got any shadows, and suddenly I have the weird sense that we aren't here at all.

"What I want you to do-" Hollinghurst starts but he doesn't finish, and we walk on again.

The air is as warm and thick as blood, and it pulls the sweat from our pores even though I'm leading him downhill. I don't look at the dug-over places, but there's a smell of fresh peat drying to dust as we pass and something else, the scent of decay perhaps.

There doesn't seem to be anyone around, but I'm sure that somewhere there must be someone watching us through the cold, blue eye of a telephoto lens. I know the shot I'd try and get in the circumstances, I can see it in the papers already, desolate and accusatory, and I hunch my shoulders against the straps of Georgie's carrier.

Simon's name hasn't been mentioned, as though by some tacit agreement, but there's a terrible sense of inevitability with each step we take. The land drops away increasingly steeply, and in less than five minutes we're at the edge of the open area but somehow no nearer the reservoir. Ahead of us is woodland proper, dense with beech and oak. Three butterflies dance in the sunlight, and although the shade will be welcome, there's something secretive, almost foreboding about the shadows. A chiffchaff calls its repetitive two-note call, and I hesitate.

"I'm sorry that I made a mistake before, but I don't know what more I can show you now," I say as Hollinghurst stops alongside me. The air has an odd opaque quality as though the sun is shining through cellophane and everything looks disconcertingly insubstantial now. "If you've already looked."

"I'd just like you to take me along the paths you used to use and to any favourite spots."

I nod, but I feel sick as the sun burns my face and

my bare arms and turns the upper surfaces of the beech leaves into sudden shivers of white light.

"Is this where you used to come into the wood?" He nudges me with his words, but still, I don't move.

Things look different now that chainsaws have erased half the familiar landmarks. I cast around to find the path, and it's nearly invisible, as though no one passes this way anymore. We follow it down the eastern flank of the wood, and the silence is oppressive beneath the canopy. Every so often a bird calls then stops again almost at once.

"Would you say that you came here often?" Hollinghurst's voice seems too loud in the deep hush and different somehow, as though I haven't quite caught the accent right.

"We played, sometimes we camped down by the water." I shrug. I don't want to think about what our innocent pleasure in the place may have led to. Instead, I walk on quickly, cupping my hands around Georgie's sleeping shape in her carrier and keeping my eyes straight ahead. There won't be anything. There can't be anything.

The path grows more distinct as it approaches the stream and suddenly the air is filled with a sickly sweet scent. Once someone must have had ideas to develop this piece of land into something other than a wild woodland and their dreams linger on in clumps of yellow-flowered azaleas and white rhododendrons that crouch close to the path. It's the scent of childhood spring, and I used to love it, but now it clings to the back of my throat threatening to choke me and vaguely I'm aware that it's too late for them, the wrong season.

"Hold on." Hollinghurst stops, then turns off the

path to his right and pushes his way through the under-growth for a few strides.

I wait, I try to stay calm, but nerves fizz through me. I don't want to look and yet I can't help myself. I follow the tight curving lines of Hollinghurst's back as he bends forward to examine something, but there is no certain message in them.

"Okay, I just thought-" Hollinghurst dusts off his hands. "It was probably an animal."

I lead the way onwards again, and within a few minutes, we're walking alongside the stream that tumbles down over granite boulders, past the remains of a derelict building and on towards the grassy area where we sometimes used to camp. Suddenly I stop and turn back to Hollinghurst. Even deep in the shade, the heat is oppressive. A spiral of insects dances above his head and away to our left a bird calls sharp and urgent.

"What do you want from me?" The moorland rescue team has been through the woodland with search dogs, and I can't help feeling that I'm missing the point of this walk. If there was anything to be found here surely, they'd already have found it.

"Like I said I just want you to show me the paths you used and the places you went to most often." He doesn't react to my question, but my heart speeds up.

The bracken has encroached on our camping spot, and now there's hardly space for onc tent let alone two or three. I stare at the wiry turf that's left, and it feels like another door into the past has slammed in my face. I'd rather not stop, but Hollinghurst turns towards the stream and casts up and down the bank for a few minutes, examining the pale crescents of gravel at the water's edge. It seems a useless gesture.

Too much time has passed for there to be any clues left.

Georgie's face is flushed, and her skin feels hot and damp when I stroke a finger across her cheek then dip it beneath her vest. A different kind of anxiety edges through me.

"I need to get Georgie back to the farm."

"Of course."

We never reach the reservoir edge. Instead, we turn onto a path that scrambles up through a stand of pines. The shade is dense and resinous, and my head throbs. We come upon the spot suddenly. The earth is rough and scraped bare of needles close to the path, and it looks as though an animal has been digging there, a big animal, a human type of animal.

I try to speak but the sound catches in my throat, and Hollinghurst pushes past me.

"Ah."

The soil is dark with peat, but there are pale pieces of granite within it, tossed to the surface by all the disturbance. Why didn't anyone notice this before? Hollinghurst kneels down and searches through the dirt with his immaculate office fingers. Grit goes up behind his nails and obscures his wedding ring. I stop watching but then there's a pause and his breathing changes. He's found something.

"No." Suddenly I'm hurrying away, not able to run because of Georgie but walking as fast as I can up the narrow path with my arms around her to stop her jolting in her sling.

"Charlotte." Hollinghurst is following me now. He wants to me to come back to see what he's found. His hands reach for me as they did for Simon.

"No."

I press on up the hill, and now he's gasping for breath behind me. I want that, to make him struggle for air, so I increase my pace until we're back out in the sun again. I have to slow down then for the horizon has a liquid tremor. A raven croaks high above us, but I can't see it against the glare.

"It's okay darling; we're going home now I promise." I adjust Georgie's sun hat then glance up. A lone figure is standing on the moor close to the wall. There's something familiar about his height and stature, I stiffen and glance sideways at Hollinghurst.

Marty walks off before we reach the gate but once or twice I catch a glimpse of him in the bracken above and slightly ahead of us as we walk back towards the road. A group of 'wild' ponies scatter out in front of him.

At the cars, we stop for a moment, and I know without looking that Marty is standing alongside his vehicle higher up the hill, watching, only it isn't the Landrover it's the dark car, the one that's been there for days.

"Thank you for your cooperation," Hollinghurst says glossing over my flight. There's sweat on his face. I don't know what will happen next and I can't ask for the heat seems to have sucked all energy, all ability to question, right out of me. I stand numbly and even though we are still my heart races as it used to in the first few months of pregnancy, a nasty out of control feeling.

"I'll follow you back to your flat," he says, and suddenly I know that we're not really having this conversation at all.

I wake early to street noises rather than birdsong outside the window and for a moment I'm disorientated, and nothing makes sense. I can't even remember what day it is, then slowly it comes back to me. I'm at the flat; today I have to see Dan, to work again. I take a deep breath, but somehow I can't quite get enough oxygen. Last night- The images are still close and something tightens at the back of my throat.

"No," I whisper. "No."

But already a little seed of panic is growing inside me, and I can't shake free of it. Should I call Hollinghurst? Should I tell him what I think even if it somehow implicates Simon even more? No, it was only a dream and yet the vision of the dark, disturbed earth is so clear, so real. I know that spot. I shake my head. Before I was almost sure that the photos were of Long-cause but now-

Should I call Simon? I stare at the bedside clock, and it's earlier than I thought, too early to call the farm and risk waking Jamie as well. Oh, God. I swallow and try to fix the time and place of the photo shoot in my head. I can't focus on them, so I climb out of bed and start to lay out Georgie's and my things for the day: cameras, nappies, notebooks, a change of clothes for Georgie and a block of muslins.

What the hell am I doing? I sit down on the edge of the bed and close my eyes for a second. Did I edit the edges of the photos in my sleep to fit my dream? If I saw them again would I be so sure that I'd made a mistake? I pick up my phone and scroll through to the incident room number, but then I don't dial it.

I need the work today. My savings are all but gone now. I have to concentrate, to get my head back where it was before all this started, before Georgie even. I know that I haven't been as sharp since she was born or as focused but perhaps I'm merely exhausted. Today London, tomorrow San Moritz. Well not quite, but today is the first step towards San Moritz. If I get it right, if I make a success of it then-

I remember Dan's confident, enthusiastic words spoken when he still trusted me. "Mr Emmerson is a new client of ours. As soon as we first met, I knew that he'd go for your work. It's exactly what he's looking for. He's already seen your portfolio; he loved the stuff you did for Celestine."

But what am I photographing? Bottled water. Plastic bottles of water being sipped by some skinny super-model. Clear water, beautiful water, healthy water in plastic bottles. All I can think about is the dark, peaty water that swirled past our campsite in the oak wood, the scent of it and the iron taste cascading down towards the reservoir.

Concentrate. I pick up my favourite lens and dust it off before putting it back in its grey foam cocoon, and suddenly I know that Dan and I will have to go our separate ways. We can't carry on working together after what I've done to him. We'll have to discuss it soon, but not today. I close my camera case and look around.

Last night, when Georgie and I arrived, the air in the flat was warm and stale, that end of a hot London day smell. A pile of unopened mail avalanched off the mat as I stepped inside and there was a layer of dust covering everything. Now after a night of half-open windows and disturbance everything seems fresher, almost back to normal, to how it always was and yet I know that's nothing but an illusion. I lean back against the bedroom door for a moment. There's a television on next door. I'd forgotten that, the sound of people through the walls.

Everything else is familiar, but the ordered emptiness that I've always loved, that used to make me feel so free, suddenly feels sterile and claustrophobic. I also have an odd, disconcerting feeling that it wasn't ever true freedom. I may have thought that it was, but Simon, Jamie, Robert and Clare were always there, shadowy figures in the background shaping my actions, turning me into the person that I've become even as I ran from them.

Georgie makes a half cry in her cot and wriggles around in her sleeping bag. I wait for a moment to see if she'll drift back to sleep but then her eyes open, and so does her mouth and I scoop her up before she can wake any neighbours that are still asleep.

"Okay, are you hungry darling?" I lie back on the bed with her, and it's reassuring to have her hot little body tucked against mine. With her there I can almost pretend that the dream was merely that, a figment of my imagination, conjured up by exhaustion after the long drive and a hot London night. Almost. I think of my short cryptic talk with Simon last night, our words kept in check by the knowledge that unseen and unknown people were listening in, and suddenly I feel hollow inside.

"No way."

When Georgie has settled and is drinking steadily I reach over her and pick my phone off the bedside table, switching it back to the normal ring tone. Before I have a chance to press the Northstone speed dial, it rings. I've never been one for personalised ring tones, and I answer it without glancing at the number on the screen, thinking it's Simon impatient and wanting to talk to me as much as I need to hear him.

"Charlotte." It's Dan, and his voice sounds a little less cool than normal. "Where are you?"

"Still at the flat. I'm just feeding Georgie, but I'll be leaving soon. What is it?"

"You haven't seen the news?"

"No." My heart speeds up, and Georgie stops drinking and looks at me. "Dan?"

"I'm coming round. I won't be long."

"What is it?" I can't reach the TV remote or the radio.

"Something's happened at the farm."

"At Northstone? What?"

"Just stay there, I won't be long."

He cuts off the call, and I scramble from the bed with Georgie in my arms squawking in protest

"It's okay darling." I try to keep my voice steady but I can't. "I just need to- Mummy needs to check something."

I switch on the TV, and there's a vista on the screen that is as familiar as my own hands and yet somehow distorted. Shock jolts through me as the camera sharpens focus and I start to make sense of the greyness.

"Oh my God." For a second I'm not sure where the smoke is coming from but as it eddies in the wind the red lettering across the back of the farmhouse jumps out at me. MURDERER. The shapes of the letters are uneven on the granite but unmistakable.

I sit quite still, and the image stays on the screen for perhaps fifteen seconds before the shot switches to an aerial scene of the farm half smothered by a dark pall of smoke. Is the house alight, or the barns, or both? My heart races. Where are Simon and Jamie?

"A further development in the case of the missing Devon schoolboy, Lee Berryman-" I grab my phone, and I've got five missed calls from Hollinghurst whilst it was on silent to avoid waking Georgie. My heart is beating hard as I press the speed dial for the farm and all the time I'm trying to make sense of the picture on the screen and the presenter's words.

"Come on, come on." The phone rings over and over and over but there's no reply, so I shut off the call and start again. Nothing. "Shit."

The camera pans in close again, and there are at least two fire engines in the yard and figures in dark uniforms dipping in and out of the smoke. It feels obscene to be in London suddenly. I spin round in a circle with Georgie clutched against me, and she cries in surprise.

"I'm sorry darling." I stop by the bed and try to call Hollinghurst back, but my phone starts to ring again before I can get my fingers to press the right keys.

"Hello. Hello?" There's no one there. I glance at the screen in confusion then realise that it isn't the phone at all but the doorbell intercom. Again the buzzer sounds and again. I press the button to silence it and remember too late that instead, I've opened the connection to the street.

"Charlotte, it's Dan. Can I come up?"

Within seconds he's in the flat. He's wearing a fresh blue shirt with the top button undone to reveal a deeply tanned v, but his hair has been cut so recently that there's a pale line of sun-starved skin across his forehead.

"Are you alright?" He averts his eyes from my exposed breast. "You've seen the news now?"

I nod. "I've been trying to call the farm, but there's no reply."

"Okay, have you tried the police?"

"I was just going to."

"Shall I take Georgie for you?" He holds out his hands, but I shake my head.

"She's still hungry."

"Charlotte, no one's called you, right?"

"Hollinghurst's tried but-"

"Has he left a message?"

"Hang on a minute," I raise my hand while I listen. "Yes, he just wants me to call him. Oh, God Dan."

"I'm sure it's going to be alright. But call Hollinghurst now." Dan's making an effort to keep his voice quiet and steady. "I'll make you a cup of tea then I'll drive you down there. Have you had any breakfast?"

"You can't do that." I stare around the room remembering something else. Today. "It's the photo shoot, we're-"

"No, we're not. Call him Charlotte."

"Has it been cancelled?" There's too much in my head suddenly, and I can't focus on this properly as well.

"Call him. We'll talk about it later."

I dial the incident room number, but the lines are jammed.

"Oh, God." I sit down on a chair for a moment. "This doesn't mean that Simon, that he- And where the hell's Jamie?"

"Jamie? Here let me take Georgie for you now." Dan

reaches for her, and somehow she's in his arms, and I'm covering up my bare breast. "Who's Jamie?"

"My other brother." I tug a strand of hair back behind my ear, and there's a sharp pain across my scalp. "They might be in the house; they might be anywhere."

I turn back towards the TV, but there's no news now, so I fire up my laptop and search the internet.

"They're saying here … it was arson. Well obviously, but there's no mention of Simon or Jamie. Look at this picture. It was started in the hay barn but the house is close and the thatch-"

"The fire brigade's there. They'll have it under control." He pauses for a moment. "I didn't know you had another brother."

"No." I glance at him and then away and sink my face into my hands, into a hot, dark, little world. I need to think clearly but everything is whirling too fast to focus on, and a headache has dug in from nowhere. "I have to speak to Simon. Oh, where is he?"

I press the Northstone speed dial again and imagine the farm phone ringing out in the smoke-tainted kitchen. It rings and rings and rings then eventually cuts through to the answering service. I shut off my phone. Maybe there are already flames in the thatch and sparks drifting in through the windows. Perhaps the curtains are alight.

"There's no answer." I think of all the beautiful, dry hay and the sweet, flowery scent of it. When you looked closely, you could see the tiny heads of clover pressed flat within it.

"Perhaps-"

"I've got to get down there. Could you hold Georgie while I get my things together?"

"I'll drive you." Dan rocks Georgie back and forth, but she looks tiny and awkward in his arms.

"No. Thank you. We'll be fine. You've got work to do anyway."

"Charlotte you shouldn't drive all that way on your own today."

"It's only Devon. I'm okay, honestly." What do I need? I grab things together into piles. "Anyway I won't be on my own, I've got Georgie."

"Exactly."

"Dan please."

Where's Simon? Who did it? I imagine footsteps in the night, soft over grass but more careful when they met the cobbles, then the hiss of a spray can followed by the splash of petrol and the whoosh of flames. Who? Did he hear them? Did the dogs? What about Jamie? The dogs, oh God.

"Charlotte." He takes my arm, but I want him to leave.

"Charlotte, let me pay for a taxi for you then."

"Thank you, but no." I shake my head, and he stares at me for a moment. "I'll need my car down there."

I have to go. I reach for my bag, running through things in my mind. I'm bound to forget something, but it doesn't matter, not now.

"Please drive carefully."

"Of course and-"

"What?"

"None of this is Simon's fault, alright. And for your information, he's the only man I've ever really loved." Even as I say it, a quiver of uncertainty stirs within me, and the air between us has an odd shimmer, like it's out of focus.

"Loved?"

"Like you already know, he's my adopted brother. It's perfectly legal."

———

I call Simon again as soon as we're out on a clear stretch of road, but still, there's no reply.

"Please, please." I let the phone ring and ring, and Georgie shifts restlessly in her seat. "Come on."

Nothing. My thoughts spin away from the farmhouse and all the smoke, out across the fields towards the village. Where are they? I redial the incident room and this time I get through.

"I'm Charlotte Elgin, I need to know, is everyone alright or have there been any, any casualties?"

My words come out in a rush then there's a hesitation on the end of the line, and I catch my breath.

"Please?"

"I'm going to pass you through to a colleague, don't go away."

The seconds flick past, and suddenly we're in a knot of traffic, and I have to concentrate on that. There's a lorry too close somehow, and then Hollinghurst comes on the line.

"Charlotte."

"Is everyone alright?"

"Where are you? I've been trying you since early." There's something about his voice that sends a chill into the pit of my stomach.

"I've been in London; I'm on my way back down."

"Okay, at least we know that now. Was anyone staying at the farm last night as far you are aware?"

"Of course they were, Simon was there and Jamie. Oh God haven't you seen them?"

"The fire officers are searching the property as we speak."

"Then?"

"I'm sorry Charlotte."

I pull out from behind a dark Mercedes and speed past. At the last minute, I think that it might be an unmarked police car and glance sideways. There's a single man inside who looks more like a sales rep.

"Is the house?" I can't bring myself to finish the sentence. I swallow, and phlegm catches in the back of my throat.

"As far as we can tell at this stage the fire started in one of the barns. The house itself is largely untouched."

"But then-"

"There's smoke damage."

Smoke. Is he trying to tell me that Simon or Jamie could be lying unconscious somewhere from smoke inhalation?

"What time do you think you might arrive?"

I glance at my watch and try to calculate.

"Charlotte?"

"I'll be there as quickly as I can."

"I'll meet you in the yard."

"Thank you." I grip the steering wheel hard and drive as fast as I dare.

23

We hit the greyness as soon as we climb away from the dual carriageway. One minute we're in bright sunshine, the next we're cruising through a strange twilight world and everything is indistinct. For a second I think it's smoke and my heart races then I wind down the window, and the air smells damp and chilly, and I let out my breath.

I have to slow almost to a walking pace and switch on my headlights. I keep my eyes on the curve of ground where the road meets the high tangled granite hedge, then we roll out over a cattle grid, and even that guidance is gone.

On either side of us, heather moorland sweeps away barely distinguishable from the road in the gloom. I have to concentrate hard to keep the car on the tarmac, and after a few miles, my eyes are aching.

"It's okay; it's okay Georgie." I talk to her as much to calm myself as anything as the surreal shapes of gorse bushes and rocks loom out of the mist on the roadside, shapes that you'd never even notice in sunlight. Our progress is so slow that I become disorientated and the curves of the road suddenly seem unfamiliar.

"Come on." I don't want to think about what I might find ahead, and yet it claws at my insides. I have to get there; I have to face it, I have to find them.

There's a chaos of people and cars all along the road to the farm entrance, but I try to keep my eyes straight ahead and my foot on the accelerator even when people walk out in front of me.

"Hey-"

"Can you tell us-?"

Cameras focus on the car and hands wave, but I take no notice. Perhaps I'm growing almost immune to them now. I haven't got time to slow, and in seconds we're being ushered through the cordon.

Part way up the farm track the fog clears as abruptly as it started and straight ahead there's a pall of dark smoke rising into the sky. Nerves shoot to the tips of my fingers, and I speed up, bumping over the potholes and sending showers of loose gravel into the hedges. Somehow I thought, or at least I hoped, that the fire would be out by now. In a few minutes, I'll be there, and I'll see it all. I take a deep breath trying to steady myself for what lies ahead.

"It's okay Georgie; we're nearly back." I glance over my shoulder, and she's asleep in her car seat, her head tilted sideways in the beautiful innocent baby way she has. It makes me want to cry suddenly. "Oh, darling."

I'm almost at the junction of tracks when I see Marty sitting in the sunshine on a rock beside Lee's 'shrine' as though he's waiting for us. He's wearing a dirty white shirt, jeans and wellies so perhaps the weather has only recently changed here.

The first bunches of chrysanthemums are nearly dead now, but there are other fresher arrangements at his feet, mixtures of flowers in yellows and burnt oranges, even some mostly white ones in a tiny tin bucket. As soon as he hears the car, he stands up and walks out onto the track. Anger flickers through me.

"Marty." I stop and wind down my window. Immediately the stench of smoke rushes into the car and cloys in my throat. "What the hell's going on?"

"Hello to you too." His hair is wild, and I notice that the top two buttons of his shirt are missing when he places a hand on the roof and leans down to the window. "Had a good time in London have we?"

"What have you done? Where are Simon and Jamie?"

"Me? Oh now hold on." His voice is slurred, and a half-empty bottle of whisky hangs from his right hand. "You tell me where my boy is first."

"I don't know."

"Really? I saw those guys in the white boiler suits going down to the reservoir. They're in there aren't they? Or at least Lee is."

"Marty, I don't know anything." I feel wrong-footed suddenly. Is he right for once? Have Clare and Lee been found, oh God, have they?

He hesitates for a moment, takes a swig from the bottle then spins around and looks up the track towards the dark smoke. "Where's Simon? Where the fuck is he?"

His voice is different suddenly, full of real anger. Was the graffiti not his doing after all? He's too far gone now to create a straight line, but he's had hours with the whisky bottle of course.

335

I need to drive on but his hand is still on the car, and he leans in towards me again, his breath rank. "I should have known he was up to no good when I saw him."

"Marty." It's tempting to put my foot down on the accelerator, but I don't dare. "I have to get back to the farm. I have to see-"

"What?" His face is flushed and sunburnt, and Georgie wakes with a whimper in the back.

I reach my arm around the seat and stroke her bare toes. "Marty please, why do you think Simon's got anything to do with this?"

"I told you, I saw him. He may have fooled you, but he hasn't fooled me." He takes another swig of whisky and turns to face the valley. "It doesn't surprise me what they're saying in the papers. He's warped, he always was. I mean living alone in a bloody houseboat, what's that all about?"

It's hot and sticky in the car. Georgie pulls her feet away from me and starts to cry.

"Marty, I need to get up to the farm and find out what's going on."

"Go on then; I'm not stopping you." He takes one step back but his movements are loose, and out of control and his free arm arcs through the air, his fingers clenched into a fist. "Just tell me where he is first."

"I don't know." A sharp pain throbs above my right eye. "That's what I need to find out."

Suddenly he steps close again and leans down as though he might reach right through the open window. His eyes are bloodshot and he smells as though he hasn't washed for several days.

"You liar."

"What?"

"You're no better than him, you never were."

"I think you should go home." I keep my voice calm and my eyes away from his.

"You think I'll do that without Simon?"

"I don't know where he is. Can't you see that?" Georgie's cries fill the car, and I want to hold her so much. "He could have been in the barn."

"Yeh, yeh-"

"Marty." Suddenly I can't wait any longer. I put my foot down on the accelerator, and the car lurches forward. I know I haven't touched Marty but glancing in the rearview mirror I see him stumble and then stagger away to the side of the track. My heart is beating hard and fast.

Soon I'll reach that point in the track where I should be able to see the house and yet what will I see? I can hardly bear to look, and when I lift my eyes, it takes me a moment or two to work out what I am seeing. Dark smoke eddies in the wind and a dusting of ash lands across the windscreen of the car. Through it, there are stark shapes, the angle of a roofline that still seems intact and then, as the smoke clears for a second, the shell of the hay barn out to the left, the roof nothing more than a broken lattice of blackened beams with wisps of smoke rising from them.

"Oh God." The smell of smoke and soot is stronger than ever, and the sides of the track are churned up by heavy vehicles, the vegetation beaten flat.

I pull over and park outside the yard gate, then lift Georgie out of her car seat and carry her in my arms towards the farm. There are two fire engines in the yard with long lengths of hose trailing from them and beyond a darker pall of smoke is still rising into the sky. I realise with a sickening jolt that the fire has spread to the other buildings behind the house. Buildings that are much closer to the house itself.

There's a loud crackling and sparks are flying up over the thatched roof. I watch as one lands and glows for a second before being doused with a plume of water from one of the hoses. Not far beneath are our bedrooms, Clare's things. My heart races. Is the fire already deep in the old oak beams of the barns, perhaps fading for minutes on end before reappearing further along? It'll lick up the centuries of dust in seconds, turning everything before it black and charred.

The hay's gone now. I think of all our hard work, and a pain stabs beneath my ribs as I step forwards. How could someone do this to us? How could they believe-? I'm hardly through the gate when a firefighter appears and holds up his hand. Georgie gives a little cry of alarm and then coughs as the smoke swirls into our faces

"Keep back please."

"But I, I live here." I can hardly get the words out and all around us, heavier and darker than the smoke, is a smell of wet tar.

"Hold on a moment." The figure waves his arm to another man further away then comes over. "And you are?"

"Charlotte Elgin. I'm the daughter." I glance around, but there's no sign of Hollinghurst. "Please can you tell me, are my brothers alright? They were here last night."

"Right. Well, we haven't seen anyone. One team went straight in to evacuate the house, but it was empty.

We have been carrying out a thorough search of the other buildings."

"But they must be here." Panic rises inside me. "Someone must have seen them."

"Okay, come over to the cab for a moment." The man gives me a quick smile but his face looks drawn and tired, and there's a smudge of soot across one cheek. When we're beside the vehicle, he takes off his helmet and runs one hand through his damp blonde hair. "We were told that some people were living here but are you sure that your brothers were here last night?"

"I, I think so. I spoke to Simon in the evening. He was here then."

"Is there anywhere they might have gone?" He glances at Georgie for a moment. "I've got one not much older at home, a little boy. Tiring but wonderful."

"Yes." Something stirs in my mind.

"As you can see the house is pretty much okay apart from-" He hesitates for a moment, and we both look at the paint. The letters are worse close to, darker and more indelible and the sight of them makes me feel sick. Will we be able to scrub them away? "I can't let you go in though until we've got the fire completely out."

"Okay."

He looks at my face. "Could they have gone to a neighbour perhaps or-?"

Doesn't he know? I stare at him for a second as something drops inside me, then I spin round. Oh, God.

"I um, I have to go."

"Is there-?"

I don't look back for I'm already half running out to the head of the track with Georgie in my arms. The stony descent is deserted. So are the meadows to the right. It's hot, but there's a strange opaque glow to the sunlight, and even the air seems to sweat. I turn to the east, and there's a movement in the far gateway. Two figures. For a moment I feel a swell of relief then as I draw closer I realise that the people are strangers. A youngish man and woman with their backs to me, dressed in shorts, t-shirts and walking boots, a perfect advert for the serious outdoors on a summer afternoon.

"Can I help you?" They both turn at the sound of my voice, and there is something, a searching quality about their gaze that catches my attention. "Have you come for some more water? There's plenty here as you can see."

"Water? No, er thank you." The woman flushes in confusion, and suddenly she doesn't look so young and smooth anymore. "We-"

"You were the ones; you called the police didn't you?"

For a moment longer they look at me uncertainly then the man gets it and nods. I clench one hand into a fist. I want them to go away; I need to find Simon and Jamie.

"We're sorry about-" The woman looks towards the smoke.

"Have you seen anyone out here?"

"No, er-"

"Okay, thanks."

Why won't they move? I glance down for a moment. Are they wearing the same boots that trod the other prints into the dust, that obliterated some of the evidence before the blood was even dry?

"This is private land you know. The track over there takes you down to the village."

"Right."

I turn away from them towards Sleepers and walk on across the next field. Suddenly through a gap in the hedge, I catch a flash of white.

"Marty." Dark flies rise out of the grass and bounce against my face as I push open the gate, but he's gone. "Marty, hang on."

By the time I reach it, the fourth field is empty. I scan the hedgerows, nothing, nothing, nothing. I look down, but the grass is too short and dry for him to leave a trace.

"Shit."

The turf is hard beneath my feet, I can't run with Georgie, but I walk as fast as I can and my heart hammers. The gate into the next field is wide open. I step through, and there's a figure digging in the dust by the water trough with a piece of stick. Nerves jolt through me and then I see that it's Jamie.

"Oh, thank God." I look round. "I thought you and Simon might-"

Jamie straightens up, picks a pale pink rose out of the hedge and grins at it.

"Where's Simon?"

Suddenly I realise that there are no dogs with him. Even if they were ranging behind, they would have heard me by now and come bounding to catch up, tails feathering. Nerves jink through me, and I take a step forward.

"Jamie, what are you doing here on your own? Where's Simon?"

He looks down at the rose and twirls it between his fingers. Up close, his skin is hot and damp.

"Jamie." I grip his shoulders with both hands and pull his attention to my face. "Jamie, where's Simon?"

He stares at me for a moment, his eyes wide and clear beneath ginger lashes, then he tries to shrug himself away. I hold on to him.

"Did someone come to talk to him?"

Still nothing but that blank and yet half-knowing look.

"Jamie, please?" In desperation I shake his shoulders, his flesh is soft over the bones. "Can't you just-"

A low moan escapes between his lips, and he turns his face away from me.

"Oh God, I'm sorry." I let him go straight away. "Jamie, look I'm sorry, I'm so sorry."

He swings around and blunders away across the grass. Over his shoulder, I catch another glimpse of white, not so far away this time.

"Marty, please wait."

Jamie heads towards Sleepers, and a knot tightens in my throat. I follow him through into a long, narrow field. It appears deserted, but I suddenly feel sure that Marty's watching us. I spin around, but there's no one in the clear sunlight behind us or up under the high hedge.

"Okay." I try to keep my breathing steady as Sleepers comes into view. The boundary hedge between our lands is rough and tangled, and a new silver strand of barbed wire cuts through the undergrowth, looped and ready to catch and tear at the flesh of the unwary. I stop. The shade is deep along the hedgeline and in the gateway but beyond the light is white and clear and dangerously exposed. Jamie walks downhill to the broken gate.

"Jamie, hold on." Reluctance grabs at me, but he

steps over the rotten rails and keeps walking as though he hasn't heard me. "Oh God."

Simon never told me exactly what happened that night in the woods all those years ago, not the bloody detail of it. The images I have I've created myself, but the aftermath was there in his step and Marty's face as well. We hardly saw him, and when we did his jaw tightened, and his words became clipped and short. I don't know if Simon ever spoke directly to a Berryman again. I certainly didn't for months.

My heart beats fast as we approach the yard. There are sheep behind the crumbled drunken walls, a mass of them penned into a corner by Gel and Bri. I catch my breath as one moves, eyeing up freedom, and Gel darts forward to turn her, belly low to the ground. Beyond them, a long granite barn blocks the path of the southeast wind. I eye two dark open doorways. Is Marty in there? Is he watching us from the shadows or is he already in the house? Has he found Simon? There's no movement, but I can't be sure of anything now.

"Jamie, can you stay here?" I look for something to hold his attention with, and there's nothing but an old car with no wheels. I wrench at the door, and it opens with a screech of protest and the dull patter of falling rust. "Look."

He bends forwards and peers into the 1970s vinyl interior. The seats are brittle and split, and it looks as though a mouse has begun to make a nest out of the foam innards. Jamie climbs in and clutches the steering wheel.

"Will you stay there?"

I don't want to close the door in case he panics, so I edge slowly backwards towards the farmhouse. Simon's inside, I feel sure, but who else? I'm half way across the yard when Jamie lurches out of the car again and steps after me.

"Jamie, please just stay there." I stand still, and he does the same. "I'll be right back, okay?"

A strange dog barks as I turn towards the house and then another and claws scratch at one of the barn doors. I'm relieved that they're still shut in as I advance on the back door, but then a snout pushes out under a rotten edge of wood, and the barrier between us feels flimsy and unsafe.

24

I haven't been up to this door since that fateful snowy day, but I remember this path so well with its worn cobbles and assortment of broken pieces of metal alongside. There's even a baked bean can rammed under a shrub and a dog bowl full of greenish water. The door itself is open, and suddenly I hear Peter's voice inside.

"Coming back for you, is he? Well, there's a surprise."

"Peter. Jamie has nothing to do with this." Simon sounds strained.

"No. He doesn't understand, does he? Doesn't know whether he's coming or going. How does that feel huh? Seeing what you've done to your little brother? He'd have been a high flier if it hadn't been for you. Dr Elgin, that's what he'd a been."

"Peter." Beyond the garden wall the sheep move, bundling into the corner as Gel flickers in and out of my sight. I step forward. The kitchen is in deep shadow, and it takes a few seconds for my eyes to adjust and make out the two of them held apart by the old table, to see

Simon stand up and Peter swing the muzzle of the gun towards me.

Instinctively I flick up a hand in front of Georgie's face in a hopeless attempt at protection.

"Simon, what the hell?" The room is crowded with furniture and debris, and it smells of stale food. There's a half-plucked chicken on the counter and a drift of pale feathers on the floor.

"Ah, now I see what you're about. Come here then." Peter raises the gun to the level of my face. "Come here."

His eyes are the same as they always were, but the skin around them is deeply wrinkled now, while his hands on the gun are knotted from years of work in the damp. I can't stop looking at those fingers on the smooth metal, they mesmerise me and draw me forwards one, two, three steps.

"Don't you dare touch her." Simon's voice is tight, but it feels too dangerous to look at him, to take my eyes off those hands.

"You bastards, did you think that you were being clever then?" When I'm less than a metre from him, Peter touches the muzzle of the gun against the side of my face. It's far colder than I expected. "Did you have this planned all along?"

"Put the gun down Peter."

"You can't fool me this easily. Where is he?"

"Lee?" I swallow. I can smell the metallic oiliness of the barrel. "I'm sorry, but I've no idea. I thought you realised that."

"I don't mean him." He laughs harshly. "I'm sure he's fine. It was only a glancing blow after all. Where's Hollinghurst?"

He smoothes the muzzle of the gun along my jaw and under my chin, his hands aren't steady and the metal jerks against my skin and all the while I'm trying to sort out his words. The meaning is so close, but still, I don't quite get it, then Georgie stretches out a tiny innocent hand, and her fingers brush against the metal.

"Please Peter, just put the gun down. I've walked over; there's no police."

"And I'm meant to believe that?"

"What else can I say?"

"I'm not going to prison. I'm not going to be locked up. It was an accident."

Simon's not two metres away, and yet I daren't turn my head to look at him. I slide my eyes sideways instead, and for a second our gaze connects.

"You're just as beautiful as you always were," Peter says. "We could have had children, you and I."

"No." I have to keep calm for my sake, for Georgie's, but the anger is hot in my throat.

"Peter, just step away from her," Simon says quietly.

"Are you jealous or something?" Peter strokes the barrel of the gun down the side of my neck.

"For God's sake Peter, think of the baby if nothing else."

"You shouldn't have come back, either of you. Why couldn't you just leave us alone?" He glances at Simon, and his voice is low and rough.

Simon is too far away, four steps, three seconds, too bloody far. I want to feel the touch of his skin again and the reassuring strength of his arms around me. I want to take his face in my hands and kiss the end of his nose right where the sun has burnt it.

"Peter put the gun down. We can sort this out."

"Oh yeh? Don't you think we've gone a little too far for that?"

He's wearing the same breed of singed, holey jumper as before, a blue one, and there's a food stain down the front. "I'm sure-"

"Hold out your hand." He leans towards me suddenly.

"What?"

"Hold out your hand. I want to look at it."

I can't do anything else. I hold out my left hand with the back to the ceiling and my heart thuds beneath my ribs. I can't get a grip on what Peter might do next, what strange, unpredictable thoughts are swirling through his brain.

"I thought as much. You don't bite your nails anymore, do you? Your hands look better for that." His skin is rough and dry against mine.

"Thanks." I try to smile as though we're just having a polite conversation but my lips won't work somehow, and Georgie starts to cry.

"Why don't you come and sit down on the sofa with me? Perhaps we can have a little talk about things there."

"No." It's the same old maroon upholstery and the same torn patchwork throw. I feel sick. "We can talk here. Please just put the gun down Peter."

"You think I wanted this?"

"I- Peter please."

There's a footstep outside, a low grunt and Jamie appears in the doorway. He sways for a moment, his face pink with exertion and sun, then raises a hand to steady himself against the doorpost. Peter moves ever so slightly towards him, and there's a ripple of sinew in

348

the back of his right hand as his tired old fingers tighten.

Simon jumps forward and Georgie shrieks but suddenly there's another movement to my left, the blur of a dirty white shirt as Marty steps through the side door and snatches at the gun in Peter's hands.

"You bastard. I knew it was you all along." His words are slurred, and there's a reek of alcohol on his breath

"Simon, Marty no!" My voice fills the room, and for a second I'm aware of it all, of Simon's taut, athletic shape and Jamie's heavy breath, of Peter staggering to maintain control against Marty's bulk, of Georgie, screaming and the end of the double barrel swinging through the air; then the gun goes off.

The noise of the shot ricochets off the granite walls, and Simon falls backwards. He catches a chair as he goes down and it squeals away across the tiles before he hits the floor with a dull thud. Seconds later an ugly earthenware vase topples off a shelf and smashes close to his head. Georgie's screams change, becoming panic-stricken and breathless, unlike any noise she's ever made before, and spatters of blood land all over us.

"Simon." His eyes are still open, and for a moment hope soars through me, but already there's blood spreading out across the front of his shirt from some-where too high and too close to his heart. "Oh God no, Simon."

It's cramped and awkward where he lies among the old scarred furniture, but I crouch down beside him and press my hand over the bloodstain. Immediately my fingers are covered, and blood runs out between them hot and sticky.

"I'm-" He tries to lift his head, to go on, but the words catch in the back of his throat with an odd wet sound.

"It's alright. Simon, Simon look at me, it's going to be alright." I reach for his hand, and I'm sure that for a second our fingers squeeze together. "I love you."

Georgie's screams rise again, and now it's hard to hear anything else above and beyond them, but the others must be there, close in the room still.

"Someone call an ambulance. Quickly." I look up and back and catch a glimpse of Peter's legs, he's wearing wellies indoors, and they're caked in old mud, but what does that matter now? "Simon."

I try to hold his gaze, to force him to keep looking at me but his eyes narrow with pain and then his lids begin to drift down. "Simon, remember Eb, remember galloping in the wind over Howden. You were always faster than me. Think about that."

"…yes an ambulance, er a gunshot wound." Peter's voice is stilted and stumbling.

"Simon, come on, I need you. When Georgie's older we'll buy some more horses, we'll race again." I hold his hand up to my lips and kiss the back of it; there's still some of the old strength in his tanned forearm. We will do it; we will ride together again with the wind in our hair. I smile down at him.

"I-" He looks straight back at me steady, and sure then his fingers slacken, and his heads rolls sideways. For moments longer I cling to the thought that he's still breathing, that somehow he'll finish his sentence, but already the cold, hard ache of knowing that he won't is spreading through me.

"No, no." I keep kissing his hand, then I hold it

against my cheek, feeling the warmth of his fingers. As always he smells of the outdoors, of earth and sun and horses.

"Charlotte." The voice comes from a long way away. So far that I want to ignore it, then Georgie's screams blast into my consciousness again, and I lay Simon's hand down on the dirty tiles and stumble to my feet.

"Alright darling, alright."

Straight ahead at eye level, the room is dirty, crowded, untidy, the same as it was but Marty's standing, not two metres away now. There's blood on his face and shirt, and his mouth is strained open. Somehow the gun is on the floor at his feet.

"What have you done? It wasn't Simon."

"He, he-" One hand flicks up to his wild hair then his mouth closes and opens but no sound comes out.

"It was- Tell him, Peter."

Marty looks from one to the other of us and Peter's neck muscles quiver. Suddenly he's an old man.

"It was you wasn't it? What did you do to Lee?"

"You? Oh my God." Marty turns towards him slowly, breathing hard. "Is he dead? Did you kill him, your grandson?"

"No-"

"Then?"

"He should have been at school." Peter's voice trembles slightly. "But he wasn't, he was there, he was with her, like always. I thought I'd go round and get him. God. I was going to put an end to it once and for all."

"And you shot him? My son."

"Don't be stupid. Lee didn't want to come back with me. I tried to grab him, and he slipped, that's all. Caught his head on the wall."

Soft, young flesh bruised and bloody. I know what that looks like.

"And Clare, what happened to Clare?"

"I didn't touch her."

Something is missing; I fumble for it in my mind, and Marty grabs at Peter's slack jumper, stretching and twisting the stained wool. "Where are they then? Come on."

"I, I don't know. I thought they'd just go to a local hospital."

"Fuck. Fuck." He releases Peter and reaches for the gun again.

"No." But already I'm turning towards the door, my arms clutched around Georgie. "Darling it's okay, it's okay, it's okay, we're going outside now, we'll find Jamie. There we are, you see it's alright, it's alright."

The garden path is bright and hot, and a robin sings in the laburnum tree near the gate, three halting bars before it flits away over the wall. There's a low moan in the yard beyond, and I know that Jamie's there somewhere, that I must go to him. "Jamie."

One step forward, two, and far away down the valley a helicopter buzzes. The air ambulance is coming like before, but this time it's too late, much too late. I glance at my right hand and already Simon's blood is drying between my fingers.

25

The rain has softened the ground, and it's strange to feel the slight give of the soil beneath my feet after so long. High above the farm, the wind is still running fast, and the pale bellies of the beech leaves flare towards the sky.

The last storm snapped one of the old beeches in two and its top lies in a tangle of limbs that half crush the moor wall. The heartwood is pale and smells of spice. Jagged splinters of it lie scattered about in the grass, and I wonder at the force it must have hit the ground.

If I look down to my left, I can just see the roof and end wall of Sleepers. I turn away quickly and lean back against a smooth grey trunk as a wave of nausea sweeps through me. All my thoughts, all my vague ideas for the future have been smashed apart. I'm just as restless as Georgie now, and even at night, all I can do is pace through the darkened rooms of Northstone until exhaustion takes me. Then I sit with Georgie in my arms, and my face pressed into the warm, sweet smell of her.

People have come to sit with Jamie and me at times, friends and strangers alike. Arthur came the first day but his eyes wouldn't meet mine, and neither of us could find the right words. Later Vicki visited, and a nurse who offered us full-scale trauma counselling, but none of them have been able to come between me and the image that seems forever seared across my mind.

I want to think about something else but I can't. I want to pull Jamie out of the corner where he sits for hours with his face pressed into his hands, but I can't comfort myself let alone him. Hour after hour my mind returns to those few minutes and to the chain of events that lead up to them, to what did and what might have happened. The things that seemed logical before, now make no sense at all. In fact, I hardly feel as though I know myself anymore.

"Did you know what Marty was planning?" Hollinghurst asked once a few days ago, but I shook my head. Who am I to judge that anymore? Who am I to say what might or might not have been true then or now?

I know that at the bottom of the lane the press vans wait, held back by the police cordon so that as long as I don't go far beyond the confines of the yard, I feel relatively safe from them. There was a helicopter overhead on the first day, it flew round and round, low enough for someone to take photos. This is the furthest I've been all week, and it feels edgy.

"Ah."

I glance around, and Jamie is lying over the fallen trunk on his belly, his head and feet hang down on either side. We used to do that as kids until all the blood ran to our heads and we had to sit up again. I'm tempted to join him now, but I still feel queasy, so I sit down on the grass with Georgie instead.

"Ah, ah." He shouts suddenly, a spurt of sound that ends as abruptly as it started and the wind picks up in the trees above our heads.

I deliberately took off my watch earlier so that I couldn't see the hours of this day scroll through with painful slowness. Now I only have an approximate idea of what time it is, but it feels as though we should have some news soon. I sat in the front room by the phone all through Georgie's thin fitful sleep, waiting for a call that never came and I can still feel the stiffness of it in my lower back.

I know that today is only the beginning. I've seen it in the papers that have continued to land on the mat each morning. Each has the same brown paper sash as the first one. Mostly it's one tabloid, once or twice another with a similar headline splashed across the front page or just inside. I don't know who brings them, and I didn't mean to read them, but after a couple of days, I found myself slitting through the sashes with my thumb-nail again.

They've used the same photo of Marty over and over. It must have been taken months ago because his face looks smooth and relaxed, in complete contrast to Simon's, which is more recent, another off-guard paparazzi shot that has caught him looking rough and watchful.

I can't bear to look at them and yet I'm drawn to the words. They reach out and coil around me, plausible enough to seem like the truth, to be the truth for anyone who wasn't there.

Once I've read them, I can't get the words out of my mind, just as Georgie can't seem to rid herself of the echo of the gunshot. She has hardly slept for days and when she does she wakes screaming, her eyes wide and her head on one side as though the sound is still trapped inside her skull.

I've tried to calm her and myself, I know what the papers are saying about today, and yet when I turn my mind to the detail of it, my heart still clenches and a light, cold sweat springs out beneath my clothes.

"Come on Jamie." Restlessness prickles me into action, and as he slides off the log, I take his hand and turn downhill. His skin is warm and slightly gritty with dirt. "We should go back."

We are in the third field when a woodcock flies straight across the sky above us from west to east, and then a few moments later the crows come.

"Look, Georgie, look," I say as the dark birds stream above our upturned faces. "They're going home to bed like you should be in a minute, madam."

Georgie squawks and waves her arms at them while the dusk creeps in, and the grass grows cool and damp beneath our feet. The crows come round again in a great restless loop that spreads and then twists tight in a dark mass of birds. Gel and Bri rush down through the orchard after them, then their barks change, growing sharper and less certain. There's someone there. Hollinghurst or-

"Not a journalist, please not a bloody journalist." I turn back to Jamie, but he's looking at the ground. "Are you okay?"

Below us, the dogs have gone quiet, and then I catch sight of them milling around a figure beside the barn. My eyes strain to see who it is, but the harder I look the more the dusk bulges and jinks. It must be someone they know, Hollinghurst then, my pulse speeds up, and I walk on. There's news. Now that it's come I'm not sure that I can face it.

The figure spots us and walks out across the grass. He has a slight limp, not Hollinghurst's smooth runner's stride, and I stop. The man is older than I first thought. As he comes closer, I see that his hair is mostly gone and his hands are empty. There's no rucksack slung over his shoulder or camera around his neck, so he can't be a reporter.

"Charlotte."

His voice is familiar before his face, but his sudden half smile takes me back.

"Eric."

"Charlotte, I'm so sorry. I set off as soon as I heard."

"You did?" I feel miles behind suddenly. I can't get my head around any of this, of him being here or what his words mean. I've been living with the gunshot for days already.

"Jamie." He looks surprised for a moment and holds out his hand, but Jamie walks past it and on down the field. "How are you?"

"It's too late. He's, he saw it all."

"Shall we go back to the house?"

He's lost a lot of weight along with the hair, and from behind, I would never have recognised him as the man who used to step in and out of our lives as though he never really went away for years at a time.

"I've been trying to get hold of you." I feel anger

suddenly, odd and sharp. It digs in at the pit of my stomach and then rises into my throat in a hot wave. "Why didn't you call me?"

As I wait to see what he will say or do, I feel how this summer should have been, I see Georgie and I taking quiet afternoon walks through drowsy London streets, I see myself holding my camera and the ordered darkness of the flat, my space.

The pasture smells of full summer and as we walk on our feet press the damp green scent of chlorophyll out of the grass.

"I … we had problems with reception on the phone. Look, Clare would like to talk to you."

"What?" I stop dead, and a jolt of nerves fizzes through my veins. "You mean-"

"Yes, they've been with me."

"All the time?" I can't quite get my head around what he's saying.

"Clare called me, in a terrible state. They both were."

"But where, how? The police have been looking everywhere."

"I've got a place up in Scotland, not much more than a bothy out on the west coast, you can only get to it by boat, or walking in over the hills." He sketches the shape of the tiny place in the air with his hands.

"All the time, all the bloody time?"

"Charlotte."

A full, early moon rises behind the beeches, and as I watch the pale, dappled globe sail out above the valley, I feel as though the ground is sliding away from me, all the thin, wiry grasses and four-petalled tormentil flowers slip into the shadows. For a moment

I stagger then Eric's hand closes around my upper arm.

"I'm sorry. Clare wouldn't go to the police, so I drove down and picked them up."

"You could have gone though." His face is deeply lined now from his years spent in the hot sun of foreign construction sites. I remember how it was, how we all pretended that we couldn't see what was going on between him and Clare.

"I know, but they were so distraught, so adamant, so on the edge. I thought if I went to the police straight away Clare might do something foolish." He shakes his head, and I think about the shotgun cartridges she bought, the stash of tinned food, the new bolts on the doors and the knife kept by her bed. "She was, I think, trying to save the son she'd already lost. I took them away to try and persuade them. It seemed like the best thing to do, at the time."

"The best-" He still loves her then. "And now?"

The air is surprisingly warm, and there are voices in the darkness, larky shouts out on the moor and the call of restless sheep.

"Clare really would like to talk to you."

"We watched him die. We couldn't save him."

"Charlotte, you need to get away from here. Come back to Scotland with me."

The irony of it hits me full in the face, and I can't look at him suddenly. He of all people had the power to stop any of this happening. The extent of his dishonesty takes away all other thought. How could he have kept quiet for so long? How could he have let us-? My initial anger turns into a blind rage that sweeps through me.

I can see it all so clearly now, but which is worse,

what Peter did in a flash of sudden temper or what Eric has done in a slow attempt to what, save Clare and Lee's feelings? In fact, does it even matter that their motives were so different, the one to scare and the other to protect when the end result was the same? They are the ones with their bloody silence who made sure that there could only be one ending to all this before Marty even grabbed the gun.

"You want me to collude with you all?"

"No."

"But that's what it is, isn't it?" I walk on ahead of him. I can't even begin to think how this goes from here, of what will happen to Lee and Clare, to any of us. "I have to go in now and feed Georgie."

"Charlotte, please?"

"I don't know." We reach the yard, and I stop. The house is shadowed and silent, and suddenly I don't want to go in and see Simon's jeans still slung over the back of a chair with a mud-stained knee, nor his denim jacket in a crumpled heap on the end of the kitchen table. "I could go to the police."

"You could." Eric hesitates. "I waited outside the court today."

"And?"

"I thought you'd be at the inquest."

"I, well Jamie and Georgie needed to stay here." I can't keep the defence out of my voice, for if I'm honest, they made a convenient excuse. It was me who couldn't face all the eyes and the words, strange and surreal in the trapped stuffy air of the courtroom.

"I understand it was adjourned. There's going to be a murder enquiry Charlotte." Eric slides an arm around my shoulders, but I shrink away from his touch. "Come back to Scotland with me."

I'm not sure how I can ever forgive him, but after a while, I nod. I know that I will go with him on the long drive through the darkness, but I don't trust the thought to words yet. Who knows where we'll be in the morning and what it'll bring?

"Jamie has to come too. I'm not taking him back to Fairfax, not after everything-"

"Of course he's coming with us."

Eric makes us all a cup of tea and waits while I feed Georgie then pack our things into two bags, my hands slow and clumsy.

"What about the dogs and, and the farm?" I look at him helplessly. I don't feel as though I've got the energy to sort any of it out anymore.

"I called Arthur earlier. He's going to look after everything."

How much has Eric told him? Does he know where we're going and who we're going to meet? Does he know that Clare and Lee are still alive? Arthur can be trusted with that secret, of course, but does Eric know that? There are so many questions that I'm too tired to ask now, but we've got a long journey ahead of us and plenty of time.

It's dark when we walk out into the garden again, but the moon is so full and high that we can still see clearly. If I close my eyes to slits, I can play that game that Simon taught me and pretend that it's the most beautiful, dazzling summer day. The shadows are just the same.

Eric and Jamie walk on towards the car, but I stop at the garden gate. Our two smooth, dark code stones lie half hidden in the dipped top of the gatepost. I look at them for a moment then pick them up and slip them into my pocket.

"Let's go, Georgie," I say and close my hand around the larger stone.

READ ON!

Thank you for reading *The Light Between Trees*. I hope you enjoyed it as much as I enjoyed writing it. If you would like to hear about my new releases and special offers then do visit my website and join my mailing list. Joining is free and you can unsubscribe at any time.

If you enjoyed this book then please consider leaving a review on Amazon. It would be really appreciated. Reviews are very important to writers and help readers to find the kinds of new books they're looking for.

www.anonarooke.com

ACKNOWLEDGMENTS

No novel is a solo project and I would like to thank the many people who have given me support and advice during the long process of creating this book. In particular my mother for believing in my writing dreams and for her practical support in bringing this novel to publication, my father for his supply of inspiring reading matter and the rest of my family for their ongoing support in a process that has often taken me away from them and into other worlds. I would also like to thank Euan Thorneycroft, Gillian Stern and Mark Stratton for their editorial advice and for giving me the confidence to keep going, and Tom and Zoe Dixon, Alice Ragg and Helen Dove for reading and offering their comments at various stages of the writing and design process. Last, but by no means least, I would like to thank Ali Hirst for checking on my progress, which often kept me writing when I might otherwise have stopped, Sam Richards for answering my technical questions and Rob Williams for all the time he put into designing the cover.

Printed in Great Britain
by Amazon